THE HIDDEN
EYES

GEORGE D. SCHULTZ

ISBN: 978-1-4669-6616-1 (sc)
ISBN: 978-1-4669-6615-4 (e)

Trafford rev. 01/29/2013

 www.trafford.com

North America & international
toll-free: 1 888 232 4444 (USA & Canada)
phone: 250 383 6864 ♦ fax: 812 355 4082

PROLOGUE

The story that unfolds, in this book, may seem almost Neanderthal. Well, by today's terrorist standards, I would imagine that it <u>is</u>.

But, in 1973—when our narrative unfolds—we'd not had <u>that</u> many years, of being exposed to such outrages. True, there had been the riots, in Chicago— at the 1968 *Democratic National Convention*. We <u>all</u> got to see that! And it <u>was</u> pretty serious stuff! Especially pre-9/11!

But, most of the terrorist activity—back then— seemed, in retrospect, to not get nearly the national exposure, so common today. Nor did they appear to have remained in the public eye, for all that long. Of course these things took place—well before the inauguration of 24-hour cable news channels. And talk radio.

The likes of Bill Ayers, Abbie Hoffman, Jerry Rubin, et.al. had all surfaced years before the ever-constant 24/7 news cycles! And their constant, continuing, rants had seemed to have become almost a part of our daily lives. Almost like the family dog being fed. Or doing the laundry.

Bernadine Dohrn, one of the founders, of *The Weather Underground*—and later married to Bill Ayers—had been involved in more than her share of terrorist activities, throughout the late-sixties, and well into the seventies. That all seemed to have become, simply, part of "The American Scene".

The outrageous explosion at the Madison campus, of the *University of Wisconsin*, occurred August 24, 1970! Coverage of that terrorist act seemed to have remained in the national dialogue, for a little while longer.

But, similar activities? Not so much.

Members of The *Weather Underground* were thought to have been assembling bombs, in a Greenwich Village townhouse—when the place blew up on March 6, 1970!

A multitude of government buildings—including the US Capitol, and many police stations and banks, throughout the country, were bombed! Explosives were used—successfully—on many other sites! Too many—far too many—to list, in these limited number of pages! Courthouses, law enforcement agencies—and even schools—as well as lawmakers' and judges' homes, were included, in the massive, nationwide, more or less semi-organized, "campaign"!

On September 17, 1971, *The New York Dept. of Corrections*, in Albany, was bombed—a protest against the "atrocious" treatment of the prisoners, incarcerated at the Attica prison! The *Pentagon*, itself, was bombed—on *Ho Chi Minh's* birthday—May 19, 1972! A "solidarity" move!

In the year, 1973—when our narrative begins, the following incidents took place:

- On May 18th, the *103rd Police Precinct*, in New York City, was bombed!
- On September 28th, *ITT's* offices in New York and Rome were bombed—a reaction to *ITT's* participation in the Chilean coup, earlier that month!

Also, in 1973, on November 6th, in Oakland, two members of the *Symbionese Liberation Army* killed school superintendent Marcus Foster—and badly wounded his deputy, Robert Blackburn—as the two men left an Oakland School Board meeting. The hollow-point bullets, used to kill Foster, had been packed—with <u>cyanide</u>!

On February 4, 1974, members of the *SLA* kidnapped newspaper heiress, Patty Hearst! On April 15th, of that year, Ms Hearst—by then, known as "Tanya"—had joined up, with members of the *SLA*! They'd proceeded to rob the *Hibernia Bank*, in San Francisco! During this "caper", two civilians were shot!

On March 6, 1974, the San Francisco office of *The Department of Health, Education and Welfare* was bombed! May 31st, of the same year, found the office of California's *Attorney General*—bombed! June 17th—*Gulf Oil's* Pittsburgh facility—was also bombed!

In 1975. *The State Department* was bombed! So were the offices of *The Department of Defense*, in Oakland!

Your memory of those extremely turbulent times—like mine—may, by now, be a little on the fuzzy side. That, most assuredly, was the case with me. But, these God-awful incidents—these few of many—

were a continuing menace, during the sixties and seventies!

It sounds almost trite, but—compared to September 11, 2001—all of these "past history" incidents (and the many other outrages that took place, back then) seem, in this day and age, to have been reduced, in so many people's memories, to the point where they've become considered to be almost "minor league" stuff!

Maybe they <u>were</u>! I guess that they <u>undoubtedly</u> were—when stacked up against such things, as the crash-bombing of the *USS Cole*! And the 1983 bombing of the *Marine Barracks*, in Beirut—where 241 of our American servicemen lost their lives!

Thankfully, other potentially horrific terrorist attempts—such as the deadly, merciless, plans of "The Underwear Bomber" and "The Times Square Bomber", among others—had been thwarted!

However, in the sixties and seventies, such things—as those listed above—<u>were</u> happening!

This story takes place at the <u>height</u> of such then-frightening activity!

ONE

"THE CAPTAIN WILL SEE YOU now," announced the heavy-set, matronly, woman—as she poked her head into the garishly-painted, cheaply-furnished, waiting room. Her voice was reminiscent of a rusty file.

It startled Victor Smigelski—from his troubled reverie.

"Right this way," she beckoned, rather impatiently.

Smigelski lifted his six-feet, one-inch, 220-pound frame—out of the uncomfortable, gaudy, orange-plastic chair—and followed the woman down a long, dank, hallway, into a small, cluttered office.

"Captain Fox," the woman intoned, "this is Victor Smi . . . uh . . . Smay . . . uh . . ."

"Smigelski, Captain," he provided. "Just call me 'Ski'.

The captain—a short, stocky, ruddy-complexioned, man—rose and shook Smigelski's hand. He indicated an uncomfortable, gaudy, bright-blue plastic chair.

Smigelski plopped himself down—as the woman left.

Captain Fox seated himself, once more, behind a mound of paperwork. Everything was in total disarray. Smigelski imagined that it was, most likely, a permanent condition. The riffle of documents, memos and notes obliterated the top of his small, seen-better-days, desk.

The stubby little man began to peruse Smigelski's application for employment—moving his lips and rasping under his breath. Then, at length, he placed the paper down on the rubble atop his desk. He leaned back in his chair—and locked his pudgy hands behind his head.

"Now," he asked, "why is it you want to get into security, Smigel . . . ah . . . Smi . . . uh . . . Ski?"

"Mainly, because I need a job. I don't have one now . . . and I've developed this bad habit. It's called eating. As you can see . . . from my app . . . I've been in the rent-a-car business for about twelve years. Last company that I was with . . . well, they went down the chute last month. These days, I can't seem to snag a job in that field."

"Why's that?"

"Well, everybody tells me that I'm overqualified. Doesn't seem to be anything available in management. I'd even been applying for counter rental-agent jobs. They still tell me that they don't have anything for me. Say they can't pay me what I need. Can't pay me what I'm worth. Sounds good . . . but, it doesn't put food on the table."

"Yeah, I imagine so."

"I tell 'em that I don't need all that much . . . but, it still hasn't done me any good. I even offered to sign an employment contract for six months . . . as a rental agent . . . at the going rate. That's about a hundred-and-a-half a week. No one'll go for it, though. They all tell me that I'll leave after six months. Even if that was true, I'd jump at it . . . if I were them. That'd be at least six months . . . in an extremely-high-turnover business . . . that they wouldn't have to worry about training anybody new. Still, dammit, no one can be bothered."

"Well, Vick," replied Captain Fox, with a broad smile, "I'm gonna call you Vick . . . do you have any idea what we pay? What we start a new man off with?"

"Not really. I figured somewhere near . . . oh . . . probably somewhere near four dollars an hour."

"Try two-fifty."

"Two-<u>fifty</u>? Captain! This is nineteen seventy-<u>three</u>! I thought that two-and-a-half dollars . . . thought <u>that</u> went out . . . <u>years</u> ago."

"No. In fact, two-five-oh is still above the minimum . . . and there's a hell of a lot of guys out there that're happy to get it. Real happy to get it. Lot'sa guys."

"I'm sure that's true, Captain. But how good . . . how capable . . . are they? How capable . . . how efficient . . . can they be?"

"Well, y'know, that's just it. Some of 'em, of course, have turned out to be pretty bad. The ones that're good, though . . . they go on, usually, to somethin' else. Bigger'n better things. Eventually, anyway. Sometimes, though . . . real quick."

"Like . . . to what?"

"Oh, you know. Sheriff's deputies. Heading up security details in various department stores. Things like that. I've been here at **Tarkenton** for sixteen years now . . . and I've started a hell of a lot of guys on their way. Lot'sa guys. Well-qualified guys. And they've wound up makin' damn good money, too. Damn good money. The field . . . well, it just doesn't pay all that much. Not startin' off, is all."

"Well," replied Smigelski, with a heavy sigh, "I'm pushing forty-years-old right now . . . and I really can't afford to make too many more changes. I was really looking to land someplace . . . and <u>stay</u>. I need to think about such things as pension plans . . . if I can still get in on one. If I put in twenty-five years at a place . . . starting now . . . I figure that I'll just about be able to slip in, under the wire, when I turn sixty-five."

"That's good thinking, Vick. We all gotta think about our futures, y'know."

"Yeah. I figure I don't have that many bites left in the apple . . . as far as jobs go. Jobs with any kind of a future. But, hell! I just can't make it! Not on a hundred bucks a week! I'm divorced. My ex-wife's got a fair-to-middlin' job . . . thank God. But, still, I've got three kids . . . and I do have a goodly number of responsibilities along those lines."

"Yeah," muttered Captain Fox, with an indifferent nod. "I see where you were used to earnin', like, a thousand . . . or eleven-hundred . . . bucks a month. I don't really know if you'd be happy . . . satisfied is what I mean . . . here."

"Oh," sighed Smigelski, "I suppose I <u>could</u> hack it . . . for awhile anyway . . . on a hundred a week. I wouldn't be thrilled, but I guess I could do it. I'd like some kind of promise, though. Something good . . .

that I'd be able to count on. Down the road. You know, I've actually had to be a little bit of a detective, myself. In the car rental business."

"Detective? How's that? What do you mean you were a detective?"

"Well, tracking down overdue cars. Things like that. I've had a few episodes that got a little hairy. Got <u>shot</u> at . . . one time! I was <u>stealing</u> . . . quote, unquote . . . back one of my own <u>cars</u>! In the middle of the night, don'tcha know! Over in Jersey!"

Captain Fox laughed. "I think you'd find that there's a hell of a lot of difference. I mean between being a professional detective . . . and just nosing around, as a amateur."

"I'm sure that's true. But, I've always thought that I was pretty <u>good</u> . . . for an amateur. Thought that jacking around, as I did, would be a fairly good start . . . at, maybe, turning pro. Let me tell you what I had in mind, Captain: I worked . . . at one time . . . for **Ballinger's Rent-a-Car**. It was a subsidiary of **Ballinger's Department Stores**. I'm sure you must be familiar with it. With them."

"Hell yeah! We used to handle security for the rent-a-car. Still <u>do</u> handle it . . . for the department stores. Big <u>account</u>! I'm not involved with it directly. That's another division. Didn't **Ballinger's** . . . didn't they drop the rent-a-car in the shit can? A few years back?"

"Right. Back in sixty-nine. I got thrown out of a job then too. Should be getting used to it. I remember, though, that <u>you</u> guys had employees over there. There were all these guys . . . a few women, too . . . who were sort of undercover agents."

"Undercover agents?"

"I know. It wasn't as exotic as I'm making it sound. They'd go in as rental clerks. Or even service agents. This was, of course, all <u>unbeknownst</u> to all the regular employees. These agents of yours . . . they'd keep an eye on things. As I understand it, they'd report back to you . . . and then, you reported to **Ballinger's**. Anyway, I was thinking of, maybe, something along those lines. As opposed to standing out in back of some manufacturing plant, somewhere."

"Yeah," grunted the captain. "Well, you see you'd have to be with us awhile . . . before you'd ever be able to get something like that. I don't even know how many rent-a-cars . . . we do that for, nowadays."

"But . . . you <u>see</u>? I <u>know</u> that I could handle that! Handle that kind of thing! Right <u>now</u>! I know I <u>could</u>! It'd be right up my <u>alley</u>!"

"Slow down, there! Ease <u>up</u>, Boy! You probably <u>could</u>, Vick. You probably could. But, you <u>still</u> have to start out as a <u>guard</u>. At two-five-oh a hour. <u>Everyone</u> starts out as a guard . . . at two-five-oh a hour."

"What kind of a future would I have here?"

Captain Fox brightened! Considerably! "Oh," he enthused, "a really <u>good</u> one! <u>Really</u> good one! Now, I don't promise that you're gonna make piles . . . not the first couple or three years. But, after that . . . why, it'd be clear sailin'! Hell, in three months or so, we'd probably make you a corporal! Maybe even sooner than that! That'd bring you a pay raise . . . right there!"

"How big a raise?"

"A quarter-a-hour! And now, that's not the end of it! In six months, you'd be eligible for sergeant! Now, I'm not sayin' you'd <u>make</u> it. But, sure as hell, you'd be <u>eligible</u>! On the other hand . . . now that I'm thinkin' about it . . . I'd bet that you'd probably <u>would</u> make it! Make <u>sergeant</u>! First time <u>up</u>! Just a feelin' I got, Vick. And, see? That'd put you at three-ten a <u>hour</u>. Plus there's usually lots of <u>overtime</u> . . . once you get to be a <u>sergeant</u>! <u>Lots</u> of overtime! Of course, there's usually a good bit of overtime . . . no matter <u>what</u> rank you are. Even startin' <u>off</u>. And, of course, you always get time-and-a-<u>half</u> for overtime."

"Oh, wow! What comes after that? After I make sergeant?"

"Well, it'd be about then, that you'd be getting' into somethin' like you were <u>talkin'</u> about. Goin' to things like rent-a-cars . . . if we still <u>service</u> any of them . . . and lots of <u>other</u> places. Or," he beamed—with genuine pride—"you could become a <u>officer</u> . . . in this <u>here</u> division! You'd wear a <u>brown</u> uniform . . . like <u>that</u> one hangin' on the wall over there! With that five-gallon <u>hat</u>! <u>Sharp</u>, hah?"

"Sharp!"

"And, see, you know there's a good chance that I could give you some overtime . . . right from the <u>start</u>. That'd be . . . like I said . . . time-and-a-half."

"How <u>much</u>? How much <u>overtime</u>?"

"Depends on what shifts you can work."

"Look, Captain. I'm divorced. I'm also the next thing to being <u>desperate</u>! I live in a little <u>room</u> . . . upstairs over a <u>bar</u> . . . in <u>Jersey</u>. My time is pretty much my own. I can work whatever shifts I <u>have</u> to. Naturally, I'd prefer days. But, it's not a really big thing. Midnights'd be all right too. I'm not exactly in love the three-thirty-to-midnight shift . . . or whatever it is. But, I could hack <u>that</u> too, if need be. For awhile anyway. Look, Captain Fox, I <u>need</u> a job! And I need one . . . <u>badly</u>!"

"All right, let me ask you somethin'. Let me ask you this: Will your livin' in Jersey . . . is that gonna give you any <u>problems</u>? Getting' to work, I mean. Most of the guard stuff is out of this office. In fact, most of it is . . . right here in Midtown <u>Manhattan</u>."

"No <u>problem</u>! <u>None</u>! I worked in Queens . . . for the last three-and-a-half years."

"Yeah. But, now I'm assumin' you had a brand new company <u>car</u>, then. Had a dependable car . . . at all <u>times</u>. What're you drivin' <u>now</u>?"

"Dodge. Sixty-five Dodge Polara."

"Hmmmm. Eight-years-old. Hunderd dollar car?"

"I guess," replied Smigelski, with a massive sigh. "Cost me a little more than that. But, it <u>is</u> dependable. Besides, the train runs a block-and-a-half from my room. And the bus stop is two blocks away. Even if the car <u>didn't</u> start, it wouldn't take me more than an hour . . . hour-and-a-half, tops . . . to get to the Port Authority Bus Station or to Penn Station, on the train. I've been <u>punctual</u> . . . all my life. I'm <u>never</u> late for work. <u>Never</u>! That was part of my problem with my former wife. She claimed I was a <u>workaholic</u>. Well, I guess she's probably <u>right</u>."

"Okay, Vick . . . Ski. Tell you what I'm gonna do with you: Now, I've got a guard's job that's open. At a warehouse . . . over on Thirty-eighth and Tenth Avenue. Right here in Midtown. Just a hoot and a holler from the Port Authority. You can go ahead . . . and take the bus in. Probably be better off. Save parkin' hassles . . . and wear and tear on the car.

Now, it's <u>midnights</u>. But, I can give you six days. So, the sixth day . . . don'tcha see . . . the sixth day would be at time-and-a-half. Plus that, there'll be times when I can get you the <u>afternoon</u> shift there, too. That is, if you don't mind workin' <u>sixteen</u> hours in a row."

"That'd be <u>no</u> problem! Especially at time-and-a-half."

"That's <u>great</u>," responded the captain—beaming. "Now, you gotta understand: You don't get no lunch hour. But you have . . . we figger . . . about ten or fifteen minutes a hour. Ten . . . maybe fifteen . . . minutes. That's, of course, once you get to know the tour. You'd have ten or fifteen minutes . . . to just sit on your ass. And have a cup of coffee . . . and, maybe, slog down a sandwich."

"The <u>tour</u>?"

"Yeah. You have to carry a time clock, see. And clock it in, at various points in the building. It's a set routine. Now, the shift runs from midnight till eight in the morning. Now, you're expected to be in fifteen minutes early . . . military courtesy kind of thing. Same as when you were in the Navy."

"Yeah, that's okay. No problem with fifteen minutes early. I assume my relief'll be in . . . also fifteen minutes early." The little man nodded—enthusiastically. "I imagine," Smigelski continued, "that I'll have a Billy club, or something."

"Right! Right you are, Vick. Yessir! We give you a Billy stick . . . <u>and</u> a sap! We provide all <u>uniforms</u>. <u>Everything</u>! What you do is . . . like I said . . . you carry this clock. Goes on a strap . . . over your shoulder, y'know. Now, you carry it with you . . . for the entire tour. Now, you have to make a complete

<u>tour</u> of the warehouse . . . each hour. That's why we say you should have ten or fifteen minutes every hour . . . eventually . . . just to sit on your ass. It's a planned tour . . . and you'll have to learn it. You have . . . like I said . . . this clock. Now, you carry it to different places in the building."

"Different places?"

"Yeah. It's all planned out. Places . . . we'll show you . . . places where there'll be a key hangin'. What they call strategic places. Usually, the key'll be hangin' on the wall, there. Now, what you do . . . is you go ahead and you turn the key in the clock. The clock'll record the number of that key . . . each key, in each different location, has got its own number. So, what it'll do is . . . it'll show what time it was when you turned the key in the clock. Ka-peesh?"

"Ka-peesh. That's so you can see where I was? And when?"

"Right! Right, Vick! And, it'll tell us if you're doin' the tour in the right sequence . . . <u>prescribed</u> manner, as we say. Now, it's gonna take you a little longer . . . until you get to where you learn the tour. So, there won't be much ass-sittin' time for the first six or seven tours. After <u>that</u>? Why, it should be duck <u>soup</u> . . . for a fella like yourself. <u>Should</u> be, anyway. You should be able to make the tour . . . and get back to the security desk and sit down on your ass for ten . . . maybe fifteen . . . minutes. Know what I mean?"

"When do I start?"

Once again, Captain Fox beamed! "<u>That's</u> the spirit," he gushed. "Like to <u>see</u> that in a man! <u>Love</u> to see that in a man! You can start <u>tonight</u>, if you want. It's . . . what the hell time <u>is</u> it?" He stared at his *Timex* wrist watch. "It's . . . lessee . . . four-thirty," the little captain muttered. "By the time the sergeant fingerprints you, and gets you to fill out all the forms for the bondin' company . . . you won't have no problems with the bondin' company, will you, Vick?"

"No. None."

"Hah! Didn't think so! Anyway, by the time we get you all processed . . . and into uniform . . . it'll probably be five-thirty or quarter-of-six. Hell, you might's well just stay on in town tonight. Go right to work. Go right on over to the damn warehouse . . . at a quarter-to-twelve. I've got a corporal doin' that trick right now. He'll stay with you the whole eight hours. After that, you're on your own. Any questions . . . why, you just go ahead and you ask him. And, Vick . . . I want you to be sure and you listen to him. You listen to whatever he says. Listen very careful. In ninety-nine percent of the cases, there shouldn't be no one . . . not a goddam soul . . . in the place. Other than yourself. If there is, well . . . then, that person . . . he's gotta have a buildin' pass."

"What time do the workers come in? The warehouse workers?"

"Good question, Ski. Excellent question. Shows you're thinkin'. Actually, they come in at about eight in the mornin'. But, see? You'll be long gone . . . . fifteen minutes before that."

Smigelski nodded.

"Now," continued the enthused captain, "if you do see somethin' suspicious, you have a little thing. Little thing . . . we call a beeper. Hooked right onto your belt. What you do is . . . you take your beeper and you press the red button. Then, when you hear the little tone . . . a kind of beep . . . you go ahead, and you speak right into it. Right into the beeper. The corporal, he'll go all over this with you. But, what it amounts to is that you just say your name and where you are . . . where you're at. What floor you're on . . . whether you're in the front or the rear of the building. Such shit as <u>that</u>. Say . . . right into the beeper . . . tell us what the hell's goin' <u>on</u>. We'll get a whole <u>bunch</u> of people over there! <u>Pronto</u>! Quicker'n <u>shit</u>! Don't get yourself <u>involved</u>! We ain't payin' you enough <u>money</u> . . . to where you need to get your <u>ass</u> shot off of ya. <u>Understand</u>?"

"You make it sound absolutely <u>delightful</u>. Are you <u>sure</u> . . . that Sam Spade got <u>his</u> start this way? Dick <u>Tracy</u>?"

"Aw hell, Vick. There <u>really</u> ain't nothin' to worry about. Only been <u>one</u> break-in at that place in the past two . . . maybe three . . . <u>years</u>. No <u>problems</u>! I don't wanna <u>scare</u> you. Just pay careful <u>attention</u> . . . to the things the corporal'll be <u>tellin'</u> you tonight."

"Don't worry," responded Smigelski. "I will. Now, what day will I be getting off? You <u>did</u> say I could work forty-eight hours, didn't you?"

"Yeah. Lessee now."

Captain Fox fished his pocket-sized desk calendar—from beneath a pile of rubble on his desk. Smigelski found himself wondering how the little man knew precisely what sheaf of papers to move— enabling the captain to, immediately, pluck the thing out so quickly, and efficiently.

"I can't b'lieve it's January the <u>seventeenth</u> already," the little man muttered, narrowing his gaze upon the calendar. "Jus' can't <u>b'lieve</u> it. God! Seems like New Years Eve was . . . like it was just a couple days ago."

Smigelski's laugh was without humor. "Well," he muttered, "when you're having fun . . ."

"Let me explain, Vick. You see? The way the pay week runs . . . the pay week runs through Sunday night. Sunday night . . . midnight. So . . . technically . . . your Sunday shift is actually Monday morning. New pay week. So, if you start tonight . . . that'd be Thursday, really . . . plus Friday, plus Saturday, plus Sunday . . . that'd give you as many hours this pay period as I can give you. You'd get paid next Friday . . . that's a week from the day after tomorrow . . . for how-ever-many hours you work through this comin' Sunday mornin'. So how 'bout . . . how 'bout you take off <u>Tuesdays</u>? That okay?"

"That's fine."

"Well, <u>great</u>! <u>Okay</u>, Ski! Okay, <u>Vick</u>! Welcome <u>aboard</u>! If you got any <u>problems</u> . . . any problems at <u>all</u> . . . why, I want you to come right to <u>me</u>. My door . . . <u>that</u> door there . . . it's always <u>open</u>! Remember my name. I'm Captain Fox. And I know you'll be a good <u>man</u> . . . and a good <u>employee</u>. I'm lookin' for great <u>things</u> from you, Vick. Now, you go on back out into the outer office and ask Miss <u>Ellis</u> . . . that's the lady that, she was the one who, brought you <u>in</u> here . . . you ask her to take you on <u>downstairs</u>. Take you down to see Sergeant <u>Forwand</u>. Now, he'll . . . he's gonna . . . <u>fingerprint</u> you. No objections <u>there</u>, is there?"

"No."

"<u>Good</u>! <u>Great</u>! Sergeant Forwand'll <u>fingerprint</u> you, and see that you fill out the bonding forms and the

W-2s or W-4s . . . or whatever the hell they are . . . and get you your <u>uniforms</u>. Now, you'll get <u>two</u> winter uniforms . . . which you'll be expected to keep 'em clean. You get a monthly <u>allowance</u>. I think it's up to four-and-a-half bucks now . . . is what it is . . . to <u>clean</u> 'em. We wantcha always to look <u>sharp</u>! Like a **Tarkenton** man <u>oughta</u> look. In the summer, why, we'll issue <u>summer</u> uniforms. Anyway, again, let me <u>welcome</u> you . . . to **Tarkenton Security Services**. I think that this <u>day</u> . . . January the seventeenth, nineteen and seventy-three . . . I think it's gonna be a real red-<u>letter</u> day, in the life of Victor Smig . . . uh . . . Smee . . . uh . . ."

"Smigelski, Captain. And thank you. I'll try and do a good job for you. But, I really am looking to move <u>up</u>! Move up the corporate <u>stepladder</u> . . . as quickly, and as steadily, as possible."

"<u>Good</u>! <u>Great</u>! Glad to <u>hear</u> it! Like to <u>see</u> that in a man! You'll go <u>far</u>, Vick! <u>B'lieve</u> me, Vick! I c'n <u>tell</u>! I'm a pretty good judge of <u>character</u>. B'lieve me . . . you'll go <u>far</u>!"

It had taken Smigelski a good deal longer than Captain Fox's estimate to wind up getting "squared away"—as Sgt. Forwand had called it. Innumerable times.

It was past 7:00 PM—before he'd gotten out of **Tarkenton Security Services'** headquarters, in Midtown Manhattan.

After grabbing a $1.89 "steak"—at one of the many production-line eateries, in the Times Square area—then, taking in a movie, he presented himself at fifteen minutes before midnight to Corporal Scotti, at the **General Appliance Corporation's** warehouse.

The eight-hour shift seemed interminable. Smigelski's legs were killing him—by five o'clock in the morning! How he'd managed to endure the last couple of tours was beyond him.

The tour—not surprisingly—required him to walk <u>incessantly</u>! Constantly schlepping up and down! Many different flights of stairs!

The tour was more difficult to learn than he'd expected. At first, there seemed to be no rhyme or reason to the routine:

Key One—turned in his traveling clock—was located on the ground floor, in the rear of the building, close by the security desk. Key Two was on the third floor—in a front section of the warehouse. Key Three was on the second story—in the center of the massive building. Key Four was back up on the third floor—at the back end of the facility. And on and on it went!

There were a total of twelve keys—located in such manner that Smigelski was required to literally walk to each corner of the entire three-story building! Each hour!

On the sixth tour, Scotti let Smigelski "lead" for the first time. Trailing behind, the corporal had had to correct the new employee twice. Essentially, though, Smigelski had the tour committed to memory. The seventh trip through the immense warehouse was done, in the same manner as the sixth. But, the "voyage" required no in-course corrections. The final sweep, Smigelski made by himself. It took him 65 minutes.

His relief—along with Corporal Scotti—was waiting for him, when he dragged himself back to the security desk, on the first floor. Scotti advised our hero that 65 minutes "wasn't all that damn bad".

"I had one guy," he explained, "really got <u>lost</u> up there. I mean, he <u>really</u> got lost. Probably be knocking around up there <u>yet</u> . . . if I hadn't gone up and fetched him the hell <u>out</u>."

Smigelski was not impressed. He was exhausted. He'd not been to bed in well over 24 hours. The constant pain—consuming every portion of his legs—brought back memories of some of his more celebrated childhood toothaches! Different location—but, same theory! And every bit as intense!

It was a monumental struggle, merely to drive back to his little room in Metuchen, New Jersey—some 30 miles south of New York City.

It was 9:30, that morning, when he'd crawled into his bed—and slept the clock around.

On his way back into "The Big Apple" that night, on the bus, Smigelski ruminated about his brief career in the wonderful world of security:

Corporal Scotti, he had been surprised to find, was a much <u>younger</u> man. Barely 22-years-of-age. He <u>looked</u> eighteen.

Although Smigelski's first impression of the corporal had been of Scotti, as the model "corporate man", Scotti had shocked Smigelski with several admissions. He'd told his new charge that he'd "ripped off" a number of items, during his tour of duty, at the warehouse! Gadgets manufactured by **General Appliances**!

"It wasn't all that much," Scotti had explained. "I did manage to snarf a table-model television, though! Color set, it was! Neat set! The rest was just nit-shit stuff. Stuff like a kitchen mixer. A blender, I guess they're called. And . . . oh yeah . . . an electric razor. Well, <u>that</u> was kinda expensive. Oh, and one of those electric frying pans. That's been pretty neat. Well, and a few strings of Christmas lights."

Scotti had paused to scratch his head.

"Plus," he continued, "one of them AM/FM digital clock radios. I <u>really</u> love that one. You can see the numbers . . . see 'em really clear at night. Also snagged one of those nifty *Mister Coffee* rigs . . . that Joe DiMaggio is always hawking on television. Works pretty good. None of the stuff was all that expensive . . . except, maybe, the tee vee. Hell, Ski! I work my <u>ass</u> off . . . and I don't make doodily-squat! <u>No</u> one does! So, I figure . . . what the hell . . . I'm <u>entitled</u>!"

Smigelski couldn't control his bewilderment. "Don't they <u>miss</u> it? <u>Miss</u> all that stuff?"

"Nah," Scotti replied with a cynical laugh. "Shit . . . they don't know, <u>themselves</u>, what they got in here. Hell, their own damn <u>employees</u> rip 'em off! Worse than <u>we</u> do . . . if anything! You should <u>hear</u> some of the things the daytime guards tell me. Employees walk out of here with all <u>kinds</u> of shit."

"Aren't <u>we</u> supposed to be . . . to be <u>stopping</u> that sort of thing?"

"Yeah. I guess you could say that. But, hell. Listen, Ski . . . they don't <u>pay</u> us enough money to get ourselves involved in a whole hell of a lot of <u>hassles</u>. Besides, you can't <u>help</u>, but <u>know</u> . . . just by the way some broad is <u>walking</u> . . . that she's got an electric can opener or something hid! Stuck up under her <u>dress</u>! What're you gonna <u>do</u>? What the hell can <u>we</u> . . . any <u>one</u> of us . . . do? <u>Knowing</u> is one thing. <u>Proving</u> is something else! What're you gonna <u>do</u>? Hike her <u>dress</u> up for her? Make her <u>show</u> you . . . that she's <u>clean</u>? Make her show you . . . show you <u>everything</u>? Scope out what kind of <u>panties</u> she's wearing? Or find out if she's wearing any panties at <u>all</u>? I'd be all for <u>that</u>! But, when you stop and <u>think</u>? Think of all the bullshit <u>involved</u>? <u>Forget</u> it! <u>None</u> of it . . . well, it ain't gonna <u>work</u>!"

"Well, I don't understand why **General Appliance** is <u>keeping</u> us! I mean, if we're not doing what they <u>pay</u> us to do, why . . ."

"It's by <u>me</u>," interrupted Scotti. "I guess they must figure that, if we weren't <u>around</u> . . . there's three or four guards on the <u>day</u> shift . . . their loyal, trusted, employees would steal even <u>more</u> shit than they do! Would steal really <u>expensive</u> shit . . . and lots <u>of</u> it . . . if we weren't on <u>guard</u>! I imagine that the fact we're <u>here</u> . . . well, it <u>must</u> intimidate 'em! At least <u>some</u> of 'em. To a <u>point</u>, anyway. It'd be a bit <u>gross</u>, I'd have to think, for a couple of guys to just simply walk on <u>out</u> of here . . . with a big, expensive, <u>stereo</u>! Or a floor-model <u>tee vee</u>! Maybe **General Appliances** figures they can <u>live</u> . . . with all the small shit disappearing, all the time. They probably <u>hope</u> that we'll <u>stop</u> the crooks, who <u>work</u> for 'em. Stop 'em from copping all the big, high-priced, stuff. I don't really know. Don't really care."

"Yeah, but a color television! Like the one you took. Don't they have some kind of record of that set? Wouldn't there be some kind of inventory control?"

"Nah," replied Scotti with a sneer. "I guess they're supposed to, y'know. Probably, they do have . . . something like that. In theory, anyway. From what I understand, it's all done by computer. Those damn things are supposed to be perfect. But, they operate off of whatever half-assed figures the people decide to feed into it. And I doubt that the employees give a shit." He smiled broadly. "I'm not worried," he went on. "They'll never trace it! Not to me! I doubt they know the damn thing's even missing. Probably, they'll never know."

"Scotti? Is this some sort of test? I mean . . . am I supposed to go to Captain Fox now? Go to him . . . and tell him? Tell him . . . what you just told me? And if I don't . . . then, I'm not doing my job? I'm fired? That kind of thing?"

"Ski, let me assure you that . . . if you ever went to Captain Fox with what I just told you . . . you'd never walk again!"

Smigelski had been astounded by the corporal's threat!

Scotti's lead-pipe serious demeanor did not diminish!

"Do you think this is the only place we guard?" he snarled. "The only place we guard? And the only one we rip off? There's guys who work, out at Kennedy Airport . . . and at LaGuardia. Listen, they rip off more shit . . . than you could ever imagine! These are guys, now, who've been with **Tarkenton** . . . for <u>years</u>! Years and <u>years</u>! They don't want to be <u>anything</u>! Not one damn <u>thing</u> . . . but <u>security</u> guards. Know <u>why</u>? They don't <u>buy</u> anything! <u>Nothing</u>! Not a damn <u>thing</u>! They <u>bank</u> . . . practically their whole damn <u>paycheck</u>! They <u>steal</u> almost everything they'll ever <u>need</u>! Do you have any <u>idea</u> how much crap goes through an <u>airport</u>?"

"I've never <u>pondered</u> it. Must be a <u>boodle</u>."

"You're damn <u>right</u>! A boodle-and-a-<u>half</u>! I just <u>live</u> for one of those guys to call in <u>sick</u>! <u>That</u> gives <u>me</u> a shot at working a shift or two out there! I'd volunteer . . . I <u>do</u> volunteer . . . so fast it makes their heads swim! But, of course, so do a half-a-million <u>other</u> guys! Just about have to be a <u>sergeant</u> . . . to score one of <u>those</u> shifts, though. I <u>did</u> manage to pull a few shifts at <u>Shea</u> Stadium. Not much out there, though. Well, I <u>did</u> manage to snag six or seven **NFL** footballs and a couple sets of shoulder pads! And a helmet or two! Even scored one of Joe <u>Namath's</u> helmets. <u>Had</u> to be his! Had number <u>twelve</u> on it . . . and everything."

"I can't <u>believe</u> this," muttered Smigelski. "Do you mean that . . . that <u>that's</u> why guys'll work for starvation <u>wages</u>? I mean . . . doesn't someone check out their <u>homes</u>? Here they <u>are</u> . . . making a hundred-and-a-quarter or a hundred-and-a-half a week . . . and they've got all this <u>loot</u>? Doesn't anyone <u>question</u> that?"

"Naah. I have the feeling that . . . down <u>deep</u> . . . that Captain Fox <u>knows</u> the way things are. But, I'm sure that he doesn't <u>want</u> to know . . . if <u>that</u> makes any sense. <u>He's</u> happy, just thinking . . . or <u>wanting</u> to think . . . that the guard profession is so <u>wonderful</u>! And so <u>noble</u>, that <u>no</u> one . . . no one in his right mind . . . would <u>want</u> to do anything else! <u>Anything</u> else! And . . . don'tcha know . . . there's just some things. that're better left <u>unsaid</u>. Let sleeping dogs lie . . . and all such shit as <u>that</u>!"

"Is it the same at all the <u>other</u> security services?"

"<u>That's</u> by me, too. I've never worked for any of the other ones. Never much <u>thought</u> about it. I suppose they <u>are</u>. I really don't <u>know</u>, though. All I <u>do</u> know . . . is that I've been with **Tarkenton** not quite a <u>year</u>! And I'm doing pretty <u>well</u>! Doing damn <u>good</u> . . . as a matter of fact! I've only been <u>pulling</u> this shift . . . for, I guess, the last eight or nine <u>weeks</u>. Don't know <u>where</u> they'll send me next. My advice to you, Ski, is <u>forget</u> . . . about taking the goddam <u>bus</u> in! Bring in your <u>car</u>! You can <u>park</u> it right out in back! Where I park <u>mine</u>! During the <u>night</u>, you put a dandy little color tee <u>vee</u> set . . . in the ol' trunk! Who'll know? Who'd ever <u>know</u>? The only thing to <u>tell</u> you is . . . when you get it <u>home</u> . . . just don't plug it <u>in</u>! Not right <u>away</u>! It gets damn <u>cold</u> . . . in the trunk of a car! Give the set a chance to warm <u>up</u>! Warm up . . . to room <u>temperature</u>! Then, you can plug it <u>in</u> . . . and turn it <u>on</u>! Then, hell, you're home <u>free</u>!"

"Are you <u>sure</u> . . . this isn't some kind of <u>test</u>? I mean, I don't know that much about the <u>law</u> . . . but, I'd have to think that this'd be something like <u>enticement</u>! Or <u>entrapment</u>! Or <u>some</u> damn fool thing! Are you trying to get me to lose my <u>job</u>? By not <u>finking</u> on you . . . to Captain <u>Fox</u>? Or . . . even <u>worse</u> . . . maybe you're trying to get <u>me</u> to cop a television! And <u>you'll</u> be sitting outside . . . with every cop in the world! Just <u>waiting</u> . . . to <u>pounce</u> upon my poor unsuspecting <u>soul</u>! Throw my ass . . . in <u>jail</u>! Get a neat <u>promotion</u>!"

"Look, Ski. Believe what you <u>want</u> to believe! I could care <u>less</u>! I'd have to <u>think</u>, though, that . . . for a man of <u>your</u> age . . . you're awfully goddamned <u>naive</u>! How <u>old</u> are you? <u>Forty</u>? And you don't <u>know</u> from such things? Maybe . . . maybe, it's <u>you</u> who's testing <u>me</u>!"

"I'm not testing <u>anybody</u>," Smigelski groused. "It's just that . . . I can't <u>believe</u> that all this . . . that all this goes <u>on</u>!"

"Well, it <u>does</u>! You can bet your <u>balls</u> on it! I hope they send me . . . next . . . to one of the **Ballinger's** locations! Or maybe **Wallingford's**! Jesus! I could have a <u>field</u> day . . . <u>there</u>! That shit . . . all that shit . . . that just <u>lays</u> out there! Just lays . . . on the <u>counters</u>! And you can just help <u>yourself</u>! I promised my wife a new <u>coat</u> . . . if I ever <u>got</u> to one of those fancy-assed places!"

"This is . . . is . . . ! How about the really <u>expensive</u> places? The really <u>excusive</u> fur salons? And all those expensive <u>jewelry</u> stores? <u>All</u> those snooty places . . . over on Fifth <u>Avenue</u>? **Bethany's**? **Baron and Calverts**?"

"Well now, over <u>there</u> they've got all kinds of <u>alarm</u> systems! And really sophisticated closed circuit tee <u>vee</u> shit. Plus, I guess they've got <u>guard</u> dogs . . . and all kinds of shit like that. I really don't think that **Tarkenton** <u>has</u> any of those outfits as clients, or whatever. If we do, <u>I</u> sure as hell don't know anything about 'em. It'd probably be handled by a different <u>department</u>, anyway. Stealing a twelve- or fifteen-thousand dollar necklace is a <u>hell</u> of a lot different than copping a three-hundred dollar tee <u>vee</u>. Or a sixty-dollar <u>recorder</u>. No, <u>I</u> ain't greedy. Just give me a few shifts . . . at **<u>Ballinger's</u>** or **<u>Wallingford's</u>**. <u>That's</u> good enough . . . for the likes of <u>me</u>. I ain't no <u>hog</u>, y'know."

"Well," Smigelski had responded, with a heavy sigh, "I want you to know that this has really been an . . . an <u>education</u>."

"An education, my Polish recruit, is only as good as what the person, who gets it, <u>puts</u> it to. In this case, it can be very, very <u>rewarding</u>. <u>Damn</u> rewarding."

TWO

S MIGELSKI MANAGED TO "HANG IN" at the **General Appliance** warehouse. The shifts he manned—and the staggering number of hours he worked—over the better part of the following three months, put a heavy-duty crimp in "what I laughingly refer to . . . as my social life", as he'd proclaimed, on many occasions. ("On too damn <u>many</u> occasions," as he'd constantly muttered to himself.)

His fiancée—June Bodner—was not, at all, pleased with the overwhelming number of those shifts! She especially was not thrilled with the <u>massive</u> number of overtime hours!

Once February had arrived—typically blustery-cold—Smigelski found himself laboring seven days! Each and every week! By the middle of February, he was putting in numerous numbers—of what Captain Fox had labeled a "double". Those translated out to be afternoon <u>and</u> midnight shifts! Virtually—well, literally—every Tuesday!

"It figures," he'd lamented to June—also on many occasions. "Tuesday was originally <u>supposed</u> to be my day off. It is to laugh. The whole thing is so typical . . . of dear ol' **Tarkenton**. Typical as hell . . . that I'd wind up working sixteen stupid hours, every damn Tuesday."

"To say nothing of most Thursdays . . . and the occasional Saturday," grumped June, in response.

There were other-than-romantic results—of his dramatic increase in hours at the warehouse! The massive work schedule—was draining Smigelski, physically!

The situation only served to make June even less enchanted with his exhausting employment situation! And she never hesitated to make her position known!

During Smigelski's first three months of "semi-gainful employment", there had been no untoward incidents. Tempted though he'd been, he'd always refrained from taking any of the many attractive appliances! Merchandise that he would walk past— each and every hour, of each and every shift! The temptation, though, was never far away! Especially, as he would become more and more fatigued—a virtually every-shift happening!

From time to time, a sergeant or a lieutenant would "spot check" him—for about 15 minutes. Just long enough to inhale a cup of coffee—and speak of everything imaginable. Generally, those "invigorating" conversations would cover anything and everything—not connected with the security business in general, or the warehouse in particular.

However, for the most part, our hero was, pretty much, left to his own devices.

On March 15, 1973, Smigelski was promoted to corporal—his stripes given to him, personally, by Captain Fox, in a surprisingly well-attended ceremony in the captain's office.

He was applauded—at great length—by Captain Fox, the matronly Hilda Ellis, Sgt. Forwand, Corp. Scotti and an impressive contingent of lieutenants and other sergeants. A few of whom, he'd never met. Impressive!

At the ceremony, Scotti informed Smigelski that he—Scotti—was to be promoted to the lofty rank of sergeant, the following week.

"I'll be damned," Smigelski observed, to June Bodner, the day following his promotion, "you'd have thought I'd just won the Congressional Medal of Honor or something."

"Or something," she'd groused. "Or some damn thing."

Six days later, he would encounter his first trouble:

As Smigelski had walked along the third floor, he'd spotted a group of six men! <u>Six</u> <u>men</u>! They were, busily, loading a goodly number of expensive floor-model television sets, onto four pushcarts!

Ducking behind another piled-high row of console TVs, Smigelski withdrew his beeper from his belt! He pressed the button on the face of the small black-and-silver contraption! Once he'd heard the expected low-pitched beep, he spoke slowly, softly—and with great care—into the instrument!

"Smigelski calling," he articulated. "**General Appliance** warehouse! Thirty-eighth and Tenth Avenue! Third floor! Front part of the building! Six men . . . they appear to be men . . . loading up console televisions! All kinds of them! I'm observing them now! They don't seem to know anybody's here! Please hurry!"

Squatting down behind the rows of televisions, Smigelski proceeded to await the "spectacular" arrival—of the veritable "army" of **Tarkenton** men! Surely, the Cavalry was, triumphantly, on its way! He could almost hear the trumpets!

He waited! And waited! And waited and waited!

Fully twenty long, suspense-filled, minutes passed! No sign of the promised reinforcements from **Tarkenton**!

The six men proceeded—the epitome of calmness—to load ten sets, onto the pushcarts! They tied them—meticulously, securely—with fabric belts! They'd been well-prepared! Remaining calm as ever, they wheeled their swag to the freight elevator—at the south side of the building!

As the gate closed on the elevator—and the car began to descend—Smigelski broke for the stairway, just behind him!

As quickly—and as quietly—as he could, he hurried down the two flights to the ground floor!

He peered out of one of the rear windows! The six burglars were in the process of, unexcitedly, loading the purloined sets—into a bus-type van! Smigelski had to marvel: They were such a highly-efficient, "business-like", group.

Once the televisions had been placed in the vehicle, the rear doors were almost-silently shut! Three interlopers scurried into the front of the truck— and, strangely, flicked on the headlights!

Smigelski fixed his stare on the license plate! He couldn't read it! The little bulb—above the plate—was out! The fact that the little truck was caked with mud didn't help!

The remaining three men hopped into a 1971 Ford LTD, four-door sedan! The plate on the sedan was half-illuminated! Smigelski was able to get all three letters and one of the three digits!

The two vehicles roared off into the night!

Smigelski raced back to the security desk—and frantically dialed **Tarkenton** headquarters! A gruff voice answered—on the fourth ring!

"**Tarkenton**! Lieutenant Brimsek here!"

"Yeah! This is Smigelski!"

"Who?"

"Smigelski!"

"What the hell's a <u>Smigelski</u>?"

"I'm the <u>guard</u> . . . over at **General Appliance's** <u>warehouse</u>!"

"Okay. You're the <u>guard</u> . . . over at **General Appliance's** <u>warehouse</u>. You expect a fuckin' <u>medal</u> or something?"

"Didn't you get my <u>call</u>?"

"<u>What</u> call? <u>When</u>?"

"I <u>called</u> you! On my damn <u>beeper</u>!" I had six <u>guys</u> in here! <u>Stealing</u>! Ripping off tee <u>vee</u> sets!"

"We didn't get no call <u>here</u>! When <u>was</u> this?"

"<u>I</u> don't know! I called twenty . . . maybe twenty-<u>five</u> . . . minutes ago!"

"And you say you called on your <u>beeper</u>?"

"<u>Yes</u>! Yes, that's <u>right</u>! And no one <u>came</u>!"

"That's 'cause we didn't <u>send</u> no one! We didn't <u>get</u> no call here!"

"You've <u>got</u> to have gotten it!"

"<u>Listen</u>, Ace! Don't tell <u>me</u> what I've <u>got</u>! Not about <u>anything</u>! How do I know that you didn't just <u>fake</u> the goddam call? <u>Fake</u> the fuckin' call . . . and <u>rip</u> all that shit off <u>yourself</u>? Now, just calm <u>down</u>, for a half-a-minute! Tell me what <u>happened</u>!"

"Well, twenty-five <u>minutes</u> ago, I was making my <u>rounds</u>! And I'd just turned number-five <u>key</u> on the tour! Look, the goddam <u>clock'll</u> . . . <u>that'll</u> tell you what time that was!"

"Yeah. It'll tell us what <u>time</u> it was . . . if the fucking thing was <u>working</u>! Those clocks get so fucked <u>up</u>, sometimes . . . that it's fucking <u>unbelievable</u>!"

"Well, I turned the key in number-<u>five</u>! And I heard some <u>noises</u>! So, I kind of crept up . . . to where the noise was <u>coming</u> from! I saw these <u>guys</u> . . . there were <u>six</u> of 'em . . . and they were loading <u>televisions</u>! <u>Big</u> ones! <u>Consoles</u>! <u>Floor</u> models! Still in their packing <u>crates</u>! <u>Loading</u> 'em! Onto these <u>hand</u> trucks!"

"Slow <u>down</u>! How many <u>hand</u> trucks?"

"<u>Four</u>! <u>Four</u> of 'em . . . I <u>think</u>! So, I ducked <u>down</u> . . . behind a bunch of <u>other</u> televisions! And I pressed the <u>button</u> . . . on my <u>beeper</u>! I heard the little <u>gleep</u> . . . at the other <u>end</u>! Then, I whispered into the <u>beeper</u>! Said <u>who</u> I was . . . and <u>where</u> I was!

And what was going <u>on</u>! Just like the instructions say I'm <u>supposed</u> to!"

"Must be somethin' wrong with the fuckin' <u>beeper</u>. Press the <u>button</u> again."

Smigelski followed instructions—and heard the same beep! "<u>There</u>!" he barked into the phone. "Hear <u>that</u>?"

"Nope," muttered Brimsek. "Didn't hear <u>shit</u>! Not a fuckin' <u>sound</u>! Not a goddam <u>thing</u>. Wonder when was the last time . . . that they ever decided to change the fuckin' <u>batteries</u> in that sonofabitch! There ain't <u>nothin'</u> comin' through, on this end! <u>Those</u> things . . . they aren't worth a <u>shit</u>, anyway!"

"Thanks a <u>batch</u>! Well, after I pressed the stupid <u>button</u>, on the stupid <u>beeper</u> . . . and gave my stupid little <u>message</u> . . . I just sort of <u>watched</u> 'em!"

"You didn't try and <u>stop</u> 'em . . . <u>did</u> you, Son?"

"<u>No</u>! Just kind of <u>watched</u> 'em! They put three or four <u>sets</u> . . . <u>big</u> sets . . . on <u>each</u>, of those hand trucks! <u>Big</u> hand trucks! <u>Huge</u> hand trucks! And they wheeled 'em over to the <u>freight</u> elevator! And they <u>took</u> 'em! Took 'em . . . on down to the ground <u>floor</u>! I took the <u>stairs</u> . . . while they were in the <u>elevator</u>! When I caught <u>up</u> with 'em, they were already <u>outside</u>! Out in <u>back</u>! They <u>loaded</u> all the tee vee sets . . . into a Ford <u>Econoline</u> van! About a sixty-<u>seven</u> . . . or sixty-<u>eight</u>! Couldn't <u>see</u> the license number! The <u>bulb</u> was out!"

"Not much <u>help</u>," grunted Brimsek.

"Well <u>three</u> of 'em . . . <u>three</u> of these guys . . . <u>they</u> got in the truck! But, <u>listen</u>! The other <u>three</u> . . . they all got into a seventy-one <u>Ford</u>! Ford <u>LTD</u>."

"How d'ya know it was a <u>LTD</u>? <u>All</u> them full-sized cars . . . they look the <u>same</u>!"

"Because . . . in seventy-<u>one</u> . . . the <u>LTD</u> had tail lights, going all the way <u>across</u>! All the way . . . across the ass <u>end</u>! The <u>other</u> full-sized Fords . . . <u>they</u> had just one <u>light</u>! One light . . . on each <u>side</u>!"

"Hey, you <u>know</u>? That's <u>right</u>! <u>Okay</u>! Were you able to get the <u>number</u>? <u>License</u> number . . . off the <u>car</u>?"

"<u>No</u>! Well . . . <u>yes</u>! Just <u>half</u> of it! One of the <u>bulbs</u> was out! But, it's something-something-seven, E-E-P. A couple of my friends are from <u>Buffalo</u> . . . and I think it's an Erie <u>County</u> plate!"

"<u>Say</u>," marveled Brimsek. "You're a <u>smart</u> sonofabitch! What'd you say your <u>name</u> was?"

"<u>Smigelski</u>. I've been in the <u>rent</u>-a-car business . . . about twelve <u>years</u>. We sometimes got cars checking <u>in</u>! Ones that had been rented . . . up in <u>Buffalo</u>! One of my <u>friends</u>, up there . . . he still <u>works</u> for **Avis**! I don't know what <u>good</u> those few <u>numbers</u>'ll do! Sorry I wasn't able to get the whole <u>thing</u>!"

"Well, we'll let the <u>cops</u> worry about it. I'll get 'em right <u>over</u> there. Look, make an <u>entry</u>, in your log! Put in everything . . . about what <u>happened</u>! Put down that you called <u>me</u>! My <u>name</u> is spelled B-R-I-M-S-E-K! When the <u>police</u> get there, just tell 'em all about what <u>happened</u> . . . and give 'em your <u>information</u>! Be sure and <u>note</u> it in your <u>log</u>! Write in, the name of the <u>cop</u> . . . who you <u>talk</u> to! Tell your <u>relief</u> . . . at eight o'clock . . . tell him. that he should tell the <u>lieutenant</u> to get that stupid-assed <u>beeper</u> fixed! Or throw it in the <u>shit</u> can! Or do <u>something</u> with it! <u>Stick</u> it . . . somewhere! You know what I'm <u>talkin'</u> about!"

He chuckled at the Ribald implication present in his remark.

"Anything else?" asked Smigelski.

"Naw. That's about it. Good work! Well done! What was your name again?"

"Smigelski. S-M-I-G . . ."

"Yeah. Well, that's fine, Smikkle-ski. Well done! Now, just watch . . . for the cops."

"How about my tours?"

"Wait'll after the cops have left. Then, have yourself a cup of coffee. Then, whatever the top of the hour is after that . . . well, you can start your tours back up again. Just hit the silly-assed clock . . . like you normally do. Be sure and put it in your log. Put in how many tours you wind up missing. And when you started doin' 'em back over again."

"Yeah, but what if I should find someone else in here? The beeper, y'know . . ."

"You won't! They ain't comin' back! But, if you do . . . if you do spot someone . . . just come on back to the guard desk! Come back, to where you are! Call me . . . on the telephone! Forget about the goddam beeper. They're no damn good anyway! I don't know why the hell they even try and use 'em! That's the third time this month . . . that someone's tried to get ahold of me, on one of the goddam things. Tried to contact me! And the damn things didn't work! And that's just me! People tryin' to get ahold of me! Okay now, Saminski, just sit on your ass! Sit on your ass . . . and wait for the law! And . . . once again . . . well done!"

Smigelski waited an hour-and-fifteen minutes for the police! By the time the officers arrived, his shift was practically over!

The cops seemed—to a man—totally <u>uninterested</u>. One officer did condescend to write down the half-license number. But, it was virtually under <u>protest</u>.

"It ain't gonna do no <u>good</u>," the policeman explained. "I'll bet my dear mother's ass, that the plates were <u>stolen</u>! Or, quite possibly, the goddam <u>car</u> was stolen! Probably, so was the goddam <u>van</u>! <u>Shit</u>, everything . . . everything in that whole <u>operation</u> . . . was probably <u>stolen</u>! Besides, by <u>this</u> time? By <u>this</u> time . . . they're long <u>gone</u>! They went right from <u>here</u> . . . broke right to the Lincoln <u>Tunnel</u>! What the hell . . . it's only five or six <u>blocks</u> away! Before you know it . . . they'll be down in <u>Camden</u>! Probably <u>down</u> there, by now! Probably <u>been</u> there a good while!"

"<u>Camden</u>?"

"<u>Sure</u>! That's where <u>all</u> the hot stuff goes! From <u>here</u> . . . and from <u>Philly</u>! Well, from <u>Newark</u> too! And even <u>Wilmington</u>! Run the biggest damn <u>fence</u> operation . . . you ever <u>seen</u>! Make you <u>dizzy</u>!"

"You <u>know</u> all that?"

"Of <u>course</u>! <u>Everybody</u> does! Fat lot of <u>good</u> it does, though! They got the Jersey <u>politicians</u> . . . along with half the <u>cops</u>, and <u>all</u> the judges . . . on the <u>pad</u>! The whole goddam <u>state</u> . . . is ass-deep in <u>corruption</u>! <u>We</u>? We can't do a damn <u>thing</u>! Can't do <u>nothin'</u>! Hell, we don't even <u>try</u> anymore! Why <u>should</u> we? <u>Frustratin'</u>! Frustratin' as <u>hell</u>!"

"But . . . but," sputtered Smigelski, "but, that's . . . that's across state <u>lines</u>! The <u>Feds</u>! Can't the <u>Feds</u> . . . can't <u>they</u> do anything?"

"Feds <u>more</u> than got their hands full. <u>C'mon</u>! Organized <u>crime</u> runs the whole shebang! They've got enough <u>federal</u> judges on the take . . . that the FBI has one <u>hell</u> of a time, trying to even <u>touch</u> 'em! <u>Any</u> of 'em! Can't get <u>near</u> 'em! You said these <u>guys</u> . . . the ones, who <u>took</u> the television sets . . . they were all young, and . . ."

"They <u>looked</u> like they were pretty young! From where <u>I</u> was."

"<u>Trust</u> me. They <u>were</u> young. That's the way the mob <u>operates</u>! They <u>get</u> these pissy-assed young bucks . . . to stick <u>their</u> necks out! Then, they pay 'em <u>peanuts</u>! A frigging <u>pittance</u> . . . for all the stuff those young studs <u>steal</u>! The <u>kids</u>? <u>They</u> risk <u>their</u> asses! And the <u>mob</u> . . . <u>they</u> make all the <u>money</u>! Mob puts the stuff in <u>places</u>! <u>Stores</u>! Ones they <u>control</u>! Ain't no one can <u>touch</u> 'em! No sense in even tryin'! So no one <u>does</u>! Just buckin' our <u>heads</u>! Buckin' 'em . . . against a goddam brick <u>wall</u>!"

"I can't tell you how <u>thrilled</u> I am! <u>Overjoyed</u> . . . with the <u>education</u>, I've gotten tonight, Officer. <u>No</u> one . . . but, <u>no</u> one . . . seems to give a <u>shit</u>!"

The cop's manner softened. His smile was indulgent. "Well," he explained, "it's not so much that no one <u>gives</u> a shit. It's just a <u>situation</u>. One where you just <u>say</u>, to yourself . . . you <u>ask</u> yourself, 'What're you gonna <u>do</u>?' You <u>get</u> to where . . . like I said . . . you're buttin' your <u>head</u>! Up against a goddam <u>wall</u>! Let's <u>face</u> it! They got us . . . by the <u>ass</u>! <u>They</u> know it. <u>We</u> know it. Not much <u>sense</u> . . . in goin' through a whole lot of <u>changes</u>! A whole lot of <u>changes</u> . . . about something you really can't <u>fight</u>! I've got the <u>information</u>! And I'll make the <u>report</u>! But . . . just between us <u>girls</u> . . . that's about as far as it's gonna <u>go</u>!"

Smigelski nodded, glumly. "Yeah," he groused. "But, that's a <u>hell</u> of a note."

"<u>Isn't</u> it! Shit, there's no <u>sense</u> . . . in <u>you</u> getting' all up-tight! What the hell? It's not as if they were <u>your</u> sets! Not like they <u>belonged</u> to you! Shit! **General Appliance** . . . they can afford the loss! I'm <u>sure</u> that your security outfit . . . they're not <u>paying</u> you enough! Not enough . . . to get yourself all worked <u>up</u>! You did <u>your</u> job! And, by damn, you did it <u>well</u>! It was good <u>work</u>!"

"Yeah," snarled Smigelski. "That and a quarter'll get me a cup of goddam <u>coffee</u>."

"That's about the <u>size</u> of it. Sorry . . . but, there just ain't a hell of a lot you can <u>do</u>, about it! Not a hell of a lot <u>I</u> can do about it! Just don't take it all too much to <u>heart</u>!" He looked at his watch. "I gotta split," he muttered. "We'll see ya around." He took two steps—and turned to face the bewildered Smigelski. "You <u>know</u>?" queried the hardened cop. "You know <u>somethin'</u>? It was <u>nice</u>! Refreshing as <u>hell</u>! <u>Talkin'</u> to you. Kind of <u>upliftin'</u>, to be able to <u>talk</u> to someone . . . a guy who still gets <u>outraged</u> at some of the <u>shit</u> that goes on these days! I think that <u>most</u> of us have such a . . . such a, well . . . such a <u>demented</u> outlook that . . ."

"Well, I'm <u>working</u> on it! Getting pretty demented, <u>myself</u>! I must seem like the most <u>naïve</u> person . . . in the entire <u>world</u> . . . to you," interrupted Smigelski.

The officer laughed. "No." he said. "But, you're probably in the top <u>ten</u>. Like I said, though, it's <u>refreshing</u>. <u>Oh</u>! One thing <u>more</u>!"

"What's <u>that</u>?"

"When you <u>see</u> someone in here . . . for <u>Christ's</u> sakes . . . just look the other <u>way</u>! Whatever you do, don't <u>confront</u> 'em! It's a hell of a lot <u>easier</u> . . . and a hell of a lot <u>safer</u>! Mark my <u>words</u>: They don't <u>pay</u> you enough money! Not to get yourself all broken <u>apart</u>!"

Smigelski sighed. "I'll try and <u>remember</u> that," he muttered.

The following afternoon—one of his few "epic" days off—Smigelski and June Bodner were sitting in one of the uncomfortable old wooden booths at **Cottleman's Cottage**, an ice cream parlor in Metuchen, New Jersey. The old-fashioned, rustic, soda fountain-restaurant was located two short blocks from Smigelski's "posh" room-over-the-bar.

"I just can't get <u>over</u> it," he muttered, spooning the glob of whipped cream off the top of his hot chocolate. "Just can't get <u>over</u> it. <u>No</u> one cares. Not one goddam <u>soul</u>! <u>Amazing</u>! Simply <u>amazing</u>!"

"Oh, Vick. I wouldn't take it all that much to <u>heart</u>. Wouldn't take it to heart . . . at <u>all</u>."

"Yeah. That's exactly what the <u>cop</u> told me, last night. 'Don't take it all to <u>heart</u>.' It's awfully damn <u>hard</u> . . . <u>not</u> to take it all to heart. It's <u>awfully</u> hard . . . not to take it <u>all</u> to heart. No one <u>gives</u> a damn! No one gets <u>involved</u>! The goddam <u>beeper</u>? <u>It</u> doesn't work! And no one <u>cares</u>! The <u>cops</u>? <u>They</u> can't be bothered taking the information. Well, they <u>hate</u> being bothered. Because the stuff's already <u>at</u> the fence's place! In goddam <u>Camden</u>! And no one <u>cares</u>! <u>No</u> one!" His voice was beginning to rise. June put her forefinger over her lips. "Well," he groused, "it's all a bunch of <u>crap</u>!" He sipped at some of the steaming, brown, liquid. "All this going <u>on</u> . . . and who <u>gives</u> a shit? <u>No</u> one! No one <u>cares</u>!"

She reached over—and covered his free hand, with both of hers. "C'mon Vick," she soothed. "You're beginning to talk a little too loudly again. Look, Honey. They're not <u>paying</u> you enough! Not enough . . . to get all hot and <u>bothered</u> about it."

"That's another thing," he muttered. "You must be the twenty-seventh <u>person</u> . . . who's told me that! <u>Including</u> the sainted Captain Fox. Must be a damn <u>moral</u> there . . . somewhere!"

June looked at him—her soft, brown, doe-like eyes locking onto his hardened, almost-green optics. That "patented look", of hers, always reduced him to, as he described it, "a quivering mass of ectoplasm".

"Look, Honey," she soothed, "it's the same all over these days. No matter <u>where</u> you go. How many times have you stood there . . . waiting to be served . . . in some store? In <u>any</u> store? And there's the clerks . . . standing around, chewing the fat! It's the same thing. No one <u>cares</u>! Just like you said. Doesn't matter <u>who</u> it is . . . or what they <u>do</u> for a living. The day when people took <u>pride</u> . . . had any <u>pride</u>, at all . . . in their work is <u>gone</u>! Ka-<u>poot</u>! Your new profession is no different than anyone <u>else's</u>."

"Nah," he growled. "There's a <u>difference</u>."

"No there's not. There really <u>isn't</u>!"

Her smile was, as always, disarming—but, it would take much more than that to blow away our hero's blue funk.

"Yes there <u>is</u>," he snarled.

His response took her by surprise. His outrage seemed so unlike "The Polack"—<u>her</u> Polack—that she'd come to know! And to <u>love!</u>

"Look," he mused. "When those clerks are standing around . . . shooting the <u>breeze</u> . . . nothing's really <u>lost</u>. Well, true . . . <u>time's</u> lost. And you're a little pee-oh'd. But, you wind up <u>buying</u> the damn thing anyway. You're swearing . . . under your <u>breath</u>! Pissed <u>off</u> . . . the whole <u>time</u>. But, you <u>know</u> that . . . if you go anywhere <u>else</u> . . . it's gonna be the same damn <u>thing</u>. The point I'm making is . . . the store owner has <u>still</u> sold what-ever-it-is. He's <u>sold</u> the merchandise . . . that you just <u>bought</u>. He just sold it a couple minutes <u>later</u> . . . than he <u>should</u> have . . . is all. And <u>he's</u> never even gonna know that, anyway. Could probably care <u>less</u>. <u>Could</u> care less! No skin off <u>his</u> nose . . . that <u>you</u> wound up highly-pissed."

"Well," she replied, "I don't altogether agree with you. Agree with that. In my case, it <u>would</u> cost the store owner. Cost him future <u>sales</u>. I won't go <u>back</u>! Not to a place . . . where the service is <u>lousy</u>."

"That'd be <u>fine</u>. If it weren't for the fact that just about any place else you <u>go</u> . . . anyplace <u>else</u> you'd go . . . you'll wind up getting treated the same damn <u>way</u>. So, you actually wind up . . . trudging back to the same <u>places</u>. And putting up with all the <u>crap</u>. And with all the crappy <u>indifference</u>. And the who-<u>gives</u>-a-shit attitude."

"Oh, Vick. We both <u>know</u> . . . that <u>you</u> didn't operate that way. Not when you were in the <u>rent</u>-a-car business."

"Yeah," he answered, with a deep sigh. "And a hell of a lot of <u>good</u> it ever did me. I'm no longer <u>in</u> the rent-a-car business . . . in case you hadn't <u>noticed</u>. Must be a moral <u>there</u>, too."

"Well, it wasn't <u>your</u> fault that your employer couldn't find <u>another</u> location . . . near the airport. It's just a damn <u>shame</u>."

"Oh, I believe they could've <u>found</u> one! If they'd <u>tried</u> a little harder. I had a couple of leads <u>myself</u>. It's just that the Arabs decided to start their stupid-assed little oil <u>embargo</u>! Sent the price of gas off the <u>wall</u>. At one point, <u>none</u> of us knew whether we were gonna even be able to <u>get</u> the stuff. All these <u>complications</u>! They just wanted . . . ! Well, with all the <u>bullshit</u> involved . . . it just made 'em pull in their <u>horns</u>! Big <u>time</u>!"

"Were they <u>that</u> worried?"

"Pretty <u>much</u>. Plus that . . . I got caught in a major <u>crossfire</u> . . . at the new car <u>dealership</u>. I was pretty much a <u>feeder</u> . . . for their used car lot. Things got to where the bigger cars had absolutely no <u>value</u> . . . on the lot, itself. They were up to their <u>fannies</u> . . . in Montereys and Montegos. They wanted <u>little</u> cars. They wanted <u>Comets</u>. <u>Those</u> little dandies . . . <u>they</u> were selling like <u>hotcakes</u>."

"I'm sure. But, what does <u>that</u> have to do with . . . ?"

"Listen, I could <u>never</u> rent Comets. Not to big-assed <u>executives</u>. Not with their fency-schmency <u>expense</u> accounts. The dealership <u>wanted</u> me to rent . . . what I could <u>not</u> rent! I couldn't rent out . . . what the dealership <u>needed</u> me to rent So . . . like the cop was saying last night . . . 'What're you gonna <u>do</u>?'."

"Well," muttered June, as she reached for her coat, "it's just a damn <u>shame</u> . . . that a good man, like <u>you</u>, has to wind up walking his <u>fanny</u> off! Has to wind up <u>walking</u> . . . up and down umpty-odd flights of stupid <u>stairs</u>! And turning a stupid <u>key</u> . . . in some stupid <u>clock</u>! A stupid <u>clock</u> . . . which may or may <u>not</u> work! Vick, I just <u>hate</u> to see you so . . . so damn <u>upset</u>! So riled <u>up</u> . . . over the fact that everyone over there's a <u>crook</u>! A <u>crook</u> . . . or else, they don't <u>give</u> a damn!"

"Probably <u>both</u>," he groused.

"<u>Probably</u> both," she nodded.

He slipped on his jacket—and they made their way out into the biting April wind. Smigelski's old Dodge was parked almost a block away. Once inside the car, they made their way to June's flat—in nearby North Plainfield.

During the drive, Smigelski glanced at his fiancée, out of the corner of his eye. She was scrunched up— eagerly awaiting the car's heater to kick in. To begin to disperse its normal, reluctant, labored, "charitable" smattering of lukewarm-at-best air.

June Bodner was a pretty blonde, 36-years-of-age, five-feet, seven-inches, with a "peaches-and-cream" complexion. She could not be described as thin—but, she, most certainly, was not heavy. Not for her height. And she possessed those always-feeling, soft, brown, doe-like, eyes . . . which, always, seemed to speak volumes. Through them, she was— always—quite transparent.

June had been divorced for slightly more than five years. She and her former husband had separated after 11 years of marriage. The union had produced two children. Both lived with their mother.

The woman had toiled at a few nondescript jobs— mostly clerical positions—since before her divorce.

She'd met Smigelski—when she'd gone to work, in the rather complicated Car Control section of the **Avis Rent-a-Car** licensee, in nearby Piscataway, New Jersey. She'd signed on with the franchisee, in 1967.

As indicated, she still had been married, at that point. So had Smigelski.

He had been leasing manager for the **Avis** licensee, until 1968, when the owners of the operation had cut back—significantly—on the firm's long-term leasing program. The reduction had, of course, affected Smigelski's earning potential. Had reduced his salary-plus-commission arrangement—also significantly.

"Cut my goddam legs out from under me," is the way he had (always) so, picturesquely, described it.

After **Avis**, Smigelski had taken a promise-laden position, in the Brighton Beach section of Brooklyn. With **Ballinger's Rent-a-Car**—an ill-fated subsidiary of the famed **Ballinger's Department Store** empire.

In 1969, when **Ballinger's** decided to get out of the car rental field—an entity it was ill-prepared to operate—he had gone to work for a Lincoln-Mercury dealership in Queens. He'd founded a rent-a-car company for the dealership. The rental subsidiary had operated out of the lobby in one of the many smaller hotels—close by the gargantuan Kennedy Airport.

By putting in 12- to 15-hour days, Smigelski had been able to build the operation to a "most decent" fleet of almost 100 cars. He'd been moderately successful in turning a profit. His main function, of course, was to provide fodder for the dealership's used car lot. An arrangement, seemingly, made in heaven.

Then, unexpectedly, the small hotel was sold to the much-larger hotel next door! The smaller building wound up being "annexed" onto the bigger one—by the simple expedient of their constructing a discotheque, which spanned the distance between the two edifices. Once the night club had been completed, it made the complex appear to be one immense building.

The sale of the hotel had coincided with the first Arab oil embargo! The combination of circumstances caused the dealership to drop its rent-a-car operation.

Smigelski was transferred—to the new car showroom. He endeavored to sell new Lincolns and Mercurys. However, his career as a new car salesman had been "spectacularly unsuccessful"—and, with obvious reluctance, the dealership had, ultimately, let him go! He was <u>crushed</u>! They'd been a wonderful employer. It was, simply, that circumstances—well beyond his control—had conspired to undercut our hero!

Going to work for **Tarkenton** didn't particularly fill him with satisfaction. But, it was proving to be, at least, steady. And—by dint of the fact that he'd usually worked 16 to 24 hours overtime each week—he'd become "reasonably solvent". ("<u>Reasonably</u>!")

Inez, his former wife, had been most lenient—and totally understanding—when it had come to his child support obligations.

She'd not worked during her marriage to Smigelski. However, in 1970, she'd taken a job at a large department store (not **Ballinger's**) in New Brunswick, New Jersey, the town in which she lived— in the house she and Smigelski had shared, until the time of their separation.

In less than two years time, she'd worked her way up to the position of department manager. Her salary wasn't overwhelming—but, it was adequate. And— base salary-wise—dwarfed Smigelski's.

Once our hero had lost his job at the dealership, Inez had never pressed him to meet his original support obligations—so long as she was convinced, she'd advised him, that he was doing his best. She'd added—almost as a footnote, a throw-away line, if you please—that she'd been convinced that he'd always done his best.

The couple had remained close friends—after their more-than-amicable divorce.

Happily, Smigelski's job with **Tarkenton**—with all the overtime involved—had enabled him to begin, once more, to fulfill his financial obligations to his children.

That being the case, when all was said and done, he was reasonably happy with his situation. This, despite the fact that the job had proven to be physically exhausting most of the time. And was continuing to sap his dexterity—on a daily basis! Exhausting, it was! And, at times, most frustrating!

His relationship with June Bodner, however, was another story.

Inasmuch as she was working days—and Smigelski was working nights—they were seldom able to spend more than a few too-quickly-gone, "stolen", hours, in the evening, with one another. Some of those most-rewarding occasions—a precious few—were spent in Smigelski's tiny room! Making love!

June was having a rough time financially. Her former husband, at that point, was making twice what Smigelski earned. A total cad, he seldom sent June any of those riches.

She was forever pursuing him in court! Petitioning to assure that her Good-Time-Charlie ex-mate would live up to his obligations. Each dollar she'd painfully extracted from him, of course, had been "akin to pulling teeth". As time had passed, June had begun to lose her zest—for the bi-monthly battle! The man, of course, knew that he was wearing his former wife to a nub! An accurate assessment of the situation!

June had a son, age 11, and a 12-year-old daughter. She lived, with her children, in a far-too-small apartment—upstairs over a grocery store, in North Plainfield.

Fortunately, her widowed mother lived only three blocks away. Every morning, June dropped the kids off, at her mother's house—to await the school bus, during most of the year—then, picked the tads up, in the evening.

Most of Smigelski's evenings were spent at the tiny apartment, in North Plainfield—with June and her two children. Except on the ever-increasing number of evenings, when Smigelski was required to work an extra shift. Tuesdays, mostly. Well, Tuesdays— virtually <u>always</u>! But another day or two always seemed to "sneak in"!

Of course, there were those few cherished occasions—when the couple would slip off, to Smigelski's "palatial" room! And make love!

June would usually wind up terribly depressed after those sessions. She was a <u>tigress</u>, in bed— but, most usually, suffered great emotional let- downs, once the love-making had ended. Hence, the traditional "uplifting" trips to **Cottleman's Cottage**— for hot chocolate (with, hopefully, generous portions of whipped cream) in the winter, and ice cream sodas in the summer. An always-needed, always-welcomed, dash of therapy.

They had spoken of marriage! Spoken of it often! However, Smigelski was reluctant to enter into a marriage—so long as his financial status remained so unstable.

On the evening in question, the heater, in the Dodge, had finally crackled to life. And June had begun to uncoil.

"Boy," she mused with a smile, "it sure takes a hell of a long time for that thing to ever kick on . . . and bestow some heat on this poor old bod' of mine."

"Whatever your bod' is," he'd replied with an overdone, sinister, leer, "it sure as hell ain't poor. And it ain't old. You gots a great bod' there, Keed."

"I hate to have to go home now. I always enjoy it, so much, up there . . . in your room. It's always so nice and warm and comfy. I know that I don't act like it . . . act like I'm all that happy . . . sometimes. But, I am, Vick. I really do like it up there. Love it up there! And then . . . dammit . . . we have to get up and come out into this bone-chilling damn weather! Bleacccchhhh!"

"Well, if I ever get back on my feet, it ain't always gonna be like this, Junie. Not even close."

"I know," she sighed, as she snuggled her nose into his shoulder. "I know."

She put her hand on the inside of his right thigh! He wrapped his arm around her shoulders!

"I guess," she continued, "that I've been down for so long . . . that it looks like up. Not original . . . but, apt." She looked up at him—and continued. "Vick, I sometimes wonder if we'll ever get there. Ever! There's always something that comes up! Always something . . . to screw us up! Screw up whatever hokey little plans we may be making! Sometimes . . . well, sometimes . . . I just get the feeling that fate has slapped us both in the fanny! With a black cat!"

THREE

THE FOLLOWING NIGHT, SMIGELSKI ENCOUNTERED his first "real" trouble—at the **General Appliance** warehouse!

The shift had begun routinely enough. His first four tours had, as usual, gone without incident. However, during his fifth sweep, through the cavernous facility, he was set upon by three young men—at approximately the same place, that he'd observed those six methodical thieves, two nights before!

Smigelski had, somehow, sensed that something was amiss! His first reaction, though, had been to, out of hand, <u>dismiss</u> the genuine uneasiness that he was experiencing!

<u>Must be getting old! I'm getting spooked too damn easily</u>!

He attributed most of the specter of foreboding to the fact that, as mentioned, he was approaching the precise location at which he'd witnessed the burglary! The "no one gives a damn" thievery—the reaction to which still had him plainly upset!

"Hell," he muttered to himself, "I've been walking by this same spot. Been schlepping through it . . . all night. And didn't feel a thing. Not a damn thing!"

He decided, however, to slow his pace! And, as a further precaution, he also withdrew his Billy club!

Obey that impulse!

In a matter of seconds, he was glad that he'd drawn what was considered his "weapon"!

The three young men leaped out at him—from behind the first row of televisions! Instantly, they knocked Smigelski to the floor! Before he'd had a chance to react, two of the three were on top of him!

As one of the two thugs attempted to swing a lead pipe at his head, Smigelski violently jammed his Billy stick, up into the youth's stomach—sending the punk reeling! And screaming! Loudly! Fortunately, the deadly pipe never landed! Well, it came to settle—harmlessly—on the cement floor!

Immediately, Smigelski's left arm shot up! His fist crashed—against the jaw, of the other young "tough"!

At the same time, Smigelski was jarred—by a shattering pain! Agony—in his own left shoulder! The third interloper had succeeded in landing a brutal blow! A ruthless smack—with yet-another lead pipe! The lethal length of pipe had, of course, been aimed at his head!

Smigelski pushed the second hood off him—and attempted to rise! Before he was able to scramble to his feet, however, the third youth swung at him again! The pipe—aimed, once again, at his head—landed virtually in the same spot, as the first murderous cut! Pain—horrible agony—seared through Smigelski's body!

The shoulder, he knew, had been broken! Of that, he was positive!

He was terrified—that he was beginning to lose consciousness! That would, he was certain, be the end! He would never wake up again! Ever!

Reaching back for "something extra", he managed to swing his club—in a vicious arc! He connected—dead on—with the pipe-wielder! The Billy stick smashed—with devastating force—into the punk's left knee! The force of the blow—sent the thug sprawling!

A second or two after Smigelski had regained his feet, the first hood—the goon, whom he'd lanced in the stomach—lunged at him! Smigelski caught him—full-force—in the face! The sickening sound of bones cracking—where Smigelski's club had blasted in—seemed to fill the entire floor!

The interloper let out a blood-curdling screech! And, as if he'd been pole-axed—he, immediately, dropped to his knees! Then, he collapsed, altogether! Sprawled out! Writhing in agony! On the floor!

The youth that Smigelski had clobbered with his fist had—obviously—seen enough! Had had enough! He broke toward the elevator! Smigelski snatched up one of the lead pipes, from the floor—and threw it at the frenzied, fleeing, hoodlum! The missile missed—ricocheting off one of the boxed televisions!

Turning to the remaining two young "toughs"— both of whom had "retained" their positions, on the floor—Smigelski noted that the thug, who'd hit him with the pipe was, seemingly, attempting to regain his feet! Bad move!

Smigelski aimed a powerful kick at the groin, of the hood! His "dainty size-eleven" landed! Scored! On target!

The young man collapsed! He laid there! Writhing—furiously! On the floor! A lot of that going around! This "tough" was clutching and clawing—frantically—at his testicles! With both hands! And shrieking! And shrieking! And shrieking! And shrieking!

Smigelski turned his attention to the remaining punk! That labored maneuver required a good deal of concentration! His own left shoulder had become a boiling inferno of blinding pain! More pain than he'd ever had to cope with before! A blood-red haze seemed to be settling in—filling his eyes! Inundating them in a frightening, almost-misty, crimson, fog! A mind-rattling shroud—consisting of he-didn't-know-what! He was certain that he was in the throes of losing his eyesight! Of actually going blind!

The youth in question had already been knocked completely unconscious, by Smigelski's club! He'd not moved—since the "weapon" had connected with what had been, in a more serene time, his face!

Looming over the fallen hood, Smigelski unleashed a bone-shattering kick—at the young thug's jaw! Direct hit! The devastating force of the vicious blow, in all probability, should've snapped the youth's neck! Somehow, Smigelski's kick didn't quite qualify! Close enough, though! Blood spurted—then trickled—from the "tough's" slack-jawed mouth!

Hovering over the two interlopers—one totally unconscious and the other still screeching at the top of his lungs, and clenching his groin—Smigelski made an arbitrary <u>decision</u>:

One of the intruders was plainly "<u>not</u> going anywhere"! The shrieking one, though? <u>He</u> was quite another matter!

Gripping his Billy club tightly—with <u>both</u> hands—Smigelski <u>launched </u>the weapon in a mighty arc! It <u>landed</u>! A <u>bone</u>-rattling blow! To the side of the hoodlum's <u>head</u>! The youth <u>stiffened</u>! His hands fell away from his <u>testicles</u>! He laid on the <u>floor</u>! <u>Still</u>! <u>Very</u> still!

An eerie—a <u>more</u> than eerie—silence filled the entire building! Smigelski ripped the beeper from his belt—and pressed the button! Hearing the tone, he spoke into the instrument—in a slow, labored, rasping, voice:

"Smigelski here! Third floor! **General Appliance** warehouse! Thirty-eighth and Tenth! Third Floor! I guess I already said that! Front part of the building! Have been attacked! By three men! Took out two of 'em! Third one got away! I'm <u>hurt</u>! <u>Bad</u>! Am heading to the security desk . . . to call in, just in case nobody's ever gotten around to <u>fixing</u> this fucking thing!"

Trying to cope with the terrible, searing, <u>pain</u>—and fighting back the overwhelming <u>nausea</u>—the troubled guard managed to stagger his way down to the guard's desk, on the first floor!

As the flow of adrenaline was definitely <u>slowing</u>, the blinding <u>agony</u> became even more and more <u>unbearable</u>! He semi-collapsed into the chair, by the weather-beaten desk!

Struggling to retain <u>consciousness</u>, he succeeded in dialing **Tarkenton's** number! On the sixth try!

The phone was snatched up on the first ring! "**Tarkenton**! Lieutenant Brimsek!"

"Yeah. This is Smigelski!"

"Smigelskawitz! What the Christ happened?"

"I got jumped! Three of 'em! Bastards!"

"Yeah! We got your message! I got four men . . . on the way! Ought to be there . . . any second!"

"Yeah. I hear 'em banging . . . on the back door! I'll see ya, Brimsek!"

Smigelski hung up the phone—and dragged himself toward the rear entrance! Halfway to his destination, he could hear the sound of police sirens! Followed closely—by the screech of tires in the parking lot!

Well, at least not everything is fucked up! Not completely, anyway!

It had become a monumental, almost-impossible, struggle by then! Everything had! But, he'd eventually managed to disengage the substantial iron-bolt lock! He attempted—to open the immense door! He managed to crack the formidable portal open! Well, wide enough—that the new arrivals were able to push it all the way!

Four **Tarkenton** men burst through! Three uniformed guards headed, immediately, toward the stairway—and the third floor. The lone plainclothes operative helped Smigelski back toward the security desk.

Before they'd moved 10 or 12 steps, six **NYPD** officers piled into the open-doored warehouse!

"Who's in charge here?" shouted one of the officers.

"Well, we're from **Tarkenton**," replied the plainclothesman. "I'm Sergeant Meeker and this man . . . he's got a long <u>Polack</u> name . . . <u>he's</u> the man who was <u>attacked</u>! Up on the third <u>floor</u>! <u>Three</u> of 'em . . . three <u>attackers</u> . . . as I <u>understand</u> it! <u>One</u> of 'em, I guess, got <u>away</u>! The <u>other</u> two? Ski, here, thinks he's knocked their <u>dicks</u> loose! Haven't had <u>that</u> much of a chance . . . to <u>discuss</u> it with him! I <u>guess</u> they still may be <u>unconscious</u>. At least they <u>were</u>! As of . . . how long ago was it, that you came down from there, Ski?"

"I <u>dunno</u>," groaned the badly-wounded guard. "Five . . . five minutes maybe. Maybe six or seven. I don't really <u>know</u>."

"Okay," barked the policeman. "I'm Officer <u>Danciewicz</u> . . . <u>also</u> a long Polack name! I'll get my <u>men</u> up there . . . on <u>three</u>! Check out what the hell's going on! Right now, though, I think we better get this man to the <u>hospital</u>! Can you <u>walk</u>, Ski?"

"Yeah. I . . . I <u>guess</u> so."

One of the uniformed officers helped Smigelski to his patrol car—and, lights blazing—sped him to the hospital! The other officers headed for the third floor!

The two punks, who'd run afoul of Smigelski, had not moved! Both were removed—on <u>stretchers</u>! They were taken, under guard, to another hospital! Where they remained under guard!

The pair of young thugs were, both, 15-years-of-age. As such, they were considered <u>juveniles</u>—by the State of New York. Their names could not be posted in the news media. Their cases would be assigned to Family Court.

If found guilty, the New York City Juvenile System would retain jurisdiction over them—until their 18th birthdays. At that point, their criminal records would, by law, be <u>purged</u>! <u>Destroyed</u>!

On the other hand, it would be a good while—before <u>either</u> hood would be released from the hospital! Both were listed in "<u>serious</u> condition", upon admission! The opinion of the admitting physicians was that both would <u>remain</u> "serious"! <u>Indefinitely</u>!

The medical experts had been exceptionally <u>accurate</u>, in their initial diagnosis! The youth whom Smigelski had kicked in the jaw would remain hospitalized—for 11 days! The other punk would settle in—for a "stay" of more than three weeks!

After having been heavily sedated for more than 12 hours, Smigelski awoke to find himself looking into the warm, loving, eyes of June Bodner. She was seated in an uncomfortable, straight-backed, chair—mere inches from his bed.

She appeared almost not to <u>recognize</u> him. Was her reaction—or lack of same—part of a <u>dream</u>? A Picasso-like <u>nightmare</u>? His in-and-out memory of the last half-day was consisting of disconnected, discordant, snippets—and snatches of the hectic, siren-laden, ride to the hospital! And a <u>horde</u> of people—prodding him, probing him, and sticking him. The entire experience—the <u>ghastly</u> experience—had taken on a highly-<u>surrealistic</u> quality.

Could it be—that he'd not really regained consciousness? That he was in some kind of a coma? That "Junie" was not really there?

His only distinct recollection was that of a faceless doctor—advising him that his shoulder was, indeed, broken! In two places! It seemed to Smigelski that, in addition, the doctor had warned that one of the breaks looked "pretty nasty"! Always an unpleasant harbinger! If true!

He was somewhat aware of the fact that they'd applied a formidable plaster cast! One that encompassed his entire shoulder! It was heavy— and still wet! And hot! Extremely hot! But then—in an instant—it was cold! He was cold! The entire procedure had been particularly agony-filled—despite the fact that they'd given him a massive series of shots! To "deaden" the pain! He could never have imagined what the experience would've been like— without the "medication"!

The sensation of overwhelming constriction— seemed, at the time, to be of equal significance! Why should that be?

He couldn't remember anyone inquiring about June! Or about Inez—or the kids—for that matter. He was certain that someone had mentioned the institution's need for phone numbers. But, he was unaware of having provided any. He was certain that he'd have been totally unable to help the hospital people—with anything like that. He'd been far from thinking coherently! Of that, he was certain! How could anyone reasonably expect him to talk—speak to anyone—intelligently? About anything?

Well—on the odd chance that he <u>wasn't</u> hallucinating—he was thankful, for June's presence! She was, most assuredly, a sight for sore eyes, as they say. And, presumably, sore shoulders! <u>Terribly</u> sore shoulders! An extremely large presumption!

Smigelski stirred two or three times! Wriggled, slightly, in his bed—looking up into the woman's tear-stained face!

"Hi!" His greeting was a raspy half-groan!

June had apparently lapsed into some sort of reverie! The sound of Smigelski's voice startled her!

"<u>Oh</u>! Oh, <u>Vick</u>! <u>OH</u>! My <u>God</u>! You <u>scared</u> me!"

"I wake up . . . and there <u>you</u> are. Here <u>you</u> are. <u>Staring</u> at me. What the hell did they <u>do</u>? Sell <u>tickets</u>?"

His attempt at a smile fell eons short.

"<u>NO</u>! No, I tried to <u>call</u> you! At your <u>room</u>! And there was no <u>answer</u>! So, I kept <u>trying</u>! And then . . . when it got to be <u>afternoon</u> . . . and I <u>still</u> wasn't . . ."

"<u>Afternoon</u>? What the hell time <u>is</u> it, anyway? What <u>day</u> is it, for God's sakes?"

"<u>Wednesday</u>! It's <u>Wednesday</u>! You were <u>hurt</u> . . . last <u>night</u>!! Rather this <u>morning</u>! A good <u>while</u> ago! A really <u>long</u> while ago! It's almost seven <u>o'clock</u>! Seven o'clock . . . in the <u>evening</u>!" She burst into tears! "Oh, my <u>baby</u>! <u>Vick</u>! Vick . . . that <u>cast</u>! It . . . it looks so damn <u>painful</u>."

"Seven <u>o'clock</u>? My <u>God</u>! I've <u>slept</u> all day! The whole damn <u>day</u>!"

"Well," she sniffled, "you're <u>entitled</u>. Anyway, when it got to be so late in the <u>afternoon</u> . . . and <u>still</u> no answer . . . I called **Tarkenton**, in New York. They didn't want to tell me <u>zilch</u>! I finally <u>insisted</u> . . . on

56

talking to Captain <u>Fox</u>! I guess I must've used my feminine <u>wiles</u>. Either that . . . or I simply became too much of a pain in the <u>fanny</u>. Anyway, I got to <u>talk</u> to him . . . to Captain Fox. He told me what <u>happened</u>! Oh, <u>Vick</u>! I don't want to <u>harp</u>, but . . ."

"So <u>don't</u>! I've got one hell of a <u>headache</u>!"

"You know what I <u>mean</u>, Vick. I just about <u>died</u> . . . when Captain Fox told me that you'd gotten into that God-awful, that terrible, <u>fight</u>! I understand there were <u>three</u> of 'em! <u>Three</u> of the bastards! Vick, we've discussed this <u>before</u>. You're not making enough damn <u>money</u>! Not enough . . . to have to <u>take</u> this sort of thing. This sort of <u>crap</u>! If you're going to <u>fight</u> . . . then, get yourself booked against Muhammad <u>Ali</u>, or someone! At Madison Square <u>Garden</u> . . . or in <u>Zaire</u>, or someplace! Make a million <u>dollars</u>! At least you'd be able to <u>afford</u> the damn plastic surgery."

She arose—and leaned over the still-struggling-to-cope-with-the-situation patient! She kissed him! Tenderly!

"Oh, <u>Vick</u>!" The tears began to flow once again. "I worry so <u>much</u> about you. I <u>love</u> you, Vick! I love you . . . so damn <u>much</u>!"

"<u>I'm</u> sorry, Junie. I didn't mean to jump down your <u>throat</u>, y'know. I guess I'm not in the best of humor. I love you <u>too</u>. I'm sorry to <u>cause</u> you all this worry."

"I just don't want you to be <u>hurt</u>, Vick. To <u>get</u> hurt. I don't want anything to <u>happen</u> to you." She rubbed her hand—lightly—over his cast. "I . . . I <u>wish</u>," she continued, "I just wish that you didn't have to <u>wear</u> that thing. It <u>must</u> be . . . must be awfully damn <u>heavy</u>. I <u>wish</u> the damn <u>rent</u>-a-car company . . . I just wish . . . wish that they hadn't gone <u>under</u>!"

"That makes <u>two</u> of us! But, it <u>did</u>," he muttered. "<u>They</u> did! <u>Nothing</u> . . . no amount of <u>wishing</u> . . . is <u>ever</u> gonna bring it back. I just have to do the best I <u>can</u>! With what I've <u>got</u>! Captain Fox must've told you that I was <u>jumped</u>! Jumped by <u>three</u> . . . <u>three</u> of those little mothers!"

"More or less. He said you'd gotten into a tussle with three <u>guys</u>! Oh <u>God</u>, Vick! That's . . . that's so <u>frightening</u>! <u>Three</u> of 'em! I can't get <u>over</u> that! <u>Three</u> of the schmucks! I figured, from what Captain Fox was saying, that <u>you</u> . . . <u>being</u> you . . . decided that your beeper wasn't going to <u>work</u>! Wasn't <u>worth</u> a damn! <u>Again</u>! <u>Yet</u>! And that you just simply <u>decided</u> . . . to take care of things <u>yourself</u>! Being as <u>unafraid</u> . . . which, in this case, is another word for <u>stupid</u> . . . as you <u>are</u>, I figured you must've <u>piled</u> into them! The <u>three</u> of 'em!"

"<u>That</u> heroic . . . that <u>stupid</u> . . . I'm <u>not</u>! Not for a couple or three bucks an <u>hour</u>! Maybe for that cool mil in <u>Zaire</u>! But, not for two or three shittin' dollars an <u>hour</u>!'

"What <u>did</u> happen, Vick?"

"I was just walking along on the third floor. And three of the little mother-hunchers . . . <u>they</u> jumped <u>me</u>!"

"Were they the same <u>guys</u>? From a couple <u>nights</u> ago?"

"<u>I</u> dunno. <u>Maybe</u>. <u>Probably</u>. Maybe <u>not</u>. Hell . . . I'm not <u>sure</u>."

"Maybe they were <u>upset</u> with you! For <u>reporting</u> them! Came back to get <u>even</u>!"

Maybe. If they even <u>knew</u> . . . that I was the one who'd <u>reported</u> them. Beats <u>me</u>! <u>Whoever</u> they were . . . they must've <u>known</u>, that I was due to come schlepping <u>by</u>! Probably decided to put me <u>away</u> . . . take me <u>out</u> . . . before I could put a <u>crimp</u> in their evening! I really don't <u>know</u>!"

"All <u>three</u> of 'em? The three of 'em . . . they <u>jumped</u> you?"

"Yeah. Well, two of 'em <u>landed</u> on me! Thank God I'd taken out my handy-dandy little <u>Billy</u> club! I just had this really <u>spooky</u> feeling . . . when I was getting to where those guys had heisted those <u>televisions</u> the other night. So, I took out my <u>club</u>!"

June nodded. "Yes," she said. "There's times, I think, when you can feel that there's something going to <u>happen</u>! Maybe it's E.S.P. or something."

"Well, anyway, thank God I took out the <u>stick</u>! These three assholes <u>jumped</u> me . . . and, like I said . . . two of 'em wound up on <u>top</u> of me! I managed to push my <u>club</u> . . . into one of 'em's <u>gut</u>! Popped the other in the <u>moosh</u>! With my <u>fist</u>!" In a reflex action, Smigelski ran his hand over his cast. "But, the <u>third</u> one," he hissed, "he <u>plastered</u> me! On the <u>shoulder</u>! With a goddam <u>pipe</u>!"

"A . . . a <u>pipe</u>?"

He nodded. "Yeah. Not the kind I light up . . . and <u>smoke</u>. This was a <u>lead</u> pipe! Like the ones that <u>plumbers</u> use. Anyway, I . . ."

"Wait a minute! You mean he . . . that he <u>hit</u> you? With one of . . . with one of <u>those</u>?"

"Yeah. <u>Sonofabitch</u>! He was probably aiming at my <u>head</u>! But, he got my <u>shoulder</u>! <u>That</u> was bad enough! Then, he <u>got</u> me! Got me . . . <u>again</u>! Same damn <u>place</u>!"

She kissed him—again. Twice. Then, a whole flurry of tear-drenched busses! All over his face! "Oh, my poor <u>Polack</u>," she rasped. "You got hit <u>there</u>? <u>Twice</u>?"

"Yeah. As I <u>think</u> I understand it . . . <u>two</u> breaks! <u>Count</u> 'em . . . <u>two</u>! I got <u>back</u> at that sonofabitch, though! Got him pretty <u>good</u>! I swung the ol' <u>Billy</u> club! Swung it . . . right at his <u>nuts</u>! Wound up hitting him in the goddam <u>knee</u>! Once I got to my <u>feet</u>, though, I was kind of <u>woozy</u>! Everything runs together after <u>that</u>! I <u>do</u> remember clobbering <u>two</u> of 'em, though! With the <u>club</u>! I think I <u>kicked</u> one of 'em! Yeah . . . pretty <u>sure</u>! Got him right in the <u>balls</u>! I <u>believe</u> I did, anyway! Hope it's nothing <u>trivial</u>! Bastard!"

Smigelski heaved a room-filling sigh. The simple act of talking, he was finding, was becoming exceptionally exhausting! The spirited description, he'd delivered had drained, from him, whatever energy may have remained.

"One of 'em," he finally managed to say, "turned <u>tail</u>! <u>Ran</u>! <u>Yellow</u> piece of shit! Hauled <u>ass</u>! I <u>think</u> I remember <u>throwing</u> something at him! Guess I must've <u>missed</u>! Dammit!"

June was crying softly. "I had no <u>idea</u>," she sniffed. "My brave Polack."

He leaned up—and, through the pain, he kissed her. "Hey Junie!" His third try at a smile was semi-successful. "<u>C'mon</u>! <u>I'm</u> all right. They'll probably have me doing push-ups in the morning."

She managed a smile. But, just barely. "Well," she responded, "any push-ups you do . . . I want to be <u>underneath</u> you."

"Blush! Embarrassment! To think that you would speak to a person . . . one as virtuous as myself . . . in such a manner. Oh, the ignominy of it all! I . . . OH!"

"Vick! What's the matter?"

"Oooooooh! Damn! Turned the wrong way! With this stupid-assed cast, I gotta really watch what I do! Hoo boy! That hurt! Strike the push-ups! At least for awhile!"

"Oh, Vick," she said. "You . . . you're hurt! Hurt so bad! So badly! I'm sorry! I'm so sorry! What can I do . . . to help?"

"Well, you could stop being so goddam sexy, for openers. I had my hands full, with you . . . when I was healthy. Now? Now, you're gonna be too much! Too much . . . altogether! I can tell! Push-ups, indeed!"

"You know, Vick . . . there was a small article on the episode in this evening's paper."

"Small? A small article? Here I lie . . . wounded, sore bestead, after an epic feat of bravery! And they give me a small article? Could they spare it? Oh, the bitter fortunes of those, who . . . OH! Ouch! Damn! Moved the wrong damn way . . . again! Mmmmmmph! Man! That's sore! What'd they say? About my little foo-fer-aw?"

"Well, they say that there were only two assholes . . . uh, punks! Not three! Plus, they're both only fifteen-years-old! So, no one knows . . . if they've got records or not! Or who the hell they are, for that matter! They can't publish their angelic little names . . . or their records . . . because, bless their glorious, sanctified, little hearts, they're juveniles! Got to move heaven and earth . . . to <u>protect</u> the delicate little darlings, don'tcha know."

Smigelski attempted to sit upright! "Juveniles, my <u>ass</u>!" he snarled. "Those mothers are as big as I am, and . . . <u>OH</u>!"

"<u>Vick</u>!"

"I'm all <u>right</u>," he panted. "Just <u>zigged</u> . . . when I should've <u>zagged</u> . . . again. What <u>else</u> did the story say?"

She smiled. "Something," she answered, "that <u>should</u> brighten your day! They're <u>both</u> in the hospital! <u>Both</u> of 'em! They're listed as <u>serious</u>! Or maybe even <u>critical</u>! Wouldn't <u>that</u> be a shame?"

"Aw. Poor babies. You're right, though. It <u>does</u> bring a smile to these parched old lips. If I knew, for sure, they <u>were</u> critical . . . that would get a chuckle. Dead . . . would've brought on hysterical <u>laughter</u>! I'd have even done all kinds of <u>handstands</u>! No push-ups, you understand. But, <u>handstands</u> I'd have done. Hell, at first, I really thought I really might've . . . actually . . . <u>killed</u> one of 'em! Must be losing my <u>touch</u>! Going <u>soft</u> . . . in my old age!"

"Well, I just wish they hadn't gotten <u>into</u> the stupid warehouse . . . in the <u>first</u> stupid place! It's not <u>right</u>! Just not <u>right</u> . . . that those little creeps should be <u>protected</u>! Just because they happen to be <u>fifteen</u>!"

"I'd <u>love</u> for them . . . not to make <u>sixteen</u>!"

"Well, it's not <u>fair</u> . . . that they happen to be under <u>eighteen</u>! Especially when you stop and consider what they did to <u>you</u>! That they might even have <u>killed</u> you! OH! Oh, my <u>God</u>! What a <u>thought</u>! What a <u>chilling</u>, God-awful, <u>thought</u>! What a horrible <u>thought</u>!"

"Nah," he tried to console her. "Didn't even come close!"

"Who do you think you're kiddin', Kid? If they'd have connected with your punkin head . . . with that damn pipe . . . they most certainly would've! Would've come close! Oh, Vick! I love you, you big lug!"

"Do people actually still say, 'You big lug'?" he asked—with as much smile as he was able to muster.

The following morning, Captain Fox was the first—and only—visitor for Smigelski. The stocky little captain had arrived, promptly, at eight o'clock—only to be advised that he couldn't see his employee till 10:00 AM.

After a good deal of ranting and raving, the feisty little man was shown into Smigelski's room at 8:20 AM. Under protest! (Those familiar with the captain, would—undoubtedly—marvel at the fact that it would've taken him those twenty full minutes to "have had his way".)

"Vick! Vick! Good to see you, Man! Good morning!"

He thrust his stubby, pudgy-fingered paw out! And wound up shaking the patient's hand—vigorously! Much too vigorously! The motion vibrated through Smigelski's entire body! Sending shock wave upon shock wave—explosively billowing up, to his shoulder!

"Good morning, Captain," he managed to rasp.

"How're they treatin' you, Vick?"

"Oh, pretty well, I guess. The nurses, I suppose, could stand to be a little sexier. But, other than that, they've done pretty well by me. Hard to tell, actually. I've been asleep most of the time. Thank God!"

The captain plopped himself down on the lower portion of Smigelski's bed—sending another lightning-based jolt through "<u>the</u>" shoulder!

"Vick," the little man began, "I want to tell you how <u>sorry</u> we all are! <u>All</u> of us! Sorrier'n <u>hell</u> . . . that this terrible thing hadda go and happen to <u>you</u>! As Lieutenant Brimsek tells it, these guys . . . I guess they all <u>jumped</u> you! Was there two, or three? I <u>heard</u> three, but . . ."

"<u>Three</u>! One got <u>away</u>! <u>Sonofabitch</u>!"

"Yeah. Well, I understand you did quite a <u>number</u> . . . on the <u>other</u> two. As far as I know, they're <u>supposed</u> to be in the hospital . . . for some good amount of <u>time</u>! For a pretty <u>good</u> while! A <u>pity</u>, hah?"

"A pity," agreed Smigelski, with a wan smile.

"How 'bout <u>you</u>, Vick? You feel like you wanna go <u>home</u> today? You can stay here as long . . . for as long you <u>want</u>, y'know. On the <u>company</u>, of course. Till they . . . till the hospital . . . throws your ass <u>out</u>. But, they told me that . . . if you want to leave <u>today</u> . . . why, they'd give you a whole shit-load of <u>pain</u> pills! You could come <u>back</u> . . . like every <u>week</u>. Or how-ever-<u>often</u>. And they could check out your <u>shoulder</u>! On a out-<u>patient</u> deal, y'know. But, you can do what ya <u>want</u>. It's all up to <u>you</u>, Boy."

"I didn't know they were even <u>thinking</u> of releasing me today. I thought they just <u>arbitrarily</u> kept you as long as they wanted . . . then just booted your ass <u>out</u>. Didn't know that I'd had any <u>choice</u> in the matter."

"Yeah. Well, that's the way it <u>used</u> to be, y'know. But, today, you hafta stay up on all the <u>modern</u> shit . . . like I do. Nowadays, y'see, they go for all the <u>psychological</u> bullshit. They figure that . . . if a patient'll do better in familiar <u>surroundings</u>, as they call 'em . . . then, he's a hell of a lot better <u>off</u>, at home. Better off at <u>home</u> . . . than at the <u>hospital</u>. But, if he's got more confidence in the <u>hospital</u> . . . or if his wife's a pain in the <u>ass</u>, or if the kids get on his <u>nerves</u> or something . . . why, then I guess they figger it's best that they <u>keep</u> him a little longer. Either way, Vick, it's up to <u>you</u>. If you want to <u>leave</u> today, they tell me you <u>can</u>. If you want to <u>stay</u> . . . why, <u>that's</u> all right too. Whatever <u>you</u> decide. Whatever you <u>want</u>."

"Uh, Captain? What about my <u>job</u>? My <u>wages</u>?"

"Vick . . . don't you worry about a <u>thing</u>. Not <u>one</u> thing. Not one damn <u>thing</u>! You just go ahead . . . and you damn well <u>relax</u>! Go ahead and get <u>well</u>! Take how-ever-long you <u>need</u>! You're on the <u>payroll</u>! Still on the ol' <u>payroll</u>! <u>Yessir</u>! And you don't come back to <u>work</u> . . . not until the doctor <u>tells</u> you that you can!"

"I'm . . . I'm on for <u>forty</u> hours a week? Forty <u>hours</u>? I've been doing <u>more</u> than that! A good <u>deal</u> more! In fact, a <u>helluva</u> lot more!'"

"I was just <u>comin'</u> to that." beamed the captain. "Not only are you still on the ol' <u>payroll</u> . . . but, you're on the payroll for forty-eight <u>hours</u>! Forty-eight a <u>week</u>! With the time-and-a-<u>half</u>, o'course!"

"Well, <u>thank</u> you. That's <u>nice</u> of you. I was <u>afraid</u> that . . ."

"Plus <u>that</u>," interrupted the enthused visitor—who was definitely on a roll, "as an added <u>bonus</u> . . . ta-<u>DAH</u>! . . . we're <u>promotin'</u> ya! To where you're now a <u>sergeant</u>! A actual <u>sergeant</u>!"

With a flourish, he reached into his breast pocket—and produced four sets of sergeant's stripes!

"Here you <u>are</u>, Vick!" He smiled—broadly. "These here are <u>yours</u>! And, with it, of course, goes a damn good raise in <u>pay</u>! Fifty-cents a hour <u>more</u> . . . in the ol' pay envelope! I'd have to bet that this is the quickest <u>time</u> . . . we <u>ever</u> promoted a man to <u>sergeant</u>! Hell . . . a <u>sergeant</u>! I may be wrong . . . but, I don't think so."

"Well, I <u>appreciate</u> it . . ."

"And <u>we</u> appreciate . . . appreciate what <u>you</u> went through, Vick! Don't think we <u>don't</u>! Why, we wouldn't've had you go through somethin' like <u>this</u>! Not for all the <u>world</u>! Not that we haven't had <u>other</u> guards get hurt . . . every now and <u>then</u>! But, I was personally <u>impressed</u> with you, Vick. Ever since the day I first <u>hired</u> you! We're keepin' a <u>eye</u> on you, Vick-Boy. You're gonna go <u>far</u> with **Tarkenton**! I c'n <u>tell</u>! Probably quicker'n most anyone <u>else</u> would of! Practically <u>anyone</u> else, anyways! You got a great <u>future</u> . . . at **Tarkenton**."

"I <u>hope</u> so," sighed Smigelski. "I sure <u>hope</u> so. My fiancée is really <u>upset</u>! She wasn't overjoyed in the <u>first</u> place . . . when I went to work for you. Now she's <u>really</u> buggaring me . . . to get my Polack butt the hell <u>out</u> of the security guard business! I should find something <u>else</u>. She's <u>convinced</u> of that!"

"Well now, Vick. Don't you worry about a <u>thing</u>! Not a cotton-pickin' <u>thing</u>! And you can tell this <u>girlfriend</u>

of yours . . . this <u>fiancée</u> of yours . . . you can tell <u>her</u> not to worry too! You just take it <u>easy</u>! Just sit on your <u>ass</u> . . . and collect all your <u>paychecks</u>! Till you're able to come back to <u>work</u>! And then, <u>maybe</u> . . . just <u>maybe</u> . . . we'll talk about another <u>kind</u> of job. Unless, of course," his expression brightened, "you'd rather stay a guard. Lots of fellas <u>do</u>, y'know. And <u>now</u> you're a <u>sergeant</u>! You <u>could</u> stay on . . . as a <u>sergeant</u>, y'know!"

"I'd really rather <u>not</u>! I was never too enamored of the <u>guard</u> thing. I figured I was just paying my <u>dues</u>. Until something <u>better</u> came along. You remember that . . . at the time of my <u>interview</u> . . . I told you that I was <u>really</u> interested in some kind of . . . well, some kind of . . . <u>undercover</u> work. Like **Tarkenton** <u>used</u> to do . . . at **Ballinger's Rent-a-Car**, for instance."

"Yeah. I <u>remember</u> that. Now, Vick, I can't go ahead . . . and promise you somethin' <u>exactly</u> like that. Not right <u>away</u>, anyways. But, when you come <u>back</u> . . . we'll have <u>somethin'</u> for you! Somethin' that, I'm sure, you'll <u>like</u> it! Probably . . . a lot <u>better</u> than stayin' a guard!" He acted as though the very thought of <u>anyone</u> opting not to be a security guard was the height of misdirected loyalty. "Only reason I mentioned stayin' a guard is because I thought that maybe you might of changed your <u>mind</u>. I've got <u>men</u> with me twenty . . . twenty-five, even thirty . . . <u>years</u>! Guys who . . . they don't wanna be anything <u>but</u> guards!"

"So I've heard. No, Captain . . . I'll be glad to get off <u>that</u> schneid!"

"Good! Fine!" The two words took a mighty effort. "Now, Vick, there's the matter of the <u>police</u>! It's important . . . pretty damn important . . . for you to make a <u>report</u>! In <u>person</u>! They made a preliminary <u>report</u>! Made it out . . . at the <u>time</u>! But, you weren't in the <u>best</u> of shape, y'know! And no one else seems to <u>really</u> know all the details . . . of what the hell went <u>on</u> up there! Now, one of the assistant D.A.s . . . he <u>talked</u> to me! Talked to me <u>personally</u>! Yesterday <u>afternoon</u>! And, Vick, he'd like to get <u>together</u> with you! As soon as <u>possible</u>, y'know! <u>Today</u>, actually . . . if we can <u>swing</u> it! Wants to get all the <u>facts</u>! All the <u>shit</u>! Now, he can either come <u>here</u> . . . or we can take you on over <u>there</u>! To <u>his</u> office! Which-ever-way you'd want to <u>work</u> it . . . is fine with <u>him</u>! And fine with <u>us</u>! Fine with <u>me</u>!"

"Well, Captain, I think I'd like to <u>leave</u> the hospital. I'll be a <u>sight</u>, I know, with this stupid <u>cast</u>, and all. But, if I <u>could</u> . . . if you could <u>have</u> someone . . . if I could go to the District <u>Attorney's</u> office this afternoon, <u>that'd</u> be fine. Get it the hell . . . out of the <u>way</u>!"

"<u>Good</u>, Vick. <u>Fine</u>! Now, we'll have a <u>car</u> here . . . right here, in front of the <u>hospital</u> . . . at, say, two <u>o'clock</u>! Two o'clock <u>sharp</u>! That'll give you time to have <u>lunch</u>, y'know . . . on the <u>hospital</u>! Of course, I don't know how <u>good</u> . . . or bad . . . their food <u>is</u> here, y'know."

"It's not that bad . . . surprisingly," replied Smigelski with an actual, bona fide, smile.

"<u>Good</u>! <u>Great</u>! Now, I'll have Sergeant <u>Forward</u> . . . he'll pick you up! Right at two o'clock, straight-<u>up</u>. It's important that we get you over to the <u>D.A.'s</u> office! As <u>soon</u> as we can! I guess <u>both</u> those little pissants'll . . . they'll be in the <u>hospital</u>, for a good while! But, before they're ready to get <u>out</u> . . . the <u>D.A.'s</u> office is gonna want to get together with the <u>Juvenile</u> authorities. Try, I guess, and get the little bastards certified as <u>adults</u>! Good luck to <u>them</u>!"

"Good luck to them is <u>right</u>!"

"Listen! Some of those <u>judges</u> . . . people who gotta <u>pass</u>, on such shit as this . . . they have their heads so far up their <u>asses</u> that . . . that . . . well, it's like tryin' ta move heaven and <u>hell</u>, to get 'em to <u>certify</u> one of those little darlin's. Those guys who <u>jumped</u> you . . . so I understand . . . they're supposed to be about your <u>size</u>! And they could've damn well <u>killed</u> you!"

"A comforting thought."

"<u>Hell</u>, Vick! You know what I <u>mean</u>! When those little shits get <u>caught</u> . . . and maybe get their precious little <u>asses</u> kicked a little bitty . . . it's <u>them</u> that's got to be protected!"

"Yeah," responded Smigelski—sighing heavily. "I guess it was ever thus."

"<u>Seems</u> like it! But, lately, it's gettin' <u>way</u> outta hand! Hell, nowadays, <u>they're</u> the ones that hafta be watched out for! What they did to <u>you</u> . . . well, it sure as shit wasn't no goddam <u>juvenile</u> crime! If they're gonna play a adults <u>game</u>, then . . . <u>I</u> allus say . . . then, they gotta be <u>prepared</u>! Prepared . . . to take the adult <u>consequences</u>!"

"I agree. But, fat chance of <u>that</u> ever happening! Probably, anyway."

"<u>Usta</u> be . . . that it was the <u>victim</u> that got all the attention! All the <u>sympathy</u>! But, <u>today</u>? Hell <u>no</u>! Those little <u>assholes</u> . . . <u>they</u> gotta have the best of <u>both</u> worlds. The hell of it <u>is</u>, Vick, they're damn well gettin' it. Yessir . . . best of <u>both</u> friggin' worlds! Damn well <u>gettin'</u> it!"

"What do you think they'll <u>do</u> with 'em, Captain?"

"<u>Shit</u>! I <u>doubt</u> they'll be able to get 'em <u>certified</u> . . . to stand trial as <u>adults</u>! I'd bet the family <u>jewels</u> on that! Bet the ol' <u>jewels</u> . . . that they wind up with goddam <u>probation</u>! And <u>then</u> . . . probably for not much longer than a few goddam <u>weeks</u>! A <u>month</u> or two . . . <u>maybe</u>! Hate to <u>say</u> it, Vick . . . certainly <u>hate</u> to say it . . . but, that's <u>my</u> guess!"

"<u>Probation</u>? Freaking <u>probation</u>? <u>Probation</u> . . . for God's sakes?" Smigelski's eyes opened to Bette Davis proportions! "<u>Probation</u>? Pro-damn-<u>bay</u>-tion? For <u>attacking</u> a man? Or a <u>woman</u>? Or <u>anybody</u>? For half-<u>killing</u> someone? Whether it's <u>me</u> . . . or anyone <u>else</u>? For <u>that</u> . . . they get fucking <u>probation</u>?"

Captain Fox nodded—grimacing violently. "That's <u>right</u>." he snarled. "Fuckin' <u>A</u>! <u>Vick</u>, with all the goddam bleedin' <u>hearts</u> out there . . . the ones who <u>make</u> these head-up-their-ass laws, <u>and</u> the assholes that run the Family <u>Court</u> System . . . well, these creeps that did <u>you</u> in, they can almost get away with <u>murder</u>! With <u>actual</u> murder, probably! If everything falls in <u>right</u> for 'em! And it usually <u>does</u>! Most <u>always</u> does!"

"Shit," muttered Smigelski. "<u>Double</u> shit!"

"It just so <u>happens</u>," advised the captain, "this here <u>particular</u> assistant D.A. . . . . the one I was <u>tellin'</u> you about, his name is <u>Conant</u> . . . he has a particular <u>hard</u>-on for <u>this</u> type of case! I guess he had his <u>grandmother</u> . . . or some maiden <u>aunt</u>, or somethin' . . . and she got <u>mugged</u>! <u>Really</u> mugged! Got <u>hurt</u>! Hurt . . . <u>bad</u>! By some little <u>shit</u> . . . who was twelve or thirteen, or somethin'! But, he was a big sonofabitch! I guess the old lady wound up with a broken leg . . . or maybe a broken hip! Broken pelvis, I think! Some damn thing! She died, though! Just a couple months later! Just a couple months, after the attack!"

"Dear Lord! That's . . . that's horrible! Especially since the kid . . . the kid, who did all this . . . was so damn young!"

"Young! Old!" Captain Fox sighed—heavily! "What the hell difference does it make? It was like this schmuck had actually killed the old broad . . . which is what he did. y'know! Anyways, the little pimp . . . he got off! Off . . . with nothin'! Scott fuckin' free! Not a goddam thing! Never saw the inside of a goddam jail cell!"

"I can't believe that those people . . . at Juvenile . . . I can't believe that they'd still operate that way. Not after all the bad publicity! Just the stuff that I've seen, in the newspapers . . . and on tee-vee! All the outrage! The real outrage . . . that's come out over the past few . . . !"

"Well, they do! They have! Seems like they always will! These assholes . . . at Family Court? They could care less! Maybe someday . . . it'll all change, Vick. But, I don't see it! No matter how pissed off the public gets! But, you gotta remember, Vick: This is still liberal ol' New York! And I'll go to my grave . . . believin' that we still got more bleedin' hearts-per-square-inch than just about anywheres! Well, maybe San Francisco . . ."

"I guess," groused Smigelski. "I wish you were wrong . . . but, you're probably right!"

"I <u>know</u> I'm right. Hell, I wish I was wrong <u>too</u>. That little <u>bastard</u> . . . the one who beat up Conant's grandma or aunt or whatever . . . <u>he</u> went right out! Went right out . . . and he <u>croaked</u> a old lady . . . <u>and</u> a old man! Just a week or two <u>later</u>! <u>Lot</u> of these creeps, y'know . . . they <u>pick</u> on <u>old</u> folks! Poor <u>bastards</u>! <u>They</u> can't fight back, y'know! Hell, these pieces of shit . . . they always <u>outweigh</u> the poor old coot! By a hunderd <u>pounds</u> or somethin'. Probably more than <u>that</u>! Plus a old guy or a old gal . . . they ain't gonna <u>see</u> you too pretty good, anyways! <u>Especially</u> if these assholes be sure and to go ahead . . . and break the old person's <u>eyeglasses</u>! Happens all the goddam <u>time</u>!"

"Did they finally throw away the <u>key</u>? When this little shit <u>killed</u> those two old people?"

"<u>Depends</u>! Depends on what you <u>mean</u> . . . by 'throwin' away the '<u>key</u>'. He got somethin' like three <u>years</u>! Maybe <u>four</u>! That's about as <u>close</u>, as they come . . . to throwin' away the fuckin' <u>key</u>, over there!"

Smigelski shook his head. "It sure isn't very <u>encouraging</u>, Captain," he muttered.

"Well, of course, this guy . . . this <u>Conant</u> . . . <u>he</u> figures that, if they'd have thrown that creep's crooked little ass into <u>jail</u>, the old couple'd still be <u>breathin'</u>. He's <u>right</u>, o'course."

"Unless some <u>other</u> young shithead decided to take out the old couple," muttered the highly-distraught patient.

"Yeah. I know <u>that's</u> right. Anyways, this Conant . . . he's got this wild <u>hair</u>, up his ying-yang! For a case . . . like <u>this</u> one. I want to do everything

I <u>can</u> . . . and have <u>you</u> do everything <u>you</u> can . . . to <u>cooperate</u> with him! With this guy, <u>Conant</u>! And as soon as <u>possible</u>! He told me that there were times . . . when <u>some</u> of those little bastards are in-and-out of Juvenile! And already muggin' someone <u>else</u>! Before his office even gets <u>wind</u> of the goddam case! Before they can <u>ever</u> lay their hands . . . on the damn <u>paperwork</u>! Maybe, Vick, we can get <u>lucky</u> on this one! Have the little sonofabitches tried as <u>adults</u>! Probably won't <u>happen</u> . . . but, it'd sure as hell be <u>nice</u>!"

"Okay, Captain," replied Smigelski—heaving another massive sigh. "I'll be ready . . . and <u>waiting</u> . . . at two o'clock. And I'll do everything I <u>can</u> . . . to <u>cooperate</u> with Mister Conant."

Once again, Captain Fox beamed. "<u>Good</u>! <u>Wonderful</u>! I knew you <u>would</u>! I just <u>knew</u> it! You're a <u>credit</u>, Vick! <u>Sergeant</u> Vick! A credit to **Tarkenton**! I <u>know</u> that you're gonna go <u>far</u>! <u>Really</u> far . . . in the <u>security</u> business. You take <u>care</u> now . . . and Sergeant Forwand'll pick you up at two o'clock, <u>sharp</u>! Be <u>sure</u>, now . . . that you don't <u>lose</u> your new <u>sergeant</u> stripes, there! Wear 'em <u>proudly</u>!"

He arose—and strutted to the door of the hospital room. Then, he turned—and grinned at his employee.

"I'll <u>see</u> ya, Vick," he said—offering a full military salute! Then, he bolted out into the hallway.

<u>Now, there's a man who's truly in love with his job. Truly in love with it</u>.

FOUR

S IX WEEKS AFTER SMIGELSKI HAD been discharged from the hospital, the two youths, who'd attacked him, were set to appear in Family Court, in the borough of Queens. The hearing was scheduled to get underway—merely one day after the second of the young men had been discharged from the hospital. He'd been more seriously injured than had first been diagnosed! <u>Much</u> more seriously!

Peter Conant had, obviously, "moved heaven and earth"—in a predictably-vain attempt to have both young men certified to stand trial as adults. He had been—as Captain Fox had sadly predicted—patently unsuccessful.

Once the big day had arrived, Smigelski had presented himself at the courthouse. Promptly at 9:00 AM—as the summons had required.

The case was—eventually—called. At 1:15 PM. However, <u>neither</u> of the young "toughs" was in the courtroom. The judge directed one of the bailiffs to determine why neither youth had reported.

At 3:00 PM, both defendants appeared—with their lawyers. Smigelski was maintaining a white-knuckled, never-let-go, grip on the side ledge of the prosecutor's counsel table—as the two hoodlums strutted into court.

<u>He's just one day out of the hospital</u>? reflected Smigelski—as the most seriously injured lad had passed by. <u>And he's strutting</u>? <u>Like some kind of a damn peacock</u>?

Both defense attorneys advised the judge that it was their understanding that the hearing was to have taken place one week later.

"I couldn't believe that Your Honor would schedule an action of this magnitude! Not so soon . . . after one of my clients had just been discharged from the hospital," pontificated one of the lawyers.

Both attorneys moved for a one-week continuance.

"So ordered," intoned Judge William Bosley, a 56-year-old magistrate—who's chief claim to fame continued to be wrapped up, in a legendary, ultra-long, flowing, out-of-control, mane of frenzied, churned, white hair. He was on the verge of retirement—and his supposedly "judicial" tone did nothing to hide his complete and utter boredom. That attitude had held true—throughout the entire day.

"Just one more <u>illustration</u>," Smigelski had snarled. "One more example . . . of the general <u>incompetence</u> that we're ass-deep in, these days. It's <u>everywhere</u>! You can't <u>escape</u> it!"

This particular complaint—one in a long, never-ending, series of them—had taken place at 7:30PM, on the evening of the aborted court action. He and June Bodner had been seated in a small booth, at the rear of a diner, The eatery was located about a half-mile from the **Avis** licensee's facility—where June was employed. The complex—where Smigelski had once "toiled" as leasing manager.

"Well," replied June, as she dug into her salad, "there's really not much you can do about it, Vick." She sighed heavily. "Just go on back . . . next week."

"I know," he groused. "But, it <u>still</u> pisses me off. No one <u>cares</u>! No one <u>gives</u> a shit! Who <u>gives</u> a damn . . . that I had to <u>sit</u> there? <u>Sit</u> there . . . and play with my <u>nip</u>? <u>Sit</u> there . . . just <u>sit</u> there . . . the whole damn <u>day</u>! No one <u>cares</u>! Who the hell am <u>I</u>, after all? Peter Conant . . . <u>he's</u> the guy I told you about. The assistant district <u>attorney</u>. <u>He</u> sat there all day, too! It cost the overburdened <u>taxpayers</u> . . . as we always say . . . a goddam <u>bundle</u>! Just because some idiot <u>clerk</u> . . . some shit-assed <u>clerk</u> . . . can't read a stupid-assed goddam <u>calendar</u>! He put the wrong <u>date</u> . . . on the summons, to those two darling kids! <u>Kids</u> . . . <u>Hah</u>! <u>Asshole</u>! They should throw <u>his</u> inept ass in jail!"

"Well, just <u>calm</u> yourself, Vick. We're going <u>out</u>! And, dammit, we're going to have <u>fun</u>." Then, in her best Nazi Gestapo voice, she whined, "You <u>vill</u> haff fun . . . undt you vill <u>enchoy</u> it!"

"Yeah. Hoo boy. Once we get the hell out of the ol' <u>stalag</u>, we'll <u>really</u> have a good time. In fact, M'Dear, I'm thinking of taking you to see a really <u>raunchy</u>

movie. About a fallen <u>woman</u>! One who lived, in sin, with <u>seven</u> . . . not one, not two, but seven . . . <u>men</u>."

"Oh, <u>good</u>! Sounds positively <u>delicious</u>! And <u>terribly</u> obscene! Gloriously <u>perverted</u>! And <u>what</u>, Sir, is this demented flick called?"

"*Snow White And The Seven Dwarfs*".

One week later, Smigelski and Peter Conant appeared once more in Family Court—only to be advised that one of the defense attorneys was involved in <u>another</u> action—in a <u>different</u> court—and could not be present!

So, of course, the same bored-to-tears judge—as expected—routinely <u>postponed</u> the hearing—for one more week.

Seven days later, it was stated that one of the defendants had fallen <u>ill</u>. His attorney, of course, presented a doctor's <u>verification</u>! And—once again— Judge Bosley granted another postponement! For one week! Also, of course!

"It's simply a goddam <u>stall</u>," Conant advised Smigelski—affirming the latter's predictable suspicion. "Nothing <u>more</u>! A damn <u>stall</u>! They're <u>hoping</u> that you'll just simply get <u>sick</u> and <u>tired</u> of dragging your butt <u>over</u> here . . . all the way <u>over</u> here . . . from <u>Jersey</u>! And . . . if it ever happens that <u>you</u> are not the one in the courtroom . . . they'll freaking <u>pounce</u>! If, for <u>whatever</u> reason, <u>you</u> should be absent . . . or maybe even a little bit <u>late</u> . . . they'll <u>spring</u>! Like the fucking rattlesnakes . . . that they <u>are</u>! <u>Then</u>, the darling <u>kids'll</u> both be <u>healthy</u>! Healthy as <u>hell</u>! No conflicting <u>court</u> actions . . . for their piece-of-shit <u>shysters</u>! <u>Nothing</u>! Not a goddam <u>thing</u>! They'll be <u>here</u>! All ready to go to <u>trial</u>! <u>Land</u> on us! <u>Cream</u> you and me! Like a ton of frigging <u>bricks</u>! Move for <u>dismissal</u>! Probably <u>get</u> it too. <u>Undoubtedly</u> get it!"

"Well, you can count on <u>me</u>, Mister Conant! I'll <u>be</u> here! I want to see those little bastards . . . those <u>schmucks</u> . . . see 'em behind <u>bars</u>! See <u>that</u> glorious scene . . . as much as <u>you</u> do! <u>More</u>, probably! Little <u>shits</u>!"

"<u>Little</u>?"

The following day, Smigelski's, beginning-to-decay, cast was—at long last—<u>removed</u>! A not insignificant change in his appearance! Especially from a <u>legal</u> standpoint!

At an eventual <u>future</u> hearing, he would present a <u>much</u> more healthy image to the judge! So—to a point, at least—the defense attorneys' delaying tactics had, apparently, borne some measure of fruit! <u>Another</u> discomfiting—one more totally <u>withering</u>—situation, for our hero! And Peter Conant!

Delay followed <u>delay</u>! Each one as <u>nebulous</u>—as <u>flimsy</u>—as its predecessor! In fact, each of the defendants' petitions seemed even <u>more</u> flea-bitten than its predecessor! The supply of excuses was, obviously, running <u>low</u>! It mattered <u>not</u>! The judge—dutifully—postponed the action, for yet <u>another</u> week! Or, from time to time—<u>ten</u> days!

It would be almost <u>three</u> months before the actual hearing would—at long last—get underway! <u>Thankfully</u>!

By the time the action began, both young men had, to all appearances, recovered from <u>their</u> injuries. That little fact did nothing to <u>improve</u> Smigelski's state of discontent!

Judge Esther Crowley had, by that time, replaced the retired Judge Bosley—and, in her most judicial voice, intoned the charges. Then, she asked each youth if he understood the severity of the allegations posed against him. Both could barely conceal a smirk!

Both attorneys answered for their clients. Both moved for dismissal of the charges—on extremely, far-fetched, highly-technical, grounds. The myriad of motions were all denied!

One of the young men—the punk who'd been most seriously hurt, in the confrontation with Smigelski—was represented by a "celebrity" attorney. One who was on an annual retainer—from the union, to which the youth's father belonged. The hoodlum was Lester Kroll. His lawyer was Guido Piccolo, a former state assemblyman, in Albany.

"This guy, <u>Piccolo</u>," whispered Conant to Smigelski, "he didn't have much to <u>say</u> before! Pretty well shut up . . . when these clowns were getting all those <u>delays</u>. He let the <u>other</u> kid's lawyer do all the talking. Do all the <u>work</u> . . . while <u>he</u> sat back and watched. Pretty damn <u>clever</u>. But, don't be fooled by <u>that</u>. Don't be <u>fooled</u> . . . by <u>anything</u> he might try. He's a high-falutin', high-<u>priced</u>, lawyer. That's not necessarily <u>bad</u> news. <u>Some</u> of those assholes wind up . . . tripping themselves <u>up</u>! Eventually, <u>most</u> of 'em, anyway . . . they'll usually wind up screwing <u>up</u>! Sometimes pretty <u>seriously</u>. Most often . . . believe it or not . . . over their own stupid <u>reputations</u>. They begin to <u>believe</u> . . . don'tcha know . . . all the <u>bullshit</u>! All the bullshit . . . that their <u>hacks</u> are continually saying, in the <u>newspapers</u>. This <u>particular</u> asshole . . . he used to be a really <u>big</u>-assed assemblyman! <u>Powerful</u> guy, he was!"

"An <u>assembly</u> man? A <u>politician</u>? And one of these little shitheads has him for a <u>lawyer</u>?"

"Yup," replied Conant, smiling broadly. "He headed up a lot of <u>committees</u>, at one time. <u>Lots</u> of silly-assed committees! In his glorious <u>heyday</u>! Was on the Evening <u>News</u> . . . all the time!"

"Yeah. I <u>think</u> I recognize the name."

"And . . . like I said . . . some of those assholes are so <u>thrilled</u> with their pissy-assed <u>reputations</u>! All wrapped <u>up</u> in them! And <u>that's</u> all that <u>matters</u> to 'em! They pick up these annual <u>retainers</u>, don'tcha know! <u>Zillions</u> of 'em! This one's . . . this retainer . . . is from some <u>union</u>! Pretty damn <u>lucrative</u>, they are! But, it's seldom that these guys actually have to get <u>involved</u>, in such <u>mundane</u> things. as this! Seldom have to . . . ugh . . . get their hands <u>dirty</u>! To actually have to <u>work</u> for their money! Most of the stuff they dick with is just nickel-and-dime, routine, stuff! Shit that they can get their <u>clerical</u> staff to do, for the most part! On the other hand, I've never run up against <u>Piccolo</u>

before! But, usually, guys like him don't bother to do their <u>homework</u>! They usually simply try to <u>bluster</u> . . . and <u>bluff</u> their way . . . through! Count on their silly-assed <u>reputation</u> . . . to work for 'em. <u>That</u> . . . and a substantial amount of <u>bullshit</u>!"

"Don't do their <u>homework</u>?"

"Naw! I'll bet the rent money . . . that this guy has just the <u>sketchiest</u> idea of what the hell the case is all about! Despite all the <u>previous</u> appearances! And I'm <u>sure</u> that he got <u>that</u> . . . from his pissant <u>client</u>! <u>That</u> data is <u>bound</u> . . . I would guess . . . to be the slightest bit one-<u>sided</u>! If he's done <u>any</u> preparation . . . any <u>real</u> preparation . . . <u>I'll</u> eat the greaser!"

It was at that moment that Piccolo rose to address Judge Crowley: "Your Honor . . ." he began.

Conant winked at Smigelski—as unvarnished pompousness seemed to gush from Piccolo's syrup-laden voice! Appeared to pour from every pore!

"I'm not all that <u>familiar</u> . . . with the evidence to be presented," he advised the judge. "However, I do wish to respectfully submit to the Court that this <u>boy</u> . . . my young <u>client</u> . . . is but fifteen-years-<u>old</u>! Now, I'm given to understand that this young man has a clean <u>record</u>! I would respectfully <u>request</u> . . . that the Court <u>view</u> these auspicious proceedings, here today, in <u>light</u> of those circumstances. I say this in all good <u>faith</u> . . . and am not attempting to . . . ah . . . <u>shade</u> anything which will take place, in this hallowed courtroom, today."

"The Court would have to take Counsel's statement at face <u>value</u>," replied Judge Crowley. "It would seem <u>obvious</u> to the Court that Counsel is, indeed, <u>not</u> familiar with the facts of this case. Further,

Counsel's source . . . pertaining to the <u>background</u> of Counsel's client . . . has not served Counsel well!"

At that point, Conant nudged Smigelski, gently, with his elbow—and fashioned an almost-imperceptible wink!

"Quite the <u>contrary</u>," continued the judge. "This young man has had <u>eleven</u> . . . <u>eleven</u> . . . skirmishes with the <u>law</u>! The most <u>recent</u> difficulty . . . prior to this <u>hearing</u> . . . involved an armed <u>robbery</u>; wherein Counsel's client was found to have <u>beaten</u> an <u>elderly</u> person! <u>Beaten</u> this person . . . <u>badly</u>! With a <u>revolver</u>! Beaten <u>that</u> particular victim . . . a goodly number of <u>times</u>! The record is <u>unclear</u> . . . as to whether the victim was male or female! Your <u>client</u>, Counselor, was given a <u>suspended</u> sentence, at that time! By <u>another</u> judge! That took <u>place</u> . . . if the Court's mathematics are correct . . . approximately <u>six</u> months ago! However, Counsel's point is well-<u>taken</u> . . . relative to Mister Kroll's <u>age</u>. The Court will, most <u>certainly</u>, consider that factor! Now, we will <u>proceed</u>!"

Conant approached the bench and presented Judge Crowley with a brief synopsis of the evidence that he intended to present.

Family Court—a much less-formal judicial system—most usually allowed both prosecution and defense much more latitude than in a normal "adult" court of law. Seldom did a "full-fledged prosecutor" involve himself in a proceeding, in that jurisdiction. Slightly more often than not, the young defendants were represented by counsel. But, the "prosecution" most usually consisted of the <u>judge</u> questioning the police officers, and/or witnesses, who'd been involved in the action—and then, virtually always, quizzing the defendants.

Sentencing—or dismissal—almost always came from such informal, "loose", hearings. Occasionally, judgment would hinge—merely on a particular judge's simple whim. So defense attorneys were not anxious to often object, during these proceedings. For fear of incurring the personal wrath of the judge.

The proceeding at hand would—by far—resemble, more closely, an actual "adult" trial. Far more "legalistic"—than a normal Family Court hearing.

Conant called to the witness stand two police officers. Each man testified that he had participated in overseeing the removal of the two defendants from the third floor of the **General Appliance** warehouse, on April 22, 1973. Both young men had been taken to *Bellevue Hospital*. Each had been totally unconscious—during the entire transportation to the hospital.

"Well," clarified one of the officers. "one of them had recovered . . . minutes before" their arrival at the Emergency Room. The other defendant had remained "out of it", for almost 75 minutes.

The officers identified Lester Kroll and the other youth—Gerald Gray—as the two young men transported to *Bellevue*.

A fingerprint expert testified that three of Gray's prints were found on one 12-inch length of one-inch-in-diameter lead pipe. Two of Kroll's prints had been lifted from another such implement.

Under cross examination, by Martin Pilnick—Gray's attorney—it was established that a palm print of Smigelski's had been found on one of the pipes.

Other, highly-technical, expert testimony was then, laboriously, painstakingly, introduced. Blood samples taken from the floor on the third level of the warehouse were determined to have come from Kroll.

Piccolo promptly moved for dismissal! On grounds that his client's blood had been taken without Kroll's permission. On grounds that "Mister Kroll" had never been advised of the purpose of the blood specimen.

Judge Crowley denied the motion. "Perhaps," she intoned, "Counsel is unaware that . . . while, certainly, a court of law . . . Family Court is much less <u>formal</u>. <u>Much</u> less formal. To the point where it is <u>unlawful</u> . . . to publish <u>any</u> of the findings of this court. If Counsel would wish to so move, the Court believes that there are ample precedents to <u>waive</u> Family Court's jurisdiction! To <u>waive</u> it! And simply let the case proceed . . . on to <u>Criminal</u> Court! To Criminal Court . . . where the various <u>appeals</u> processes could be brought into play! Technical <u>constitutional</u> issues!"

"Counsel would <u>withdraw</u> the motion, Your Honor," replied Piccolo. He projected an image of undiluted magnanimity—seemingly oblivious of Judge Crowley's obvious rebuke.

Finally, Conant put Smigelski on the stand.

After establishing that Smigelski was a bona fide employee, of **Tarkenton Security Services**—and was so employed on April 22, 1973—Conant asked the witness if he'd had occasion to encounter either or both of the two defendants, in the course of his duties, on the date in question.

"<u>Yes</u>, Sir! I <u>did</u>! Yes. <u>Both</u> of them! <u>Both</u> men!"

"Would you then relate to the Court, Mister Smigelski, the details of that encounter?"

Smigelski shifted in the witness chair—and faced Judge Crowley. "Well," he began, "I was, as Mister Conant has said, a security guard . . . employed by **Tarkenton**. I worked the midnight-to-eight-in-the-morning shift, at the time. My duties were to make a tour . . . through the entire <u>warehouse</u>. Did that . . . once each <u>hour</u>. In the course of my <u>fifth</u> tour . . . through the building . . . I was <u>set</u> upon! <u>Attacked</u> . . . by three <u>men</u>!"

"Do you," asked Conant, "see any of those men, in this courtroom today?"

"<u>Yes</u>, Sir! <u>Two</u> of them! The <u>defendants</u> . . . over <u>there</u>!"

"Would you point the two men . . . point them out . . . to the Court?"

Smigelski arose—and directed a finger at each of the young men. Then, he reseated himself in the witness chair.

"Let the record show," said Conant, "that the witness has pointed at Defendant Kroll and Defendant Gray. Now then, Mister Smigelski, what happened . . . when those three men set upon you?"

"Well, at first, I didn't <u>realize</u> what hit me. Couldn't <u>fathom</u> what was happening! I was on the <u>floor</u> . . . before I could really <u>react</u>! <u>Two</u> of them . . . <u>two</u> men . . . wound up on <u>top</u> of me! I'm not altogether sure <u>which</u> two! It <u>seems</u> to me that . . . one of them was Mister <u>Kroll</u>! And, I <u>think</u> that the <u>other</u> . . . was the <u>third</u> man! The one who got <u>away</u>!"

"Then what happened?"

"Well, I pushed my <u>Billy</u> club up into the stomach, of <u>one</u>! And <u>hit</u> the other one! <u>Hit</u> him . . . in the <u>face</u>! With my <u>fist</u>! <u>That</u> got . . . well, it got <u>both</u> of 'em off me! Then, <u>another</u> man . . . Mister <u>Gray</u>, I believe . . . <u>he</u> hit me in the <u>shoulder</u>! <u>Hit</u> me in the shoulder . . . with one of those lead <u>pipes</u>! I believe all <u>three</u> of 'em had lead pipes! Anyway, the man who'd hit me, in the <u>shoulder</u> . . . well, he hit me <u>again</u>! Same <u>place</u>! My shoulder . . . it turned out . . . was <u>broken</u>! <u>Broken</u>! Broken in two <u>places</u>! I <u>did</u> manage to . . . to <u>get</u> the guy! The one . . . who'd <u>hit</u> me! Got him in the <u>leg</u>! Got him pretty <u>good</u>! With my <u>club</u>! Knocked him <u>down</u>!"

"Mister . . . Smigelski is it?" Judge Crowley had asked the question. The fact of the judge inserting herself was an unexpected complication, for the witness!

"Yes, Ma'am? Yes, Your Honor?"

"Mister Smigelski," she said with an expression on her face—one that could best be described as expressionless, "I just want to take this moment to <u>advise</u> you. Advise you to <u>try</u> . . . to do your best . . . to remain <u>calm</u>. Since you've begun your testimony, your voice has risen an <u>octave</u> . . . at least. As I've already suggested . . . to Mister <u>Piccolo</u> . . . this is a more <u>informal</u> type of court. The Court is mainly <u>interested</u> . . . in merely your telling your story."

"Yes, Ma'am?"

"The Court <u>realizes</u> that . . . in a moment of extreme <u>anxiety</u> and <u>pressure</u> . . . the Court <u>knows</u> that it's not easy to <u>remember</u> who was exactly in <u>what</u> spot, at any given <u>time</u>! Do you see what I'm <u>getting</u> at? Mister Conant has already <u>established</u> . . .

through other <u>testimony</u> . . . the <u>presence</u> of the defendants at the scene! The scene . . . immediately <u>following</u> the incident, that you are now <u>describing</u>! With that <u>foundation</u> having been established . . . it's not overly <u>critical</u> that you be pin-point <u>precise</u>, in recollecting each and every <u>detail</u>."

Smigelski seemed almost <u>stunned</u> at what he'd initially feared might be a rather harsh <u>rebuke</u>! Such an <u>admonishment</u> would seem to fit in—perfectly— with his lowly regard to the efficacy (and efficiency) of the entire proceeding!

Judge Crowley—sensing his despondency— smiled down at him. Warmly. "The Court is certain," she explained, "that defense counsel will <u>thoroughly</u> test your memory of the situation. Before defense counsel <u>objects</u>, let the Court state . . . for the record . . . that the Court is merely commenting on the fact that a <u>foundation</u> has been laid, by the prosecution. The Court is not commenting upon the <u>quality</u> or <u>competence</u> . . . of that foundation. Not at this <u>time</u>. That factor <u>will</u>, of course, be considered . . . in whatever verdicts may be issued from these proceedings. You may proceed, Mister Conant."

"Thank you, Your Honor," replied Peter Conant. "Now, Mister Smigelski, as the Court advises, please try and remain as calm as possible. Every person connected with these proceedings is aware of the fact that you are describing a highly <u>traumatic</u> experience. <u>Highly</u> traumatic! Now, as I remember, you'd testified that you had hit the third man . . . with your Billy stick! Had knocked him to the floor! Is that correct?"

"Yes, Sir."

"He was the man who had hit you . . . <u>twice</u> . . . in the <u>shoulder</u>? Had <u>broken</u> your shoulder? In <u>two</u> places?"

"Yes, Sir."

"Would you, then, please continue?"

"Well, I managed to get to my <u>feet</u>! I remember <u>one</u> man was <u>running</u>! I picked up one of those <u>pipes</u>! From off the <u>floor</u>! And I <u>threw</u> it at him! I'm sure I <u>missed</u> him! He got <u>away</u>! After <u>that</u> . . . to be perfectly <u>truthful</u> . . . it's all a little <u>blurry</u>! The <u>pain</u> . . . the pain, in my <u>shoulder</u> . . . the pain was terribly <u>intense</u>! I remember <u>kicking</u> one of the men in the . . . in the . . . well . . . in the <u>testicles</u>! I'm pretty <u>sure</u> that I hit the other one . . . hit him, in the <u>face</u>! Hit him a pretty <u>good</u> one! I <u>probably</u> hit them . . . hit <u>both</u> of them . . . a few more <u>times</u>! I wanted to make <u>sure</u> . . . that they wouldn't be getting <u>up</u>! Either <u>one</u> of 'em! Not any time <u>soon</u>!"

"What did you do then?"

"Well, I called in my <u>report</u> . . . on my portable beeper. I <u>did</u>, then, manage to get back down to the <u>guard's</u> station . . . on the first <u>floor</u>! By <u>that</u> time, **Tarkenton** had four of <u>their</u> men on the scene! A minute or two later, the <u>police</u> . . . **NYPD** . . . got there! <u>Someone</u> . . . an officer . . . at that point, took me to the <u>hospital</u>!"

Conant smiled—also warmly—at his witness. He bowed toward the defense table and smiled! "Your witness, gentlemen."

Guido Piccolo arose and strode to the rail, close by the witness chair. "Now then, Mister . . . uh . . . Smi . . . uh . . . Smig . . . uh . . ."

"Smigelski," furnished the witness.

"Yes. Thank you. In <u>any</u> case . . . if you don't mind my saying as much . . . you <u>related</u> your testimony. Your <u>testimony</u> . . . to the Court! Testified . . . very <u>efficiently</u>! Yes. <u>Most</u> efficiently!"

"Thank you."

"In fact, <u>some</u> might feel that you told it . . . almost <u>too</u> efficiently! Is it not true . . . that you would've been <u>coached</u>? Coached at great <u>length</u>? By the <u>prosecution</u>? By Mister Conant . . . and who-ever-<u>else</u> they might've dredged <u>up</u>?"

"No, <u>Sir</u>." The degree of offense, at the accusation, was clearly evident in Smigelski's tone of voice! "No, <u>Sir</u>," he repeated—even more strongly. "I was <u>not</u>! Mister Conant just advised me to simply get up, on the <u>stand</u> . . . and to tell what <u>happened</u>. So, I got up on the <u>stand</u> . . . and <u>told</u> what happened."

A slight titter ran through the courtroom.

"Well, Mister . . . Smigelski, is it?"

"Yes, Sir?"

"Well, Mister Smigelski, I have <u>always</u> been one to call a spade a spade. And so . . . let me <u>tell</u> you. <u>Tell</u> you . . . what's on my mind. Tell you what's <u>bothering</u> me. Get it out in the <u>open</u>, I always say."

"Fine," replied a back-to-being-slightly-bemused Smigelski.

"Now, Mister Smigelski, I don't know quite how to <u>say</u> this . . . ah . . . but, putting no . . . uh . . . <u>onus</u>, as it were, or casting no unflattering <u>reflections</u> on your particular <u>station</u> in life . . ."

Piccolo made a production of wringing his hands. Then, he looked up at Judge Crowley—as though they, alone, were sharing a deep, personal, secret.

"I, for one," he began again, "happen to feel that the security guard profession is one of the <u>finest</u> callings a man can have. Positively one of the finest of <u>callings</u>."

"<u>I'm</u> sorry, Mister Piccolo," said Smigelski. "I don't understand what you're <u>getting</u> at."

"Well, Mister Smigelski, let me put it <u>this</u> way. When you <u>think</u> of a <u>security</u> guard . . . you <u>picture</u> him as <u>talking</u> in a . . . well, in a . . . in a certain <u>way</u>. Do you <u>understand</u>? Understand what I'm <u>saying</u>?"

"I never <u>thought</u> much about it."

"In any case, to hear you <u>relate</u> your story, to the Court, it doesn't come <u>across</u> . . . not to <u>these</u> ears, anyway . . . as being <u>told</u> the way a <u>security</u> guard would, you know, <u>tell</u> it! It comes <u>across</u> as . . . well, as . . . as being from someone who'd been significantly <u>coached</u>! Who'd, actually, been <u>well</u> coached! <u>Very</u> well coached! <u>Probably</u> . . . by the assistant district <u>attorney</u>! Now, if <u>that's</u> the case, why, you should just simply <u>say</u> as much! All we <u>want</u> to get here . . . as the Court has <u>explained</u> . . . are the <u>facts</u>! And, if the <u>prosecution</u> is . . . uh . . . putting . . . ah . . . <u>words</u> in your mouth . . . now, I'm not saying that that's the <u>case</u>, no sir . . . but, well, if that <u>is</u> the situation . . . why, then we should <u>know</u> that! <u>Know</u> those things!"

"Well, Mister Piccolo, I really can't <u>help</u> . . . the way I <u>talk</u>. I'm <u>telling</u> you here and now . . . under <u>oath</u> . . . that neither Mister Conant, nor anyone else, <u>coached</u> me! <u>Ever</u>! I told Mister Conant my <u>story</u> . . . as you so indelicately <u>put</u> it . . . and he <u>asked</u> me a few questions! Then, he told me to tell it to the <u>Court</u>! At no <u>time</u> . . . did he suggest any <u>changes</u>! Any <u>deletions</u>! Or anything <u>else</u>! And I <u>resent</u> the fact that you <u>suggest</u> that such was the <u>case</u>! To ease your mind, though, I've not always <u>been</u> a security guard! Not all my <u>life</u>! In fact, I was <u>on</u> that job for only a little better than three <u>months</u> . . . before I got <u>jumped</u> by your estimable <u>client</u>! Him . . . and two other <u>guys</u>! Therefore, I really haven't had a chance to <u>perfect</u> my security guard vernacular! I've done a couple years of <u>college</u>! And I've managed a few <u>rent-a-car</u> operations over the past twelve or thirteen years! So, if I don't say 'dese', 'dem' and 'dose' . . . like some dumb Polack <u>security</u> guard . . . then, I'm <u>sorry</u>! My <u>apologies</u>!"

Laughter rocked the courtroom!

"That will <u>do</u>, Mister Smigelski," admonished Judge Crowley—fighting, mightily, to conceal a smile. "However, I <u>do</u> think that your point is well-taken. <u>Should</u> be well-taken! Do you have any further questions, Mister Piccolo?"

"Just one or two, Your Honor." Another lack of perception—as to the thrust of the judicial rebuke. "Now, Mister Smigelski? You say you were attacked by <u>three</u> persons?"

"Yes, Sir."

"What happened to the <u>third</u> man?"

"He turned tail . . . and <u>ran</u>!"

"I see. And has he been apprehended?"

"No, Sir. I don't <u>think</u> so. Not as far as I <u>know</u>, anyway. It's my understanding . . . that the two defendants have <u>refused</u> to cooperate with the police! Have <u>not</u> cooperated . . . in establishing who the <u>third</u> man was!"

Gray's attorney was on his feet in a flash! "<u>Objection</u>, Your Honor! That's <u>hearsay</u>!"

"Sustained."

"Now," continued Piccolo, "as to this other man . . . did you describe him? Describe him . . . to the police?"

"Yes, Sir. As much as possible. As much as I could."

"What do you mean . . . as much as you could?"

"Just what I said! I told them . . . that he was a white male! About my size . . . and, I believe, about the age of the two defendants."

"And that," Piccolo asked, incredulously, "that . . . is all?"

"Yes, Sir."

"Do you realize, Mister Smigelski, that there must be thousands of white males of that height and age . . . in a city this size?"

"Yes, Sir. That's what the police said! I assume that's one reason why he hasn't been apprehended!"

"Well," huffed Piccolo, "do you expect this Court to believe that . . . after having given such an inadequate description of the one man who got away . . . do you expect the Court to believe that you can make a credible identification, of the two defendants?"

"Mister Conant?" interrupted Judge Crowley. "Do you wish to object?"

Pete Conant arose and replied, "Thank you, Your Honor. I appreciate the Court's concern. However, I feel that the witness is doing all right . . . and doesn't really need any protection."

"You may answer the question, Mister Smigelski," the judge said, with a smile.

"Well, Mister Piccolo," responded Smigelski, "describing someone is one thing! Recognizing him . . . is something else! I'm certain . . . certain as I could be . . . that I could recognize the one who got away! If I ever saw him! But . . . in his absence . . . I really can't describe him! Not any better than that! I'm certain, however, that both of the defendants could!"

"That'll be enough, Mister Smigelski," admonished the judge, still fighting, valiantly, to conceal another smile. "Merely answer the question."

"Well," Piccolo pressed on, undaunted, "it would seem to me that, with such a sketchy description of the missing assailant . . . if, indeed, there is a missing assailant . . . it would seem to test your credibility! Test your credibility . . . that you could, indeed, recognize the two defendants."

Conant arose and addressed Judge Crowley.

"Your Honor," he began, "I believe that I will, at this time, object! I feel that both the Court, and The Prosecution, have given Counsel the utmost . . . the most liberal . . . latitude, in this cross examination! It is becoming apparent, though . . . more than apparent . . . that Counsel has begun to badger the witness! A fact, in evidence . . . for a good while now!"

"The Court agrees! Mister Piccolo, you will keep your questions on a plane . . . one that is substantially higher, that those past few."

"Your Honor," replied Piccolo, "if it please the Court, Counsel has every right . . . to test the credibility, of this witness!"

The only person in the courtroom who was oblivious of Judge Crowley's obvious irritation appeared to be—Guido Piccolo!

"Mister Piccolo," responded the judge, "Counsel does not have the right to hector the witness! In the Court's view, that's exactly what Counsel is engaged in! It would appear, to the Court, that the witness' ability to describe a third assailant . . . or to not describe a third assailant . . . is a moot point!"

"But, Your Honor . . ."

"Mister Conant." interrupted the judge, "has established, to his satisfaction . . . and, quite frankly, to the satisfaction of this Court . . . that the two defendants were, in point of fact, on the third floor of that building! That they were there . . . just mere minutes, after the incident, that Mister Smigelski has described, took place! Further, the Court has positive proof . . . of the fact that they were in the precarious physical condition, that Mister Smigelski has testified they were in! Now, the Court would suggest that Counsel alter . . . substantially . . . the line of questioning, of this witness! You may proceed!"

"I have but one more question, Your Honor," stated Piccolo—the picture of abject martyrdom.

"Mister Smigelski," he began. "Has it occurred to you, that you . . . that you almost killed my client? You could've killed him! As well as the other young man! Over there . . . at the defense table! Has that . . . ever . . . gotten through to you?"

"Yes, Sir! Yes, it has! But, it has also occurred to me that . . . if I'd have gotten nailed, on the head, once or twice, with one of those lead pipes . . . the person killed could, very easily, have been me! So, you'll excuse me . . . if I don't seem all that broken-hearted over the condition of your sainted client! Also, I'd like to point out, that . . . had your client not been in the warehouse, in the <u>first</u> place . . . neither <u>one</u> of us would've gotten <u>hurt</u>! Neither would the <u>other</u> young man . . . over at the <u>defense</u> table!"

He leveled withering—an icy—stare! First at Kroll—then at Gray! "Those two <u>creeps</u>," he seethed, "had no <u>business</u> . . . no business <u>whatever</u> . . . in that <u>warehouse</u>!"

Virtually everyone who'd had business in the courtroom broke into spontaneous <u>applause</u>! Each person had sprung to his or her <u>feet</u>—clapping <u>fervently</u>!

Judge Crowley banged her gavel! Furiously! "<u>Enough</u>!" she half-shouted. "<u>Order</u>! Order in the <u>court</u>! Any <u>further</u> outbursts . . . will bring <u>contempt</u> citations! By the <u>dozens</u>!"

Piccolo—still exuding pomposity, finally intoned, "No further questions, Your Honor."

Kroll and Gray were both found guilty of Juvenile Delinquency!

They were sentenced to one of New York State's juvenile detention homes! <u>There</u> they would <u>remain</u>! In <u>theory</u>, anyway! Until their 18th birthdays! A sentence of approximately 2½ years! Upon <u>release</u> from detention, their criminal records would be <u>destroyed</u>!

The third assailant was never apprehended!

FIVE

TWO WEEKS AFTER THE HEARING in Family Court, Smigelski was back at work—full-time—with **Tarkenton**. During the extensive litigation period, he'd wound up working various guard shifts—at varying sites. (None of which had been the warehouse, where he'd been attacked.) Most of these "hit-and-miss" assignments were even <u>day</u> shifts. Truly, he felt, his "cup runneth over"!

He was certain that Captain Fox had seen to it that he'd drawn assignments which offered minimal amounts of risk. And minimal amounts of physical dexterity. "<u>Extremely</u> minimal"—as he'd said to June Bodner, "early and often".

He'd been—for the most part—a sergeant, assigned to working with rookie guards. He was gratified to find that his diminutive boss had begun to see to it—that he would work "an extra shift or three" every week. And at his "new and improved" pay grade!

He'd reflected—many times—upon the gratifying changes, in his varied assortment of "soft" assignments, since his return to work.

Sitting in one of his employer's renowned plastic chairs, he had listened quietly—and patiently—as Captain Fox had delivered himself of an extensive (really extensive) "Welcome Back" speech.

"Vick," he'd begun, "I know that . . . if I was you . . . I'd be a little gun-shy right about now. And that's all right. We expect that. I mean, you did get popped! Popped . . . pretty good! By the way, how's the shoulder?"

"It's okay. Still a little tender . . . well, a lot tender. But, it's coming along."

"Good! Great! Wonderful! See, that's somethin' that some of us never learn. Time's the great healer . . . the great healer, Vick! No matter what ever happens, time is always on your side. It's on your side, Vick. Now, I can't do you no bigger favor . . . than makin' you realize that fact. Y'see, Vick? You can go into any kind of skirmish . . . and not really have to worry! Never have to worry . . . about gettin' hurt! Eventually . . . in time . . . the pain's gonna pass! I do a lot o' readin', Vick. That probably goes without sayin'. But, some of them head-shrinkers . . . they'll tell you that most people are a little bit cowardly! I mean . . . let's face it . . . we're all afraid of somethin'! Everyone has his or her own fears! Our own private hells, y'know! We all got 'em! But, accordin' to these here doctors, the reason a man'll back down from another man . . . and sometimes even a woman . . . it's because he's afraid he's gonna get hurt! But, y'see? That's the secret! Don'tcha see? That hurt . . . it's there! But, for only just a little while! It goes away! Eventually! But, it . . . the pain . . . it does go away!"

"That'd be a good title for a song," Smigelski had replied, with a half-smile.

"That's the spirit! That's what I like to <u>see</u>, Vick! I mean, I like to see you <u>joke</u> about it! That <u>pleases</u> me . . . your <u>attitude</u>, I mean!"

"I really don't think I'm seeing all <u>that</u> much hilarity in the thing. Not yet. anyway. But, I'm not going to be all that <u>intimidated</u>. Oh, I would imagine that . . . I'll be a little more <u>spooked</u>, than usual," Smigelski responded, sighing deeply. "At least, until I get back into <u>harness</u> again. Get my feet wet again."

"<u>Right</u>, Vick! <u>Right</u>! <u>That's</u> the way I like to hear you talk! Now, what I'm gonna <u>do</u>, with you . . . I'm gonna do <u>this</u>: I'm gonna <u>try</u> and give you some <u>soft</u> stuff . . . until you can kind of work your way back! Back into the <u>groove</u>! Know what I <u>mean</u>?"

And the ebullient little man had been true to his word.

Our hero continued on, with his "softball" assignments, for almost 10 months. Well into 1974.

Smigelski had this unusual—this foreboding, unshakable, albeit unexplainable—feeling that something ominous was in store for him! This chilling sensation overtook him—that almost-full-year, after he'd returned to work! This all came to pass—when the captain had called him into his office.

"There's a midnight-to-eight trick out at *Shea Stadium*," the little man had advised his employee. "That slot is important! Damn important! Important for this division! Well, important . . . for the whole damn company! Listen, this slot is real important! All year 'round! Always a really critical thing, y'know! The Mets . . . they're still out there, of course! Well, actually I think the season's just about shot in the ass. I believe they might even be outta town right now. Out on a road trip, y'know. But, the Jets . . . they're gonna be comin' in PDQ. Probably have some of their gear . . . probably lots of their gear . . . out there, even now."

In 1974, *Giants Stadium*—in New Jersey's Meadowlands—was not yet a gleam in anyone's eye. It would've been thought, at that point in time, to have been totally impossible—that New York City would even come close to losing one of their professional football teams! The Giants! Especially to a glitzy new stadium—located in "some swamp . . . over in Jersey"! Let alone the totally implausible fantasy—that, eventually, the city would ever find itself bereft of both **National Football League** franchises!

But, that ghastly scenario is precisely what—a mere few years later—would, spectacularly, happen! Then, in 1984, the Jets joined the Giants—in that reviled Meadowlands "swamp"! In 2010—both **NFL** teams moved to even glitzier *MetLife Stadium*, in the same New Jersey area! The substantial number of years—since the initial Giants-to-Jersey transformation—have gone relatively smoothly! Not close to the horror that would've been imagined—had anyone <u>dared</u> to speak of (or even <u>think</u> of) such an "atrocity", in the mid-seventies!

In the "antiquity" of 1974, however, the Giants had plied their wares in *Yankee Stadium*—and the Jets had called *Shea Stadium* home.

"Anyway," Captain Fox had continued, "there's really not a hell of a lot to <u>do</u> out there . . . especially on the <u>night</u> shift . . . but, to just go ahead, and sit on your ass. I was gonna say that you could, maybe, get caught up on your readin', out there. Lotta <u>dead</u> time, y'know."

"Yeah. That'd be nice. What does the job entail, Captain?"

"Well, you see, I was comin' to that, Vick. This slot we're talkin' about here . . . well. it's really a <u>sergeant's</u> job, y'know. On this one, you don't hafta fart around, y'know. Fart around . . . with <u>tours</u>! Or stickin' goddam keys, in goddam clocks! Nothin' like that! You just sit on your ass! Sit on your ass . . . in one of the <u>equipment</u> rooms, under the stands. They got a desk, in there. And a phone . . . and everything else. All set up in there. <u>Beepers</u>? They don't <u>work</u> too pretty good out there. Not under all that cement and mortar . . . and whatever."

"Well, <u>that'll</u> be different."

The little man ignored the thinly-veiled barb. "Anyway," he continued, undaunted, "you take a stroll through the place . . . once or twice . . . durin' a shift. But, mostly, they got six or eight of them new-fangled . . . those closed-circuit . . . them television cameras, out there. <u>Them</u>, you hafta watch! The whole set-up gives you a pretty good <u>picture</u> . . . of the entire <u>stadium</u> . . . from what I understand.

There's never been any kind of break-in out there. Not as far as I know."

No . . . but, there's a helluva lot of thievery goes on, out there, reflected Smigelski—remembering the many things that Corporal Scotti had advised him, on his first night "in the fold". Our hero seemed to recall that Scotti had purloined a Jets helmet. One that had, apparently, belonged to Joe Namath.

"Main thing, I guess," expanded Captain Fox, "is that they worry, a lot, about fire! Especially, y'know, when there's a big crowd out there! Shouldn't be all that many crowds . . . not on your shift, anyways! That's, y'know, where all the television camera bullshit comes in! The tee vee cameras are in the places where they figure, y'know, they're most likely to be where a fire could start! How's that job sound, Vick?"

"Sounds pretty good. I never thought I'd hear myself saying something like this. Not about a security guard job, anyway."

"Fine! Great, Vick! That's the way I like to hear a man talk! And, Vick, you'll go a long way with this here outfit! Believe me! I think I told you that before! Believe me, though, you will! I shit you not. Now, for the long haul, we're thinkin' along the lines of somethin' else for you here! Somethin' . . . well, maybe down the road a bit! Like I said . . . we're talkin' long haul!"

"What's that?"

"Well," beamed the feisty little captain, "I can't really get too much . . . into particulars. Not right now, anyways. We don't have all our ducks in a row . . . like they say. Not yet, anyways. But, let's just say that it'll be somethin' . . . fairly much along the lines that you was talkin' about. Talkin' about . . . when you first applied here. You remember how you was talkin'? All about those guys? The ones that . . . they was workin' as sort of undercover agents for us? When you were at **Ballinger's Rent-a-Car**?"

"Yeah. That's really why I applied."

"I know! I know that, Vick. And I think that . . . pretty damn soon now . . . I think that we'll be able to get you into somethin' like that! Somethin' we think, is a helluva lot like that! And with more money to boot! Main thing, right now, though, is we get you really back in harness! Doin' real sergeant stuff. That's what we got in mind for you . . . right at this present moment! Do you feel like you can get yourself cranked up . . . to sergeant speed? Like, starting tonight?"

"Yup."

"Good! Fine! Now, tell you what you do: You report out to *Shea*! Tonight . . . at midnight. Well, quarter-of, you know. We've got a small stand . . . under Section Thirty-nine! And you'll meet . . . uh, lemme see now . . . you'll meet Corporal Tiefenauer. The corporal . . . he'll show you where your duty station is! And he'll stay with you . . . probably through most of the shift! He's not happy, y'know . . . about comin' off the assignment! But, what the hell! You are a sergeant . . . and he is a corporal. Rank has its privileges, y'know. He'll show you around out there! And then he's gonna go ahead and leave you . . . when he's really sure that you got it! But, it ain't like you hafta, you know, learn some really complicated, shit-assed, tour!"

Smigelski arose—rubbing his backside, which had fallen asleep. He shook hands with his boss.

"Thank you, Captain," he said, with a warm, totally-sincere, smile. "I really <u>appreciate</u> everything you've done for me. I've <u>always</u> appreciated your giving me all that time <u>off</u>! To recuperate! And to jack with all the <u>court</u> crap! I'll do my <u>best</u> . . . out there at *Shea.* I'm <u>anxious</u>, of course, to get into that <u>other</u> thing that you mentioned!"

"Of <u>course</u> you are, Vick! Of <u>course</u> you are! And I don't mind tellin' you that I been <u>pushin'</u> for you, Boy. Been pushin' . . . like a <u>sonofabitch</u>!"

"I'm sure you have."

"<u>Pushin'</u>, y'know! Like nobody's <u>business</u>! I think that you probably came <u>along</u> . . . faster'n anyone <u>I</u> ever seen here! But, I really <u>feel</u> like you . . . like you'll be a <u>good</u> one! Like you <u>are</u> a good one! And I'm doin' everything I <u>can</u> . . . to, you know, to get you on <u>ahead</u>! I <u>know</u> . . . that you ain't gonna let me <u>down</u>, Vick."

"I <u>won't</u>, Captain! I <u>assure</u> you . . . I <u>won't</u>!"

"<u>Good</u>! <u>Wonderful</u>! Now, you'll meet Corporal <u>Tiefenauer</u> . . . out there tonight! And good <u>luck</u>! You'll be <u>hearin'</u> from me . . . just as soon as I can turn up somethin' <u>new</u> for you! Somethin' that <u>befits</u> a man like yourself! But, don't you <u>worry</u>, Vick! It won't be long <u>now</u>!"

"It never <u>was</u>," replied Smigelski, sardonically.

The Ribald reply had gone completely over Captain Fox's head.

For the better part of four months, Smigelski worked nights at *Shea Stadium*—six nights each week. He'd thought it "interesting" that—unlike Corporal Scotti—Corporal Tiefenauer had not come close to launching into a diatribe—concerning any items that he may have lifted from the confines of the facility, in Queens. Captain Fox had, of course, mentioned the corporal's reluctance to yield the spot. Scotti had, many months previous, innumerated the many light-fingered reasons that <u>any</u> guard might be extremely reluctant to give up the potentially ultra-profitable gig!

Over the passage of time, the original, highly-ominous, feeling of foreboding had, slowly, <u>eroded</u>. For that, Smigelski was grateful. He was much less appreciative of the fact that Captain Fox's promise of "bigger, better, things" had not yet materialized. The thought was that, quite possibly, the little man had <u>forgotten</u> his pledge. Or, then again—maybe he had <u>not</u>!

During that time, nothing out of the ordinary had ever occurred, during the course of Smigelski's many shifts! <u>That</u>, of course, was something for which to be <u>really</u> thankful! On the other hand, there'd been substantially less overtime—which had made June happy, but was becoming a bit of a fiscal concern, to our hero!

The baseball season had wound down. In 1974, the New York Mets had played to a disappointing 71-91 record—and had finished a <u>really</u> disappointing 5th place, in The National League East Division. The season had been a <u>special</u> letdown for a team that had fared so wonderfully the previous season.

Manager Yogi Berra—who'd led the Mets to a remarkable record, in 1973—managed to survive the team's forgettable, dismal, 1974 performance. However, the even-then-legendary little man was eventually sacked—during the 1975 campaign. The highly-quotable (to this day), rotund, ever-popular, athlete/philosopher was replaced, in '75, by Roy McMillan.

The Mets, of the seventies, were the proud possessors of a "sweetheart" contract with the City of New York—which owned *Shea Stadium*, in the Borough of Queens. The club's "Deal" even affected the **National Football League's** New York Giants—despite the fact that the Giants, in the early-seventies, played their home games, as mentioned, at *Yankee Stadium*, in The Bronx.

The contract between the City and the Mets stipulated that absolutely <u>no event of any description</u> could be booked into *Shea,* during the baseball season. Well, not without the Mets' specific approval. The consequences were substantial! Many potentially lucrative football dates—involving the Jets (and, in numerous cases, the Giants)—were not permitted, by the Mets' management.

Most notable—by far—of the potentially-lucrative events, that had been summarily vetoed by the baseball club, was the always-looked-forward-to, spectacularly-popular, mega-profitable, annual, preseason Jets/Giants football game. The citizens of "The Big Apple"—who'd helped support *Shea,* with a multitude of their tax dollars—were required to make "The Long Schlep", up to the *Yale Bowl* in New Haven, Connecticut, to attend the game!

An active security guard once more, Smigelski, on occasion, had arrived at *Shea*—to assume his station before the Mets players had dispersed. A "star-gazer" all his life, he'd found himself <u>reveling</u> in the close proximity to the athletes. They were not commonly referred to as "jocks" in 1974. Certainly not in mixed company. The "culture" has come a long way since then. As our hero would grouse—usually to June— "<u>Progress</u>! Ya can't <u>beat</u> it!"

Several times, Smigelski was able to discuss with a number of Mets players the fact that no football games or concerts could be booked into the stadium during the baseball season.

To a man, the players had always <u>justified</u> the ban. A concert, they'd claimed, had never failed to bring too many people, onto the field. The situation, inevitably, resulted in the playing surface being torn up. "Grievously scarred"—as one of the more literary players had described it.

That same justification, of course, was used— for the most part—to keep the always-intriguing Jets' games out. It was, forever, the baseball team's position—and that of the players—that football cleats always heavily damaged the field! Wrought havoc— without exception! To the point, in the consensus of opinion, where their use consistently affected— in major ways—the play of the Mets, and their opponents!

"I'll tell you what," muttered one of the players. "I damn near broke my ankle on the field! Out in Saint Louis! And it was the day . . . after they had a damn

<u>football</u> game played there! It really screws up the <u>field</u>!"

Once the World Series had been completed, other activities began to find their way—at long last—into *Shea*.

It was during a January, 1975, rock concert, at the stadium, that Smigelski recorded his second "incident", during his tenure with **Tarkenton**!

He'd been assigned to this particular concert by Captain Fox, of course. He would merely "show up early" for his shift. He would be paid for an extra, separate, eight-hour workload. Instead of pursuing his normal course of employment—beneath the stands—he would roam a particular section, of spectators' seats. "To assist . . . in any emergency".

"It's just a one-shot deal, Vick. But, what the hell. It'll give you a little overtime. A little more overtime, y'see. Like I said, I'm really pushin' for you, Boy. I really am. Plus . . . and besides . . . there'll be <u>other</u> concerts, down the line! Concerts and <u>wrestling</u> matches! <u>Boxing</u>! And who-<u>knows</u>-what other shit they'll have out there! I'll <u>see</u> . . . that you get your share! <u>More</u> than your share!"

As with virtually every concert of that type, extra security was a <u>must</u>! Smigelski was well aware of the fact that—despite the captain's talk of only "emergencies"—<u>any</u> guard's main function was that of crowd control! The long-dormant specter of <u>foreboding</u> had, immediately, rushed back to the surface! Once again, all <u>sorts</u> of troubling scenarios "danced in his merry little head"! Our hero found himself wishing—mightily—that they had <u>not</u>!

Even with the always-required added security, history is rife with incident-upon-incident of public misbehavior. <u>Deadly</u> situations where, in some cases, the entire crowd had gotten completely out of control! To Smigelski's way of thinking, the throng had usually "started <u>out</u>, semi-out of control"!

Most usually, there were great amounts of marijuana smoked—as well as overwhelming evidence of harder drugs being used—at those concerts! Virtually without exception! There was ample evidence of these things being in play—at virtually <u>all</u> rock concerts!

June Bodner, as might've been imagined, had been terribly <u>upset</u>! She'd physically <u>shuddered</u>—at the "spooky" prospect, of Smigelski working the highly-publicized, sold-out-for-weeks, event!

She was certain that he would wind up becoming involved in some imbroglio with some person—or persons—who were either "high", or "on a trip". "If I know <u>you</u> . . . you'll wind up, in the damn <u>center</u>, of some damn-fool outburst, or something," she'd groused! She'd repeated that chilling lament—numerous <u>times</u>! (<u>Numerous</u> times!)

Smigelski assured her that he would <u>absolutely</u>—<u>positively</u>—steer clear of anything of that nature. "Nothing even <u>close</u>," he'd promised—solemnly.

He'd even offered to buy June a ticket to the concert if possible—"so you can keep a wary eye on me".

"No thanks," she'd replied, shuddering once more. "It's not my kind of <u>music</u>. Now, if it were Henry

Mancini . . . or someone like that . . . it'd be a helluva lot different! On the other hand, I wouldn't worry so much . . . about you working a Mancini concert! Whole different clientele! Altogether different! One that's a little more . . . ah . . . earthbound!"

"Of course it is. I've never heard of them booking extra security for a Mancini concert. Or Tony Bennett . . . or Peggy Lee."

"Oh, Vick! Promise me! Promise me . . . that you'll be careful! I'm so worried . . . worried about you!"

"Of course! Certainly . . . I'll be careful! I'm not so screwed up . . . that I relish problems! Don't want no problems! I'm not looking forward . . . to getting clobbered again! That ain't no fun! There won't be any problems! Zero problems! None! Trust me!"

"You, I trust. It's your half-assed sense of righteousness . . . that I worry about."

"Fie, Woman! You borrow trouble. A pox upon your warped imagination! Nothing's going to happen! Really, Junie. Tell you what. I'll try and call you a couple . . . or three times . . . during the concert! Listen, I don't know where they'll have me stationed . . . so I don't really know if I'll have access to a pay phone."

Obviously, this conversation had taken place well before the advent—and common usage—of cell phones.

"I promise you, though," continued Smigelski, "that . . . if I can possibly call you . . . I'll give you a ring! If you don't hear from me . . . it's simply because I just could not get to a phone! But, I'll try! I will! That, I promise you! I will try to call you!"

Once he'd left her warm living room—to try and coax his Dodge's heater into springing for a more generous allotment of heat, than it was most always reluctant to provide (and <u>far</u> more quickly)—Smigelski found himself <u>glad</u>! <u>Glad</u>—that he'd brought the word "<u>try</u>" into play! And so <u>often</u>! And—each and every time—with such <u>emphasis</u>!

During the first three-quarters of the concert, nothing untoward took place. A rather <u>large</u> surprise to/for our hero. (<u>Rather</u> large!)

Smigelski was able to call June—twice—from the stadium. Each time, she'd been <u>noticeably</u> relieved! <u>Noticeably</u>!

Shortly before 10:00 PM, though, five young men—obviously "on" something—began harassing two young ladies! The incident was taking place—six rows, in front of where Smigelski happened to have been standing!

The women—both of them—were attempting, vainly, to <u>ignore</u> the unwelcomed hassle, coming from the hell-bent-on-having-their-own-way youths! That, of course, only <u>spurred</u> the troublemakers on—to even <u>more</u> obnoxious conduct! It didn't take <u>much</u>!

Smigelski became aware of the ruckus—once he'd spied one of the youths putting his hand—<u>firmly</u>—on the breast, of one of the troubled young women! She, immediately spat an <u>obscenity</u> at the molester—and pulled <u>away</u>!

One of the other punks <u>grabbed</u> the frightened young lady! He yanked her <u>up</u>—and out of her chair!

The first man, then, began to—violently—rub both of his hands across her <u>breasts</u>! With extreme "<u>vigor</u>"!

The other woman, at that point, attempted to <u>rise</u>! And to <u>flee</u>! She was thrown <u>back</u>! Thrown <u>down</u>— into her seat—by two of the <u>other</u> youths!

Literally dozens of people sitting alongside—and in the rows behind—paid absolutely no <u>attention</u> to the plight of the frightened, and embarrassed, victims!

Smigelski <u>rushed</u> to the scene—and ordered the five young men to <u>desist</u> and <u>disperse</u>! (His actual, spoken, command was a little more "flowery" than that!)

"Did you hear <u>that</u>, Richard?" whined one of the punks. "Ol' <u>Dad</u> here . . . <u>he</u> wants us to fuckin' <u>leave</u>!"

"<u>Indeed</u>, my dear William! <u>Indeed</u>! Perchance the old fart can't <u>count</u>! Otherwise, he'd have <u>noted</u> that there are <u>five</u> of us! And only <u>one</u> of him!"

William continued to fondle the young woman's breasts!

A "kindly" patron—comfortably seated directly <u>behind</u> the poor struggling young lady—told Smigelski to "take a <u>hike</u>"! The guy was, obviously, trying to listen to the musicians—on the stage! The "<u>diversion</u>" was, of course, <u>unforgivable</u>!

Smigelski ignored the boor in the next row! But, not William!

"I'm <u>telling</u> you, goddam it," he shouted, grabbing the youth's arm—<u>firmly</u>! "Telling you . . . to get your punk ass <u>out</u> of here! Leave her <u>alone</u>!"

William was able to pull away from Smigelski's grip! In so doing, he wound up <u>pushing</u> the badly-

shaken, trembling, woman—back into her seat!
Violently!

At that moment, one of the other hoods cracked
Smigelski! A monumental blow! Across his back! The
youth had had both of his fists doubled together! The
staggering blow sent the guard trundling forward—
into Richard! The latter had remained—threateningly
hovering over the second terror-stricken young lady!

Richard attempted to bring his knee up—headed,
directly, for the somewhat-rattled Smigelski's
stomach! However, there had not been sufficient
room—for him to inflict his intended damage! The
maneuver, in fact, wound up causing Richard to—
significantly—lose his balance! He tumbled to the
cement! With Smigelski—on top of him!

"Look out!" screamed one of the young women.
"He's . . . he's got a knife!"

Smigelski rolled off—of Richard! He unleashed a
merciless kick, of his own! It was aimed—at the knife-
wielder's groin! The kick collided—with its intended
target! At the exact moment when the hoodlum made
ready to lunge at him—his switch-blade open! The
force of the blow—sent the young "tough" to the
cement! Screaming—in pure agony!

Jumping to his feet, Smigelski hurled himself—
onto the other two men! Both of them had been—
critically—unsteady! Thanks to whatever "freedom-
from-earth" substance that they were "on"! That
wobbly-legged fact proved helpful! Extremely
helpful!

All three men rolled down the concrete steps—as
Smigelski pummeled each of the two hoods, with his
fists! One of the boorish troublemakers came out of

the skirmish—with three less <u>teeth</u>, than he'd <u>brought</u> to the contest! The other had sustained a broken jaw! The official diagnosis wound up reading, "Multiple Fractures"!

The youth who had tried to stab Smigelski lay on the cement deck—writhing, and clutching, frantically, at his <u>testicles</u>! His face had <u>contorted</u>—into a frenzied mask, of agonizing <u>pain</u>!

Richard had not regained his feet! William—reaching an "executive decision"—opted to make a run for it!

Smigelski, once again, got to his <u>feet</u>! He withdrew his trusty Billy club, from its sheath! He <u>swung</u> the weapon! And <u>connected</u>, dead-on! With William's <u>head</u>! The one-sided collision produced a <u>sickening</u> thud! The punk <u>dropped</u>—as though he'd been pole-axed!

Richard was, foolishly, attempting to <u>rise</u>! At the exact <u>moment</u>—when Smigelski was refocusing his attention, on that young worthy!

As the ill-fated Richard was attempting to climb to his feet, Smigelski swung his club once again! The crushing blow caught Richard full in the <u>face</u>—shattering his left <u>cheekbone</u>! His <u>nose</u> also turned out to be an especially-<u>bloody</u> casualty!

By that time, two uniformed <u>New York City police officers</u> had rushed to the scene! Mere seconds behind "New York's Finest", clamored four of **Tarkenton's** men! And one <u>woman</u>! <u>That</u> was a surprise. To <u>Smigelski</u>, anyway.

At that point, as you might well imagine, none of the young hoodlums were going anywhere!

In 1975, the populace of New York City had apparently come to expect that neither security guards—nor anybody else—would bother to involve themselves in a "regrettable" situation, such as the one in which Smigelski had found himself immersed, vis-a-vis the five "disturbed" youths.

Tales abounded of people who had purchased front-row seats—at considerable expense—to myriad numbers of concerts, sporting events, etc. etc. etc.— only to find themselves in a situation where a group of young "toughs" had simply usurped their seats!

In most (well, virtually all) cases, the bona fide ticket holders could not persuade anyone—security personnel, or even police officers—to remove the poachers! Not by force—nor by any other means!

Such happenings—as well as blatant gate-crashing; wherein hordes of people, all without tickets, simply stormed the turnstiles—in overwhelming numbers. It had become an accepted fact of life, in "The Big Apple". Therefore, it was virtually unheard of—for a single, unarmed, man to take on a group, of young rowdies!

Added to the prevailing philosophy, of non-involvement, was the ominous fact, that the come-lately "Drug Culture"—in which frightening numbers of young people had been caught up—had fostered an alarming, seemingly universal, disrespect for virtually all elements, and vestiges, of authority! Any authority! It was, in fact, considered to be exceptionally "cool" to "put down" anything even remotely "establishment"!

The leader of the rock group—performing, at the height of the battle between Smigelski and the five punks—had screamed into his mic, "Fucking pigs!" He was gesticulating, wildly, at Smigelski—who, clad in a blue, police-type, uniform, was close enough to being "the real thing . . . the fuzz" for the "entertainment personality's" judgment!

Most of the crowd had, of course, applauded the rock star! A few spectators, though—those seated adjacent to the troubled young ladies—had actually shown the out and out temerity to boo their obvious disapproval, of the performer's epithet! Considered a sacrilege in "the culture"!

Immediately after the skirmish, Smigelski was interviewed by a young woman correspondent. She represented one of the area's smaller, independent, television stations. The reporter had been covering the concert—and was to submit an audio report, to be aired on the station's 11:00PM newscast. No cameraman had been assigned to the event.

The television personality was an attractive black woman, in her early-twenties. She was sporting the wildest Afro hairstyle that Smigelski had ever seen.

The New York Police—whose presence, at the scene of the confrontation, had been swelled to seven at that point—were in the process of removing the five young men from the area! The operation had required a "goodly amount" of effort. Two of the "toughs"—would wind up in the hospital! For a "good, long" stay!

It was at that moment that the reporter had approached the still-rattled Smigelski—shoving a microphone into his face.

"Hi," she said brightly. "I'm Lottie Ann Holt . . . Channel Thirty-Six. Can I talk to you a minute? It should wind up . . . on the air."

"Yeah," panted Smigelski. "I guess so."

"I understand," Lottie Ann began, having flicked on her portable recorder, "that you were involved . . . with a few young men, there."

"A few. Yeah."

"What happened?"

"Well," Smigelski was still short of breath, "they were . . . were annoying a couple young . . . a couple young ladies there. And . . . chee! . . . I can't seem to catch my breath! Must be getting old!"

"Perfectly all right, Mister . . . ?"

"Smigelski. Vick Smigelski. Victor Smigelski."

"Just take your time . . . and catch your breath . . . Mister Smigelski. I appreciate your talking to us."

"Anyway," continued the haggard security guard, "there were these five punks . . . down here. They were flat-out harassing two young women . . . and they out and out wouldn't stop! Would not stop! So, I figured it was up to me to . . . to, well . . . to make 'em stop!"

"You took on five of 'em? All five of 'em?"

A young woman spectator—seated two rows behind Lottie Ann—hollered, from over the reporter's shoulder, "He sure as hell did!".

"That's amazing," responded Lottie Ann. "What did you do? How did you get them to stop, Mister Smigelski?"

"I pulled one of 'em <u>off</u> one of the girls . . . off one of the young women. Then, the <u>other</u> four creeps . . . <u>they</u> decided that <u>they</u> were going to get involved!"

At that point, the lady who'd been molested by William cut in:

"Excuse me," she said, breathlessly. "This man came to my <u>aid</u>! There were <u>five</u> of these jerks! And <u>one</u> of 'em, he was . . . well . . . he was putting his hands all <u>over</u> me! And he wouldn't <u>stop</u>! My <u>girlfriend</u>, here, and I . . . we just couldn't <u>do</u> anything! <u>No</u> one . . . no one <u>around</u> us . . . was going to <u>help</u>! All those <u>guys</u> there? <u>Nothing</u>! Wouldn't get <u>involved</u>! Not <u>one</u> of 'em . . . had <u>balls</u> enough! Didn't <u>any</u> of 'em . . . have <u>balls</u> enough, to get <u>involved</u>! Then this man, <u>here</u> . . . this <u>guard</u> . . . <u>he</u> asked 'em to stop! They <u>wouldn't</u>! They <u>didn't</u>! They started <u>in</u>! Started in . . . on <u>him</u>! One of those bastards pulled a <u>knife</u> . . . a damn <u>knife</u> . . . on <u>him</u>!" She put her hand on Smigelski's arm! "But, <u>he</u> . . . this guy <u>here</u> . . . he took 'em <u>On</u>! Took 'em <u>all</u> on," she continued. "Every damn <u>one</u> of 'em! It was a <u>tremendous</u> thing! A <u>wonderful</u> . . . a really <u>brave</u> . . . thing! I've never seen <u>anyone</u> so brave! Anyone that <u>brave</u>!"

"Or <u>stupid</u>," muttered Smigelski, with a wan smile.

"What's your name?" the reporter inquired of the young woman.

"Melody. Melody Blair. And this is my friend . . . Janice Mullet."

Turning from Melody, Lottie Ann asked, "Is what Miss Blair <u>said</u> . . . is it really <u>true</u>, Mister Smigelski?"

"Yeah. I <u>guess</u> so. It was over so <u>fast</u> that, I really don't <u>remember</u> . . . remember too many of the <u>details</u>! I guess the thing that <u>bugged</u> me . . . almost as much as those scumbags harassing the <u>girls</u> . . . was the fact that there must've been twenty or twenty-five able-bodied <u>men</u>! <u>Men</u>, dammit! <u>Men</u> . . . sitting within <u>shooting</u> distance of these girls! And not a <u>one</u> of those assholes <u>did</u> anything . . . not a damn <u>thing</u> . . . to <u>help</u> them! Not on damn <u>thing</u>! <u>Nothing</u>!"

"Well, I can <u>see</u> that you're still . . . uh . . . still <u>excited</u>, Mister Smigelski. Still have the old adrenaline <u>flowing</u>! I want to thank you so <u>much</u> . . . for <u>talking</u> with us. This is Lottie Ann Holt . . . Channel Thirty-Six News . . . at *Shea Stadium*."

Smigelski was eventually able to call June Bodner. He did his best to explain what had happened at the concert—advising her to watch the 11:00 PM news on channel 36!

"When are you coming home, Vick?" she asked, icily. "Or <u>are</u> you coming home?"

"Not for awhile. They want me to go to the hospital, you know, and . . ."

"Oh, <u>Vick</u>! Vick, Vick, <u>Vick</u>! <u>Damn</u> it all! You're <u>hurt</u>!" The chill had left her voice! <u>Immediately</u>! "I <u>knew</u> it! Dammit! I just <u>knew</u> this would happen! I <u>knew</u>! I just <u>knew</u> it!"

"I'm not <u>hurt</u>, Junie! <u>Honest</u>! I'm <u>not</u>! I just took a little bit of a crack . . . across my <u>back</u>! I'm sure nothing's <u>wrong</u>! It's just a little <u>sore</u>! <u>That's</u> all."

"Your <u>shoulder</u>, Vick! How's your <u>shoulder</u>?"

"My shoulder's <u>fine</u>! Nothing <u>wrong</u> with it. Nothing wrong with <u>anything</u>. I think the people who booked the concert . . . I think <u>they</u> want me to go to the hospital! Want to get me checked <u>out</u>! Maybe it's the powers-that-be at *Shea*. I don't know. <u>Someone's</u> just trying to cover his or her legal-action <u>ass</u>. They don't want me <u>suing</u> 'em . . . I'm sure . . . for some half-assed <u>injury</u>, somewhere down the road!"

"<u>Vick</u>! <u>Listen</u> to me, Vick! You've <u>got</u> to get out! Get <u>out</u> . . . of this damnable business! You've simply <u>got</u> to! Otherwise, you're going to get yourself <u>killed</u>! I'm <u>telling</u> you, Vick! I'm <u>worried</u> . . . worried <u>sick</u>! Worried <u>sick</u> . . . about you! I really <u>am</u>! Sooner or <u>later</u> . . . something's going to <u>happen</u> to you! Something <u>bad</u>! I <u>know</u> it! I can just <u>feel</u> it! I just <u>know</u> it! I . . . oh, <u>Vick</u>! Vick . . . <u>please</u>! <u>Please</u>!"

"C'mon, Junie. I don't <u>mean</u> to upset you. I <u>know</u> that you worry! You worry your pretty little <u>fanny</u> off! Worry it <u>off</u> . . . over me! And I <u>hate</u> it! Hate the fact that I <u>always</u> seem to be putting you . . . putting you through all <u>kinds</u> of hell! But, what else can I <u>do</u>? <u>Jobs</u>! Jobs are awfully damn hard to <u>come</u> by, nowadays! <u>Damn</u> hard!"

"Oh, <u>Vick</u>! I've talked to Mister <u>Hennings</u>! <u>Talked</u> to him . . . about <u>you</u>! Any <u>number</u> of times! Any <u>number</u>!"

Sylvester Hennings was one of the two partners— one of the pair of owners—of the **Avis Rent-a-Car** licensee, where June was presently employed. Smigelski had left their employ—in 1968.

"Junie . . . <u>look</u>! We've been all <u>through</u> that," he replied—sighing heavily. The conversation, thankfully, seemed to be entering a lower—less intense— key. "I <u>know</u> that I'm being stubborn! And . . . quite probably . . . a total <u>asshole</u>! But, I simply <u>can't</u>! Can <u>not</u> go back to <u>work</u> there! Don't ask me <u>why</u>! I don't really know . . . <u>myself</u>! It's just that . . . just that I can't <u>do</u> it!" His voice tailed off—to an almost-whisper. "I'm sorry," he muttered.

"I <u>guess</u> I understand," she responded, around her own, even louder, massive sigh. "I don't know," she groused. "Maybe I <u>don't</u> understand! Maybe I don't understand <u>anything</u>! Not one damn <u>thing</u>! I'm <u>not</u> trying to lay one of those if-you-really-<u>loved</u>-me-you'd-<u>do</u>-it trips on you! I'm honestly <u>not</u>! You're a big <u>boy</u> now!"

"Yeah," muttered Smigelski. "So I've been <u>told</u>! The world's biggest . . . and oldest . . . juvenile <u>delinquent</u>."

"You <u>know</u> what I mean."

"I guess. <u>Look</u>, Junie! Captain Fox has been <u>talking</u> to me! <u>Talking</u> to me . . . about <u>not</u> getting my Polack butt, into a situation like this. He's talking about a job . . . where there's not really any physical danger. A situation . . . where there's not really any physical <u>danger</u>! Well, <u>practically</u> none, anyway! Something like I was talking about <u>before</u>! You know, with all that <u>undercover</u> stuff . . . at **Ballinger's**. <u>Look</u>! I'll tell you <u>what</u>: I'll give him a more-or-less <u>ultimatum</u>!"

"More or <u>less</u>?"

"Yeah. I'll <u>tell</u> him that . . . unless he can get me into a position like that <u>undercover</u> thing . . . that I'm just gonna pack it <u>in</u>! Even . . . God help me . . . go talk to Sylvester <u>Hennings</u>, dammit!"

"Oh, <u>Vick</u>! You'd do <u>that</u>? You'd do that . . . for l'il ol' <u>me</u>?"

"Only because you're so damn <u>sexy</u> . . . and have such a cute <u>butt</u>! Not necessarily in that <u>order</u>. But, probably, <u>in</u> that order."

"I try. God knows, I try. Are you sure you're not saying all this . . . not telling me all this . . . just to calm me down? I mean . . . listen, old Polack of mine . . . I'll go along with whatever you want to do! I may go along kicking and screaming . . . but, dammit, I will go along! I just worry, Vick! I worry so much! I worry . . . about you! I do! I don't want you to do something, though! Something you don't want to do! Just to placate me! Really . . . I don't!"

"I'm not trying to placate you. It does sound like fun, though." In his most sinister Snidely Whiplash voice, he asked her, "Have you been placated . . . lately?"

"Behave yourself!"

"I'm not just talking, Junie! I figure that I should've proved myself by now! I've paid my dues . . . as they say! Tarkenton may not think so . . . but, I think so! So, if they can't move me into something a little less physical . . . a little less risky . . . then, I will! I'll chuck it! Pack it in!"

"Most of me believes that, Vick."

"Most of you? Which parts of you?"

"Hush," she said softly. "Listen, Vick. There are times . . . when I think you actually enjoy these conflicts! Like tonight! You're Captain Marvel! You're Superman! You're off to rescue some damn damsel . . . in distress!"

"Aw, Junie! Someone had to do something! That sonofabitch . . . he just wouldn't keep his hands off that poor girl's boobs! If you could've seen her . . . why, you'd have done the same thing I did!"

"Yeah," she answered with another massive sigh. "Yeah. Someone had to do something! Trouble is that . . . today, <u>these</u> days . . . <u>no</u> one does <u>anything</u>! <u>No</u> one does <u>shit</u>! <u>No</u> one . . . except for people like <u>you</u>! And, I think that a major <u>part</u> of people like you . . . a great big <u>part</u> of people like you . . . is, I think, the <u>enjoyment</u> you get! Or the <u>gratification</u>! Or <u>whatever</u>! The <u>satisfaction</u> that you get . . . out of seeing those bastards get <u>theirs</u>! Like those five little <u>shits</u>! The ones . . . that you grappled with <u>tonight</u>! I think . . . I really and truly <u>think</u> . . . I think that you might probably groove <u>out</u>! Groove <u>out</u> . . . on seeing them get <u>theirs</u>!"

"My! Aren't we <u>psychological</u>."

"I don't have to be a <u>shrink</u>. I've been to enough movies with you! Enough flicks . . . that I can see the <u>euphoria</u> that comes over you! When the bad guy gets <u>his</u>! We <u>all</u> like to see the heavy get what's <u>coming</u> to him! Unless, obviously, we happen to <u>be</u> the heavy! But, you almost get an <u>orgasm</u> . . . when you see the villain get his come-<u>uppance</u>! The other side of the <u>coin</u> . . . is that you get all <u>depressed</u>! It's a real <u>downer</u> for you . . . when you read of some poor old <u>geezer</u>! See someone like that . . . getting <u>mugged</u>! Being kicked <u>silly</u> . . . by a couple or three young <u>bucks</u>! Especially when they really <u>hurt</u> the old guy . . . or the old <u>gal</u>! That's always a real <u>downer</u> for you!"

"Of <u>course</u> it's a downer. It'd be a downer . . . for <u>anyone</u>! For <u>everyone</u>!"

"Not like it is for <u>you</u>! That's why I <u>worry</u>! Worry that you may . . . knowingly or <u>unknowingly</u> . . . <u>enjoy</u> the real-life conflict! Enjoy the real-life <u>confrontation</u>! I can <u>tell</u>, that . . . even <u>now</u> . . . you're on a bit of a <u>high</u>! Knowing you <u>saved</u> that lady from . . . that little bastard! The one . . . that was <u>pawing</u> her! I also <u>know</u> . . . that you're probably <u>hurt</u>! <u>Hurt</u> more . . . than you're letting <u>on</u>! Even if it's nothing really serious! Hey . . . <u>Shazam</u>! You're *Captain Marvel*!"

"C'mon, Junie! I'm <u>not</u> *Captain Marvel*. And I really <u>don't</u>! I do <u>not</u> enjoy the physical challenge! Or anything that goes <u>with</u> it. Do you really <u>think</u> that the reason I've stayed on with **Tarkenton** . . . and won't come back to work at **Avis** . . . is because I've got some kind of stupid, some silly-assed, *Superman* complex?"

"I dunno," she lamented. "Yeah. Maybe. Possibly. That's <u>part</u> of it! I <u>believe</u> that's part of it, anyway! I really don't <u>know</u> . . . can't <u>imagine</u> . . . what the <u>percentage</u> is! Don't know how <u>much</u> it is . . . what <u>percentage</u> it is . . . of the entire <u>Polack</u>! But, I'm just as <u>sure</u> as I can <u>be</u> . . . that it's a monumental <u>part</u>! A <u>gigantic</u> part . . . of the damn <u>equation</u>! You just can't <u>stand</u> . . . to see evil go <u>unpunished</u>! It makes you <u>nuts</u>!'

"Well, don't you worry, My Little Chickadee! I'll do <u>exactly</u> . . . what I <u>told</u> you I'll do! I'll issue Captain Fox an <u>ultimatum</u>! It won't even <u>be</u> a more-or-less one, either!"

"<u>Part</u> of me . . . well, <u>most</u> of me . . . is <u>overjoyed</u>! Overjoyed and <u>relieved</u> . . . to hear you <u>say</u> that! But, <u>part</u> of me worries! Worries like <u>hell</u>! Worries me . . . that I'm <u>pushing</u> you! Pushing you, too <u>hard</u> . . . to do something that you'd rather not <u>do</u>! Just <u>tell</u> me, Vick. Just tell me to butt <u>out</u>! I <u>mean</u> it!. I <u>truly</u> don't want to be <u>pushy</u>! I <u>do</u> want you to know, though! Know how <u>concerned</u> I am . . . about you! I <u>love</u> you, y'know!"

"I <u>know</u> you do," he added with yet another sigh. "I know you <u>do</u>! And . . . if I had any <u>class</u> at all . . . I wouldn't <u>put</u> you under all this crappy <u>stress</u>! Make you worry your cute little <u>fanny</u> off!"

"My cute little fanny and I <u>thank</u> you. Mostly <u>me</u>, though. Flattery will get you <u>everywhere</u>."

The following day, the New York media played up Smigelski's scuffle with the five youths—to the <u>maximum</u>!

Noon found three television crews—and scores of radio and newspaper reporters—outside the little Metuchen, New Jersey, building, in which his "luxurious" single-room dwelling was located. In such a small town, the attendant commotion represented quite a "happening".

Smigelski spoke with eight different reporters from television, radio and the press.

No sooner had he been convinced that the media was, at long last, dispersing—when a television crew arrived from Philadelphia. He'd had to replay the entire adventure—all over again.

Three days later, an attorney—ostensibly representing Gregory Lovett, one of the five rowdies that Smigelski had confronted, at the rock concert— announced that Lovett was suing *Shea Stadium*, **Tarkenton Security Services**, the rock concert aggregation, and the promoters of the concert! For seven million dollars!

Lovett was the young man Smigelski had kicked in the groin! He was also the youth who had, so innocently, playfully pulled a lethal switchblade <u>knife</u>, during the skirmish!

Lovett's attorney was William Cuthbertson— long identified with "civil rights" causes and ultra-liberal organizations. It had been the celebrated Cuthbertson—who had sought out Lovett. He would be representing the "offended" young man—on a pro-bono basis.

Whether he would eventually win the case or not— the widely-reported suit would make for excellent, wildly profitable, publicity, for Cuthbertson!

The attorney called a press conference—to announce the suit! And, of course, to deliver himself of an emotion-filled sermon! The message denounced, of course, the use of force by "those in authority . . . or those who <u>think</u> they are in authority. <u>Especially</u> those who think they are in authority!"

He called upon the District Attorney's office—to arrest and prosecute "this gorilla, Mister Smigelski", for his "vicious, ruthless . . . and certainly uncalled for . . . attack" upon his "put upon" client!

The media—as usual—had, dutifully, hung upon every word that he'd seen fit to utter! Of course, they—also dutifully—reported his every thrust! His every parry! His every nuance!

Two of the City's newspapers editorially applauded the well-known, very compelling, Cuthbertson's "heart-felt campaign to rid the City . . . of a most dangerous element! An underground element!

An over-simplistic, self-righteous, 'law-and-order', mentality! Of a 'law-and-order' <u>fantasy</u>"!

In every portion of the lengthy, seemingly never-ending, diatribe, Smigelski was referred to, consistently, as "The Lowest Of The Low"!

Captain Marvel—indeed!

SIX

TWO WEEKS—TO THE DAY—AFTER THE celebrated rock concert, Captain Fox led Smigelski into a posh office, two floors above his own. Noticeably ill at ease, in such "lavish" surroundings, the stocky little captain—rather hesitantly—approached the receptionist.

"Captain Fox and Sergeant Smigelski . . . to see Mister Nype," he announced—almost under his breath.

"Certainly, Captain," the young lady replied, in a soft, seductive, voice—and with an infectious smile. "Mister Nype is expecting you, Sir. Go right in."

Captain Fox pushed through the large, oaken, door, to the left of the receptionist's desk, and— followed by Smigelski—entered an even more posh inner office.

A tall, slender, tanned, silver-haired man, in his mid-fifties, rose from behind a monstrous, gridiron-sized, gleaming, mahogany desk—and welcomed his two visitors, his hand outstretched. Mr. Nype was the epitome of the word "distinguished"!

"Captain Fox!" Nype's resonant, deep-pitched voice filled every corner of the huge room. "So good to see you, Captain. And this? This must be the man you've been telling me about. Mister . . . Smigelski, is it?"

Captain Fox shook hands with Nype, and answered, "Yes, Sir. I'll bet you're the first person who could ever pronounce his name right. First off, anyways."

The captain introduced the two men: "Mister Leland Nype . . . this here is Victor Smigelski. Now, I've told you a lot about this man. And you've read about him in the newspapers . . . and he's even been on tee vee."

"Indeed! Indeed, I most certainly have read about him. Mister Smigelski, Captain Fox has really gone to bat for you. I head up . . . what's referred to as . . . our 'other' division. It's probably not as exotic as you've been led to believe."

"I don't know, Sir," replied Smigelski. "From what I've heard . . ."

"We simply go in," elaborated Nype. "Go in, and . . . stripping away all the bullshit . . . we spy on people! It's as simple as that! Also, I think that you'll find we're not quite as military up here, as they are . . . and by necessity . . . in Captain Fox's division. We're a little more . . . ah . . . relaxed in that particular area. We do, though, have a distinct chain of command . . . as you'll discover! Anyway, Mister Smigelski, I'm glad to finally get a chance to meet the man . . . I've heard so much about! I'm sure that you'll fit right in . . . with our little operation! Fit in just fine."

"Thank you, Mister Nype," replied Smigelski. "It's certainly nice to meet you."

The three men seated themselves—Smigelski and the captain in luxurious Corinthian-leather, high-backed, visitor's chairs. Quite a departure from the garish plastic dandies—featured so prominently, two floors below.

"Now then," Nype began, "Captain Fox tells me that you've had a more-or-less . . . a nodding . . . <u>acquaintance</u> with our operation, up here."

"Well," replied Smigelski, "probably more nodding . . . than acquaintance. As I'd mentioned to Captain Fox, I'd been in the car-rental business . . . for a little over twelve years. And a substantial part of my illustrious career . . . included a tour of duty, at **Ballinger's Rent-a-Car**. I know that you used to have operatives, at **Ballinger's**. Is that the correct word? Operatives?"

"Well," laughed Nype, "that sounds a little on the intrigue-ey side. Agents would probably be a better word. But, even agents sounds a good deal more exotic . . . than what the position actually is. Or was. For the most part, we simply refer to them, around here, as employees. Quite a come-down, I would imagine, from the picture the general public has. But, go on, Mister Smigelski."

"Well," resumed the newly-minted "agent", "some of your employees worked there . . . at **Ballinger's**. I'd <u>heard</u> about a few of 'em. I imagine that there were a good many <u>more</u>. Ones that I didn't <u>know</u> about! That <u>none</u> of us knew about!"

"If they were doing their <u>job</u> . . . doing it correctly, doing it <u>professionally</u>," Nype replied, with a half-smile, "you <u>shouldn't</u> have even <u>known</u> about them! <u>Any</u> of them!"

"Well, some of it was, you know, second hand stuff . . . although, I did consider most of it to be factual! Some of it scarily factual!"

Nype leaned back, in his high-backed, Corinthian-leather, executive chair and asked, "Well, from what you know . . . first-hand, second-hand, hearsay, whatever . . . what do you think, Vick? May I call you Vick?"

"Yes. Yes, Sir. Certainly. To answer your question, though, I've always felt as though there's nothing more dangerous than someone who thinks he knows everything about something . . . and doesn't know anything at all! I wouldn't want my reply to sound like I'm coming off as some kind of expert! I admit it . . . I know practically zilch about this end of the business! But, from what little I do know, I believe . . . I honestly believe . . . that I could do the job! I've always been a bit of a frustrated detective! Amateur! And highly frustrated! Highly frustrated!"

"How's that?" asked Nype, with an indulgent smile. "I mean the part about your being an amateur . . . albeit frustrated . . . detective."

"Well, in the quite-a-many years, that I've been in the rent-a-car business, I've been called on to track down . . . a goodly number of cars! Cars that were overdue! That, in some cases, the customer went and converted the unit . . . to his own use! To be completely honest, some of the gumshoe stuff took nothing more than a phone call or two. The renter, in those situations . . . once I was able to speak to him or her . . . they'd bring the car back! No problem!"

"No problem?"

"Well, there was usually a hellish <u>bill</u> involved . . . but, the car <u>was</u> back. Other times, it meant simply getting in my car . . . and driving out to the renter's <u>residence</u>! Or, maybe, his or her place of <u>business</u>! But . . . and I <u>swear</u> this is the truth . . . there were <u>many</u> times when it led to a good <u>deal</u>, of <u>investigative</u> work!"

"How so?"

"Oh, there were times when someone was able to <u>flim</u>-flam the rental agent into <u>renting</u> him the car, in the first place! When, for instance, it turned out, the <u>information</u> that he'd given . . . <u>address</u> and <u>job</u>, and stuff like <u>that</u> . . . had become badly <u>outdated</u>! Or, sometimes, out-and-out <u>false</u>!"

"Don't the rental agents . . . aren't they <u>supposed</u> to check those things <u>out</u>?"

"They're <u>supposed</u> to! They're <u>certainly</u> supposed to! But . . . every now and then . . . one'll get <u>by</u>! Most usually, it's a <u>borderline</u> case! A customer . . . that you've <u>had</u>, for a long time . . . maybe! At first, you're very <u>careful</u> with him! Always get a large enough <u>deposit</u>! And recheck his <u>information</u>! But then, he <u>always</u> brings back the car . . . when he <u>says</u> he will! And . . . human <u>nature</u> being what it is . . . after awhile, you tend to become a little bit <u>lax</u>, with the guy! A little <u>careless</u>! Sometimes, a <u>lot</u> careless!"

"Like <u>how</u>?" Nype was obviously intrigued.

"Well, say the man <u>moves</u> . . . after six or eight months! Or six or eight <u>years</u>! The agent keeps writing the contract . . . <u>showing</u> the renter's old <u>address</u>! If the agent would simply <u>ask</u> the man . . . as he's <u>supposed</u> to do . . . whether that's his <u>current</u> address, the renter would simply say, '<u>No</u>'! And . . .

in most cases . . . he'd be <u>glad</u> to give the agent the <u>correct</u> address! There's <u>probably</u> no sinister reason why he doesn't <u>offer</u> it! But, he <u>doesn't</u>!"

"There's probably some deep-seated . . . some psychological . . . <u>reason</u>," interjected Nype. "Sub-consciously, he now <u>knows</u> that he's got a <u>leg</u> up on you! And, he probably <u>figures</u> . . . that it couldn't <u>hurt</u> to hold <u>on</u>, to that advantage!"

"Yeah. I'd never really <u>looked</u> at it, that way . . . but, you're probably <u>right</u>, Mister Nype. Anyway, all of a sudden, the man loses his <u>job</u>! Or, maybe, his <u>wife</u> catches him, in the sack, with another <u>woman</u>! And so she hits him with a <u>divorce</u>! Any <u>number</u> of things could happen! And sometimes, they <u>do</u>! I've seen cases where the guy cleans out the joint <u>bank</u> account! And <u>splits</u>! Gets the hell out of Dodge! With our <u>car</u>! Or, he simply <u>loses</u> his job! And now, he 'needs' the car . . . quote, unquote . . . to find another <u>job</u>! Like they say, 'there's eight-million <u>stories</u> . . . in the naked city'! But, the sum and <u>substance</u> of the situation, is that . . . from time to time . . . I'd have to get off my Polack <u>butt</u>! And go out . . . and <u>find</u> the stupid car!"

"I'm beginning to see what you <u>mean</u>," responded Nype.

"There were <u>times</u>," continued Smigelski, "when it really took some <u>doing</u>! But, thank God, I virtually <u>always</u> managed to come up . . . with my <u>car</u>! Sometimes, it was just a question of driving through parking lots, at some <u>airport</u>! There <u>were</u> times, though, when I staked <u>out</u> . . . I guess you'd say . . . a <u>bar</u>! Or a <u>girlfriend's</u> house . . . or something! Got many <u>cars</u> . . . <u>many</u> cars . . . back that way! Anyway,

I'd always <u>been</u> kind of intrigued . . . with that <u>aspect</u> of the job! As much as any <u>other</u> part of it! Whenever I <u>think</u> about it . . . I guess that I <u>did</u> do pretty good! For an <u>amateur</u>! If I <u>do</u> say so myself."

Nype's face reflected the degree to which the newcomer had impressed him. "I can see where you're not <u>exaggerating</u>, Vick," he observed. "You certainly <u>did</u> have to be a bit of a detective! Even driving through airport <u>parking</u> lots . . . qualifies as <u>detective</u> work! You had to know <u>where</u> to look, don't you see! I've never <u>thought</u> much about it . . . but, it's <u>obvious</u>, that a certain amount of investigative work <u>would</u> have to have gone into your position! A certain amount of '<u>gumshoe</u>' work . . . as you so colorfully <u>put</u> it!"

He reached for a silver humidor on his desk, opened it, and offered a very expensive cigar to Captain Fox—who'd readily accepted it—and to Smigelski, who'd declined. Nype removed one for himself, closed the cover of the humidor—and produced an engraved, silver lighter. He lit Captain Fox's cigar—and then his own. He exhaled a monumental cloud of blue smoke—then, languished back, into his sumptuous chair.

"Let me <u>tell</u> you something, Vick," he said, removing the cigar from his mouth—and studying it. "<u>Most</u> people have this <u>image</u>, of a detective . . . or a private investigator. <u>Everyone</u> has read detective books. Ones about . . . oh . . . Mike <u>Hammer</u>, or Michael <u>Shayne</u>, or Phillip <u>Marlowe</u>. Consequently, <u>everyone</u> has this <u>image</u>! All <u>manner</u> of action! All <u>kinds</u> of excitement! This image . . . of a detective, being a sort of Sam <u>Spade</u>! It's <u>universal</u>! And it just

ain't <u>so</u>! Most <u>detective</u> work is . . . well, it's deadly
<u>dull</u>! Boring as <u>hell</u>! It's ninety-five percent <u>routine</u>!
Maybe even ninety-<u>eight</u> percent! Most <u>police</u>
detectives, for instance, are so bogged down in
<u>paperwork</u> . . . that they really don't have a <u>hell</u> of
a lot of time for <u>derring</u>-do. <u>Private</u> investigators will
spend <u>weeks</u> . . . sometime <u>months</u> . . . just watching
a single <u>cash</u> register! Or a stupid <u>trash</u> can! Or
something <u>equally</u> as thrilling!"

"Well, Mister Nype, at my age, I'd just as soon
not get involved in a whole lot of <u>derring</u>-do! The ol'
<u>ticker</u> . . . and the ol' <u>bod</u>' . . . they <u>sure</u> ain't what
they <u>used</u> to be!"

"That ain't <u>true</u>," injected the virtually-forgotten
Captain Fox. "He took on three big <u>guys</u> . . . guys
who <u>jumped</u> him, Mister Nype . . . and he flat-assed
<u>cold</u>-cocked two of 'em."

"Yeah," muttered Smigelski. "And I got my <u>shoulder</u>
broken . . . for my trouble! No <u>thank</u> you! I'd just as
soon <u>avoid</u> such things, in the future! <u>Long</u> term . . .
and <u>short</u> term!"

"Well, Vick," said Nype, with a warm smile. "We're
going to put you to <u>work</u> at . . . are you ready? . . .
Ballinger's Department Store. One of their <u>stores</u>!"

"Hoo <u>hah</u>!" responded Smigelski. "My alma
<u>mater</u>!"

"Not quite," said Nype—his smile broadening. "As
you know, they're out of the car rental business. <u>Been</u>
out . . . for a good while."

"I know. I never could figure out why the hell they
got <u>into</u> the business . . . in the <u>first</u> damn place,"
mused Smigelski. "They didn't have the <u>foggiest</u>
idea . . . of what they were <u>doing</u>! Or <u>trying</u> to do!

They were a bunch of <u>department</u> store people . . . trying to be <u>rent</u>-a-car people! And it didn't <u>take</u>! In <u>spades</u> . . . it didn't take!"

"Well," advised Nype, "we're going to put you on in . . . as an <u>appliance</u> salesman! We've, of course, phonied <u>up</u> an employment history! I've got a <u>copy</u> of it here . . . somewhere!" He reached for some papers on his desk.

At that point, Captain Fox arose, took a deep pull on his cigar, exhaled a copious amount of smoke, and announced, "Well, gentlemen, I'll go ahead an' I'll leave you two alone . . . to really get into the thing. I do wanna say, Vick, that I know I'm losin' a good man. Hell of a good man. I hate to lose you. To see you go. If you ever wanna get back into the guard end of the business again . . . why, you just go ahead and you let me know. On the other hand, I know that you're gonna do real well . . . up here, with Mister Nype."

Smigelski got up—and shook the little man's hand. "Captain," he said, "I <u>appreciate</u> . . . all you've done for me. I've <u>enjoyed</u> working for you. Really and truly, I have. I wasn't all that <u>thrilled</u> . . . when I <u>started</u>! It was sort, you know, . . . kind of an any-port-in-a-<u>storm</u> deal! But, now that I've gotten <u>in</u> to it, I'd have to say that it's really a good <u>field</u>! A really <u>great</u> field! I've gotten to where I actually <u>like</u> it! And I know that you've gone ahead . . . and stuck your <u>neck</u> out for me! Here with Mister <u>Nype</u>! I want you to know that I really <u>appreciate</u> that! I really <u>do</u>! And I'll do my very best to vindicate your <u>judgment</u>! <u>Yours</u> . . . and Mister <u>Nype's</u>!" His genuine affection—for the feisty little man—was evident

"I know you <u>will</u>, Vick," beamed the captain. "I just <u>know</u> you will." He turned to Leland Nype. "Mister <u>Nype</u>," he implored, "be sure you take <u>care</u> . . . of my favorite <u>Polack</u>!"

Nype arose—and bowed! "Rest <u>assured</u> that I will, Captain. Rest assured that I <u>will</u>."

Captain Fox departed—leaving Nype and Smigelski to reseat themselves.

Nype lifted a file folder from his desk—and rifled through a sheaf of papers. He handed a copious number of them to Smigelski.

"Now, then," said the silver-thatched man, "you can see where you were <u>supposed</u> to have been an appliance salesman. At **W.G. Lee's**. Their store in <u>Astoria</u>. You <u>specialized</u> . . . in <u>televisions</u>. If you look through those papers, you'll see where we've got **Lee's** <u>house</u> brand names. Have 'em . . . all broken <u>down</u>. As you can see, all the stuff with their <u>nameplate</u> . . . it was all made by some national manufacturer or another. I don't know which <u>ones</u> . . . not off the seat of my pants. But, read <u>through</u> that stuff! Read through <u>all</u> of it! It's <u>important</u> . . . hell, it's <u>critical</u> . . . that you <u>familiarize</u> yourself with it! So that . . . obviously . . . you can talk, intelligently, with the <u>other</u> people in the Appliance Department! Your fellow employees . . . over at dear old **Ballinger's**!"

"Okay. So far, so good."

"In addition, Vick, we'll be paying you two-hundred-and-twenty-five dollars a <u>week</u>! **Ballinger's** is putting you on their payroll at a hundred-and-twenty-five! Plus <u>commission</u>! I want you to <u>know</u> . . . that we'll make up whatever <u>difference</u> there is! If you make a hundred-and-seventy-five, on <u>their</u> payroll, <u>we'll</u> pay you the other fifty over here! If, on the other hand, you have a particularly <u>good</u> week . . . and huff in three- or four-<u>hundred</u> dollars . . . you're entitled to <u>keep</u> it! Keep it <u>all</u>!" He effected a villainous laugh— and advised, "But . . . if <u>that</u> happens . . . you ain't getting' <u>nothin</u>' outta <u>us</u>, over here!"

"That's . . . that's <u>wonderful</u>, Mister Nype. <u>Thank</u> you!"

"Well, I <u>would</u> remind you, though, that your primary <u>role</u> over there is <u>investigating</u>! Not selling damn <u>television</u> sets! It may well <u>be</u>, that . . . if you wind up making a <u>fortune</u>, selling boob tubes . . . you might just want to <u>quit</u> here! And actually go to <u>work</u>! Go to work . . . for wondrous **Ballinger's**!"

"I doubt that I'd <u>ever</u> want to work for **Ballinger's**! And I really can't <u>see</u> myself . . . as a tee <u>vee</u> salesman! Not on a permanent, full-<u>time</u>, basis."

"Truthfully, I can't either. But, I'll bet the <u>rent</u> money that . . . a <u>year</u> or so ago . . . you would never have been able to see yourself, as a <u>security</u> guy either. Either in Captain <u>Fox's</u> division . . . or <u>mine</u>."

"This is <u>true</u>."

"I <u>do</u> want to see you make a good buck, Vick. Really, I <u>do</u>! Now, you've got to <u>satisfy</u> everyone . . . everyone in the <u>Appliance</u> Department, over there at **Ballinger's** . . . that you actually <u>are</u> a professional salesman! And that you're really <u>motivated</u>! And that you're out to <u>move</u> their stupid-assed televisions! As a matter of fact, that's been one of the <u>problems</u> I've been having . . . with whoever I <u>put</u> over there: They've got their **Tarkenton** paychecks coming! Whether or <u>not</u> . . . they <u>sell</u> anything! So, they just sit on their <u>butts</u> over there! Don't do a damn thing! Could care <u>less</u> . . . about making <u>nice</u>, with prospective buyers! So, I'm expecting <u>you</u> . . . to <u>sell</u> some of their idiot-lanterns for them! If you <u>do</u> . . . you can make a pretty good <u>buck</u>! It's as simple as <u>that</u>! It's just that I wouldn't <u>expect</u> you to <u>do</u> it . . . to the <u>exclusion</u>, of everything <u>else</u>! It's a fine <u>line</u>, Vick! Can be an <u>exceptionally</u> fine line! I <u>do</u> expect you to walk it, though!"

"I don't think I'll have any problem with <u>that</u>, Mister Nype."

"No. I don't expect you <u>will</u>. Now, what we want you to <u>do</u> . . . is to keep your <u>eye</u> on things there! There are five <u>other</u> people . . . in the department! Televisions, of course, are the <u>biggie</u>! But, there are <u>other</u> appliances . . . cassette tape players, clock-radios, table model stereos, blenders, mixers, electric knives, coffee pots, hair dryers! <u>That</u> sort of thing! <u>Those</u> are all <u>smaller</u> things! Stuff . . . that's more likely to walk <u>out</u> of there! <u>Walk</u> out of there . . . without being <u>paid</u> for."

"It shouldn't take me long to learn the merchandise."

"I'm sure it <u>won't</u>," replied Nype, with another smile. "What we want you to try, and find out for us . . . is <u>why</u> they lose so much of the small stuff. They don't really have a helluva lot of <u>shrinkage</u> . . . in the <u>large</u> appliances! But, all <u>kinds</u> of small stuff . . . marches on <u>out</u> of there! Twenty-dollar <u>toasters</u>! Thirty-dollar <u>blenders</u>! Stuff like <u>that</u>!"

"<u>Shoplifting</u>?"

"<u>Some</u> of it . . . <u>certainly</u>! But, we feel . . . with good <u>reason</u> . . . that some of the <u>employees</u>, over there, are involved! None of the <u>other</u> operatives I've sent over there have been able to <u>document</u> anything!

I'm <u>convinced</u> that the reason for <u>that</u> . . . is that your predecessors just never got off their <u>asses</u>! Male <u>or</u> female! Never worked . . . never tried their hand . . . at <u>convincing</u> the other folks, over there, that they were <u>salespeople</u>! Made the employees <u>suspicious</u>! Or, at least, that's the <u>theory</u>! So, we need <u>you</u> to move some of the glorious <u>merchandise</u>!"

"I'll do my <u>best</u>, Sir! Especially . . . if it means a few dollars, in the ol' <u>paycheck</u>!"

"I'm <u>sure</u>! <u>Oh</u>! One thing I want you to <u>know</u> . . . and <u>remember</u> this: We've got <u>another</u> man working out there . . . at the store! On the <u>shipping</u> dock, over there! His name is Edward <u>Blaine</u>! If you're <u>ever</u> . . . ever in <u>trouble</u> . . . seek him <u>out</u>! But, <u>only</u> if you're in <u>trouble</u> . . . which you <u>shouldn't</u> be! If you have any <u>questions</u> . . . any questions, at <u>all</u> . . . call this <u>office</u>! Only in an <u>emergency</u> . . . should you go to <u>Blaine</u>! Likewise, <u>he'll</u> know about <u>you</u> . . . and, in an emergency, <u>he</u> would call on <u>you</u>! For Christ's <u>sakes</u>, if that should <u>happen</u> . . . which it <u>won't</u>, but if it <u>should</u> . . . do whatever you <u>can</u>, to help him out! Understood?"

"<u>Understood</u>! But, now, about the employees. Why would you suspect <u>them</u>? Be so <u>positive</u> that it's <u>them</u>?"

"The rip-off rate . . . in smaller appliances . . . is positively <u>startling</u>, Vick! <u>Mind</u>-boggling! We <u>believe</u> . . . that some of the employees are working, with <u>accomplices</u>."

"Accomplices?"

"<u>Accomplices</u>," nodded Nype. "Most likely members of their own <u>families</u>! Maybe a few close <u>friends</u>!"

"I'm not sure I see . . ."

"Well, we think that maybe the employees are wrapping up the appliance . . . an electric coffeemaker, we'll say . . . without writing it up! Or ringing it up! In a situation like that, the accomplice can just simply walk on, through the store . . . ostensibly shopping! Continuing to shop! He or she has this wondrous little coffeemaker . . . in his or her bright-green **Ballinger's** bag! After a reasonable amount of time, he or she . . . just walks on out! Walks out of the store! Simple as that!"

"Holeh mackell! How can I watch for that sort of thing? Without . . . you know . . . hovering over whoever the salesperson is? That'd surely tip 'em off! Wouldn't it?"

"You're exactly right! It surely would! No, Vick, the last thing, in the world, that we want is for you to make 'em suspicious! We can't let 'em think that we're on to them! That probably was our problem . . . with the others, that we'd sent over! The other employees were . . . I'm positive . . . suspicious of 'em! Suspicious as hell! We just want you . . . to observe! For instance, if the same customer comes back . . . say, three or four times a week . . . and spends an inordinate amount of time, fingering the merchandise, chances are, he or she is a shoplifter. But, if he or she seems to be waiting . . . all the time . . . for the same salesclerk, then you'd want to watch the transaction, that takes place! Watch it very closely. Well, as closely as possible! Without tipping your hand, of course."

"Watch it closely?"

"Try and determine what amount . . . if any . . . the clerk rings up on the cash register! If they ring it up . . . at <u>all</u>! They have to ring <u>all</u> sales . . . both cash <u>and</u> charge . . . on the handy-dandy <u>register</u>! They just use different <u>keys</u>. The figures they punch in are large enough to be <u>seen</u> . . . to be <u>observed</u> . . . well, from a reasonable <u>distance</u>! So, simply keep an <u>eye</u> peeled . . . to see if they're ringing up the proper <u>amount</u>! Of if they're ringing up <u>any</u> amount at all."

"It sounds <u>simple</u> enough."

"Not as simple as it may <u>seem</u>, Vick! <u>Uncomplicated</u> . . . that might be a better <u>word</u> for it!"

"Well, I . . . I <u>hope</u> that I've got enough smarts to be able to pull this thing <u>off</u>! Without blowing my <u>cover</u>!"

"I'm <u>counting</u> on you . . . doing just <u>that</u>, Vick!"

"What shift'll I be working?"

"Well, it's kind of a swing shift . . . which is <u>exactly</u> what we want. It'll be mostly days, though. However, the store is open two <u>nights</u> a week, and . . . as the junior employee . . . you'll probably have to work <u>both</u> nights. Which . . . from our perspective . . . is <u>great</u>! You'll probably pick <u>up</u> a good buck-or-two on those nights. I know that . . . if <u>I</u> were a sales guy . . . <u>I'd</u> want to work those nights. While there are <u>six</u> employees . . . counting yourself . . . in the department, seldom will there be more than <u>four</u> of you on the floor at any one time. Sometimes, I guess, just <u>three</u> of you."

"Now that I'm actually getting into something like this, Mister Nype, I'm starting to get really <u>excited</u>! I was <u>afraid</u> that . . . once I'd gotten myself up to this <u>position</u> . . . that I'd decide that I really didn't <u>want</u> to go ahead with it! Cold <u>feet</u> . . . and all that! But, really, I'm <u>excited</u> about it! I really <u>am</u>."

"Good, Vick. I could tell . . . that you were getting mentally involved! Could tell that . . . as we talked! I can't tell you . . . what a refreshing change that is! Just remember that, if you see a customer just hanging around . . . especially when you're all busy . . . and then heading for his or her favorite clerk, that'd be a tip-off! With Blaine keeping an eye on things on the shipping dock . . . and a man of your caliber in appliances . . . we should be able to cut down on a whole lot of this hocklejock! Save **Ballinger's** a boodle!"

"I'll do my best, Mister Nype. I honestly will."

"I'm sure you will! Now, in that bundle of papers I gave you, you'll find a copy of the *General Instructions for Employees* for this section. For this division . . . of our glorious company. You'll have to submit a report . . . every week! Every week . . . without fail! There's some forms in there . . . and instructions that'll tell you how to prepare 'em. Not all that much mentally challenging stuff in there. Also, it gives you a comprehensive outline . . . of what to look for! Far more comprehensive . . . than I could possibly give you, verbally! I've told you . . . generally . . . what to look for. This thing goes into many more particulars than I've covered here. Many more!"

"When do I start?"

"That's the spirit. Captain Fox told me . . . assured me . . . that you were a good man! An ambitious man. I must admit, though, that I'd harbored a few . . . well, a few reservations!"

"Reservations? You did?"

"Yes. Look, when you piled into all those . . . all those . . . those assholes! Out at *Shea*! I thought,

'Damn . . . just another dumb <u>Polack</u>'! A <u>courageous</u> one . . . to be sure! But, nonetheless, a <u>dumb</u> one! Only <u>two</u> things could've prompted you to have taken <u>on</u> those creeps: It had to be <u>dumbness</u> . . . hell, out-and-out <u>stupidity</u> . . . or pure <u>dedication</u>! I have to <u>admit</u> that . . . at first . . . I'd thought it was the <u>former</u>! Having <u>spoken</u> with you, though . . . having actually <u>met</u> you . . . I now know that it was the <u>latter</u>! I <u>congratulate</u> you, Vick! Dedication like <u>yours</u> . . . is hard to <u>come</u> by, in this day and age! Especially in <u>our</u> business! In <u>our</u> business . . . sad to say . . . dedication is practically <u>nonexistent</u>! I <u>apologize</u> to you . . . for having <u>thought</u> of you, as I <u>did</u>!"

"No apology <u>necessary</u>, Mister Nype. I've been thought of . . . and called . . . worse things than a 'dumb Polack'."

"I guess you probably <u>have</u>, responded the silver-thatched man—ever so wistfully. "I guess we <u>all</u> have . . . from time to time! But, the point is, you <u>shouldn't</u> have! Should <u>never</u> have been called <u>anything</u> like that! Especially by someone like <u>me</u> . . . who's made a career of telling himself exactly how <u>tolerant</u> he is! Especially by someone like me . . . who's not <u>supposed</u> to be given to thinking in terms of <u>stereotypes</u>." He sighed heavily. "I can see where I've acquired a rather <u>demented</u> outlook, Vick," he acknowledged. "A <u>really</u> demented outlook! Going to have to <u>work</u> on that!"

Smigelski laughed, uncomfortably. Shifted in the comfortable—almost unshiftable—chair.

"But, I <u>digress</u>," continued Leland Nype. "You'll start <u>Monday</u> . . . at **Ballinger's** Manhattan store!

Do you know where it is? Third Avenue and Fifty-fourth?"

"Yes, Sir. I know where it is. What time do I show up?"

"Nine o'clock in the morning! Sharp! You'll have to report to Mister Bill Rutherford! He's head of Personnel! Now, bone up . . . on all that stuff, I gave you! That'll keep you off the streets . . . keep you out of trouble . . . till Monday, anyway!"

Nype rose—and extended his hand. "Vick," he said, "I know that you're going to do one hell of a job for me!"

Smigelski got to his feet—and shook hands with his new boss. "I'm glad to be here, Mister Nype. Especially in this division!"

"Well, it's good to have you with us! I can see why Captain Fox said he was losing a good man! He didn't really want to turn you lose, y'know! But, of course, he knew! Knew that it really was the only way that **Tarkenton** could keep you! Some people laugh . . . at him! At Captain Fox! But, they really shouldn't! Should not! He's the epitome . . . of the company man! In a way, he's the soul of our company! **Tarkenton** should have a hundred Captain Foxes! A million Captain Foxes! We should be that lucky!"

Smigelski could barely wait to telephone June Bodner—at work—with the news of his new position! He fervently hoped that she would be as excited as he was!

SEVEN

MONDAY, FEBRUARY 3, 1975—AND SMIGELSKI wondered where the two years had gone. Those he'd spent in the security business.

The preceding night, he'd mused to June Bodner how swiftly the time had passed.

They'd stopped at "Ptomaine Gulch"—the little diner near the **Avis** licensee, in Piscataway, New Jersey—after having taken in the Barbra Streisand/Robert Redford movie, *The Way We Were*, at a little theater in Plainfield.

"It's certainly been a tidy period for you," June had observed. "You've come up with a broken shoulder, gotten your melodic voice on tee vee . . . as a big ol' hero . . . and now you're on the verge of becoming **Tarkenton's** answer to <u>Bond</u>. <u>James</u> Bond."

"You make it sound more than it really is, Junie. Much more. I've spent a <u>lot</u> of time . . . just sitting on my butt! <u>Long</u> time for that stupid-assed <u>court</u> thing! A <u>generous</u> amount of time . . . recovering from that damn <u>shoulder</u>! The company's been very <u>good</u> to me . . . all things considered. All <u>kinds</u> of time off!"

"Maybe. Probably. Vick? Look, I'm sure that these past couple of years have gone fast . . . probably really fast . . . for you! But, not for me! The time sure hasn't gone fast for ol' Junie! Maybe it's because I worry about you! More than you worry about you! To me, it's been a damn rotten couple of years! A damn . . . really, really, really rotten . . . period! Piss poor . . . as Shakespeare or Voltaire or one of those high-falutin' Greeks have said."

Her outburst had surprised—and somewhat dismayed—Smigelski. Well, more than "somewhat".

"I suppose," he answered, with a deep sigh, "that you've got a valid reason to be upset."

"Yes, I suppose," she'd groused. "And it really doesn't look like it's going to get much better!" Her mood was souring—rapidly! "Not anytime soon, anyway. Look, Vick! I just wish . . . that you'd get out! Get the hell out! Out of that goddam business! Just get the hell out! Now! The sooner the damn better!"

Obviously, his unbridled enthusiasm, for his new assignment, was—most assuredly—not shared by his "significant other".

Promptly, at nine o'clock, the following Monday morning, Smigelski reported to the head of **Ballinger's** personnel department. After an extremely brief—totally-dispassionate—interview, our hero was dispatched to the store, up in The Bronx, where the chain retained a doctor-in-residence. The newest "employee" was given what was laughingly referred to as a "physical examination".

"All it amounted to," he would advise June, later that evening, "was a 'look to the left . . . and cough' kind of thing."

Returning to the Manhattan store, from The Bronx, at 12:15PM, he was escorted to the Appliance Department—on the fourth floor—where he was introduced to the two other employees, who were "working the floor" at that time.

The day wound up being interminably long!

Though Smigelski had studied, intensely, the "propaganda" dispensed by the manufacturers of the various appliances—and had become as knowledgeable as possible about each line—he'd felt terribly clumsy. He'd found himself hoping—fervently—that his natural ease, in meeting (and talking to) people would cover a goodly portion of what he perceived to be an alarming lack of confidence. Confidence—and knowledge.

It was <u>vital</u>—<u>critical</u>—according to Leland Nype, that the other employees, in the department, accept him, as being a bona fide, experienced, appliance salesman.

Before the day had expired, the troubled newcomer would be introduced to the three other salesclerks, assigned to the department. The store was open till 9:00 PM—and the three late-comers would work the evening shift. Their newest member would begin working the later hours. But, not until the following Thursday.

Three men, two women—and Smigelski—now comprised the celebrated sales staff of the storied, fabled, Appliance Department.

That evening, at "Ptomaine Gulch", Smigelski replayed the day—replayed it, over and over—to June Bodner, who did her best to feign enthusiasm.

"I really feel like a damn fish out of water," he'd lamented.

"<u>Nonsense</u>," she'd replied. "I'm sure you'll do <u>fine</u>. I'm sure it's not a news bulletin for you that I'm not <u>thrilled</u> with the situation . . . but, I have no <u>doubt</u> that you'll do all right! That you'll do <u>fine</u>. dammit! Probably too <u>damn</u> 'fine'!"

"I dunno," he'd answered—practically filling the eatery with a deep sigh. "I really don't <u>know</u>, Junie. Old <u>dogs</u> and new <u>tricks</u> . . . and all such crap as <u>that</u>, y'know."

"Oh, Vick. Once you get a couple or three days under your belt, it'll be as though you've been hawking those stupid appliances all your <u>life</u>. Let's <u>face</u> it. **Tarkenton** wouldn't have <u>put</u> you there . . . if they'd had any <u>doubt</u>, about your ability to do the <u>job</u>. And do it <u>well</u>."

"I don't know," he said, letting go another sigh. "From what I understand, a helluva lot, of my predecessors, were total <u>screw</u>-ups! I wish . . . I just wish . . . that <u>I</u> had the confidence in me that <u>you</u> have in me. Well, you . . . and Leland <u>Nype</u>."

Despite his trepidation, Smigelski <u>was</u> adapting well—to his new situation! Happily—and surprisingly, to himself—he seemed to possess an inborn knowledge of the appliance field. In addition—having successfully dealt with the public, over the 12 years he'd spent in the car rental field—he'd always, generally, presented an efficient and dedicated personage. For, virtually, his entire professional life! Consistently! Apparently, a truly believable one!

His first paycheck, at **Ballinger's**, totaled in excess of $300! A source of unbridled joy! Of unprecedented joy! Especially for someone who'd considered himself grossly underpaid—during his entire career. He was probably unaware of this—but, a major portion of Smigelski's psyche had, totally, given up—on the prospect of ever seeing a paycheck that would've contained a large number of zeros on its face! Such a situation would never be a part of his life! Of that, he was positively convinced!

In his new spot, he had—faithfully—submitted his required weekly reports. Had—meticulously— filled them out, each and every Saturday, in his room. In each instance, he'd reported no unusual happenings.

The paucity of any "juicy stuff" worried him— more than slightly! The last thing, in the world, that he'd wanted—was to be sent back to Captain Fox's division! His greatest fear! He believed that he was going to wind up, as Sgt. Smigelski, once more! He was petrified that this would be his fate! It seemed likely—unless he proved himself capable of sniffing out a multitude of sinister, dastardly, deeds! Well, a few of them, anyway! And quickly! Damn quickly!

On March third, Smigelski, with much trepidation, telephoned Leland Nype—and expressed his concern. Nype had laughed—heartily.

"Don't worry about a thing, Vick," he'd reassured his employee. "I'm certain that you're keeping your eyes open. Just between us girls, the store hasn't had anything . . . nothing of earth-shaking import . . . taken out of that department! Not since you've been there! Couple of small cassette recorders, I guess. You'd have to expect, you know . . . to lose a few of those little gems! Lose 'em . . . to out and out shoplifters! Besides, you can't be there . . . like twenty-four hours a day!"

"There've been some days . . . when I've felt like I've been there that long. But, not real often! Mostly . . . as strange as it seems . . . it's like the day's not long enough! Especially when it occurs to me . . . that I've not solved anything! Not one damn thing!"

"Well, I'd rather have you reporting . . . that nothing's going on! Than to have you invent something! Report nefarious stuff . . . just for effect! God knows, I've had enough people pull that kind of shit, on me! More than enough! Look, if any of their employees are into something, you can bet . . . that they'll make some kind of move! Eventually! Probably before long! Just stay alert . . . and you'll pick it up! I'm sure! All I can tell you . . . is to just hang in there! Keep the old eyes open! Make your reports! It's certainly not costing us much . . . to keep you there! I understand you had a helluva week, last week! One of many! My sincerest congratulations!"

"Doing <u>pretty</u> well. Grossed about four-and-a-<u>half</u>, I guess. I've been somewhere between three-and-a-<u>half</u> and four-<u>hundred</u> . . . just about every <u>week</u> now! Denks God! <u>That</u> part of it has been <u>great</u>! But, fear <u>not</u>! I'm <u>not</u> considering <u>quitting</u> . . . and going to work for dear, beloved, old **Ballinger's**."

"That's <u>great</u>, Vick! I'm glad to <u>hear</u> that! I'll tell you something <u>else</u> . . . again, just between us <u>girls</u>: Captain Fox had been <u>hoping</u> . . . that I could get you into something like <u>this</u>! For the <u>Christmas</u> season! He'd <u>wanted</u> you to pick up a few extra bucks . . . for the <u>holidays</u>! We just couldn't pull it <u>off</u>! Not back <u>then</u>! He <u>has</u> been looking out for you! For the longest <u>time</u>! He thinks you're the <u>top</u>! Thinks the sun <u>shines</u> . . . out of your back <u>pocket</u>! Keep up the good <u>work</u>, over there, Vick. And, of course, if anything <u>happens</u> . . ."

"You'll be the <u>first</u> to know!"

It was two days after Smigelski's phone conversation with Nype—that "something <u>happened</u>"! One of the employees "made a <u>move</u>":

Virginia Enio—a very attractive young woman of 23—wrapped a *Mister Coffee* system, and handed it to another young woman. Presumably to a customer.

Smigelski was certain he'd seen the shopper in the department, from time to time. However, he was unsure whether Virginia had been the clerk who had <u>waited</u> on her—exclusively.

He was certain of one thing, though: Virginia had neither put cash in the register—nor had she written up a charge slip for the coffeemaker. In either unauthorized case—as determined by Smigelski—the sale was to have been rung up, on the cash register! It was not!

Our hero calculated the amount of the sale—selling price, plus tax—then, left the floor, for the employee's restroom area, in the rear of the building!

Immediately outside the men's room, was located a pay phone! Dropping a dime into the slot, he quickly dialed the number—listed in his voluminous instructions, from **Tarkenton**.

The phone buzzed on the other end—and was answered before the second ring had fully finished. The bulk of the "business" done in Nype's section—was performed on the second floor of the **Tarkenton** headquarters. The floor between Nype's office and that of Captain Fox.

"Lieutenant Broderson here."

"Yes, Lieutenant. This is Victor Smigelski. I'm assigned to work at **Ballinger's Department Store**, in Manhattan. Appliance Department. Fourth floor."

"Right, Smigelski. What've you got?"

"Employee! Virginia Enio! Wrapped up a *Mister Coffee* . . . and handed it to a youngish lady. Early-to mid-twenties, I'm guessing. Didn't ring up the sale! Service sells for thirty-nine, ninety-five! Sales tax is seven percent! Another two-eighty! Total sale should be forty-two, seventy-five! I'm not privy to the cash register tape, of course. But, I'm certain . . . that the sale was not rung!"

"When? When did the transaction take place? That's vital . . . for when they check the register's tape!"

"Only eight or ten minutes ago."

"Okay, Smigelski. We'll handle it from <u>here</u>! Don't <u>worry</u>, anymore . . . about the thing! We've got a regular <u>procedure</u> we follow . . . from <u>here</u>! They'll check the <u>register</u> . . . at the end of the day! And all such shit as <u>that</u>! So, if you don't hear anything <u>more</u>, about it, in the next <u>day</u> or two, don't <u>worry</u>! We've got it <u>covered</u>! And we're on <u>top</u> of it! It <u>might</u> be what we've been <u>looking</u> for! What something like <u>this</u> usually means . . . is that they <u>trust</u> you now! Usually, when a new <u>employee</u> comes into the department, like that, they won't hardly <u>try</u> anything! They'll size you <u>up</u> . . . know what I <u>mean</u>? Apparently, they've decided that you don't pose any kind of a <u>threat</u> to 'em! Stay <u>loose</u>! This is probably only the <u>beginning</u> . . . if past history is anything to go by! Anyway, good work! We don't give 'well-dones' up here! Not like in Captain <u>Fox's</u> division. But, it <u>is</u> a good beginning for you, Smigelski! Like I said . . . it's probably only the <u>beginning</u>, folks!"

The phone went dead in Smigelski's hand. Slightly bemused, he went into the men's room, washed his hands, and combed his hair. Then, he returned to the floor.

The following day, Virginia Enio did the exact same <u>thing</u>—with the same young <u>woman</u>! In that instance, the appliance turned out to be a deluxe blender!

Smigelski thought it best not to leave the floor— <u>immediately</u> after Virginia's "sale". Instead, he made a mental calculation of the amount of money, which should've gone into the cash register!

Forty-five minutes later—feeling that he'd observed a decent interval—Smigelski was beginning his dutiful mission to the pay phone, when one of the male employees, Stanley Piepczyk, caught his eye! The man was placing a small, compact, <u>stereo</u>—in one of the world-famous, bright-green, **Ballinger's** bags. Smigelski stopped to observe—as Piepczyk handed the package to an older man!

No <u>record</u> of the transaction was made—of that, Smigelski was <u>positive</u>!

Piepczyk was a tall, stocky, man—in his mid-thirties. The "customer" appeared to be in his late-fifties or early-sixties.

Making a note of the supposed "transaction", Smigelski decided to wait until the end of his shift—and, hopefully, to note any further irregularities.

It did not take long to add to the list:

Piepczyk, within an hour, had placed a *Mister Coffee* service in a bag—and had handed it to a middle-aged woman! As time had gone on, he'd performed the same act—with a hair dryer! And then, with an electric knife!. In each case, the two items were given to a younger man! These "sales" occurred—about 90 minutes apart!

By the end of the afternoon, Virginia Enio and Stanley Piepczyk had dispensed <u>four</u> different appliances! <u>Each</u>! Every <u>one</u> of these items—at an attractive 100% <u>discount</u>!

Once his shift had ended—at 6:00 PM—Smigelski left the store, made his way to a sidewalk pay phone, then dialed the **Tarkenton** number!

"Lieutenant Meiser here," came the prompt answer.

"This is Victor Smigelski. I made a report yesterday . . . on a Virginia <u>Enio</u>! I work at **Ballinger's** . . . in Manhattan. Appliance department. Fourth floor."

"That's <u>right</u>, Smigelski. The Enio girl gave <u>away</u> a *Mister Coffee*!"

"Why . . . why that's <u>right</u>! You . . . you <u>knew</u> that?" Smigelski was <u>aghast</u>! And unable to keep the <u>surprise</u> from his voice!

Meiser laughed. "Thought we didn't have the <u>report</u>! <u>Right</u>?"

"Well, when I was in Captain <u>Fox's</u> division . . . sometimes you couldn't be all that <u>sure</u>!"

"That's <u>diplomatic</u> talk," laughed Meiser again, "meaning they all had their heads up their <u>asses</u>, down there."

"Well, I don't know that I go so far as to say <u>that</u>."

"<u>I</u> would! But, enough of this brilliant <u>repartee</u>. What've you <u>got</u>, Smigelski?"

"Uh, same <u>girl</u>! Virginia <u>Enio</u>! She did the same thing today . . . with an **Apex** <u>blender</u>! Retail is twenty-nine, ninety-<u>five</u>. With sales tax, it <u>should've</u> been thirty-two-oh-<u>five</u>! <u>Happened</u> at about a quarter-after <u>one</u>!"

"I <u>love</u> that. '<u>Should</u>'ve been'. That's <u>great</u>!"

"Also, she gave out an **Apex** <u>toaster</u> oven! Retail is forty-four, ninety-<u>five</u>. Total of forty-eight-ten . . . with <u>tax</u>! That was at a little after three <u>o'clock</u>! In addition, she gave out an **Apex** electric <u>grill</u>! <u>Retail</u> on the grill is the same as the <u>toaster</u> oven . . . forty-eight-<u>ten</u>! Close to five-<u>thirty</u>!"

"**Apex**, I take it, is the house brand?"

"Right. But, this girl now . . . she's an equal opportunity crook! She also gave out a **General Appliance** cassette recorder!"

"Hmmmm. Busy girl!"

"You know it! Retail on the recorder is fifty-nine, ninety-five!"

"Isn't that a little . . . a tad . . . expensive?"

"Not for this one! Top of the line! Lots of bells and whistles on it! Total sale should've been sixty-four-fifteen! This happened just fifteen or twenty minutes ago!

"Was that it . . . for our little pooh-pooh?"

"Yeah."

"Hmmmm. She had a pretty productive day, I'd say."

"I agree," replied Smigelski. "And she wasn't the only one!"

"Oh? More?"

"One more! Fella named Stanley Piepczyk!"

"Stanley what?"

"P-I-E-P-C-Z-Y-K!"

"Thanks. I needed that."

"Anyway, he packaged up four items too: A *Mister Coffee* . . . same arithmetic . . . as Miss Enio's little caper, yesterday!"

"Big demand for those, I guess."

"I guess. That came shortly before noon! Also a small **Apex** stereo . . . just fifteen or twenty minutes later! Sixty-nine, ninety-five! Total sale should've been seventy-four, eighty-five! One **Apex** hair dryer . . . at about four-thirty! Twenty-nine, ninety-five! Thirty-two-oh-five . . . with the tax!

"Okay, that's <u>three</u>! What was the <u>fourth</u> little trinket?"

"**Apex** electric <u>knife</u>! Gave it to the same <u>person</u> . . . the one he gave the <u>hair</u> dryer to! Only, probably, a little over a couple hours <u>later</u>! Knife sells for sixteen, forty-<u>nine</u>! Total sale <u>should've</u> been seventeen, sixty-<u>four</u>! <u>None</u> of these . . . I'm sure . . . will show up on the register tape!"

"That's <u>it</u>?"

"Yep."

"Okay, Smigelski. <u>Listen</u>! Good <u>work</u>! In a case like <u>this</u>, they usually wait till a new employee settles <u>in</u> . . . before they really <u>begin</u> making their nefarious little <u>moves</u>! Apparently, you've <u>arrived</u>! Passed the <u>test</u>! They've gotten to where they <u>trust</u> you. Does <u>that</u> make you proud . . . or <u>what</u>?"

"I can't tell you how <u>honored</u> I am."

"It's all part of the <u>action</u>! Keep at it, Smigelski. Let us know . . . if anything <u>else</u> happens over there! Well, let us know . . . <u>when</u> anything else happens over there! It surely <u>will</u>!"

As Smigelski hung up the phone, he shook his head in wonderment. <u>I'll be damned</u>! <u>Those guys are pretty good</u>! <u>What an upset</u>!

Over the next three days—through Saturday evening—Virginia Enio and Stanley Piepczyk—plus a third employee, a slender man in his mid-thirties, named Marvin Gershenson—indulged in the theft of from four to seven <u>items</u> each day! Each and <u>every</u>

day! Smigelski wondered if he might've <u>missed</u> previous thefts—perpetrated by Gershenson.

Saturday evening, as he'd accounted for the four previous day's 100% percent discount "events", Smigelski set forth the full roster of names—as well as a complete listing of items taken, along with each unit's price, to **Tarkenton**.

"A tidy week," he mumbled to himself—as he scratched out his weekly report.

Monday morning and early afternoon—as Smigelski would later explain to June Bodner— "lightning struck the shithouse"!

Piepczyk, Gershenson and Virginia Enio were each called into the store's security office! Each was questioned—thoroughly—as he or she had reported to work! Each was informed of his or her rights! Each wound up—charged with petit <u>larceny</u>! Each was taken to the nearby <u>precinct</u> station—and <u>booked</u>! Each was, eventually, released on his or her own <u>recognizance</u>!

No trial dates were set!

That was not to be the end of that particular issue for Smigelski:

Two weeks later—on a Friday night, just before 11:00 PM—he stepped off the commuter bus, in Metuchen, New Jersey. The disembarking site was located two blocks from the room, in which he lived!

As he'd walked up Hillside Avenue, Smigelski's path required him to pass an alleyway—behind the long row of stores, all of which fronted on Main Street, the thoroughfare, on which he'd exited, from the bus!

Three people lunged <u>out</u>—of the darkened alley!

One of the murky figures attempted to <u>hold</u> Smigelski—as a second attacker murderously swiped a large, switchblade <u>knife</u>. in the direction of his <u>abdomen</u>!

Lurching, with all his might, Smigelski managed to throw the thug—the one, who'd been, furiously, attempting to hold him—to the <u>ground</u>! He <u>almost</u> managed to <u>dodge</u> the oncoming, lethal, blade! <u>Almost</u>!

He felt the searing <u>pain</u>—under his right rib cage! Immediately, he became aware of the rush of <u>blood</u>—from the frightening <u>wound</u>! It was—already—beginning to discolor his <u>topcoat</u>! The knife had sheared through the rather substantial garment—as well as his suit coat, his shirt and his undershirt! With one God-awful <u>swipe</u>!

Lashing out at the knife-wielder, Smigelski <u>caught</u> the figure—flush on the <u>jaw</u>! It was a <u>vicious</u> punch—immediately knocking the assailant to the <u>ground</u>! The knife took a <u>separate</u> path to the cement!

At that precise moment, the <u>third</u> shadowy figure barreled <u>into</u> him! The intended victim—weakening, <u>rapidly</u>, from the already-massive loss of blood—lost his <u>footing</u>!

The <u>first</u> attacker—the one Smigelski had thrown off—had, by then, regained his <u>feet</u>! He piled on <u>top</u> of the embattled "detective"—while the <u>second</u> player, in this critical, life-and-death, drama was doing his best to recover the potentially-lethal <u>knife</u>! In a matter of three or four fright-filled seconds—he'd <u>succeeded</u>!

As the one with the deadly weapon <u>lunged</u> toward him, Smigelski had managed to throw off the <u>first</u> attacker! The one who'd been on <u>top</u> of him! The intended victim pushed the thug off to the side! Quickly, he aimed a desperate <u>kick</u>—at the <u>groin</u> of the person, with the knife! <u>Bull's eye</u>! Smigelski's foot scored—exactly where it had been <u>intended</u> to land! With <u>devastating</u> force! With mind-boggling <u>impact</u>!

The knife hit the ground once more—followed, closely, by the <u>assailant</u>! The latter <u>laid</u> there! <u>Writhing</u> and <u>flailing</u>! <u>Frantically</u>! Gagging <u>violently</u>—on the pavement! <u>Thrashing</u> about! <u>Furiously</u>! In great, almost unimaginable, <u>agony</u>!

Once again, the <u>third</u> figure <u>dove</u> at Smigelski! With a mighty <u>heave</u>, the beleaguered security agent pulled himself <u>erect</u>! His last-ditch-effort fist <u>caught</u> the lunging <u>adversary</u>! Slammed <u>in</u> to his assailant! <u>Squarely</u>! In the pit, of the shadowy person's <u>stomach</u>!

The blow brought a blood-curdling <u>cry</u>! Then, a horrible <u>moan</u>! It was <u>then</u> that the intended-victim discovered—that the <u>third</u> attempted assassin, was a <u>woman</u>! She'd already hit the <u>ground</u>—also writhing about, <u>frenetically</u>—before the shocking gender fact finally <u>registered</u> with Smigelski!

Struggling to remain standing, he turned his attention to the <u>first</u> assailant—the one who'd, unsuccessfully, attempted to hold him! Hold him <u>steady</u>—for the intended onslaught, of the <u>knife</u>! <u>That</u> worthy was trying—mightily—to get back to his (or her) feet! Smigelski launched another vicious <u>kick</u>! It smashed against the still-shadowy figure's <u>nose</u> and left <u>cheekbone</u>—with a sickening, bone-shattering, <u>thud</u>!

The person <u>collapsed</u>! <u>Immediately</u>! Who-ever-it-was fell back—howling, in abject <u>agony</u>—onto the sidewalk! The overwhelming, panic-stricken, gurgling, gasps <u>seemed</u> to be coming from a male! Smigelski didn't know—whether <u>that</u> was good or bad!

The knife-wielder? <u>He</u> continued to <u>squirm</u>, madly, about! On the cement! In violent <u>pain</u>! His hands raked, wildly, at his <u>groin</u>! His legs <u>churned</u>—wildly— in every direction! The animal sounds were <u>especially</u> eerie! Taking deliberate <u>aim</u>, Smigelski brought his <u>heel</u> down—squarely <u>impacting</u> the upper part, of the right <u>cheekbone</u>, of the fallen knifeman! His scream <u>dwarfed</u> the gurgling sounds—still <u>pouring</u>, from the first assailant!

It was at that moment that Smigelski <u>recognized</u> the man—whose jaw he'd just <u>shattered</u>! It was Marvin <u>Gershenson</u>! Blood continued to <u>gush</u>, from the fallen man's nose—and <u>mouth</u>!

Smigelski stooped for a closer look at the other man. He needn't have <u>bothered</u>! It was <u>Piepczyk</u>, of course!

The remaining member of the life-threatening trio would, obviously, be Virginia Enio! <u>She</u> was, at that moment—ever so shakily—getting to her feet!

Smigelski <u>lunged</u> at her—but, missed! <u>Missed</u> the woman—by a <u>substantial</u> distance! Virginia turned and <u>ran</u>—toward Main Street! It was a valiant <u>effort</u>— given her physical condition!

Bleeding badly, Smigelski took out after the frenzied, fleeing, woman! It turned out to be—not much of a <u>race</u>! He <u>caught</u> her! <u>Well</u> before she'd even reached the corner!

Grabbing her, viciously, by the <u>arm</u>, he painfully <u>pinioned</u> the limb—up into the small of her <u>back</u>! She managed to turn her head—and to <u>glare</u> at him! Her face was an ugly contortion of <u>pain</u>—and unadulterated <u>hate</u>!

"You fucking <u>stool</u>-pigeon" she hissed. "You fucking <u>stoolie</u>! I'll <u>kill</u> you! I'll fucking <u>kill</u> you!"

"Not <u>tonight</u> you, won't," he seethed. "I want you to march your rotten little <u>ass</u>! March it . . . up to the <u>police</u> station! It's two <u>blocks</u> from here, Sweetheart! You give me any <u>shit</u>, Bitch, and I'll <u>break</u> your goddam <u>arm</u>! And if you don't <u>believe</u> me . . . just give me an <u>excuse</u>! Just <u>one</u> goddam excuse! Just <u>one</u> . . . Bitch!"

He gave the limb an insistent <u>push</u>! The maneuver sent a frenzied bolt of <u>pain</u>—coursing through Virginia's <u>body</u>! <u>Head</u> to <u>toe</u>!

Smigelski's entire right side, by then, had become <u>saturated</u>—with his own <u>blood</u>! The pain was <u>overwhelming</u>! His strength was <u>ebbing</u>! With a <u>rush</u>!

He'd had to literally <u>shove</u> Virginia Enio—for the entire two <u>blocks</u>! Finally, he was able to push her— <u>violently</u>—into the Metuchen <u>police</u> station! He'd found himself. at that point, drawing from a hidden-till-then fount of <u>strength</u>! One he'd never known he'd <u>possessed</u>!

Stumbling into the reception area, he <u>threw</u> the woman—with great <u>resolve</u>—onto a hard, wooden, bench! She landed with a resounding <u>thud</u>! Skidding in on her right <u>hip</u>—and her right <u>arm</u>! It had been a <u>final</u>—a <u>desperate</u>—<u>thrust</u>!

Her captor fell—<u>heavily</u>—onto the other substantially built bench, located across the narrow waiting room!

The desk sergeant snapped awake, from a semi-nap—and pushed the large, red, alarm button! The resultant "loud" clanging of the giant bell on the far wall filled the entire area! He, immediately, rushed from behind the high counter—his revolver <u>drawn</u>!

Within 30 seconds, three <u>other</u> officers—burst into the reception area!

Smigelski endeavored to <u>describe</u> the attack, to the assembly of policemen! The sergeant nodded—and gestured, <u>frantically</u>, to one of the other cops! "Gariepy!" he shouted. "Put this broad in the <u>lockup</u> . . . till we find out what the hell's goin' <u>on</u>!"

Turning to a second officer, he ordered: "Larkins, get on the <u>radio</u>! Get both <u>patrols</u>, out there . . . get 'em to <u>Hillside</u>! Just north of Main! <u>Supposed</u> to be two <u>men</u> there! They . . . I guess . . . they went and <u>attacked</u> this man here! One <u>caution</u>! One of 'em's <u>supposed</u> . . . to have a <u>knife</u>! Bring <u>both</u> their asses in!"

To the third cop, he pointed at Smigelski! "Get this man to *JFK*! Right <u>away</u>! He's lost a hell of a lot of <u>blood</u>! <u>Stay</u> with him! Till we can figure this whole thing <u>out</u>!"

The bleeding Smigelski was led through police headquarters—and into the garage! The officer helped him into a police cruiser—and rushed him to the *John F. Kennedy Hospital,* in nearby Menlo Park!

The passenger lost <u>consciousness</u>—in the patrol car!

The next hours were nothing more than a fitful haze to Smigelski! He would regain consciousness—periodically—only to "go under" again! Would relapse—in a minute or two! Sometimes—in a <u>second</u> or two!

He believed that the hospital personnel were preparing him for surgery! He would be unable to answer the question, "Based on <u>what</u>?". He <u>was</u> aware of at least two blood transfusions! At <u>least</u>!

He did his best to ask the nurses to <u>contact</u> June Bodner. He was far from certain that he'd been able to <u>do</u> so! Couldn't <u>imagine</u> the possibility—that he'd been even <u>remotely</u> capable of saying <u>anything</u> even halfway coherent!

Eventually, the more permanent, ever-beckoning, <u>blackness</u> swept over him! Mercifully, it plummeted him into a deep, dark, <u>abyss</u>!

When Smigelski awoke, it was light outside! He blinked his eyes—repeatedly! Each open-and-shut maneuver was shockingly <u>painful</u>! It seemed as though he'd never be able to get the "orbs" to adjust, to the inescapable, the blinding, glare of sunlight—which, without letup, poured through the overhead window, and onto his bed.

He was able, at length, to discern that he was, indeed, in some hospital—somewhere! In a semi-private room!

Asleep on the other bed—was June Bodner!

Junie? In the other bed? Nah! Can't be! I gotta be dreaming!

He clenched his eyes shut! After holding them scrunched tight, he snapped them open, once more! June still lay there! Sleeping—on the other bed!

He spotted a call button—it was lying next to his pillow—and pressed it. Thirty seconds later, a prim, middle-aged, woman—in a crisply-starched, gleaming-white, uniform swept into the room.

"Ah," she said softly. "Sleeping Beauty has awakened. How do you feel, Mister Smigelski?"

He attempted to speak. His lips moved—but, no sound came from them!

"Throat's dry, hah? Okay. Let ol' Elsie get you a pitcher of water. I'll be right back."

With that, she was gone.

A minute later, the woman was back—bearing the promised, most welcomed, pitcher of water. Pouring out a glassful, she bade him drink. The water, as Smigelski wolfed it down, was both delicious—and painful! Still, he readily accepted a second glass—and, quickly, downed half of the refill.

"Now," asked Elsie, softly. "Does that feel better?"

Smigelski nodded.

"Good," she smiled. "How do you feel?"

"I . . . I don't know." Was that his voice? It sounded like a foghorn—one badly in need of repair. Looking over at June, he asked, "How long's she been here?"

"Oh, since the middle of the night. I came on at eight this morning . . . and she'd <u>been</u> here, for a good while, then. Sitting up in that stupid <u>chair</u>. Hadn't <u>slept</u> . . . poor thing. I <u>pointed</u> her at the vacant bed. Told her that <u>I</u> wouldn't say anything . . . if <u>she</u> didn't."

He started to reply—but the only thing that came was a hoarse rasp!

"Sore <u>throat</u>, hah?" asked Elsie, smiling.

He nodded. "Head hurts like hell, too," he grumped.

"Well," she answered, "throat'll <u>be</u> sore . . . for awhile. That damned <u>anesthetic</u>, don'tcha know. Once the ol' saliva starts flowing again . . . <u>really</u> flowing . . . you'll be all right. I'll see if I can get you something for the <u>head</u>." Looking over at June, she asked, "Want me to wake her <u>up</u>?"

Smigelski shook his head—which only made the mind-boggling headache worse. "No," he managed to say. "Let her <u>sleep</u>. I've caused her more than <u>enough</u> sleepless nights."

"Well," observed Elsie, "you'll probably be interested to <u>know</u>: There's two <u>other</u> fellas here! As <u>guests</u> . . . of the Middlesex County <u>Sheriff's</u> Office. These guys <u>also</u> were pretty sleepless, last night. Understand they <u>jumped</u> you! Over in <u>Metuchen</u>, was it?"

He nodded—painfully—once more.

"One of 'em," elaborated Elsie, "has a broken <u>nose</u> and <u>two</u> broken cheekbones! The one cheekbone's a real <u>doozer</u>! Oh, and he has a smashed <u>jawbone</u>!" Then, she smiled. "He's also got a problem with his symbols-of-<u>manhood</u>!" Her laugh was one of the most obscene that the patient had ever heard. "They're about the size of <u>grapefruits</u>!"

"Pity," responded her patient—a wan smile crossing his face.

"The <u>other</u> one? You rearranged <u>his</u> face pretty good too. Not quite as <u>thorough</u>, as the first one . . . but, not <u>bad</u>! Not bad at <u>all</u>! It'll <u>do</u>! I'd give <u>it</u> . . . about a seven-point-<u>eight</u>! First guy is definitely a perfect <u>ten</u>!"

"If you don't mind a little stupidity, Miss . . . Miss . . . uh . . ."

"Elsie. Just Elsie. What <u>manner</u> of stupidity are you fixin' to lay on me?"

"What <u>day</u> is it?"

"<u>Saturday</u>, Love. Saturday . . . February Twenty-<u>Threeth</u>. You wound up losing a lot of <u>blood</u>, y'know. Still, just <u>between</u> us, I'd have to imagine . . . that you'll be <u>out</u> of this vale of tears <u>tomorrow</u>! If I had to <u>guess</u>! They <u>always</u> do their best to get the troops out of here . . . as quickly as possible. That's my unofficial <u>prediction</u>. <u>Tomorrow</u>!"

She gazed over at the still-slumbering June. "Your <u>wife</u>?" she asked.

"No," he muttered. "My Veteran <u>Fiancée</u>, June Bodner."

"Fixin' to <u>be</u> your wife?"

"I <u>hope</u> so! I <u>love</u> her . . . very <u>much</u>!"

"She must love <u>you</u>! Sat in that stupid damn <u>chair</u> . . . most of the <u>night</u>, I guess . . . just <u>lookin'</u> at you! Isn't that <u>all</u> it takes? <u>Love</u>, I mean!"

Once again, Smigelski was able to smile—albeit briefly. "Well, I guess you can't do much <u>without</u> it. <u>Love</u>, I mean. But, the past couple <u>years</u> . . . well, things have been really screwed <u>up</u>! <u>These</u> days, I always seem to get myself beat <u>up</u>! Get the <u>hell</u> beat out of me . . . for a <u>living</u>! A million <u>laughs</u>! Understandably, she's not too <u>thrilled</u> with that! It's been just a couple of <u>months</u>, now . . . that I've gotten to where I'm beginning to make any <u>kind</u> of money, at all! I don't know how much <u>that's</u> going to <u>count</u> for . . . now! I'm sure we'll <u>make</u> it . . . <u>eventually</u>! Sure as hell <u>hope</u> so!"

"Not if you wait for <u>everything</u> . . . to be just <u>right</u>. Take it from <u>me</u> . . . things are <u>never</u> just right. Absolutely, <u>positively</u>. <u>Never</u>!"

"So . . . now you're Ann Landers?"

She laughed. "I <u>try</u>," she said. "God <u>knows</u> . . . I <u>try</u>. I can't seem to do too well for <u>myself</u>, y'know. But, hell, I've got the <u>answers</u> to everyone <u>else's</u> problems!"

At that point, June began to stir! Raising her head, she did her best to blink the sleep from her semi-bloodshot eyes! Then, she locked them—onto Elsie and Smigelski!

"<u>Vick</u>! Oh, <u>Vick</u>! Are . . . are you all <u>right</u>?"

"Apparently," he replied. "Got a terrible . . . God-awful, splitting . . . <u>headache</u>. And my side is . . . well, it <u>hurts</u>! Hurts . . . like forty-'leven <u>hells</u>!"

June arose and hurried to him—disregarding Elsie completely! She leaned over him—between the patient, and the more-than-understanding nurse!

"<u>Vick</u>! Vick . . . this <u>can't</u> keep . . . can't keep going <u>on</u>!" She leaned over and kissed him! "I can't worry . . . worry every <u>day</u>," she continued. "I can't <u>do</u> it! Worry every damn <u>day</u> . . . when you go off to <u>work</u>! Worry that maybe . . . maybe they're going to bring you <u>home</u>! In a <u>basket</u> . . . or something!"

She kissed him again—taking care not to jostle him. Then, she eased herself down into a sitting position, on the bed. Still between him and the nurse—who'd, eventually, risen, to a standing position.

"<u>Really</u>, Vick," she went on. Her eyes were beginning to overflow. "<u>Really</u>! I can't <u>take</u> this anymore! I <u>thought</u> that this latest assignment . . . I thought it was <u>supposed</u> to be safe! Goddam <u>safe</u>! No more patrolling stupid damn <u>warehouses</u>! No more shit-assed <u>rock</u> concerts!"

"Junie, look . . ."

"Now I find out that there are three <u>people</u>! People . . . ones you <u>caught</u>! Caught . . . stealing all <u>kinds</u> of stuff! All kinds of <u>shit</u> . . . at goddam **Ballinger's**! Three damn <u>creeps</u>! And they . . . they <u>jumped</u> you! <u>Jumped</u> you, for God's sakes! <u>Vick</u>! You could've been . . . <u>could've</u> been . . . could've been <u>killed</u>! <u>Vick</u>! For God's <u>sakes</u>! Get <u>out</u>! Get the hell <u>out</u>! Get out <u>now</u>! <u>Please</u>, Vick! Please get <u>out</u>! <u>Please</u>! For <u>me</u>, Vick! For <u>me</u>! <u>Please</u>! You've <u>got</u> to!"

"I . . . I dunno, Junie. I don't know <u>anything</u>. Not a God damn <u>thing</u>! Who <u>knew</u>? Who the hell <u>knew</u> . . . that those three <u>assholes</u> were going to decide to take me <u>out</u>?"

"It's not just <u>that</u>, Vick. According to . . . to the <u>nurse</u> here, I understand that you put <u>one</u> of those guys out of commission! Did him <u>in</u> . . . pretty <u>good</u>!

The <u>Jewish</u> guy. She said you broke up his <u>face</u>! Broke up his <u>entire</u> face! Totally broke it <u>up</u>! And she said you <u>also</u> kicked him in . . . <u>kicked</u> him . . . <u>kicked</u> him in the . . ."

"Kicked him in the <u>balls</u>, is what I'd told her," furnished Elsie—with a broad grin.

"<u>Vick</u>," resumed June. "You <u>got</u> to . . . you've simply <u>got</u> to . . . get your Polack fanny <u>out</u> of the damnable <u>security</u> business! While you've still <u>got</u> a Polack fanny! You've <u>got</u> to! You've simply <u>got</u> to! Now that you've busted those guys <u>up</u> . . . how do we <u>know</u> that <u>they</u> don't have <u>friends</u>? <u>Lots</u> of friends? Friends who're gonna come <u>after</u> you? Or even with <u>connections</u>? Connections . . . in the <u>Mafia</u>? How do we <u>know</u> . . . that they won't <u>get</u> someone? Get someone <u>else</u> . . . to take you <u>out</u>? We can't <u>know</u> that! We <u>can't</u>! We simply <u>can't</u>!"

"Nah," he answered. "They're simply nickel-and-dime, piss-ant, <u>thieves</u>! They don't have any <u>connections</u>! Doubt that they've got any <u>friends</u>!"

"Yeah? Well, they <u>were</u> giving all that <u>stuff</u> . . . all those damn coffeemakers, and stuff . . . they were <u>giving</u> all that crap to . . . to <u>someone</u>!"

"Look, folks," broke in Elsie. "I'll see if I can get something for Mister Smigelski's <u>headache</u>. I'll be right back." Directing her gaze at June, she mildly admonished, "Honey, take it <u>easy</u> on him! He's not <u>that</u> long . . . out of <u>surgery</u>! These things can be <u>discussed</u>, at a more . . . at a more <u>beneficial</u> . . . time!"

Smigelski gestured toward the nurse—and muttered to June, "Mind what she <u>says</u>, dammit. She's Ann <u>Landers</u>."

Elsie grinned—as she headed toward the door. "Smart aleck," she laughed. "Forget what I <u>said</u>, Miss Bodner. Give him <u>hell</u>!"

"Oh," muttered Smigelski, returning his attention to June, "the woman . . . Virginia, her name was . . . she was giving the stuff to a <u>girlfriend</u>. And to her <u>mother</u>. And, I <u>think</u> . . . to a stupid damn <u>uncle</u>. Piepczyk? He was giving his loot to his father. And, I think, to his sister. I can't <u>remember</u> . . . about Gershenson. <u>Seems</u> to me . . . it was, maybe, his <u>girlfriend</u>. And, maybe, a <u>brother</u>. I'm not <u>sure</u>. Hell. It hurts . . . hurts like <u>hell</u> . . . just to <u>think</u>, for God's sake."

"Vick," June pleaded. "Vick, I <u>thought</u> that . . . now that you're in a different <u>part</u> of the business . . . well, I <u>thought</u> that you'd be <u>safe</u>! That you'd be better <u>off</u>! Not still risking your <u>neck</u> . . . and every <u>other</u> part of you! But, with those creeps <u>jumping</u> you . . . like they did . . . you're no better <u>off</u>! Not any better off . . . than when you were schlepping around that stupid damn <u>warehouse</u>! <u>Please</u>, Vick! I want you to get <u>out</u>! Get out <u>now</u>! <u>Now</u>! <u>Please</u>, Vick! For <u>me</u>! <u>Please</u>!"

He sighed heavily. "<u>All</u> right," he groused, after 30 or 40 long, tension-filled, seconds. "All right, <u>Baby</u>. This whole thing's just about as screwed <u>up</u> . . . as it can possibly <u>be</u>! Don't really feel like getting <u>into</u> it with 'em . . . but, I'll (sigh) <u>talk</u> to Mister Nype! Talk to him . . . <u>tomorrow</u>! <u>Promise</u>!"

"Are you going to tell <u>Inez</u>? Or the <u>kids</u>? About what <u>happened</u>? You'll probably be <u>seeing</u> 'em, y'know . . . in a <u>day</u> or two!"

"<u>Nah</u>! Maybe they won't <u>notice</u>!"

"They'll <u>notice</u> all right. You know that as well as <u>I</u> do! You also know how <u>upset</u> they all were . . . when those scumbags jumped you, in the warehouse! Inez even called me! I didn't ever tell you . . . but, she asked me if I couldn't talk you out of the thing! The whole crappy business . . . of continuing with **Tarkenton**! She even told me that she could probably get by . . . with less money, from you!

"Yeah? Well . . . there for awhile . . . I couldn't have given her a helluva lot less. She's never really complained!"

"Well, she even told me that she could get by . . . with no money . . . if it meant your not getting the hell beaten out of you! Her words . . . not mine!. Bless their hearts, Inez and the kids . . . they do worry about you! Worry about you . . . just as much as I do!"

"God! You guys! You're all ganging up on me."

"It sure as hell hasn't worked, has it!"

Once again, Smigelski sighed. "You're right," he rasped. "I'll have to tell 'em. Tell 'em what happened!"

He ran his fingers up and down her cheek.

"Your kids," he noted, "they worry about me too. Don't they?"

She nodded. "Yes," she acknowledged. "Yes, they do! We all do! Inez! Your kids! My kids! And . . . last but not least . . . ol' Junie herself! That's why you've just got to get out! Get out of this damn thing! Get into something civilized! Something safe! Something . . . where we're not going to have to go through all kinds of changes, every day! Every stupid, stinking, goddam, shittin', mother-you-know-what day! Wondering whether you're ever going to make it home! Home from just your goddam work! If you're gonna ever make it home . . . from stupid work, for God's sakes! From work! Work! Goddam work! You've got to get out, Vick! That's all there is to it! You've simply got to!"

At that point, Elsie, the nurse, made her triumphant return.

"Really had a hell of a time," she announced, brandishing a hypodermic! "One hell of a time . . . getting someone to authorize something for your head! But, trusty ol' Nurse Landers . . . to the rescue! Medication akimbo! Turn yourself over!"

It took a good bit of what little dexterity that had remained, but Smigelski managed to roll over onto his stomach—as June got to her feet. Elsie pulled the sheet down off of him! The nurse pulled his gown up—exposing his behind!

Smigelski winced—as the needle bit into his left buttock!

Elsie withdrew the implement—once she'd successfully emptied the vial of painkiller into her target. Then, she slapped him, lightly on his right cheek, pulled his hospital gown down—and covered him again!

Smigelski labored to roll over onto his back, wincing—emphatically—at the pain, ricocheting up and down his side!

"Well," noted June, with a broad grin," I can see that you're in the best of hands, oh Polack of mine."

"I'd have to agree," he replied. "Especially since ol' Nurse Landers, here, is standing over me like that. I'm afraid that . . . if I was to really offend her . . . she'd dust off that old square needle! The one we used to fear, so much, in the Navy!"

Elsie laughed heartily. "I'm well aware, Mister Smigelski, as to where that square needle <u>went</u>," she advised. "Well, where it was supposed to <u>go</u>! And you're right! If you're not a good boy, I <u>will</u> dust off the ol' square needle!" She refilled his water glass and set it back on the nightstand. "But, <u>enough</u> of this uplifting conversation," the nurse continued. "I'll <u>leave</u> you two lovebirds alone . . . to thrash things <u>out</u>! Let you go best-two-out-of-three-<u>falls</u>! Catch as catch <u>can</u>!"

As she approached the door, Elsie turned to the couple—and admonished, "<u>Look</u>, you two! Make <u>nice</u>! Things'll work <u>out</u>! Be <u>good</u> . . . to one another! I <u>envy</u> you! Envy the <u>hell</u> out of you! Envy what you <u>have</u>! Envy <u>everything</u> you have!" The smile left! Her face clouded over! "I <u>mean</u> that! I <u>do</u> envy the thing . . . the thing that you guys <u>have</u>! Have . . . <u>between</u> you! Envy the <u>hell</u> out of you! You don't <u>know</u>! You <u>can't</u> know . . . just how <u>lucky</u> you are!"

Once Elsie had disappeared, June looked at Smigelski. "I have to <u>wonder</u> . . . wonder what she <u>meant</u> by that," she mused.

Smigelski began to shake his head—but, stopped abruptly, with a wince.

"Poor <u>Vick</u>," soothed June. "Head really <u>killing</u> you, huh?"

He started to nod—and thought better of it. "You <u>know</u> it," he rasped. "<u>Side's</u> no bargain either. I don't know <u>what</u> she meant, either. She's a <u>deep</u> one . . . that Elsie."

"By the bye, ol' boy . . . where <u>did</u> that square needle go?"

"You're going to <u>hate</u> yourself, for asking" he answered. "It was supposed to go in the left <u>nut</u>! Listen, I'd <u>believed</u> it! For . . . I think . . . a <u>year</u> or two! Scared the <u>hell</u> out of me! <u>Always</u> scared me to death!"

She broke into laughter! Almost hysterical laughter. The tension was broken! "I guess I should've <u>known</u>," she finally remarked. "I really <u>should've</u> known. You'd think that I'd learn to keep my big <u>mouth</u> shut."

She began laughing again! Gales of laughter!

He pulled her close! The laughter stopped! As suddenly as it had started! Then, the <u>tears</u> came! <u>Multitudes</u> of tears! The dam had certainly <u>burst</u>!

"Take it easy, Junie," he soothed. "I'll get <u>out</u> of the thing. I really <u>will</u>, Baby. But, I'm going to need a place to <u>land</u>. I can't just walk <u>away</u> from it . . . not without a place to <u>go</u>!"

She attempted to speak! To <u>answer</u>! For three or four long, never-ending, minutes! It was a lost cause!

"Oh, <u>Vick</u>," she was finally able to plead. "Vick . . . <u>please</u>! Please . . . <u>please</u> try and find something <u>else</u>! <u>Anything</u> else! I <u>beg</u> of you! <u>Please</u>! I'm <u>sure</u> they'll give you some time off . . . to <u>recover</u>! To get over <u>this</u> injury. <u>Please</u> use the time, Vick! <u>Use</u> it to find something <u>else</u>! <u>Anything</u> else! <u>Inez</u> isn't going to press you to . . ."

"Okay Junie." Neither one of them had ever heard him speak—in tones nearly as subdued. "I <u>will</u>! I'll <u>try</u>! I honestly <u>will</u>! Hey! That <u>reminds</u> me! As far as I know, **Tarkenton** doesn't know <u>zilch</u> about what <u>happened</u> last night. They'll be <u>expecting</u> me to show <u>up</u> . . . <u>bright</u>-eyed and <u>bushy</u>-tailed . . . at **Ballinger's**, <u>tomorrow</u>!"

"I <u>called</u> **Tarkenton**! Called 'em, last <u>night</u>," advised June. "I was <u>honored</u> . . . that you'd told the hospital to call <u>me</u>! And not <u>them</u>!"

"All part of the <u>soivice</u>. What'd **Tarkenton** say?"

"I don't know <u>how</u> . . . but, I managed to get hold of the night <u>dispatcher</u>, or something! He kept telling me . . . <u>assuring</u> me . . . that he'd <u>see</u> that Captain Fox got the <u>message</u>! I kept trying to <u>explain</u> . . . that you don't <u>work</u> for Captain Fox anymore! I must've <u>told</u> him that . . . fifteen damn <u>times</u>! Fifteen times . . . <u>minimum</u> . . . that you <u>now</u> work for Mister <u>Nype</u>! I really don't <u>know</u> . . . if I was <u>ever</u> able to <u>convince</u> him of that! Finally, I just gave the hell <u>up</u>! I figured that . . . if the idiot ever <u>got</u> the message . . . to Captain Fox . . . that, <u>eventually</u>, Mister Nype <u>would</u> find out what happened!"

"I'm <u>sure</u> he will. I'll call him in the morning. Hmmmmm."

"What puts you so deep in thought . . . oh, Polack of mine?"

"Those three assholes that <u>jumped</u> me. I wonder what they're gonna do with <u>them</u>! What the authorities have in <u>mind</u> for the bastards!"

"<u>That'll</u> be interesting, all right," she answered, sighing deeply. "It'll be awfully damn <u>interesting</u>!"

EIGHT

MARCH 2, 1975. ALMOST ONE month had passed since Smigelski had been set upon— by the sainted three ex-employees of **Ballinger's Department Stores**.

He'd been discharged from the hospital on that Sunday—as had been predicted by Elsie the nurse. He'd remained "blest"—with an extremely <u>painful</u> left side! Thankfully, the constant headaches had subsided—to some extent. There were still far too many mornings, though, when the dull, throbbing, pain would return! Sometimes <u>spectacularly</u>!

It had turned out—that a number of tendons, in his side, had been severed! They'd needed to be surgically repaired. Fortunately, the hospital's skilled staff had responded to his condition—almost immediately! Dedicated surgeons had performed the precarious (for the day) surgery—within <u>minutes</u> after his arrival, on that red-letter, "celebrated", Friday night!

Some four weeks after the attack, Smigelski could still feel the muscles inside, as they strained and

pulled—whenever he stretched or bent. No matter how slightly.
He'd not returned to work, since the attack.

Much to the overwhelming, usually-tearful, chagrin of June Bodner, he was to begin "a brand spanking new job"! With **Tarkenton!** The new position would be completely different—as Leland Nype had explained:
Smigelski had spoken with Nype, over the phone, on Monday—the day after he'd left the medical facility. He had—at that time—tendered his resignation.
However, the ever-persuasive Nype had talked our hero into "dropping in". "Let's, at least, discuss the situation," the supposedly-erstwhile employer had suggested. The (so called) former employee had "bitten"! On February 14th, the two men had gotten together.
"Vick," Nype had begun, "I've never seen anything like this before! Ever! Nothing even close! Look, I've been in the business . . . almost thirty years! And I've never encountered a man . . . who's had the propensity for getting himself into all kinds of physical confrontations! Not like you do! The battles you've been involved in . . . in just a couple of years . . . would be a whole career for most of our guys. In many cases . . . hell, in most cases . . . it'd be more than a career! Way more than a career!"
"Yeah. Well, it's been a career for me, Mister Nype! Complete . . . and total career! And . . . if nothing else . . . it's been exciting! Stimulating as hell! But, it jolly well is a career! A completed career!"

"Well now, don't be so <u>hasty</u>, Vick. I think you've probably used <u>up</u> . . . used up <u>all</u> your lifetime's worth of such crap!"

"Well, you know, Mister Nype, that fracas at the <u>warehouse</u> . . . and the thing last <u>month</u> . . . those were not really <u>my</u> doing! In both cases, I was <u>jumped</u>! <u>Blind</u>sided! I, sure as hell, didn't go <u>looking</u> for 'em. I have to admit, though, that . . . at *Shea* . . . I pretty well <u>did</u> pile into those assholes! But, I certainly did <u>not</u> set out . . . <u>looking</u> for a fight. I'm too <u>old</u> for that sort of thing. I've <u>always</u> been too old for that sort of thing."

Nype had nodded. "I know Vick. I know. I'm not saying that you went looking for <u>anything</u>. Call it the fickle finger of fate . . . or whatever. For some reason or another, though, it just seems to be your <u>lot</u>! Your lot . . . to simply <u>find</u> yourself, in some sort of physical situation."

"Yeah. And my fiancée . . . <u>she</u> is <u>really</u> upset by it! So's my former <u>wife</u>! And my <u>kids</u>? The <u>kids</u>? Don't even <u>ask</u>!"

"I don't <u>blame</u> her. I don't blame <u>them</u>! I don't blame <u>any</u> of them. If I were any <u>one</u> of them, <u>I'd</u> damn well be upset too."

"Yeah, well, they <u>are</u>! Junie's upset . . . to the point where I promised her I'd drag my Polack butt <u>out</u> of the security business. Just like I told you, on the phone. Well, Inez . . . and the kids . . . <u>they</u> were happy to hear that, too. <u>Exceptionally</u> happy!"

"I <u>understand</u>, Vick. Believe me I <u>do</u>."

"I don't know that you <u>do</u>, Mister Nype. If you could <u>see</u> how Junie looks at me! <u>Looks</u> at me! All the <u>time</u>!

How she . . . out and out . . . suffers! Then, you'd understand! But, lacking that, you really can't . . ."

"Listen, Vick. As much as I'd hate to lose a good man, I certainly wouldn't want to be responsible . . . for your breaking a promise! To . . . Miss Bodner, is it? I'd hate to be a party . . . to making her unhappy! She seems like a wonderful woman!"

"She is. Believe me . . . she is."

"All I'm asking, Vick . . . is for you to just simply hear me out."

"Well, . . ." Smigelski had muttered.

"I want you to take the next three weeks off. Or how-ever-long you need. How many days . . . or weeks . . . it'll take you to get completely well. With full pay, of course! We're . . . also, of course . . . we're going to pay you, for the time you've lost after this latest little . . . ah . . . latest little adventure, of yours! As we speak, you're still on the ol' payroll! No matter what decision you come to . . . after our little chat!"

"You know, Mister Nype," Smigelski had responded, with an ironic smile, "I've been with **Tarkenton** a couple of years, now. I don't think I've actually worked . . . performed my duties . . . for even half of that time! Maybe not even a quarter! I always seem to be recuperating! In sickbay! From some damn thing or another!"

"Well, that's neither here nor there. Company policy is that . . . if you get hurt in the line of duty . . . you get all the recuperation time you need! And all the compensation required! We never . . . as in ever . . . press the employee . . . in that area! Ever! I don't . . . and I'm sure that Captain Fox never has! Absolutely positive of that!"

"No. Of <u>course</u> not! Of <u>course</u> he didn't! He's <u>always</u> been <u>more</u> than fair with me! So have <u>you</u>! You <u>both</u> have!"

"Yes. Well, we <u>try</u> to be."

Nype had sat straight up, in his mammoth chair—and, rather ceremoniously, had folded his hands on the desk, in front of him. His gaze was steely! And <u>very</u> penetrating!

"I do," he'd gone on, "have another <u>position</u> in mind for you, Vick. It's a <u>really</u> behind-the-scenes thing. <u>Way</u> behind the scenes!"

"Behind-the-<u>scenes</u>? <u>Way</u> behind the scenes? What does <u>that</u> mean?"

"Well, I don't believe there's a way to put this <u>delicately</u> . . . so, I won't even <u>try</u>! You see, Vick, we also monitor the <u>johns</u> . . . the employee's <u>restrooms</u> . . . at **Ballinger's**! At <u>all</u> of their stores!"

"You <u>what</u>?"

Nype had forced an extremely tight laugh! It had required a goodly amount of forcing.

"Monitor the <u>johns</u>," he'd repeated. "We've got a <u>mic</u> and a <u>camera</u> . . . in <u>each</u> employee restroom! Throughout the entire **Ballinger's** <u>system</u>! When you worked at their Manhattan store . . . well . . . ah . . . <u>you</u> were on 'Candid Camera'! Whenever you . . . ahem . . . <u>relieved</u> yourself!"

Smigelski had begun to <u>rise</u>! Then, for some reason—unbeknown to <u>himself</u>—he'd thought better of it. He found himself plopping back down onto his leather visitor's chair! Teetering—precariously—on the very edge of it!

"Why . . . why," he'd sputtered, "that's ridiculous! That's flat-out outrageous! It's fucking out-and-out stupid! Why, you're . . ."

Nype had held up a hand! "You'd be surprised, Vick, at what we're able to learn," he'd responded, in an almost-embarrassed tone.

"I'm sure! I can just imagine . . . that you can learn one hell of a lot! All about who's got the runs! And who's constipated! All such wonderful crap . . . excuse the pun . . . as that!"

He had laughed—nervously—and was on the verge of getting up again.

"Look, Mister Nype," he'd announced, at length. "I'm not really interested in monitoring the toilet habits of **Ballinger's** employees! Not interested at all! No sale! Thanks . . . but no thanks!"

Nype had nodded—his demeanor as placating as possible. "I know," he'd acknowledged. "I know, Vick. It sounds horrible!"

"Sounds horrible? It is horrible! Fucking horrible! I can't even imagine . . ."

"It gets even more horrible! Sometimes, Vick, we're not able to assure that a man will monitor the men's' room . . . and that a woman will monitor the ladies' room!"

"You're kidding . . . right?"

"Nope! Dead serious!"

"Oh, that sounds like a barrel of laughs! I guess Junie was more right . . . than she'd ever even thought!" He'd shuddered—from head to toe! "This is a creepy-assed business! Really is!"

"Yeah. Like you say . . . a million laughs! Listen, Vick. We try not to . . . but, there are times when we simply <u>have</u> to have someone of the <u>opposite</u> sex! Have 'em looking <u>in</u>. I don't really <u>know</u> how <u>upset</u> our people get . . . boys <u>or</u> girls . . . when you're called upon to watch the wrong sex's <u>potty</u>! And that statement goes for <u>women</u> . . . as well as <u>men</u>!"

"That just goes to further <u>prove</u> that I'm not cut <u>out</u> for this . . . this shit-assed <u>business</u>! Junie was righter than she <u>thought</u>! Than she could <u>ever</u> have thought!"

"Vick. I want you to try and <u>look</u> at this! Look at it . . . with an open <u>mind</u>!"

"You . . . you're <u>serious</u>, aren't you! You're goddam <u>serious</u>!"

"Never more serious in my <u>life</u>! Don't get me <u>wrong</u>! It offends <u>my</u> psyche too! But . . . and you've got to <u>believe</u> this, Vick . . . it's <u>necessary</u>! A necessary <u>evil</u>! And I'm <u>not</u> rationalizing! It's a <u>vital</u> operation! It really <u>is</u>! And I'll tell you <u>why</u>!"

"Oh, <u>brother</u>," Smigelski had thundered—heaving a giant sigh. "<u>This</u> . . . is going to be <u>good</u>!"

"Well, not <u>good</u>, Vick. But, not as <u>bad</u> . . . as you're <u>picturing</u> it! It's really <u>not</u>! Not <u>nearly</u>!"

"<u>Yeah</u>? Well, it <u>sounds</u> pretty damn bad to <u>me</u>, y'know! Pretty <u>ridiculous</u>! Actually . . . <u>goddam</u> ridiculous!"

"I know." Nype's response was barely audible. But, his voice took on new strength—as he continued. "Obviously, we don't go out of our <u>way</u> . . . to <u>publicize</u> the fact, that we <u>play</u> this dirty little game!"

"I don't imagine you <u>do</u>! Wouldn't <u>imagine</u> you would!"

"Well, people could get the wrong <u>idea</u>! It <u>happens</u>, you know."

"Who could <u>possibly</u> get the wrong idea?" Smigelski had asked—his voice dripping with sarcasm.

"Well, for openers, <u>you</u> could, Vick. Get the wrong <u>idea</u>, I mean. In fact, you already <u>have</u>! And it's perfectly natural that you <u>would</u>! In fact . . . if your eyes had lit <u>up</u>, at the prospect . . . the prospect of monitoring rest rooms . . . I'd have been quite <u>worried</u> about you! About the whole <u>offer</u> to you! That's <u>one</u> reason . . . that I usually blurt it! <u>Blurt</u> out . . . <u>lay</u> out . . . the whole <u>project</u>, in the <u>first</u> place! Rather than . . . you know . . . beating around the <u>bush</u>! Do that with <u>everyone</u>! Rather than trying to set a person <u>up</u>! Set 'em <u>up</u> . . . for the big <u>revelation</u>!"

"Yeah. Well, it's a <u>revelation</u>, all right!"

"Vick, do you have any <u>idea</u> . . . any idea, <u>whatever</u> . . . as to how much <u>money</u> is lost? <u>Lost</u> . . . in employee <u>thefts</u>? It's <u>billions</u> . . . <u>literally</u> billions . . . on a <u>national</u> level. <u>Billions</u> of dollars . . . every damn <u>year</u>!"

"<u>That</u> I can understand. I can <u>understand</u> your wanting to cut down . . . on that sort of thing. But, it sure as hell <u>doesn't</u> give you . . . not you, or any-damn-body <u>else</u> . . . the right to watch some perfectly <u>innocent</u> little girl! Watch her <u>piddle</u>! Watch her <u>piddle</u> . . . just because some damn <u>crook</u> may, or may <u>not</u>, come into the john! Come in . . . sooner or <u>later</u>!"

"Your point is well taken, Vick. But, you'd be <u>surprised</u> . . . <u>shocked</u>, actually . . . at how many perfectly <u>innocent</u> little girls that there are <u>not</u>! Piddling . . . or <u>otherwise</u>! You'd be <u>aghast</u> . . . at the number of people we find, taking <u>merchandise</u>! Or even <u>embezzling</u>! Stealing <u>money</u>! Taking <u>cash</u>! And we <u>learn</u> this stuff . . . just from bugging the <u>johns</u>!"

"Mister Nype, I've done some awfully stupid <u>things</u> in my life . . . and. hell, a number of out-and-out <u>rotten</u> things! But, I damn well draw the <u>line</u> . . . at peeking into <u>johns</u>! Particularly the <u>ladies'</u> john! If there is one perfectly <u>innocent</u> little girl . . . just <u>one</u> . . . and she's in there, <u>piddling</u>, then that's enough for <u>me</u>! <u>More</u> than enough for me . . . to reject the whole goddam <u>thing</u>! <u>Reject</u> it . . . out of <u>hand</u>!"

"Now, Vick . . ."

"Now Vick . . . <u>shit</u>! I think the whole <u>thing's</u> probably against the goddam <u>law</u>! Not only against the <u>law</u> . . . but positively <u>disgusting</u> as well! I think it's lower than <u>whale</u> shit . . . and <u>that's</u> right at the bottom of the friggin' <u>ocean</u>!"

Smigelski's voice had risen—substantially. In both tone and decibel level! "I really think," he'd spouted, "that something like what you're doing should be <u>exposed</u>! Poor choice of <u>words</u>, I guess! I knew that there were <u>seamy</u> sides . . . <u>many</u> seamy sides . . . to this horse-shit business! But, I could <u>never</u> have guessed anything . . . anything even <u>close</u> . . . to what <u>you're</u> talking about! Junie's <u>right</u>! I've been in this <u>cesspool</u> . . . appropriate <u>word</u> . . . too damn <u>long</u>!"

"I <u>understand</u> what you're saying, Vick. But, I <u>do</u> have a legitimate <u>proposition</u> for you! A bona fide <u>offer</u>!"

"Save your <u>breath</u>, Mister Nype! I'm not <u>interested</u>! In <u>spades</u> . . . I'm <u>not</u> interested! Not in the <u>least</u>! Not in the damn <u>least</u>!"

"<u>No</u>! Hear me <u>out</u>! You <u>owe</u> me that!"

Once again, Smigelski had heaved a deep sigh—then, had slumped back, into his suddenly-confining chair. "All right, Mister Nype," he'd groused. "Proposition <u>away</u>! It won't do any <u>good</u>! The whole goddam <u>idea</u> is . . . well, it's out in left fucking <u>field</u>! <u>Way</u> out in left field! I won't have <u>anything</u> . . . anything to <u>do</u> with it! <u>Refuse</u> . . . to even <u>consider</u> it!"

"<u>Fine</u>! <u>Don't</u> have anything to do with it. <u>Refuse</u> to consider it. But, I want you to <u>listen</u>! Listen . . . to what I have to <u>say</u>! Okay?"

"You'd be better off . . . saving your <u>breath</u>," muttered the disgruntled employee. "Saving your <u>time</u> . . . and <u>my</u> time! No <u>way</u> . . . no goddam <u>way</u> . . . am I <u>ever</u> gonna get involved, in some shit-assed scheme like <u>that</u>! No goddam <u>way</u>!"

"Completely <u>understandable</u>, Vick! But, it's <u>important</u> . . . <u>vitally</u> important . . . that you hear me <u>out</u>! First of all, I probably shouldn't have <u>mentioned</u> the part where . . . <u>sometimes</u> . . . <u>men</u> have to monitor the little <u>girl's</u> room! And vice <u>versa</u>! Not at <u>first</u>, anyway, should I have brought <u>that</u> part of it up! This <u>happens</u> . . . but, damn <u>seldom</u>! <u>Damn</u> seldom! Practically to the point of never happening at <u>all</u>."

"I don't know if I <u>believe</u> that, Mister Nype! You <u>did</u> say that you don't have too many <u>employees</u> . . . ones <u>refusing</u> to monitor the other gender's can!"

"That's what I <u>said</u>! And that's what I <u>meant</u>! What I didn't <u>mean</u> to <u>convey</u>, though, was the illusion that it happens all the <u>time</u>! It <u>doesn't</u>! Does <u>not</u>! I guess I was probably trying to make <u>light</u> of something! Something that I <u>shouldn't</u> have. I was simply trying to get <u>everything</u> . . . all the <u>drawbacks</u> . . . out, onto the table! Take my <u>word</u> for it, Vick! It happens damn <u>seldom</u>! But, it <u>does</u> happen! And I wanted you to <u>know</u> that! Know that . . . going <u>in</u>! If I had to put a <u>number</u> on it, I'd guess that it happens . . . oh . . . maybe two or three times, in a <u>year</u>! Certainly not much <u>more</u> than that! Plus . . . in the <u>women's</u> toilet . . . you can't really <u>see</u> anything! <u>None</u> of the cameras are inside the <u>stalls</u>!"

"Well," Smigelski had growled. "It's still a damn <u>travesty</u>!"

"I don't know that I'd go <u>that</u> far, Vick. It's certainly <u>distasteful</u> . . . to <u>me</u>, anyway! On the other hand, you'd be <u>surprised</u> . . . at how many <u>women</u> would, actually, be <u>excited</u>! Excited as <u>hell</u> . . . if they thought some man was <u>watching</u>! And . . . you can <u>bet</u> . . . vice versa."

"Yeah. And <u>you</u> don't know . . . how many would be <u>shocked</u>! And vice-damn-<u>versa</u>!"

"I'm sure that's <u>true</u>. In any case, Vick, what I <u>propose</u> to you . . . what I'm asking you to <u>do</u> . . . is to do <u>one</u> day! Just one single <u>day</u> . . . of <u>monitoring</u>! <u>One</u> damn day! One lousy <u>day</u>. And <u>that</u> would be . . . whenever you'd want to come back to <u>work</u>! Whenever you feel as though you <u>could</u> come back to work! I wouldn't want you to come back <u>before</u> then!"

"Well, I . . ."

Nype had held up his hand again. "Listen, Vick. I'm not so <u>naïve</u> . . . as to believe that you won't be <u>looking</u>! Looking for another <u>job</u> . . . while you're <u>recuperating</u>. I'm sure that <u>I'd</u> be looking . . . if I were in <u>your</u> shoes. You've been in the rent-a-car field . . . for <u>years</u>. Obviously, you <u>enjoy</u> it. And I'm just as sure as I can <u>be</u> . . . that you're very <u>good</u> at it. I <u>do</u> feel, though, that you've been reasonably happy . . . in this hallowed field! The . . . ah . . . unfortunate physical setbacks notwithstanding! Maybe I'm wrong, but I really believe that . . . deep inside . . . I'm convinced, that you actually do enjoy this business!"

"Oh," Smigelski had sighed. "I guess I do. Hate to admit it. Even to myself." Another room-filling sigh! "Beats hell out of starving for a living, anyway."

"True! But, in my estimation, if you didn't enjoy it . . . get, at least, something out of the game . . . you never would've stayed! Not for a couple whole years! You'd have gotten out! Immediately! Right after your little go-around . . . over at the warehouse!"

"I . . . well, I guess. Yeah. You're probably right! I guess that I probably have enjoyed it! Except, of course . . . when I'm getting the shit kicked out of me! Those are not moments I've treasured! But still, that doesn't make the thing with . . ."

Again, Nype had held up his hand! "I do understand how you feel, at this moment, Vick," he'd said. "Believe me, I do. And, with the pressure that Miss Bodner . . . and your former wife . . . are exercising at this point, I'd be a fool to think that you'd not be looking around. Especially when you've actually got a goodly amount of convalescent time . . . to do it in. Listen, Vick, if you find something good . . . really good . . . then, God bless you! Take it! Jump on it! Jump all over it! With my blessing! And my most sincere good wishes! But . . . and please take this to heart, Vick . . . if it's not something totally earthshaking . . . totally outstanding . . . then, please give what I have in mind for you a try! Just for one stinking . . . pardon the pun . . . day!"

"I dunno, Mister Nype. I really don't <u>think</u> that . . ."

"What I'm saying is that I <u>hope</u> you won't be looking . . . looking just simply to be <u>looking</u>. Seeking to simply find a place to <u>land</u>. If it's a choice between just someplace to <u>go</u> every day . . . even at about the same <u>salary</u> . . . or taking <u>me</u> up on <u>my</u> proposition, then, please <u>take</u> me up on <u>my</u> proposition! For <u>one</u> single day! I assure you . . . you won't be <u>sorry</u>! You really <u>won't</u>, Vick. I <u>promise</u> you!"

"You started to <u>tell</u> me <u>what</u> . . . <u>exactly</u> what . . . your proposition <u>was</u>, Mister Nype. Your <u>offer</u> to me! <u>Moneywise</u>, I'm guessing! And <u>hours</u>! <u>That</u> sort of thing! The <u>particulars</u>!"

"What's that? Oh! <u>Right</u>! I guess I <u>do</u> tend to digress. They <u>call</u> that senility."

For the first time, Smigelski had surrendered to his normal, warm, smile. "Whatever <u>else</u> you may be, Mister Nype," he'd said. "<u>Senile</u> . . . you're <u>not</u>!"

"Nice of you to say, Vick. But, sometimes I wonder. Here's the <u>proposition</u>: I'd like for you to work that one <u>day</u> . . . just one single <u>day</u>, Vick . . . monitoring the <u>men's</u> room! Not at the <u>Manhattan</u> store, of course! Too many people <u>know</u> you there!"

Smigelski's smile had vanished. "Yeah," he'd grumped. "Do they <u>ever</u> know me there!"

"I'm thinking of **Ballinger's** Rego Park store! <u>Huge</u> facility! Out in Queens! <u>No</u> one out there . . . is going to <u>know</u> you! Now, if this thing turns out to be the total <u>turn</u>-off that you <u>feel</u> it'll be . . . then, I'll give you something <u>else</u> to do! I <u>promise</u> you that! I can't really <u>tell</u> you . . . what it'd <u>be</u>! Not at this <u>point</u>! Mainly, because I don't <u>know</u> what it'd be! But, I give you my <u>word</u>, Vick . . . my solemn word . . . that it'll be <u>far</u>

removed, from what you've been doing! I really want to <u>keep</u> you as an employee, Vick! I really <u>do</u>! At this moment, my most <u>pressing</u> need . . . <u>really</u> pressing need . . . is in Rego Park! But, I'll do <u>anything</u> . . . within <u>reason</u> . . . to <u>keep</u> you!"

"That's pretty heady <u>stuff</u>, Mister Nype! I'm <u>honored</u> . . . <u>truly</u> honored! I mean . . ."

"I really <u>don't</u> want to lose you, Vick! I can <u>see</u> you . . . and I'm not <u>bullshitting</u> you . . . I can see you, sitting in <u>this</u> chair! <u>Eventually</u>! Somewhere down the <u>road</u>! Please <u>believe</u> me . . . I'm not trying to <u>borax</u> you! I can honestly <u>see</u> you . . . taking my <u>place</u>! Like I said, <u>eventually</u>! But, I <u>can</u> see it!"

Smigelski had sighed—heavily—once more. "Well," he'd replied, "that's <u>always</u> nice to hear! Especially after this past year-or-so! I guess I <u>needed</u> . . . to hear something like that!"

Nype then brought his infectious smile into play. "It's <u>true</u>, Vick! If it wasn't . . . if I wasn't sincere . . . I wouldn't <u>say</u> it! We get so many <u>bodies</u> . . . come through here! Dear <u>Lord</u> . . . Captain Fox . . . <u>he</u> gets <u>zillions</u> of 'em! I really don't know <u>how</u> that man keeps his <u>sanity</u>. But, even in <u>this</u> division . . . <u>we</u> get more than our share of <u>stiffs</u>. So, if it were just a question of wanting to keep a warm <u>body</u> around . . . why, we wouldn't be <u>sitting</u> here, having this <u>conversation</u>. Bodies I can <u>get</u>! Can <u>always</u> get! By the <u>thousands</u>! I want to keep <u>you</u> because . . . well, first <u>off</u> . . . you're a good <u>man</u>! A <u>conscientious</u> man! A devoted-to-<u>duty</u> man! But, in <u>addition</u>, you've got a whole <u>lot</u> of potential . . . for this <u>business</u>! <u>Potential</u> . . . up the poopie-dooper! I <u>mean</u> that sincerely, Vick! Anyway . . . <u>please</u> . . . work just that one day! Okay? Just one freaking day! One! Then, we'll talk! All right?"

"Damn! Dammit . . . I don't know, Mister Nype! I really don't know! The whole idea is so . . . well, it's so damn offensive! To me, anyway! If I was going to be true to myself . . . and everything I believe in . . . I think that the first thing I ought to do is to run to the media! Run like hell . . . to the media! Spill my guts! Tell the whole story! Big scoop! For somebody!"

Nype had begun to say something—but, was halted by Smigelski's upheld hand. "Don't worry," he had assured. "Don't fret, Mister Nype. I'm not going to fink on you. But, let me tell you: The fact . . . that I'm not going to spill my guts . . . that worries me! Worries the hell out of me!"

Smigelski, by then, had slouched down in his chair! Deflated! Almost as though someone had let all the life—drain out of him.

"It kills me," he'd continued. "Kills me that . . . not only am I not going to expose this crappy little game . . . but, apparently, I'll be contributing to it! Makes me feel . . . well . . . makes me feel dirty!"

"I really think that you're actually making a mountain . . . out of a molehill, Vick! I really do! I think you'll find that . . . after you get yourself involved . . . I think you'll find that it won't be nearly as offensive as you're picturing!"

"Yeah," Smigelski had muttered, absently. "I don't know, Mister Nype! I just don't know! Junie! Well, Inez, too! And the . . . the kids! Jesus! If any of them . . . any of them . . . knew! Why, they'd all flip out! Flip their corks . . . altogether!"

"Well . . . for the present . . . we're only talking about one <u>day</u>. Maybe it'd be best . . . not to <u>tell</u> them! <u>Any</u> of them!"

"I <u>doubt</u> that! Well, with <u>Junie</u>, anyway! We <u>always</u> talk! <u>Always</u>! Talk . . . about <u>everything</u>!" He'd stared—with great intensity—down at his shoe tops. "<u>Everything</u>." The last word was barely audible.

Nype had nodded. "I <u>understand</u>," he'd acknowledged. His voice was becoming a slight bit raspy. "Okay, Vick. I'm all <u>through</u> . . . with my <u>sales</u> pitch. I'm not going to try and talk you <u>into</u> it. Not any more . . . than I already <u>have</u>. My reasoning in wanting you in such an important . . . yes, <u>important</u> . . . position, is not at <u>all</u> illogical! Do you <u>think</u> . . . that we're interested in some <u>goofball</u>? Some idiot . . . stealing four <u>postage</u> stamps? Or a damn <u>pencil</u> . . . or something? Hell no. Penny <u>ante</u> stuff. <u>Many</u> of the operatives, we've had out there . . . on that detail . . . they'll <u>panic</u>! Go running . . . to <u>report</u> someone, who takes a nineteen cent *Bic* <u>pen</u>! That's where that '<u>bodies</u>' thing comes in! While they're <u>away</u>, from their station . . . reporting the theft of a damn <u>pen</u> . . . all <u>hell</u> could be breaking loose!"

"All <u>hell</u> breaking loose?"

"Well, <u>that</u> may have been a poor choice of <u>words</u>. But, what I'm <u>looking</u> for is someone . . . an <u>employee</u> . . . with enough <u>smarts</u>, to observe a man tearing up a <u>charge</u> slip! Watching him throwing it in the <u>trash</u> can! Then . . . once the man <u>leaves</u> the john . . . I'd like the <u>operative</u> to have enough <u>snap</u> to go fish <u>out</u> the pieces of the slip! Piece it <u>together</u>! If it's for a color tee <u>vee</u> . . . or even a suit of <u>clothes</u> . . . I'd like to see <u>that</u> operative report it!

If a store employee was to take <u>money</u> out of his suit coat pocket . . . or his shirt pocket . . . and put it in his <u>wallet</u>, we'd like to <u>know</u> that! It's the <u>big</u> things that we're interested in! And <u>some</u> of these dickheads, we've employed . . . well, they don't know the <u>difference</u>! No sense of <u>priorities</u>! That's why I <u>need</u> someone . . . someone with some <u>snap</u>! Someone like <u>you</u>! Someone like you . . . <u>out</u> there! On that <u>detail</u>! I'd like to put my best <u>agent</u> . . . Glenn Hayes . . . on it. But, I need <u>him</u> . . . for other things! He's deeply involved in something <u>else</u>! <u>Deeply</u> involved! Something really <u>crucial</u>! I'm, <u>honestly</u>, not trying to make a <u>voyeur</u> out of you, Vick! I . . . really and truly . . . <u>do</u> need your expertise, out there! And . . . for the <u>record</u> . . . as soon as <u>possible</u>! As soon as damn <u>possible</u>!"

"<u>Expertise</u>? I don't <u>know</u>, Mister Nype. This has all <u>hit</u> me . . . has hit me, all so <u>suddenly</u>! I <u>suppose</u> that I shouldn't <u>be</u> so . . . so taken <u>aback</u>, so <u>shocked</u> . . . by the thing, but . . ."

"Why <u>not</u>? <u>I</u> certainly would've. Would've been taken aback . . . pretty damn <u>good</u>! I <u>expected</u> you to be . . . well . . . <u>shocked</u>! Maybe not <u>quite</u> to the degree that you <u>were</u>! To the degree that you <u>are</u>! But, I <u>did</u> expect you . . . positively <u>expected</u> you . . . to go through a few <u>changes</u>! And you <u>did</u>! You sure as hell <u>did</u>!"

"I think what <u>bothers</u> me," Smigelski had muttered, "what bothers me more than anything <u>else</u> is . . . well . . . you hear <u>stories</u>!"

"<u>Stories</u>? What <u>kind</u> of stories?"

"Well, when I was with **Ballinger's Rent-a-Car**, I was pretty good <u>friends</u> . . . with this one girl.

This one <u>woman</u>. She worked up at the location on Thirty-eighth Street . . . across from the Airline <u>Bus</u> Terminal."

"Yes?"

"Well, one day she told me about one of the **Tarkenton** <u>operators</u>! This was a <u>woman</u>! And Nancy <u>saw</u> this happen! With her own <u>eyes</u>! If you knew <u>Nancy</u>, you'd <u>know</u> that . . . if she <u>says</u> it happened . . . then, it jolly well <u>happened</u>! <u>Period</u>! <u>Paragraph</u>! I <u>believe</u> her! Without <u>reservations</u>!"

"What did she say?"

"Well, one day, this <u>woman</u> . . . the one who <u>worked</u> for you . . . she went up to the <u>manager</u>! The manager . . . at Thirty-eighth Street . . . and asked if she could <u>snitch</u> a couple gallons of <u>gas</u>! Gas . . . for her own personal <u>car</u>! It was <u>Monday</u>, or something . . . and payday wasn't till <u>Wednesday</u>! She <u>told</u> this poor guy that she didn't have enough gas to get herself <u>home</u> . . . and back . . . for the next <u>day</u>, or two! Now, you're <u>aware</u> of the fact that putting company <u>gas</u> . . . in your own <u>personal</u> car . . . is a big fat <u>no</u>-no!"

"Yes. Yes, of <u>course</u>! Of <u>course</u> it is!"

"Anyway, I guess the manager told the broad . . . that she couldn't <u>do</u> it! Couldn't have any <u>gas</u>, for her car! Well, this babe . . . who, Nancy said, was built like a brick <u>shithouse</u> . . . kind of <u>rubbed</u> herself up <u>against</u> this poor bastard! Asked him <u>again</u>! <u>Still</u> no! So, according to <u>Nancy</u>, this gal just about <u>ground</u> her boobs into this guy! Of course, he was beginning to get a little <u>shaky</u>! Starting to <u>sweat</u> . . . a lot! To make a long story longer, this poor clown could only <u>take</u> so much of what this babe was <u>doing</u>!

Plastering herself . . . <u>firmly</u> . . . up against him! So, I guess he finally caved <u>in</u>! Told her that, yeah, she could go ahead . . . and <u>take</u> a couple <u>bucks</u> worth! At <u>that</u> point, this <u>bitch</u> . . . that was <u>Nancy's</u> word for her, and Nancy <u>never</u> swears . . . she pulls out her **Tarkenton** badge! She got this poor character <u>fired</u>! <u>Gone</u>! He's frigging <u>gone</u>! No longer frigging <u>em</u>-damn-<u>ployed</u>! Now, goddam it, <u>that's</u> entrapment! Or <u>enticement</u>! Or <u>some</u> goddam thing! Pure and <u>simple</u>! If <u>anyone</u> . . . other than <u>Nancy</u> . . . had told me that story, I doubt that I'd have <u>believed</u> it! But, it <u>was</u> Nancy!"

"Vick, calm <u>down</u>! You're working yourself into a <u>snit</u>! I don't <u>recall</u> the incident. I don't even know who the woman could've <u>been</u>! We <u>did</u> have a hell of a lot of 'em working in the hokey little rent-a-car drama . . . over the years! We've got a hell of a lot of 'em working <u>now</u> . . . at the various **Ballinger's** stores! If what your friend . . . this <u>Nancy</u> . . . if what she says is <u>true</u>, and I don't <u>doubt</u> it for a minute . . . that just points up what I've been <u>telling</u> you!"

"What you've been <u>telling</u> me?"

"Yes. <u>Exactly</u>! My whole <u>point</u>. This woman was, obviously, a warm <u>body</u> . . . although one that was apparently pretty well <u>stacked</u>! And, like I said, we've got <u>boodles</u> of 'em! Got <u>plenty</u> of 'em! They don't use their <u>heads</u>, at all! I guess <u>some</u> of them use <u>other</u> parts of their anatomy! So <u>many</u> have no damn <u>sense</u>! None at <u>all</u>! On the other <u>hand</u>, the security business really isn't <u>that</u> much different . . . in that <u>area</u>! Not a helluva lot <u>different</u> . . . than, virtually, any <u>other</u> field! I'm <u>sure</u> that . . . in the <u>rent</u>-a-car business . . . <u>you</u> had <u>more</u> than <u>your</u> share of absolute <u>stiffs</u>!"

Smigelski had nodded. "Yeah," he'd acknowledged, sourly. "I guess we <u>did</u>."

"Well, that's what <u>this</u> broad was! A damn <u>stiff</u>! <u>That's</u> why . . . in critical <u>situations</u> . . . I've <u>got</u> to have someone who doesn't have his or her head up his or her <u>ass</u>! And . . . <u>again</u>, believe it or not . . . this position, we're talking about, <u>is</u> critical! But, you're never going to <u>know</u> that! Not unless . . . and until . . . you <u>see</u> that, for yourself. I think that you and I have pretty good <u>rapport</u>. <u>Despite</u> that, though, I don't know if <u>I'd</u> believe what I'm <u>telling</u> you, if I were you. That's why it's so <u>important</u> . . . so damn <u>critical</u> . . . that you take a look for <u>yourself</u>! Give it <u>one</u> day! One lousy <u>day</u>! That's all I <u>ask</u>! One damn <u>day</u>! If the whole thing makes you <u>gag</u> . . . then, that'll be the <u>end</u> of it! I think you'd have to <u>agree</u>, Vick, that I've <u>tried</u> . . . done my <u>best</u> . . . to be <u>fair</u> with you! So did Captain <u>Fox</u>. If this wasn't something that was so damn <u>important</u>, I really wouldn't <u>press</u> it! But, it <u>is</u>, Vick. It really and truly <u>is</u>! <u>Damn</u> important. I really <u>believe</u> that, if you'll give me <u>one</u> day . . . one pissy-assed <u>day</u> . . . you'll <u>see</u>! See that I'm telling you the <u>truth</u>! The gospel <u>truth</u>! What <u>sayest</u> thou?"

Once again, Smigelski had sighed deeply. "What can I <u>say</u>, Mister Nype? <u>Okay</u>. I'll feel totally <u>insipid</u>," he groused. "But, I'll give it a damn <u>try</u>! I'm going to <u>hold</u> you . . . to that one day stipulation, though."

Nype had smiled broadly. "<u>Good</u>," he'd said. "<u>Great</u>! I <u>will</u> stand by my promise. I gave you my <u>word</u>! And I'll <u>honor</u> it! If the thing <u>upsets</u> you . . . really and <u>truly</u> upsets you . . . I'll find something <u>else</u> for you. But, <u>please</u> Vick, give it a legitimate <u>shot</u>! A purely open-<u>minded</u> chance!"

"All right," Smigelski had semi-growled. "I'll give it a <u>shot</u>! I haven't the foggiest <u>idea</u> . . . what I'm going to <u>tell</u> June! Or <u>Inez</u>! Not the <u>foggiest</u>! And I don't even want to <u>think</u> about my kids!"

As he'd walked down the corridor—heading away from Leland Nype's office—he had found himself muttering aloud: "I don't know <u>how</u> the hell I keep getting myself talked <u>into</u> these stupid-assed things."

He was still muttering—as he entered the elevator.

NINE

S MIGELSKI'S "INEVITABLE" FIRST DAY ON the job—in his new **Tarkenton** bailiwick—was not as terrible, nor <u>nearly</u> as disgusting, as he'd expected. He'd discovered no immediate need for the "barf bag".

For one thing, the cameras—there were two of them, in the men's room—were not situated where the observer would actually watch a man relieving himself. In fact, one camera angle was very poor. Half of the lens was obliterated by a sizable portion of the aluminum paper towel dispenser. The other camera, however, did allow an adequate overview of the lavatory—outside the four stalls.

Smigelski found himself wishing that June Bodner could see exactly how <u>innocuous</u> the entire situation was. Then, he'd out and out <u>shuddered</u>—and, immediately, fled from the ever-too-hasty thought process!

The couple had experienced one of their more <u>spectacular</u> rows—on the evening, that he'd advised his fiancée of his decision to give his new assignment a one day trial.

June had refused to speak to him for two days!

Though she'd eventually relented—to a point— she continued to make no secret, of her complete unhappiness! Her complete unhappiness—and her abject disappointment—were never far from the surface! The employment situation would cast an almost-never-ending pall on the relationship! A pall— that seemed not destined to end soon! The result was a consistent almost-armed-truce status between the couple! One that was remaining most troubling—for the both of them!

Shortly after three o'clock on Smigelski's first afternoon, on the job, a young man had stepped just inside the door, of the restroom—and had quickly taken four or five "scrunched up" bills from his sport coat pocket! He had nervously stuffed the currency— into his wallet! Then, he'd hurried out of the lavatory!

Smigelski, seated behind a scruffy desk, closely studied the two monitors, with another man. His partner was Richard Gladwynne—a middle-aged, slender, black man, who'd worked the "watch" for almost two years. Nype had endorsed Gladwynne— as ("thank God") one of his most competent agents.

Their outpost was a small, stuffy, windowless, room—located right next to the men's restroom.

Gladwynne—who'd been unable to recognize the man that had switched the money—gave Smigelski a hurried order! Smigelski left the scruffy, little, room—and trundled down the hall. He arrived at the elevator, a few seconds after his quarry had pressed the "down" button. Some 30 seconds later, the elevator doors opened. Both men stepped into the car. The man pressed the button for the second floor. Smigelski made a pass at the same panel destination—and pulled his hand back, once the "Two" button had lit up. The pair exited, at the second floor. Smigelski watched—as the other man entered the clothing department, and made his way behind the showcase/counter.

Smigelski picked his way through a half-dozen shirts—then, returned to his fifth-floor post.

After a hurried conference with Gladwynne, he picked up the phone on the desk—and dialed the extension of the store's director of security, Donald Hens.

The phone was picked up—on the second ring. However, no sound came from the other end.

"Mister Hens?" Smigelski began.

"Yeah." It was more a growl than an answer.

"Smigelski . . . Victor Smigelski . . . one of the **Tarkenton** people. I'm in the observation post for the employees' men's room."

"Yeah. Okay. What you got?"

"Young white man . . . twenty-seven or twenty-eight . . . just transferred money! I'm guessing . . . forty or fifty bucks! Transferred it from his coat pocket . . . into his wallet! Tall slender guy! Sort of blondish! I followed him . . . down to the second floor! He works . . . in Men's Clothing!"

"Yeah? How do ya know that?"

"I saw him walk behind the counter, down there!"

"Very good! What'd you say your name was?"
"Smigelski. First name is Vick."
"Hell of a lot easier . . . than the last one. Okay . . .
fine, Vick! We'll handle it . . . from here! Very good!"
Abruptly, the connection was broken.

Fifteen minutes later, Smigelski and Gladwynne
heard a key being turned in the lock—in the door, to
their cubbyhole office! A huge man—fully six-feet,
six-inches and, easily, 265 pounds—entered! The
soggy stub of a cigar jutted from his mouth. The cigar
bobbed up and down—whenever the man spoke. His
yellowed teeth gave witness—to years of neglect.

Looking at Smigelski, he snarled, "Are you Vick?
The guy with the long Polack name?"

Smigelski nodded.

"Good. I'm Hens." Thrusting two trading-card-sized
items at Smigelski, he continued, "I got two guys . . .
who fit that description! They're working the floor,
down there . . . even as we speak. Was your guy . . .
one of these?"

Smigelski scanned the cards. Gladwynne
peered over his shoulder. The pasteboard forms
were *employee identification cards*. They listed the
employee's name, address, phone number, social
security number, age, date of employment, number
of dependents and employee number. In the upper
left corner of each card was a passport-sized photo.
Neither picture was particularly flattering.

Handing one of the cards back to Hens, Smigelski
confirmed, "It's this one! Darrel Warwick!"

"You sure?" Hens' stare narrowed. "Because . . . if
it's not him . . . I'll have your ass!"

"I'm sure."

"He's the guy," added Gladwynne.

"You guys . . . you'd goddam better be, fuckin' well, shit-sure," growled Hens.

With that, he snatched the other card from Smigelski's hand—and stormed out of the tiny room!

"Holy shit," muttered Smigelski. "Is he . . . is he for real?"

"A real pussycat, isn't he?" responded Gladwynne, with a mirthless laugh.

Smigelski shook his head, slowly. "I've never seen . . . never seen . . . anyone like that before," he muttered. "Man! He can reduce you to a pile of rubble . . . with that stare of his! I don't think I've ever had such a chill! What'll they do . . . with this guy? This Warwick?"

"Oh, they'll track down what he would've sold . . . just before he pocketed the money! They're supposed to have a wondrous . . . completely foolproof . . . inventory system here. But, I really think that it's probably not all that great. They may not be able to figure out exactly what it was . . . that he glommed! If they can't nail him today, you can bet your sweet ass . . . that they'll be watching him like a damn hawk. **Tarkenton's** supposed to have security people . . . in every department, I guess! They might even . . . send in a shopper!"

"Someone . . . who acts like a customer?"

"Yeah," Gladwynne nodded. "Comes in . . . and picks out a sport coat or something! Merchandise that looks like eleven-million other coats, on the rack! The shopper always gives the guy a wonderful chance . . . to steal the money! Creates a beautiful opportunity for him! Then, they nail him! Nail his ass . . . good! If you don't <u>believe</u> me . . . just conjure <u>up</u>, the choirboy <u>countenance</u>, of Mister Donald <u>Hens</u>, in your mind! Once you get <u>that</u> noble picture, into your brain, If you think that he's <u>not</u> going to <u>crucify</u> that Warwick guy, why . . ."

"I <u>believe</u> you! I <u>get</u> the picture! I <u>fair</u>-thee-well <u>believe</u> you!"

"Getting on to about time . . . to be going on home," observed Gladwynne, with a yawn. "Been an uneventful <u>day</u>. My <u>relief's</u> always ten . . . or fifteen . . . minutes <u>late</u>! I've stopped <u>covering</u> for him! **Tarkenton** lets him get <u>away</u> with it. I <u>guess</u> they've had trouble . . . <u>filling</u> the slot! <u>He's</u> been working <u>alone</u> . . . since <u>forever</u>!

Gladwynne's statement made Smigelski recall Leland Nype's explanation—as to his difficulty, in finding people to man the station.

"Do you get many <u>people</u> . . . <u>many</u> people . . . like <u>this</u> guy?" asked the newcomer. "This <u>Warwick</u>? I mean . . . stashing money in their <u>wallet</u>, like that? <u>Lots</u> of people . . . doing that?"

"Oh, from time to <u>time</u>. More <u>often</u>, though, we'll pick up a <u>conversation</u>! A little <u>exchange</u> . . . between a couple of <u>employees</u>! Making a <u>deal</u>!"

"What do you mean . . . 'making a deal'? What kind of deal?"

"Well, say I worked in <u>Receiving</u>. And <u>you</u> worked in . . . hell, you could work almost <u>anywhere</u>. Anywhere in the <u>store</u>. <u>I'd</u> come to you . . . and <u>tell</u> you, that we're going to be unloading a shipment of . . . say . . . of camelhair <u>coats</u>. Coats that'll be coming in right after <u>lunch</u>. They're <u>supposed</u> to sell for . . . I dunno . . . maybe a hundred-and-ninety-five bucks. I tell you . . . that I'll pick off one of those little dandies for you. You tell me, 'Swell' . . . and you slip me fifty bucks. Or . . . most likely . . . you tell me you'll pay me on payday. I go ahead . . . and swipe the coat. In your size, of course. I arrange to dump it some place! Some place that's safe . . . obviously! Then, when you get off work, you just sashay by . . . and you pick it up! Voila! You've got a glorious winter coat! Don't know as you'd really be well advised to wear it around here, though." He yawned once again. "That sort of thing happens! Happens . . . all the time! Around here! Not the wearing . . . but, the very clever theft!"

"Really?"

"Trust me! Turnover down in Receiving . . . is out of this world! Hell, turnover in every department is, probably, out of this world."

"Why? Why would that be? Is it the same in every other department store . . . in town?"

"Naw. I don't think so, anyway. **Ballinger's** treats their employees like shit! They all have to take a polygraph . . . as a mere condition of employment! Have their picture taken! Fingerprinted! The whole bullshit! There's security people . . . lurking all over the goddam place! The johns are bugged! I'm not any kind of expert, of course, but I'd hazard a guess that . . . if an employee hadn't already thought about stealing anything, when he or she is first hired . . . it wouldn't take much to get 'em thinking that way! From the very first day!"

"I see what you mean," Smigelski replied, gloomily.

"And that's not all, Ski! You should see . . . gaze at the damn employment application the poor stiff has to fill out! It's damn well demeaning!"

"Demeaning? How so?"

Gladwynne's smile betrayed his distaste. "Well, for openers," he explained, "you have to finish . . . some shit-assed sentence! Some gem . . . like, 'My greatest failing is . . . ', Or, how about this? One question asks, 'What would you do . . . if you had a black bowel movement?'!"

"Really? They put that . . . on freaking applications?"

Gladwynne nodded—emphatically. "Damn right they do," he grumped. Then, he laughed. "One guy," he continued, "is reputed to have answered, 'Wipe my ass'!"

"Yeah, but . . . if they're such sons of bitches, why would anyone work for 'em?"

"Come on, Ski. Didn't you tell me that you just about starved? When that one company went out from under you? The woods are full . . . of people looking for jobs. People who need jobs. Need 'em badly! And here comes along the chance to work for a . . . quote, unquote . . . prestigious department store! I read a study once . . . all about employers! Ones . . . who put their people through all the bullshit! Stuff that **Ballinger's** does! The writer . . . who did the report . . . summed up, by saying something like, 'I'm convinced that employers, who resort to such tactics, virtually always wind up with the worst possible employees'. And he went on to say that they jolly well deserve 'em."

Once their shift had ended, Gladwynne and Smigelski were replaced by one man. Gladwynne's fabled relief!

As soon as he'd left the store, Smigelski found a pay phone on Queens Boulevard. He placed a call to Leland Nype's private number, at **Tarkenton**. Once the connection was made, he heaved a massive sigh.

"Okay, Mister Nype," he said. "I'll stay with it! For awhile, anyway!"

"Wonderful, Vick!"

"Let me be honest, Mister Nype. I'm not hooked on it. Not by any means! But, you were right. It's not as bad . . . not as flaming obscene . . . as I thought it'd be! I'm sure that I'm able to rationalize though. Rationalize with the best of 'em!"

"Rationalize?"

"Yeah. The old bit about . . . if I wasn't doing it, you'd just have to hire someone who would! The operation's not going to stop! So, why shouldn't I make the money? Rationalization . . . pure and simple!"

His superior laughed—heartily! "Oh, I think you're being a wee bit too harsh on yourself, Vick. As I told you before, it's an important slot! Extremely important!"

"I'll tell you what, Mister Nype! That Hens character . . . he scares the beJesus out of me!"

Nype's laugh was surprisingly enigmatic—a laugh Smigelski had never heard before. "He scares the beJesus . . . out of everyone! Out of . . . literally . . . everyone!"

The rest of Smigelski's first week on the "watch" turned out to be literally uneventful. With one exception: He and Gladwynne did overhear a number of conversations: One man—who worked in the Receiving Department—had sold a multitude of merchandise to various other employees! He'd enumerated a goodly number of these capers to two friends. The rather-complete alliteration of such nefarious transactions were then, dutifully, reported to Donald Hens.

On the Monday—beginning Smigelski's second week—Darrel Warwick again pulled a number of scrunched-up bills from his pocket and transferred them to his wallet! This appeared to be a much <u>larger</u> wad of currency—than he'd shuffled, the preceding week!

Earlier in the day, Warwick had sold a $159.95 overcoat to a "plant"—another **Tarkenton** operative— and the cash transaction had never appeared, on the cash register tape.

The **Tarkenton** man had paid Warwick—almost surreptitiously. Behind one of the many winter coats/ winter jackets racks. He'd, obviously, made it almost-<u>ridiculously</u> easy—for the clerk to pocket the money! Which, of course, Warwick <u>did</u>! The agent had, of course, given Warwick the sale amount—in "marked" bills!

As soon Smigelski had reported the transfer of money, Hens had—<u>immediately</u>—ordered that Warwick be brought to his office! He'd succeeded in "persuading" the frightened young sales clerk to produce <u>all</u> of the money in his wallet. Examining the currency beneath a fairly-high-tech (for the times) ultra-violet light, Hens was able to show Warwick the distinct <u>markings</u> on each of the "hot" bills!

Under the intimidating glare of Donald Hens—and in the presence of the **Tarkenton** agent—Warwick, tearfully, <u>acknowledged</u> what had happened! Then, he signed a document <u>admitting</u> the theft!

Hens immediately had the erstwhile employee arrested! Once the officers had led Warwick away, Hens phoned Smigelski—and barked, "Good fuckin' <u>work</u>!". Hens' voice never failed to send <u>shivers</u> up (and down) Smigelski's back!

Tuesday brought a situation—which was to change Smigelski's life! <u>Forever</u>:

Nothing out of the ordinary had occurred—until almost 3:15PM. At that point—while Gladwynne was on his break, and out of the broom closet office—Smigelski watched a young, slender, black man walk into the lavatory. The young man sauntered, leisurely, to a large, "frosted", window—and lit a cigarette. A not-unusual action.

Five minutes later—as the man had thrown the butt into one of the urinals—an even-younger white man, pushed his way through the door.

"About damn <u>time</u>," the black man growled.

"Oh, wow! I had a hell of a <u>time</u> . . . trying to get my ass out! That goddam <u>broad</u> . . . my glorious <u>supervisor</u> . . . she's a first class pain in the <u>ass</u>! I kept <u>telling</u> her I had to go . . . and she just kept finding something <u>else</u> for me to do! She's <u>really</u> got the rag on today! Finally, I <u>told</u> her . . . that she'd damn well <u>better</u> let me go! Before I <u>pissed</u> . . . all over her bright new <u>carpeting</u>! She finally got the <u>message</u>, I guess."

"Probably the only reason she let you <u>out</u>," replied the black man, with a smile. "Ah, the lovely and gracious Marcie," he continued—his tone noticeably softened. "She's a real <u>winner</u>!"

The young white sighed. "Look, Clark," he said, "I don't have all that much <u>time</u>, up here. That dippy broad's just in the mood to come barreling <u>in</u> here . . . and drag my ass right off the goddam <u>commode</u>! You'd better fill me <u>in</u>! <u>Fast</u>!"

Clark, the black man, withdrew a list from his inside pocket. "Look," he said, "I've got this <u>list</u> here! It's all the stuff we're gonna <u>need</u>! Some of the others . . . they'll be contributing <u>some</u> of this shit, I'm sure! So, the only things they really expect <u>us</u> to get . . . is just the stuff with the <u>checkmarks</u> next to 'em."

Hurriedly, the white man looked over the piece of paper Clark had given him—his lips moving, rapidly, as he'd scanned the text.

"I dunno," he protested, glumly. "<u>Most</u> of this crap, the store doesn't even <u>handle</u>! I <u>really</u> don't think they handle <u>any</u> of it! And I'm not sure that I've got anywhere <u>near</u> the <u>connections</u> . . . to get even <u>half</u> of it!"

"God <u>damn</u> it, Frank! The hairiest things are going to be the <u>blasting</u> caps! And I already <u>told</u> you . . . that <u>I'd</u> get 'em! My uncle . . . he's a superintendent at a <u>construction</u> site! I figure I can get, maybe, two <u>dozen</u>

of 'em! It won't be easy! But, I'll get 'em. Should take care of us . . . for a good long time! Now, goddam it, you've got to get the rest of this stuff! And no one really gives a shit . . . where you get it from! Or how! This thing isn't just creeping up on us, anymore! It's closing right in! With a fucking rush!"

Frank grunted. "Okay," he grumped. "All right. I'll do what I can! But, it's sure as shit going to take some doing! And with that stupid-assed broad, downstairs . . . with her climbing all over my ass . . . it's gonna be . . ."

"You can do it, Kid," encouraged Clark, with a smile. "You'll be there . . . tomorrow night?"

Frank nodded—tentatively.

"For sure?" Clark persisted.

"I said I would. Now, back off, dammit. Back fucking off! I've got enough hassles! My mother's having a goddam bird . . . about my being away from the fucking apartment so often. Between her . . . and that Marcia bitch . . . I don't know if I'll ever be able to deal with broads! Any broads! In my whole fucking lifetime!"

Clark's booming, almost-hysterical, laugh filled the entire room! "Shit," he responded, still chuckling. "Twenty-one-years-old! Un-fucking-married! And pussy-whipped as hell! I don't know anyone else . . . who could manage all that! Not at your age, Frank."

"Get off my back," seethed Frank. "I'll see you tomorrow night! Now, let me get back down on the floor! Before that shit-assed bitch . . . comes stalking in here! After me!"

Both men left the room.

Smigelski—the color drained from his face—waited till Gladwynne returned. Then, he bolted out of the little room—and headed directly for Donald Hens' office!

Once admitted to Hens' inner sanctum, Smigelski began—with no formalities: "Mister Hens! I think we've got a biggie! A real biggie!"

"Aaaahhhhh. They're all biggies. Sit down. Take a load off. What was your name again?"

"Smigelski! Now, there were these two guys . . . in the men's john, and . . ."

Hens held up a grimy hand. "Calm down," he cautioned. "Calm down! Christ! You've been here long enough now . . . that you shouldn't be getting so goddam upset, over some goddam theft."

He re-lit his cigar—and indicated, once more, that Smigelski should seat himself.

"That's just it," protested Smigelski, seating himself on the very edge of one of Hens' surprisingly-comfortable visitor's chairs. "It's not a theft! It's something bigger! Much bigger! A hell of a lot bigger!"

Hens smiled—something Smigelski had never seen before. He'd always thought, as a matter of fact, that such a phenomenon would be well outside the realm of possibility. "Like what? What the hell are you talkin' about?" The security chief's voice was laced with sarcasm.

"Like these two guys! That's what I'm trying to tell you! They're gonna blow up something! Or someone!"

"What something? What someone?"

"I . . . I don't know! I . . . they were just talking! Talking about blasting caps! And . . . and getting some other stuff! Stuff that's . . . I'm pretty sure . . .

not legal! One gave the other a list! There's some kind of meeting . . . they're going to! Going to . . . tomorrow!"

"Aw come on, what-was-your-name-again?" snarled Hens. "You're building up . . . building up a whole big fuckin' thing! Probably over nothing! Over . . . probably . . . not a goddam thing! What you had was two silly-assed guys! Two guys . . . that were just simply playin' with their nips!"

"I'm not! I'm not building a whole big thing! I know what I heard them say!"

"Well, there ain't nothin' . . . nothin' I can do about it!"

Smigelski came up out of his chair! "What do you mean you can't do anything about it?" he screamed.

"What do I have? A goddam impediment of fuckin' speech? What'd I just say? There's not a fuckin' thing . . . not one fuckin' thing . . . I can do about it. Is that clear enough . . . for your comic book mentality?"

Hens' steel-grey eyes bored into Smigelski's forehead.

Smigelski made no attempt to hide his disgust! "Look, Mister Hens," he seethed. "This isn't something you can just dismiss! These guys are up to . . . up to something! I want to know who they are! We've got to . . . well, we've got to keep our eyes on 'em!"

Hens shifted his rancid cigar to the other side of his mouth. "Yeah," he snarled. "That's what the fuck we're payin' you for. Keep your eyes on 'em! Every time they come in to take a shit! And . . . if you hear 'em plannin' to steal something . . . steal something from the goddam store . . . then, you come, and you

<u>tell</u> me about it! Just like <u>always</u>! Outside of that . . . I don't want to <u>hear</u> it. It's not <u>my</u> fuckin' <u>problem</u>!"

Smigelski glared down at Hens! "You <u>disgust</u> me," he hissed. "You fucking <u>disgust</u> me!"

Hens waved his grubby hand—a gesture of dismissal! "I could fuckin' care <u>less</u>," he answered, with a half-smirk. "It's no skin off my <u>ass</u> . . . if you fuckin' love me! Or if you goddam <u>hate</u> me! But, you fuckin' <u>will</u> obey me! You'll do as I fuckin' <u>say</u>! <u>Understood</u>?"

Smigelski turned—and stormed out of the office! Returning to his outpost, he slammed the door—and threw himself into his chair!

"Hey <u>Ski</u>!" Gladwynne had never seen his partner in such turmoil! He seemed completely unable to determine—how to deal with Smigelski. "What <u>gives</u>?" he continued. "I can see the <u>smoke</u> . . . coming out of your ears . . . from <u>here</u>! Have a little <u>tiff</u> . . . with our esteemed director of <u>security</u>?"

"That <u>sonofabitch</u>," seethed Smigelski. "That no-<u>good</u> . . . that <u>rotten</u> . . . <u>sonofabitch</u>!"

"Yep. That's the <u>one</u>. <u>He's</u> the guy . . . I was <u>talking</u> about."

Smigelski sat back up in his chair—his expression taking on a new dimension. "Dick," he pressed. "Dick . . . is there some woman named <u>Marcie</u>? Does she run a <u>department</u>? <u>Downstairs</u>?"

"Yeah! Does she <u>ever</u>! That'd be Marcie <u>Brenner</u>. Heads up the <u>Carpeting</u> Department. Why? What's <u>up</u>? Surely, <u>she</u> didn't come roaring into the . . ."

"Do you know a <u>Frank</u>? White fella! One . . . who works in that <u>department</u>?"

213

"No. But, <u>that</u> doesn't mean anything. I don't really know a <u>soul</u> in that department. There's a really sharp <u>turnover</u>, down there! Marcie . . . in the true **Ballinger's** tradition . . . is a real <u>bitch</u>! Pure <u>hell</u>, to <u>work</u> for . . . so I understand. Kids <u>today</u>, you know . . . they won't put <u>up</u> with it. Put up with anything <u>close</u>! Average tenure . . . in her fiefdom of a department . . . is about twenty <u>minutes</u>, I'm guessing."

"Well, do you know a <u>black</u> man? Young fella. Named <u>Clark</u> something?"

"Uh . . . no. Not <u>really</u>. Wait a <u>minute</u>! There's a young black guy up in <u>Personnel</u>! I <u>think</u> his name is Clark! But, hell, I'm not absolutely <u>positive</u>!"

"Damn. I'm getting' <u>nowhere</u>! <u>Fast</u>!"

"Hey, <u>Ski</u>! What's <u>up</u>? What the hell's come <u>over</u> you? What're we <u>doing</u>? Playing *Twenty Questions*?"

"I don't <u>know</u>," groused Smigelski. "Maybe I'm barking up the wrong <u>tree</u>! But . . . goddam it . . . something's <u>up</u>! <u>Something's</u> up!"

"What do you <u>mean</u> 'something'? Hell . . . what do you mean '<u>up</u>'? What do you mean . . . by <u>any</u> of this?"

"This guy . . . this <u>Clark</u>! He was talking to a man named <u>Frank</u>! <u>White</u> guy . . . who, I guess, works in <u>Marcie's</u> department! And Clark . . . he <u>gives</u> this guy, Frank, a list of <u>stuff</u>! A list of stuff . . . to <u>get</u>!"

"<u>Get</u>? For <u>who</u>? What <u>kind</u> of stuff?"

"Well, <u>blasting</u> caps . . . for <u>one</u> thing! I don't <u>know</u> what else! And I don't know . . . for <u>who</u>!"

Gladwynne let out a low whistle! "<u>Christ</u>, Ski! <u>Blasting</u> caps?"

Smigelski nodded. "Yeah," he muttered. "And I don't recall <u>exactly</u> what they said. But, they were <u>talking</u> . . . talking about <u>bombs</u>, for Christ sakes! That much, I'm <u>sure</u> of! I don't give a shit . . . <u>what</u> that asshole, <u>Hens</u>, thinks! This is damn <u>frightening</u>, Dick! <u>Awfully</u> damn frightening!'

"So, you told <u>Hens</u> about it? What they were <u>talking</u> about?"

"<u>Yeah</u>! <u>Sonofabitch</u>! He didn't want to <u>hear</u> it!"

"He <u>didn't</u>? Why the hell <u>not</u>?"

"Because . . . they weren't fucking <u>stealing</u> anything! Not from his precious <u>store</u>! That's all he <u>knows</u> . . . is <u>theft</u>! So <u>what</u> if they're, maybe, gonna blow <u>up</u> the goddam place? Not his <u>problem</u>!"

"They . . . they're gonna blow the joint <u>up</u>?"

"Hell, <u>I</u> don't know." Smigelski had deflated— noticeably. "<u>This</u> place . . . maybe! Some <u>other</u> place . . . maybe! But it <u>was</u> bombs! It was <u>bombs</u> . . . that they were <u>talking</u> about, Dick! Fucking <u>bombs</u>!"

"<u>C'mon</u> now, Ski. Calm <u>down</u>! You may be bending yourself all out of <u>shape</u> . . . and for <u>nothing</u>! For no reason at <u>all</u>! You may be jumping . . . <u>way</u> to one hell of a false <u>conclusion</u>! To one <u>hell</u> of one!"

"Yeah," Smigelski mumbled. "I suppose. And, then again, I may <u>not</u> be jumping to one hell of a conclusion! I <u>know</u> what I <u>heard</u>, Dick! And he <u>said</u> . . . he <u>did</u> say . . . <u>blasting</u> caps! As plain as <u>hell</u>! That's what . . . that <u>has</u> to be scary! <u>Damn</u> scary! I'm at a total <u>loss</u>! I don't know <u>what</u> to do! Not the <u>foggiest</u>!"

Gladwynne sighed. "Well," he tried to be reassuring, "we can keep an <u>eye</u> on 'em! At least . . . when they go to the <u>crapper</u>! But, Ski, that's about all we <u>can</u> do! You <u>did</u> report it, y'know! So, you're <u>covered</u>!"

"Yeah," he sulked. "Yeah, I'm <u>covered</u>! Fat lot of good <u>that'll</u> do . . . when we're <u>all</u> covered! Covered with eleven million <u>tons</u> . . . of goddam <u>rubble</u>!"

"Well, at this point, I think all you can <u>do</u> . . . is to, maybe, call Mister Nype! Put it in your <u>report</u>! Your <u>written</u> report! I mean . . . as we <u>speak</u> . . . what else <u>can</u> you do? <u>Look</u>, Ski! Maybe they'll <u>do</u> or <u>say</u> something . . . something that'll tip their <u>mitt</u> . . . in the next <u>day</u> or two! <u>Then</u>, we'll be able to . . ."

Smigelski slammed his fist on the desk—causing a clipboard and a chewed-up *Bic* pen to go clattering to the floor.

"God <u>damn</u> it, Dick!" he roared. "I don't even <u>know</u> . . . if we've <u>got</u> a day or two! <u>One</u> of 'em . . . I don't remember which <u>one</u> . . . said that this <u>thing</u> . . . <u>whatever</u> it is . . . that it's closing <u>in</u> on 'em! Closing <u>in</u> . . . with a goddam <u>rush</u>! With a goddam <u>rush</u>! That's what he <u>said</u>! I'm scared <u>shitless</u>, Dick! You <u>hear</u> about people! People blowing up <u>banks</u> and <u>embassies</u> and foreign <u>offices</u> . . . and a whole <u>shitload</u> of places! Even *McDonald's* . . . and <u>post</u> offices! And *Burger Kings*! A whole <u>shitload</u> of places! Goddam <u>colleges</u>! <u>Airports</u>! Even <u>libraries</u>! Some <u>real</u> assholes . . . <u>they</u> tried to blow up the Statue of <u>Liberty</u>, for God's sakes! The Washington <u>Monument</u>! The New York City <u>Police</u> Headquarters! It wasn't that <u>long</u> ago . . . when all this shit took place! Those yahoos, they scare the <u>shit</u> out of me . . . I don't mind <u>admitting</u>."

"<u>Okay</u>, Ski! All <u>right</u>! We'll keep our <u>eye</u> on 'em. I don't know what <u>else</u> we can do . . . except to, maybe, tell Mister <u>Nype</u>! Maybe something'll turn <u>up</u> . . . in the next <u>day</u> or two!"

"I know," growled Smigelski. "You <u>said</u> that."

TEN

A S SOON AS HIS SHIFT was over—at five o'clock that afternoon—Smigelski donned his overcoat and took the elevator, down to the Carpeting Department, on the 3rd floor.

Ostensibly browsing through the many varieties of rugs and carpeting, he watched the man—the one he knew as Frank. Studied him—as the latter, busily, waited on a customer.

His mind spinning—desperately attempting to formulate some sort of intelligent plan—the frustrated "eye in the john" decided to simply vacate the department. Let the clerk finish his shift. He imagined—that his quarry would probably be through at 6:00PM.

Leaving the store, Smigelski ducked into a luncheonette across Queens Boulevard—and attempted to read *The Daily News*, while all-too-quickly downing three cups of gamey, God-awful, coffee.

He knew that he should phone Mr. Nype. But, what would he <u>tell</u> him? Leland Nype would probably be just as skeptical as Donald Hens—albeit with much more class. There was nothing—on which to go! Nothing provable!

At 5:50 PM, Smigelski returned to **Ballinger's**. He positioned himself in such a way as to appear to be browsing at the men's toiletries counter—adjacent to the bank of elevators, on the ground floor. He'd watch—ever so carefully—for his target! He wound up—waiting for 25 minutes!

Finally, Frank emerged from the far elevator—and made his way to one of the Queens Boulevard exits! Smigelski followed—at what he hoped was a discreet distance!

Once outside the store, Frank descended into the subway, fished a token from his coat pocket, inserted it into the slot—and hurried through the turnstile!

Smigelski—cursing under his breath—pushed into line at the token booth! After what seemed an eternity, he made his purchase—and dashed through the turnstile!

Frank was nowhere to be seen!

"Fine fucking detective you are," snarled the disappointed pursuer—loud enough to startle some poor elderly lady, who was striving (valiantly) to get out of his way! "Sit on your ass, drinking coffee," he continued to mutter. "When you should've been buying goddam subway tokens!" He looked, desperately, for his man—while trying to convince himself that there was absolutely no way he could've known that Frank would take the "stupid subway".

It was sure as hell a possibility. You should've thought of that!

In a fast-paced jog—covering each platform, on the first level—the sinking feeling eventually plummeted into full-scale depression! There was no sign of the elusive Frank!

Taking the steps two and three at a time, our hero barreled down to the next floor! As he landed on the second level, he spotted Frank—as the latter entered one of the front cars of a Manhattan-bound train!

Barely negotiating himself into one of the middle cars, of the same train—crucial seconds before the relentless doors closed—Smigelski slowly made his way forward! It was 6:30PM—and the day's rush was, at long last, beginning to wind down.

Cautiously working his way through four cars, he stopped before entering the fifth! Looking through the window of the door, he spotted the calm-appearing Frank! His quarry was seated in the fifth car! The epitome of non-worry! Seemingly at peace with the world! Smigelski decided it would be prudent to remain "once removed".

The train clattered into Manhattan, squealing and squeaking its way to the Third Avenue exit—at Fifty-third Street—where the hopefully-unsuspecting Frank disembarked!

Smigelski, became more and more apprehensive! He and Frank had been the only passengers to leave the train at that station! He followed the young man—from as far behind as he'd dared! His prey made his way, up the stairs—to the street!

Frank headed north on Third Avenue—to Fifty-sixth Street. Smigelski followed—at what he'd, again, hoped was a safe distance!

Turning right on Fifty-sixth, Frank headed in the direction of Second Avenue. Crossing Second, the young man hurried to the second apartment house on the north side of the street.

Once Frank was out of sight, Smigelski broke into a run! He headed toward the same apartment house! Then, abruptly, he decided it would be foolish to draw attention to himself—with his "hokey trot"! So, he slowed himself down! To a brisk walk!

Where the hell am I going in such a hurry? I don't have the foggiest idea where he might've gone, inside there!

Entering the vestibule, he tugged on the door to the lobby! It was locked, of course! The troubled "detective" quickly scanned the directory of tenants—located above the many tainted mailboxes—then, found himself laughing out loud!

What're you looking at names for, Stupid? You don't have the faintest idea what Frank's last name is! You don't even know if he lives here! Lesson Number Two . . . in becoming a detective: Find out who the hell it is . . . that you're damn chasing! You could've found out his name . . . before you even left the goddam store!

He wondered how important it could've been to follow Frank that evening—"in the first damn place".

The meeting, Dumbkopff, that's why! The freaking meeting . . . which is tomorrow night!

Our hero left the building—and, dejectedly, walked back to Third Avenue. It took him fully five minutes to find a pay phone that hadn't been vandalized! One that was even workable!

He dropped a dime in the slot—and called the **Ballinger's** store, in Rego Park. Once the call was answered, he asked the switchboard operator to connect him with the Carpeting Department. He heard a click—and then a buzz.

Then, a husky female voice answered, "Carpeting". Smigelski assumed that he was speaking—with the celebrated, the sainted, the virtuous, Marcie.

"Yeah," whined Smigelski, in his most nasal—hopefully, a thoroughly irritating—tone! "I'm tryin' to reach Frank . . . uh . . . Frank . . . Frank . . . hell, I don't recall his last name."

"It's <u>Crimmins</u>," came the reply, the woman's voice crackling with impatience. "And he's not <u>here</u>! Gone <u>home</u>! And you can <u>tell</u> him, for <u>me</u>, that . . . if he gets one <u>more</u> God damned personal <u>phone</u> call from any of his faggot <u>buddies</u> . . . you just <u>tell</u> him, <u>Queer Boy</u>! <u>Tell</u> him that his ass is fucking <u>grass</u>! He <u>knows</u> . . . goddam <u>well</u> . . . who has the goddam <u>lawnmower</u>!" So saying, she—charmingly—slammed the phone down, into its to-be-pitied cradle!

"Hoo <u>boy</u>," muttered the stunned caller. "Nice <u>lady</u>!"

Hurrying back to the apartment house, the re-enthused Smigelski's heart sank, once more! No Crimmins was listed in the directory of tenants.

Heaving a sigh—constructed of deep, deep <u>frustration</u>—he made his way to *The White Palace* hamburger restaurant at the corner of Fifty-seventh Street and Second Avenue.

Once inside the eatery, he seated himself—at the far end of the counter, and ordered a burger—and yet another cup of (much better than the stuff in Queens) coffee. While he pondered his next "intelligent" course of action. They'd all yielded so many <u>wonderful</u> results. He had no <u>idea</u>—what his next "brainstorm" would be!

He second-guessed himself—as to the wisdom of even <u>following</u> Frank, on that night! Inasmuch as the big-deal "<u>meeting</u>" was scheduled—for the <u>next</u> evening—he probably could've better <u>prepared</u> himself! (<u>Much</u> better prepared himself!) Had he waited just one more day—he could've, <u>then</u>, tailed Frank! <u>Tailed</u> him—directly to the actual <u>gathering</u>! Then, too, there was <u>this</u>: It would be extremely <u>doubtful</u>—that he could, <u>successfully</u>, shadow his target again! Not <u>two</u> days—in <u>succession</u>! <u>Certainly</u> not without arousing all manner of <u>suspicion</u>!

The hamburger—and a refill of his coffee mug—appeared before him. Although he'd seemed to not notice, he began noshing on the burger. His overworked brain was still trying to fight its way through the maze of what to do next!

<u>Supposing I follow him tomorrow</u>? <u>What if he walks into another apartment house</u>? <u>A different one</u>? <u>And there's no goddam Crimmins listed there either</u>? <u>What do I do then</u>? <u>Go get another fucking hamburger</u>?

He was, obviously, still without a plan of action!

<u>Go home</u>, <u>Stupid</u>! <u>You have no idea where ol' Frank is</u>, <u>in that stupid damn building</u>! <u>Or what he's doing</u>! <u>Or what the hell he's up to</u>! <u>It could be a damn whorehouse</u> . . . <u>for all you know</u>! <u>Probably not a whorehouse</u>, <u>though</u>! <u>Not if dear</u>, <u>sweet</u>, <u>lovable old Marcie was right on</u>! <u>Unless it's some kind of gay</u>

joint! Face it . . . you have no idea when he's coming out! Or if he's coming out! All this bullshit . . . and all over some stupid-assed overheard conversation! A silly-assed conversation . . . which, maybe, you completely misinterpreted! Nice going!

"Naw! I didn't misinterpret it," he said, aloud.

"What'd you say?" asked the waitress—a pretty, young blonde, who was in the process of refilling his mug.

"Huh? Oh, nothing. Just talking to myself."

"They say that's all right," she'd replied, with a warm smile, "as long as you don't start getting answers."

"I'm getting answers, all right," he'd muttered. "All over the stupid place! Only, they're wrong kind!"

"Welcome to the club. I wrote the book."

He smiled—for the first time in a long time. "Maybe," he mused, as the pretty lady had withdrawn, "I should just go on home. Get out of these wet clothes . . . and into a dry Martini."

As he reached for his wallet, he stopped abruptly, and began, quickly to stare—with great intensity—at his coffee cup!

Entering the restaurant, at that moment, were Frank, Clark, another white man, and three black women! They seated themselves in the booth furthest to the rear—completely out of Smigelski's earshot! Our hero ordered a refill—for his hastily-drained mug.

"Changed your mind, hah?" chided the waitress.

Smigelski answered, with an impatient nod—and did his best to concentrate on his coffee cup. He strained—to do his best, and listen in on the sextet's conversation! It was proving to be a vain effort!

He noted that the men's room was just behind that rear booth. The trying-to-act-as-a-real-detective "gumshoe" arose—and strode past the three couples! He entered the washroom!

Once inside, he pressed his ear—flush—against the rather-flimsy wooden wall, which separated him from the six. He was able to pick up mere snatches of dialogue—coming from the booth! Some wisps of their exchanges—were a little more articulate than others! Many, thankfully, were coming through fairly clearly!

He was able to hear Clark say, "The Premier is definitely gonna make it tomorrow!" The next voice— from further distance—was unintelligible!

"I still think the Premier's as power-hungry as the goddam imperialists," cut in a third voice—that of a woman.

For what seemed an eternity, another voice had droned on. And on and on. Smigelski was unable to pick up any of the overlong diatribe! He was unable to determine—whether it was even a man or a woman!

Then, he recognized Clark's voice once more. The young black man seemed to be speaking louder—than any of his companions: "Well," he said, "once we've got ourselves . . . got ourselves, on the map . . . it's gonna be a whole different ballgame! You'll understand! You'll see! See what I've been talking about," he proclaimed. Clark was the one— who appeared to be in charge! "When this whole thing evolves," he continued, "we're going to be the ones . . . who're gonna be in control! You just watch! Then, all the work we've done . . . it'll all be rewarded! But, shit! I'm thrilled! Just to be on the cuttin' edge!

<u>This</u> is going to be one of the greatest political <u>coups</u> . . . in the history of the whole fuckin' <u>world</u>! Just <u>think</u> about it! Your <u>kids</u>! And your <u>grandkids</u>! They'll <u>all</u> be reading . . . all <u>about</u> you! About <u>all</u> of us! <u>Reading</u> about <u>us</u>! <u>Forever</u> . . . in their goddam <u>history</u> books! In their fucking <u>history</u> books!"

There were two more voices—both garbled. One or the other had rambled on—for fully five minutes.

While Smigelski could not understand what they were saying, the tenor of the voice of one of the participants—a woman—seemed to be terribly <u>argumentative</u>! The other—a nasal-voiced male— tended to <u>rant</u>! <u>Endlessly</u>!

At that point, Smigelski decided it would behoove him to not remain in the men's room any longer. Making his way to the lone stall, he flushed the toilet. Then, he washed his hands—making sure to press the button sending the noisy hot-air hand dryer into action.

Walking back to his position at the counter, he was satisfied that the six in the rear booth had been—and remained—completely <u>oblivious</u> of his presence!

After another six or eight minutes, the three couples began to stir—making preparations to <u>leave</u>. Smigelski paid his tab, left the waitress a bigger tip than he could really afford, put on his coat—and sauntered out of the restaurant!

Outside, he walked a half-block west on Fifty-seventh, then stopped—ostensibly to look into a store window. He saw the six emerge from the coffee shop! They <u>dispersed</u>! In all <u>directions</u>!

Our hero hailed a cab—another "luxury" he could ill-afford—and headed straight for **Tarkenton** headquarters!

It was almost 9:00 PM—when Smigelski arrived. And was advised, very forcefully, that no one—but, no one—was permitted on the third floor, where Leland Nype's office was located! Nor would he be allowed onto the second floor—where Nype's minions were located! The only person who would deign to speak with him—was a burly lieutenant, from Captain Fox's division! And he was most uncooperative!

"Look, Buddy," the lieutenant had snarled, "ain't no way you're gonna be able to talk to Mister Nype! Not tonight! Not a chance in hell! He's gone home! And there ain't no one gonna give out his private number! And . . . when he ain't here . . . ain't no one in God's dear earth allowed on two! Let alone three! Not after six o'clock, anyways. Now, whyn't you be a good little boy? And just run your ass on home? And don't cause me no more grief! Okay?"

"Suit yourself. But, I just want you to write down . . . I want to see you put it in your log . . . write down that I was here! My name is Smigelski." Patiently, he spelled his name—three times—to the bemused officer. Then, he continued: "Just so that my ass is covered! I sure as hell don't want to be on the hook! Not when there's hundreds-of-thousands of dollars . . . worth of damages!" He sighed—for effect! "At least, I'm doing my duty! Trying to . . . making a good-faith effort to . . . report it."

He looked at the grizzled veteran's badge. "Now," he pressed, "you're Lieutenant who?"

"Capolla."

"Okay. That's with a 'C'? Or is it a 'K'?"

227

"'C'. Hey . . . what the hell is this?"

"I just wanted to be able to tell them . . . tell them, who it was! The person who wouldn't put me in touch with Leland! When lightning strikes the shithouse, I want to be in the clear! Completely in the clear! I'm just covering my ass, Lieutenant! Just covering my Polack ass!"

"Well, if it's so goddam important . . . then, tell me!"

"Can't! I work for Mister Nype! And this is so damn important . . . so damn important . . . that it's for his ears only! Critical! Critical as hell! Can't divulge any of this stuff! Not to anybody else! Now, if you want to take that responsibility . . . the awesome responsibility . . . for seeing that he's not disturbed, well then, that's fine, with me! At least it lets me off the frigging hook!"

"All right, goddam it," snapped Capolla. "Just wait a goddam minute!"

He produced a book from the top drawer of the battered old desk—and dialed a number from it. Smigelski shifted from one foot to the other, while the phone continuously rang—endlessly, it seemed—on the other end!

Finally, Capolla spoke into the instrument: "Yeah, Mister Nype. Look, Mister Nype . . . this is Lieutenant Capolla. Well, I hate to have to go ahead . . . and to bother you at home! But, I got one of your men here! An' he says . . . it's a matter of life and death! Somethin' about all kinds of millions of dollars! Millions of dollars . . . worth of damage! Or some goddam thing! His name? Long Polack name! Lessee, I got it down here! Right here . . . in my log. Uh . . . Smeegel . . . uh . . . uh huh. <u>Yeah</u>! Yeah, <u>that's</u> it! That's <u>him</u>! Okay, Mister Nype, I'll put him <u>on</u> to you!"

Capolla directed Smigelski to pick up one of the extension phones—located on a long, battle-scarred table across the room! The latter snatched the receiver from its cradle!

"Mister <u>Nype</u>? I wouldn't bother you at <u>home</u>! Unless it was a matter of <u>terrible</u> urgency!"

"I <u>know</u> that, Vick. What's up?"

"Well, I know this sounds <u>terribly</u> cloak-and-daggerish . . . but, I really and truly cannot <u>tell</u> you! Can't <u>say</u> any of this . . . over the <u>phone</u>! It's God-awful <u>important</u> . . . that I <u>see</u> you! Face to <u>face</u>! Meet you . . . <u>somewhere</u>! As soon as <u>possible</u>!"

"<u>That</u> urgent?"

"<u>Yes</u>, Sir. That <u>urgent</u>! I hope you know me well <u>enough</u>, by now, to know that I <u>really</u> wouldn't <u>tell</u> you that . . . if I was just whistling in <u>Dixie</u>! It's <u>really</u> . . . really and <u>truly</u> . . . something that can't <u>wait</u>, Mister Nype! It really <u>can't</u>! I've <u>got</u> to . . . got to <u>see</u> you!"

"Now you've got <u>me</u> worried! Worried as <u>hell</u>!"

"Technically, it's <u>nothing</u> to worry about! Not as far as **Tarkenton** . . . the company <u>itself</u> . . . is concerned! At least not right <u>now</u>! But. it's actually a helluva lot <u>bigger</u>! As far as <u>I</u> can figure it, anyway. Oh . . . <u>look</u>! <u>Look</u>, Mister Nype! It's all screwed <u>up</u>! <u>All</u> screwed up! The more I <u>talk</u> to you . . . without <u>telling</u> you anything . . . the <u>worse</u> it's going to <u>sound</u>! The more <u>scary</u> . . . it's going to <u>sound</u>!"

"It's scary enough <u>now</u>! <u>All</u> right. It'll take me about twenty . . . maybe twenty-five . . . minutes, to <u>get</u> there! I'm on my <u>way</u>! <u>Wait</u> there for me!"

"Fine! Thank you, Mister Nype! I'll be waiting . . . right here!"

Thirty-five minutes later, Leland Nype hurried into **Tarkenton** headquarters! Still impeccably groomed, he motioned Smigelski to a dark, open-door, elevator, adjacent to the reception room. Hurriedly, the two men entered the car. Nype turned a key in the control panel. The elevator sprang to life! An overhead light snapped on! The door closed! And the car began to move—rapidly—upward!

"I just hope this isn't some kind of wild goose chase, Vick. I want you to know that . . . if it'd been any other man than you . . . I'd have told the good lieutenant to tell you to go screw yourself! But, I do respect your priorities! And you do have a really troubling propensity for blundering . . . probably a poor choice of words . . . into the damndest things!"

The elevator reached the deserted third floor—and the door opened. The two men disembarked—and Nype groped for a light switch, next to the elevator door.

"Sheeeee," exclaimed Smigelski. "It's sure dark up here. I'd have imagined that you'd have some kind of dispatcher . . . or some kind of supervision officer . . . up here! Twenty-four hours a day!"

"He's on the second floor. Little cubicle . . . approximately above Captain Fox's office, down on the ground floor! They're all on two. No need . . . for anyone to be on this floor. Not at night."

Once the area was illuminated, the pair headed toward Nype's office.

As they made their way down the corridor, Smigelski muttered, "The thing that <u>bothers</u> me, Mister Nype, is that you may well think that this might very well <u>be</u> some kind of a wild goose chase! As soon as you've <u>heard</u> . . . what I've got to <u>say</u>! But, I think . . . I <u>hope</u>, anyway . . . that you'll <u>understand</u> my thinking! My <u>thinking</u> . . . in <u>doing</u> it this way! Doing it . . . hopefully . . . the <u>right</u> way!"

Once inside Nype's office, Smigelski seated himself in one of the posh chairs—across from the older man.

"<u>Now</u>, Vick," Nype began, his hands folded on the gleaming surface of the desk in front of him. "Suppose you <u>tell</u> me . . . what this whole emergency thing is all <u>about</u>!"

"Well, Mister Nype, I wish I <u>could</u> tell you . . . <u>exactly</u> . . . what it <u>is</u> all about! I wish to hell that I <u>knew</u> enough about the thing! Enough to tell you . . . everything there <u>is</u> to tell!" Nype's expression—one of total chagrin—was <u>not</u> encouraging. "Let me tell you," augmented the anxious Smigelski. "Tell what I <u>know</u>! Let me start . . . from the <u>beginning</u>!"

"That's always a good place to <u>start</u>," muttered Nype, with a discouraging amount of sarcasm. "<u>Always</u> a good place."

His employee recounted the entire series of events—from the overheard conversation in the men's room, to his chance encounter with the six at *The White Palace*.

"What am I supposed to <u>do</u>, Mister Nype?" he asked, at length. "I really <u>believe</u> . . . that I'm <u>on</u> to something! Something awfully damn <u>serious</u>! Frigging <u>critical</u>!"

Nype shook his head slowly. His face was expressionless. "I don't <u>know</u>, Vick," he finally answered, a multitude of pressure-packed minutes later. "I really <u>don't</u>! This is so far out of left <u>field</u> . . . that I don't really know quite <u>what</u> to think!"

The silence hung—heavily—in the office! Nype slouched back into his huge, luxurious, chair! A maneuver which surprised his employee! The older man looked almost <u>beaten</u>—as opposed to the vibrant, in-charge, executive; the image that he normally conveyed!

"You <u>could</u>, I suppose," he resumed darkly, "have gone to the <u>police</u>! Still <u>could</u> go to 'em . . . for that matter. Puts <u>me</u> in a bit of a bind, though! From a <u>corporate</u> standpoint! As you can well <u>imagine</u>, I'd like not to <u>publicize</u> . . . to the local <u>constabulary</u> . . . the fact that we're in the questionable business, of bugging <u>privies</u>!"

"Yeah," nodded Smigelski. "Plus, I don't know how much of this I'd be able to <u>prove</u>! Probably . . . now that I <u>consider</u> it . . . I couldn't <u>prove</u> a damn thing! Not a damn <u>thing</u>! Not at <u>this</u> point, anyway! I <u>guess</u> that that's one of the reasons . . . that I knew that I had to get with <u>you</u> on this! <u>That</u> . . . but, mostly, the fact that I know it'd be <u>embarrassing</u>! Embarrassing as <u>hell</u> . . . if it got out that we're bugging the johns, at **Ballinger's**! And . . . I would imagine . . . at numerous <u>other</u> places!"

"Yeah." muttered Nype—sighing deeply. "But, all that <u>pales</u> . . . pales <u>totally</u> . . . when you consider the prospect of a goddam <u>bomb</u> going off over there!

Your <u>informing</u> their flower-of-the-security-world . . . the sainted Mister <u>Hens</u> . . . is probably <u>sufficient</u>! Probably <u>sufficient</u> . . . to cover our <u>corporate</u> ass! But, obviously, that's <u>secondary</u>! Secondary, when you look at the potential for . . . God help us . . . a <u>huge</u> loss of <u>life</u>! Well, loss of . . . possibly . . . <u>everything</u>!" He grimaced. "Especially . . . God forbid . . . if the store should be really <u>crowded</u>!"

Smigelski found himself slouching too. "The potential for loss of life is <u>great</u>," he groused. "No matter <u>where</u> they decide to set the damn bomb . . . set it <u>off</u>! That's what <u>scares</u> the hell out of me, Mister Nype.! There doesn't seem to be a hell of a lot . . . that I can <u>do</u> about it! Not much <u>anyone</u> can do about it! I know that <u>I'm</u> spinning <u>my</u> wheels! Playing amateur detective . . . and all such shit as <u>that</u>! And doing it very <u>badly</u>!"

Nype reassumed his executive position—sitting straight up, his hands folded, once more, on the surface of the desk. "You've done <u>better</u> . . . a <u>helluva</u> lot better . . . than a good many <u>professionals</u> would've done, Vick," he responded, at length. "I don't <u>know</u>! Maybe the <u>answer</u> . . . is to go into a holding pattern! Wait and see what <u>develops</u>!"

Disgust contorted Smigelski's face. "What . . . what do you mean by <u>that</u>, Mister Nype?"

"Well, listen. You've covered a lot of <u>ground</u>, Vick! You truly <u>have</u>! And you've accomplished a hell of a <u>lot</u>! Even if <u>you</u> don't think so. But, you have to keep in mind . . . that his whole thing has come from a <u>wisp</u> of a conversation! A <u>conversation</u> that you <u>overheard</u>! In the <u>can</u>! Now, if they've got something really <u>big</u> brewing . . . and I'd bet the rent money that

233

they do . . . then, chances are that they'll have to hold a few more meetings, or whatever! I'd have to guess that they'd have a helluva lot more things to say, about it! If this thing was that crucial, by now! They wouldn't be gathering at the stupid *White Palace*! I'm guessing that there'd be many more things for these sweethearts to go over! Hopefully, some of it'll be . . . in the men's room . . . at **Ballinger's**!"

"I don't know, Mister Nype."

"None of us do! Listen, I'd have to imagine, that they have to communicate some kind of updates . . . from time to time! If we keep our eyes . . . and ears . . . open, maybe we'll be able to pick up on it! Maybe pick up on lots of it."

Smigelski's reply was sullen: "Maybe. And . . . then again . . . maybe not!"

"Vick, face it! If we were to try and act tonight . . . we'd be shooting in the damn dark! Scatter-shooting! And way in the dark! What would we do? What could we do? What do we actually know? Who would we talk to? Who could we talk to? What would we tell the authorities? How much hard . . . concrete . . . evidence do we have? Zilch!" His features softened— and he slumped back into his chair. "Listen, Vick," he resumed, "if you can come up with some brilliant plan . . . I'll be glad, to go along with it. But, as it stands . . ."

"Shit! I've been trying to hatch a brilliant plan all freaking night! And nothing's come! Not a smidgen!"

"That's exactly what I'm saying! If two brilliant minds . . . such as ours . . . can't come up with anything, why . . ."

"It's debatable . . . how brilliant I've been."

Nype laughed—bitterly. "Pretty damn brilliant, I'd have to say, Vick. Pretty damn brilliant! It's just that I can't see anything . . . not right now, anyway . . . that us brilliant-types can do! Not tonight, anyway! Except to spend a goddam sleepless night!"

"I'm sorry, now . . . that I bothered you at home, then."

Nype held up a hand. "No need to worry about that," he assured. "No need to worry at all! I'm actually glad you did what you did! You did what was best! What was right! You done good, Vick! I'd have done the same thing! Here . . . let me give you my home number!" Nype wrote the number on a memo pad, tore off the sheet—then, handed it to Smigelski. "Don't hesitate . . . don't ever hesitate . . . to call me at home, Vick," he soothed. "I mean that! You've got enough horse sense . . . to know when to call! No need to go through the hassle with those 'scholars' downstairs, when you need to get ahold of me."

Both men rose.

"Well, Mister Nype, I appreciate your coming down . . . and letting me bend your ear. Especially since it was a no-questions-asked deal, on your part."

As the two men walked back up the corridor, Nype stopped—halfway to the elevator—and turned to Smigelski. Placing his hand on his employee's arm, the older man said, "Look, Vick, I know how you are! How dedicated and all! I know that our not being able to do anything tonight is really grinding on you! Really eating at you! But, I want you to promise me . . . promise me, right here and now . . . that you won't do anything stupid! That you won't attempt something that's patently idiotic!"

"Stupid? Idiotic"

"Yeah! Stupid! Idiotic! You know damn well . . . what I'm talking about! Under no circumstances do I want you to follow these clowns! Or attempt to infiltrate 'em! Or try to put the kibosh on 'em! I don't want you to even think . . . of attempting to put the kibosh on 'em! Not in any way! These people are not . . . repeat, are not . . . like the dipshits at Shea! Or the assholes that jumped you . . . near your home! Apparently, these bastards have some kind of expertise! Damnable expertise . . . probably . . . in the fine art of building bombs! And that's out of your league, Vick! It's most certainly out of mine! Please, Vick! Please! Promise me, that you won't go ahead . . . and do something stupid!"

Smigelski sighed heavily. Twice "Okay. All right, Mister Nype," he finally answered, sighing heavily, once more. "Okay. I promise . . . that won't do anything stupid! I fare-thee-well promise!"

Now, how the hell am I gonna know what's stupid . . . and what's not?

ELEVEN

THE FOLLOWING DAY, SMIGELSKI'S CONDITION could best be described as distraught.

He was almost praying for a spate of overheard <u>thievery</u> interplay! <u>Anything</u>—to fill up the space! <u>Anything</u> to keep his mind from being continually <u>consumed</u>—by the happenings of the previous afternoon, and evening.

Richard Gladwynne had observed, that morning: "<u>You</u> look like a sack-full of assholes"!

And, in our hero's mind, that—most likely—had been an <u>accurate</u> description! He'd slept precious <u>little</u>, the night before! A goodly portion of his God-awful sleeplessness—had been caused by his not advising June Bodner, of the tenuous Clark/Frank situation! Deliberately not speaking to her—about the increasingly-<u>tense</u> situation! He'd seen no reason to "<u>bother</u>" his fiancée with his disturbing discovery! And what it might <u>lead</u> to! She'd <u>remained</u> unhappy enough, at the prospect of his being party to a <u>disgusting</u>—and, she'd believed (not without good reason), a totally illegal—operation!

At 3:15PM, that afternoon, Smigelski and Gladwynne both observed an illegal transaction, in the men's room. Gladwynne had left the claustrophobic room—to report the incident to Donald Hens. Smigelski remained behind—to maintain observation of the lavatory.

At the exact moment that Gladwynne <u>returned</u> to the monitoring room, Smigelski burst up—and out of his chair! <u>Frank Crimmins</u> had just walked into the men's room!

"That's <u>him</u>!" Smigelski shouted. "That's <u>him</u>! That's the <u>Frank</u>! The one I <u>told</u> you about . . . <u>yesterday</u>!"

Gladwynne nodded! "Then," he observed, "<u>that</u> must be . . . <u>what's</u> his name? <u>Clark</u>?"

As he'd spoken, the black man had walked into the restroom.

Immediately, the "spied-upon" pair began to speak. Frank was in an obviously nervous—highly agitated—state! He gestured graphically—flailing his arms in every direction! He moved his lips! Yet, no sound came out!

Smigelski reached for the volume control—an unnecessary exercise. Clark almost <u>deafened</u> the two observers—as he spoke!

"Simmer <u>down</u>, Frank," advised the black man, the epitome of rock-calmness.

"I . . . I don't <u>know</u>, Clark!" Frank had gotten his voice back. Albeit just barely. "I fucking . . . <u>really</u> don't know! I don't think . . . I probably <u>shouldn't</u> . . . I <u>never</u> should've let myself get <u>talked</u> into . . . talked <u>into</u> . . . into this fucking <u>thing</u>! <u>Christ</u>, Clark! You <u>can't</u> . . ."

"Oh, cut the bullshit, Frank! You are in it! Ass deep! Now, get hold of yourself! You're in it! Up to your armpits! So, spare me the crap! Besides, I don't know what the hell you're so scared of! Look . . . it's all going to go off! Go off . . . like a goddam charm! Hell, it's not everyone . . . not everyone . . . who gets a chance, to make history! Literally make absolute fucking history! Listen, Frank! If you weren't with us . . . you wouldn't have been there last night! You're all right! Just getting a little bit . . . a tad bit of stage fright! That's all! A few butterflies! That's fucking all!" He added a mirthless laugh. "You'll be fine," he continued. "You just watch! Just fine!"

"Look, Clark! Listen! Clark . . . the only reason I was there, last night, was because . . . because, well . . . because I wanted to see what was going on! See what was actually happening! I didn't realize . . . didn't have any idea, none whatever . . . what a big deal this was gonna be! What a big fucking deal! Jesus Christ, Clark! We'll never be able to pull this thing off! Not ever! Not in a million fucking years!"

"Oh, don't be so pessimistic, Frank! Of course we will! I really thought that last night's get-together was going to last a little longer . . . than it did. Do a little socializing, maybe! If you get my drift! Those three broads were . . . they were really fine! Really fine!"

"Broads . . . schmauds! I don't know how you can stay so fucking calm! I didn't sleep at all last night! Not a goddam wink!"

"That makes two of us," muttered Smigelski, under his breath.

"Aw c'mon, Frank," encouraged Clark. "Like I said . . . all you got is a little case of the butterflies.

Now, relax! Just relax! And don't you worry! We're gonna pull it off! Pull it off . . . big time!"

"Clark!" Frank seemed to be unraveling even further. "Clark . . . do you realize? Realize what we're talking about? I mean . . . this isn't like some little shit-assed scene! Not like what the guys on television talk about! What they call 'civil disobedience'! This is fucking real, Man! Fucking real!"

"Of course it's real!" Clark's words were clipped! Close-cropped! A frightening degree of coldness had—suddenly—crash-landed into his voice. "Of course it's real," he repeated. "What'd you think? That we're all running around . . . in some kind of freaking fantasyland, or something? Look, Frank! We all have our job to do! Just one single job! A simple one, when you look at it! All we have to do . . . is our one single job! And it'll work! It's gonna work! It has to work! Can't fucking miss!"

Frank had held his breath—during Clark's diatribe! Now he exhaled! With a whoosh! "Clark!" His voice was barely a hoarse whisper. Both Smigelski and Gladwynne had to strain to hear what the obviously-frightened man was saying! "Clark . . . listen! I had no idea! No idea, that there were gonna be so many . . . so damn many . . . all of those bombs! So many bombs! Clark! Scares the shit out of me! All . . . all those . . . those goddam bombs!"

Clark's voice, in his reply, seemed to take on a renewed degree of indulgence: "This is the only way! It's gonna work, Frank! This is the only way, though! Hell, a bomb goes off at **Chase Manhattan** . . . or at one of the embassies, or at the U.N. . . . and no one pays any attention! Nothing! No one hardly even

notices, these days! That's the <u>problem</u>! Don't you
<u>see</u>? That's our big <u>problem</u>, nowadays! <u>None</u> of those
other groups were ever <u>united</u>! <u>None</u> of 'em! <u>We</u> are!"

"How 'bout . . . how 'bout The <u>Weathermen</u>?"

"Small <u>potatoes</u>! We're talking <u>much</u> more
<u>manpower</u>, here! Much more <u>firepower</u>! <u>Much</u> more!
A shitload . . . more than the <u>Weather Underground</u>!
More than they ever <u>dreamed</u> of! Not even <u>close</u>!
When eight or ten <u>bombs</u> go off <u>here</u> and in <u>Chicago</u>
and in <u>L.A</u>. . . . plus six or eight in <u>Washington</u> . . . as
well as all the ones that I don't even <u>know</u> about, <u>then</u>
they gotta sit <u>up</u>! Sit <u>up</u> . . . and take fucking <u>notice</u>!
The immoral establishment's <u>got</u> to see that we're for
<u>real</u>! They don't have any <u>alternative</u>! No <u>choice</u>! It's
the old bullshit about having to hit the <u>mule</u>! Hit the
mule . . . over the <u>head</u>! With the <u>two</u>-by-four! Only
way to get his <u>attention</u>!"

"This is more than <u>that</u>, Clark! We're talking, here,
of more than a fucking <u>mule</u> . . . and a goddam <u>two</u>-
by-four! A <u>lot</u> more! <u>Eons</u> more! <u>Bombs</u>! We're talking
fucking <u>bombs</u>!"

"Naw! Same damn <u>thing</u>! Same <u>theory</u>! <u>That's</u>
why there has to be so <u>many</u>! A whole <u>shitload</u>! In
each <u>city</u>! And all going off . . . at the same <u>time</u>!
Only way we can <u>weaken</u> the system! Hopefully,
<u>destroy</u> the fucking system! Don't you <u>see</u>? Don't you
<u>understand</u>? We've <u>got</u> to bring down the <u>system</u>,
Frank! The whole fucking <u>system</u>! Blow the <u>hell</u> out
of it! Otherwise, we don't have a snowball's chance
in <u>hell</u>! No <u>chance</u> . . . of winning! The whole goddam
<u>revolution</u> . . . it'd go right down the old <u>crapper</u>!"

"Yeah. But <u>listen</u>! <u>Listen</u>, Clark! <u>Listen</u>! All those
<u>people</u>! All those <u>people</u>! Getting fucking <u>killed</u>! All

those people! I'm almost sick to my stomach, Clark! Sick to my stomach . . . at the thought of all those people! So many! Being . . ."

Clark put his hand on the distraught man's shoulder. "Frank," he began—his voice dripping with sadness, "listen to me! Listen, they couldn't be sacrificed . . . could not be sacrificed . . . for a better cause!" The sympathetic tone then vanished! As suddenly as it had arrived. He went on. "There's just no other way . . . to do it, Frank! Look! You can't stop it! Neither can I! The important thing is that . . . the pigs . . . they can't either! They don't have a chance . . . not one chance, in hell, to stop it! Not one shittin' chance! This time the fucking fascists . . . have fucking well had it!"

Frank's saucer-like eyes—had progressed from fright to out-and-out horror! "You . . . you," he stammered, "you sound just like . . . just like one of those goddam pamphlets, Clark! Just like one of those scary-assed pamphlets!"

"Yeah? Well, that's not a bad way for anyone . . . for everyone . . . to be," replied Clark, laughing nervously. "It's not a question of sounding like some damn pamphlet! The only way . . . the only way . . . we're going to make people aware, of what we're trying to do . . . what we've got to do . . . happens to be something like this! Has to be something like this! Something . . . that's fucking earth-shaking! There's . . . believe me . . . there's no other way."

"I dunno, Clark. What about the kidnapping? Them snatching Peggy Devonshire?"

"Well, that . . . that was actually a fuck-up! They weren't supposed to have pulled that snatch! Not till we were <u>all</u> ready! Ready to make our <u>move</u>! It was all <u>supposed</u> to have been <u>coordinated</u>! Coordinated . . . with our brothers and sisters <u>here</u>! And in <u>Chicago</u> . . . and in <u>Washington</u>. I don't know <u>why</u> they couldn't keep their peckers, in their <u>pants</u>! You see what I'm <u>saying</u>, Frank?"

"I dunno, Clark," came the muffled reply. "I . . . just really don't fucking <u>know</u>!"

"<u>Yes</u> you do! We've gone all <u>over</u> this . . . <u>all</u> of this . . . before! Look, Frank! Kidnapping a big-deal department store <u>heiress</u> . . . well, it <u>did</u> make news! But, it didn't do a damn <u>thing</u> . . . to bring down the goddam <u>system</u>! Sure, people were <u>worried</u> about her . . . for <u>awhile</u>! And it made the evening <u>news</u> . . . for a fairly-long time! But . . . don't you <u>see</u>? Before long, the novelty wore <u>off</u>! The novelty <u>always</u> wears off! <u>Always</u>! Just a matter of <u>time</u>! So, what the hell <u>good</u> . . . did snatching the Devonshire bitch <u>do</u>?"

"Well, they . . ."

"I'll <u>tell</u> you what good it did: <u>Zero</u>! <u>Zip</u>! <u>Zilch</u>! <u>That's</u> why we gotta <u>do</u> this thing! And do it <u>right</u>! Like the premier <u>says</u> . . . this whole thing is a magnificent <u>crusade</u>! <u>Magnificent</u>! And it's gonna <u>take</u> something like this! Something, <u>exactly</u> like <u>this</u> . . . to make the American people <u>realize</u>! Realize just how <u>rotten</u> things are! How fucked <u>up</u> everything <u>is</u>! How rotten the <u>system</u> is! How <u>repressive</u> it is! And it's getting more and more <u>rotten</u> . . . by the <u>day</u>!"

"See? You're back to sounding like a goddam <u>pamphlet</u> again! '<u>Repressive</u>'! That's <u>pamphlet</u>-talk!"

"<u>Listen</u> to me, Frank! <u>You</u> listen to <u>me</u>! This thing . . . this <u>mission</u> . . . is even <u>more</u> important! The <u>people</u> . . . they're gonna <u>realize</u>, that these are forces of good! Forces of good! And forces of love! And forces of hope! That these forces . . . us . . . that we're all out here! Out here . . . doing something about it! Doing something to right all these goddam wrongs! It's wonderful! Wonderful, Frank! Just like the premier says! The whole thing is fucking magnificent!"

"I know, Clark," moped Frank. "I . . . I agree. I agree with what you're trying to do. With what we're trying to do. But, Christ . . ."

Clark was totally wound up by then: "Well, then you've got to be willing to do something about it! About things! Make a goddam contribution! Show some balls!

"It's not a question of . . . of whether I'm showing balls or not."

"Yes it is! It fucking is! Where the hell do you think this country would've been . . . two hundred years ago . . . if it weren't for a bunch of really brave revolutionists? Why, we'd still be British subjects! Paying outrageous taxes! Without any kind of representation! And now? We've come full circle! That's the situation . . . today!"

"I don't know as I'd say 'full circle'. I mean, we've gone a . . ."

"Dammit! Don't you see? We have! We've got the whole same fucking thing . . . again! Same damn thing! Right here! Right now! It's the same goddam thing! You and me . . . we're paying some kind of enormous taxes! And who the hell represents us? No one! Not a fucking soul! That's who! The goddam politicians . . . all they're interested in, is one thing! In feathering their own crooked . . . their corrupt . . .

nests! And the big companies? Like **Ballinger's**? They just keep ripping us off! The government? They throw the rebels . . . and the revolutionaries . . . throw 'em all in jail! And they throw away the goddam key!"

"Yeah, but you'd think that . . ."

Clark was not to be sidetracked! "The system we've got now?" he seethed. "It shit-cans the elderly! It beats its children! It drinks itself to death! It's a terrible culture, Frank! A terrible culture! It's going to take dedicated people, Frank! Dedicated! People like you and me . . . and our brothers and sisters! Gonna take all of us . . . to overthrow what's become an oppressive fucking government!"

"That's what I'm saying, Clark! Overthrowing the government? People get sentenced to death . . . for shit like that!"

"That's why it takes brave revolutionaries! Frank, listen! The only way we're gonna be able to accomplish our goal . . . is out-and-out war! Fucking war! That's why we're fighting, Frank! And that's what we're fighting! We're fighting a goddam war! You know what they say, Frank. War is hell!"

"Yeah, but . . ."

"But, hell! Frank, we've simply got to know our enemy! And we've got to identify our enemy! Kill our enemy! Not only that . . . but, we've got to identify ourselves!

"Identify ourselves? What the hell does that mean? I've got no real need . . . to get myself executed!"

"Just what I said! Identify ourselves . . . regardless of the damn consequences! That's where the bravery . . . the dedication . . . comes in! Identify ourselves . . . to the public! Identify ourselves . . . to the <u>people</u>! It's the <u>people</u>, Frank! <u>They're</u> the ones who're . . . when all is said and <u>done</u> . . . <u>they're</u> the ones, gonna make this thing <u>work</u>! We've just got to let 'em <u>know</u>! Let 'em <u>know</u>, that they're more than <u>welcome</u>! <u>Welcome</u> . . . to <u>join</u> us! We gotta <u>welcome</u> 'em! <u>Welcome</u> 'em . . . to take up <u>arms</u>!"

"Take up <u>arms</u>? Clark, this is <u>really</u> beginning to . . . ! Even the <u>premier</u>, last night, didn't say <u>anything</u> about . . ."

"How else we gonna <u>do</u> it, Frank? We gotta <u>encourage</u> 'em . . . to club the <u>establishment</u>! <u>Club</u> the establishment . . . into out-and-out fucking <u>surrender</u>! It's a <u>wonderful</u> cause, Frank! <u>Magnificent</u>! Just like the premier <u>says</u>! Let me <u>tell</u> you! I'm proud to be just a simple <u>part</u> of it! <u>You</u> should be too! Proud as <u>hell</u>!"

Watching the monitor, Smigelski's face had—long since—become beet-red! He was muttering obscenities, under his breath—as the disturbing conversation, in the men's room, had continued! He couldn't fathom how Gladwynne—also listening to the diatribe—could remain so seemingly unconcerned!

In the lavatory, Frank was shaking his head slowly. "I really don't <u>know</u>, Clark," he muttered. "I don't <u>know</u>. I <u>guess</u> you can . . . well, you <u>can</u> . . . I guess you can deal me <u>in</u>. When I'm with <u>you</u> . . . with you, or any of the <u>other</u> people . . . I get myself all hyped <u>up</u>! The adrenaline gets to . . . you know . . . really <u>flowing</u>! I feel . . . feel really <u>good</u> about it! But, when I'm by <u>myself</u>, Clark . . . when I'm all by <u>myself</u> . . . I get <u>scared</u>! <u>Really</u> scared! Scared as <u>hell</u>!'

Frank's declaration—tepid as it was—seemed to be the tension-breaker!

"Don't <u>worry</u> about it," beamed Clark. "Listen. We're <u>all</u> scared! But, anything <u>worthwhile</u> . . . anything at <u>all</u> . . . well, it involves <u>risk</u>! A <u>turtle</u> doesn't get anywhere . . . unless he sticks his <u>neck</u> out. Frank, this is such a <u>magnificent</u> cause! <u>Magnificent</u>! And it's <u>gonna</u> work! It'll work <u>wonders</u>! Almost like a magic <u>cure</u>! A <u>magic</u> cure . . . for what <u>ails</u> the country! The whole . . . the entire . . . <u>country</u>! <u>You'll</u> see! You <u>did</u> get all the stuff, didn't you?"

"Yeah. Almost. Just <u>about</u>. I'll have <u>everything</u> . . . by <u>tonight</u>!"

The euphoric tone left Clark's voice! Replaced by the cold, calculating, tightly-clipped, dimension that had come into play early in the conversation: "Be goddam <u>sure</u> . . . that you <u>do</u>," he admonished, sardonically. "Be <u>damn</u> sure you <u>do</u>!"

"I will, Clark. I will." Frank's tone sounded almost defeated.

"Did you get the <u>paint</u>?" asked Clark—his tone much less icy.

"Yeah, responded his partner—nodding nervously. "Yeah. Getting the cans <u>out</u> of the store . . . <u>that</u> was no big deal! Even with that <u>number</u> of cans! No <u>problem</u>! I just <u>bought</u> them! <u>No</u> problem! Getting it all back <u>in</u>, though . . . getting <u>all</u> of it back in, with all the <u>bombs</u> inside . . . <u>that's</u> gonna be the rub! I mean, what reason could I possibly <u>have</u> . . . for bringing paint back <u>in</u> to the store? Eight <u>gallons</u> . . . of the shit?"

"<u>C'mon</u>, Frank! You're just <u>borrowing</u> trouble! Just tell 'em it's the wrong fuckin' <u>color</u>! Tell 'em your girlfriend didn't <u>like</u> it!" Clark snickered, at the irony of Frank speaking of a girlfriend. "Tell 'em it's a shade or two off, or something," he advised. "Just tell 'em it's the wrong damn color! Be firm!"

Frank's voice remained filled with defeat: "Okay," he grumped, with a heavy sigh. "Let me get back to work . . . before Marcie comes up here and drags my ass back down to the floor. The meeting . . . it's the same place as last night, is it?"

"Right," nodded Clark, emphatically. "Right! Seven o'clock! The premier's gonna be there! Don't be late, now! Whatever you do, Pal . . . don't be fucking late! And be damn sure . . . be fucking sure . . . that you've got everything! Everything!"

Frank turned and left the lavatory. Thirty seconds later, Clark followed suit.

In the observation post, Smigelski banged his fist on the desk—causing the monitor to jump!

"There," he seethed. "Now, for Christ's sakes, do you believe me? Can you see how serious this is?"

"I believed you yesterday, Ski. It's just that I thought you might be misinterpreting . . . what they were talking about. Obviously, you weren't! What're you gonna do now?"

"I'll probably wind up with cleat marks all over my ass again . . . but, I'm gonna go down and talk to shit-assed Hens! Again! This time . . . well, he's got to listen! This time I can tell him something! Tell him . . . something constructive! Tell him something . . . about his beloved store! Like they're gonna blow the fucking thing up! Blow it out . . . from under his glorious ass!"

Smigelski stormed down the corridor—to the security chief's office! He demanded to see Donald Hens! Sweeping past the more-than-reluctant receptionist, he burst into Hens' inner office! In two strides, he was at the latter's desk!

"That biggie I told you about yesterday? Do you remember that? Well, it's bigger than you think," he barked. "Bigger than I ever thought! Bigger than . . ."

"What biggie," snarled Hens, looking up cynically. "What the hell are you talking about? What fucking biggie are you yapping about? Are you still bull-shittin' . . . about that silly-assed, cockamamie thing with the stupid-assed bombs and shit? Listen, Asshole! You been watchin' too many boys! Too many boys . . . makin' pee-pee! It's affected your piss-poor excuse for a mind!"

"Yeah? Well, think again, Hens! These guys are gonna blow your precious, goddam store! Blow it right off the fuckin' map! Maybe you with it! One could hope!" Then, in a half-whisper, he added, "We should all be so lucky!"

Hens sloshed his soggy cigar to the front of his mouth. "Bullshit," he responded, the disgusting butt almost becoming a poisonous, pollution-producing, projectile.

"Don't give me any of your 'bullshit', Hens! I heard it! With my own dumb Polack ears! What's more, Dick Gladwynne heard it! I'm telling you! Telling you that these piss-ants are gonna blow your worthless ass . . . blow it right out of that goddam overstuffed chair! How does a couple bombs . . . maybe five or six bombs, maybe <u>eight</u> or ten bombs . . . every <u>one</u> of 'em planted in cans of your store's glorious <u>paint</u>? How does <u>that</u> grab you?"

"What the fuck are you <u>talkin'</u> about?"

A look of almost-helpless frustration encompassed Smigelski's face—as Hens removed what was left of his cigar and examined it.

"What I'm talking about," hissed his "guest", "is that there are two asshole <u>employees</u>! Employees . . . of <u>yours</u>! And they're fixing to blow <u>up</u> your goddam <u>store</u>! Is <u>that</u> fucking <u>plain</u> enough for you? Or is it <u>me</u> . . . with some kind of goddam impediment of <u>speech</u>? <u>Boom</u>! Do you <u>dig</u>? <u>Boom</u>! They're gonna put <u>bombs</u> . . . in a few gallons of your precious store's <u>paint</u>! And the bombs are going to <u>explode</u>! <u>Boom</u>! <u>Boom</u>! They're gonna go <u>off</u>! Fucking <u>explode</u>! <u>Bombs</u>, Asshole! I'm talking about <u>bombs</u>! <u>Exploding</u>! All <u>over</u> the goddam place! That's not <u>good</u> . . . in case you didn't know! Not <u>cool</u>! Your precious, frigging, <u>store</u>! <u>Think</u> about it! It's going to be just a pile of <u>rubble</u>! <u>That's</u> what I'm talking about! What <u>part</u> . . . of your dim-assed, Mortimer Snerd, <u>mind</u> can't fucking <u>understand</u> that?"

"<u>Bombs</u>? In <u>cans</u>? <u>Paint</u> cans?" Hens was totally bemused!

Smigelski uncorked a massive sigh—and nodded. "Well," he growled. "I'm <u>finally</u> getting <u>through</u> to you," he hissed. "You catch on <u>quick</u>! "<u>Yes</u>! Bombs! In fucking <u>paint</u> cans! There's this <u>white</u> guy . . . Frank <u>Crimmins</u>! He works in <u>Carpeting</u>! And this <u>black</u> guy . . . <u>Clark</u> something-or-other. I <u>think</u> he works in <u>Personnel</u>! Not <u>sure</u> of that! They . . . both of 'em . . . belong to some kind of, <u>shit</u>-for-brains, anti-<u>government</u>, outfit! Some kind of <u>cult</u> . . . or something! What-ever-in-hell you want to <u>call</u> it! They're gonna blow stuff <u>up</u>! Blow up <u>lots</u> of things! Including . . . are you <u>ready</u> for this? . . . this blessed <u>store</u>! Maybe <u>other</u> **Ballinger's** stores! Maybe a whole <u>lot</u> of other **Ballinger's** stores . . . although I didn't hear 'em <u>mention</u> another store! I guess they already <u>got</u> the paint cans! Got 'em . . . out of <u>here</u>! Now, they're gonna bring 'em all <u>back</u>! <u>Frank</u> is! Complain that something's <u>wrong</u> with the stuff! Wrong <u>shade</u> . . . or <u>some</u> damn thing!"

"How can they put a fucking bomb in a goddam can of <u>paint</u>? It'd get all <u>wet</u>! It wouldn't <u>explode</u>!"

"How the hell do <u>I</u> know? Plastic <u>bombs</u>, maybe? Who <u>knows</u>? <u>I'm</u> no bomb expert! But, it <u>sounds</u> like <u>they've</u> got a whole <u>shitload</u> of experts! A whole <u>bunch</u> of 'em! On <u>their</u> side!"

"Yeah? When they gonna do <u>that</u>?"

"I don't <u>know</u>, dammit! But, it's gonna be <u>soon</u>! Damn <u>soon</u>! Gladwynne'll back me <u>up</u> on this! My <u>feeling</u> . . . is that they're gonna be putting bombs together! Like <u>tonight</u>! Manufacturing fucking <u>bombs</u>! <u>Tonight</u>! Well, <u>probably</u> tonight! Hell . . . I don't really <u>know</u>! <u>Listen</u>, Hens! <u>Listen</u> to me . . . for a goddam change! We don't have any <u>time</u>! Of <u>that</u>, I'm <u>certain</u>! No time to <u>waste</u>! They're <u>talking</u> . . . seriously <u>talking</u> . . . about blowing up a whole <u>lot</u> of things! A whole <u>shitload</u> of things! Not only <u>here</u>! Not only in New <u>York</u>! But, in <u>Chicago</u>! And Los <u>Angeles</u>! <u>Washington</u>! God only <u>knows</u> where else!"

"<u>C'mon</u>, fa Christ sakes! How fuckin' <u>gullible</u> do you think I <u>am</u>?"

"<u>Look</u>! <u>Don't</u> believe <u>me</u> . . . if you don't <u>want</u> to! Why don't you haul your lovable ass on down to our lovely Taj Mahal <u>outpost</u>? Ask <u>Gladwynne</u>? Ask him what <u>he</u> saw? Ask him what <u>he</u> heard?"

Hens jammed his cigar stub back in his mouth—and began patting, furiously, at piles of the papers on his desk. He was in search of a book of matches.

"How do I <u>know</u> that you're both . . . the <u>both</u> of you . . . how do I know you're not fuckin' puttin' me <u>on</u>?" he snarled—as he filched a beaten-up pack of matches from underneath the fourth or fifth stack of ruins. "How do <u>I</u> know . . . that you're not tryin' to get me to put my <u>foot</u> into something? I'm <u>not</u> universally <u>loved</u>, around here, y'know."

Smigelski bunched his hands into fists, placed them on Hens' desktop—and leaned forward! "If you just keep on <u>sitting</u> there," he snarled, "with that goddam <u>cigar</u> in your lovely face, you won't have to fucking <u>worry</u> about it! You won't have to fucking worry about <u>anything</u>! They'll be scraping you <u>up</u> . . . scraping <u>up</u> your miserable ass . . . from all over the <u>neighborhood</u>! And a few <u>adjacent</u> ones!"

Hens pulled himself to his feet. It seemed almost an overwhelming effort. "Okay," he groused. "Let's go see Gladwynne. But, goddam it . . . if you guys are <u>shittin'</u> me, it'll be the last time you <u>ever</u> shit anyone! Either fuckin' <u>one</u> of you! You hear what I'm <u>sayin'</u>? You hear what I'm fucking <u>tellin'</u> you?"

"Yeah. I <u>hear</u> you! Save your bad <u>breath</u>! Let's <u>go</u>!"

The two men filed out of Hens' office—heading back up the hallway to the observation post. When Hens pushed the door open, they found Gladwynne engrossed in the monitor.

"What the fuck's goin' <u>on</u>?" shouted the director of security.

"Just what he <u>told</u> you! <u>That's</u> what's going on," answered Gladwynne. "There's two <u>guys</u> . . . who were in there! They were talking about blowing <u>up</u> the joint!"

"Not only <u>talking</u> about it," added Smigelski. "They were jolly well making <u>plans</u> . . . to <u>do</u> it!"

Gladwynne nodded his agreement.

"<u>Sheeeeee-iiiiiit</u>!" replied Hens, in a mighty exhale. "Are you two fuckin' <u>sure</u>?"

Gladwynne nodded. "We're fucking <u>sure</u>," he affirmed. "Ski and I . . . we listened to the whole <u>thing</u>! They're going to a meeting <u>somewhere</u>! <u>Tonight</u>! And . . . judging by what we both <u>heard</u> . . . it <u>sounds</u> as though they're gonna be manufacturing frigging <u>bombs</u>! I don't know how much Ski's <u>told</u> you . . . but, they were talking about bringing <u>bombs</u> in here! Right into the <u>store</u>! In cans of <u>paint</u>!"

Hens removed the cigar from his mouth—and scratched the back of his head. "I'll be a sonofabitch," he muttered.

"That may very well <u>be</u>," snapped Smigelski. "The <u>important</u> thing is . . . what're we gonna <u>do</u> about it? What the hell are <u>you</u> gonna <u>do</u> about it?"

Hens jammed his cigar back into his mouth—and shook his head, spraying tobacco juice, in a fine mist. "<u>Christ</u>," he muttered. "I <u>dunno</u>! I ain't never <u>had</u> anything like . . . <u>nothin'</u> like . . . like <u>this</u>, ever <u>happen</u> before. Jesus <u>Christ</u>! I <u>guess</u> we could maybe watch 'em! Keep a <u>eye</u> on 'em, y'know! And, when they bring the fucking paint <u>in</u> . . . why, we could <u>nail</u> their asses! Nail their asses <u>then</u>!"

"You don't <u>understand</u>, Mister Hens," responded Gladwynne, with a sigh. "You just don't <u>understand</u>! What you're proposing . . . well, it may solve <u>your</u> problem! Your problem . . . <u>here</u>! But, how about the stores in <u>Manhattan</u>? Or <u>Westchester</u>? <u>Brooklyn</u>? How 'bout the ones over in <u>Jersey</u>? I'd have to <u>think</u> that . . . if they're gonna blow up this <u>store</u> . . . that they're gonna blow up one or two <u>others</u>! Maybe a whole <u>shithouse</u> . . . of other ones! <u>Probably</u> a whole shitload of other ones! We don't know how <u>many</u>, of those lovable little dandies . . . how many might work at <u>other</u> **Ballinger's** stores! Not even a <u>glimmering</u> . . . of a goddam <u>clue</u>! There could <u>be</u> these assholes . . . these bastards . . . working in every **Ballinger's** <u>store</u>! <u>All</u> of 'em, maybe! They could, possibly, be planning . . . to blow <u>all</u> of 'em! Blow 'em all . . . off the frigging <u>map</u>!"

"We don't even <u>know</u> how many of them . . . how many of these dipshits . . . there <u>are</u>," augmented Smigelski. "No <u>idea</u>! Could be ten or <u>twelve</u>! Could be sixteen <u>thousand</u>! Who the hell <u>knows</u>?"

Hens was totally befuddled! He snatched his dead cigar from his nicotine-stained lips—and flipped it into the wastebasket, narrowly missing Gladwynne's leg. He rubbed his chin. The sound of fingers scraping against an abundance of stubble seemed to fill the little room.

"I . . . I <u>dunno</u>," he said, at length. "I don't fuckin' <u>know</u>!"

As Smigelski was about to reply, he was stopped in his tracks—by Hens! The latter had launched—into screaming out, a string of unprintable oaths!

"Fuck it!" the director added, at a lower decibel level. "Fuck it! That ain't my fuckin' responsibility! I'm the director of security at **Ballinger's**! **Ballinger's** . . . in Rego fucking Park! Period! Fucking paragraph! That's all! That's as far as my responsibility goes! If I nail these two assholes . . . then, I'll be doin' my fuckin' job! Anything else? It ain't my department! Ain't my responsibility!" (Had the saying, "It's above my pay grade" been in vogue, in the seventies, rest assured, that Hens would've delivered himself of that "classic".)

"I don't believe this," Smigelski shouted. "I don't fucking believe it! Don't you realize . . . you horse's ass . . . that they're not going to set off bombs, just around here? These schmucks are talking about other places! A lot of other places! Many other places! Setting off fucking bombs! In lots of other places! Dozens of places! Maybe hundreds of places! All over the country!"

Hens reached for a fresh cigar—from his shirt pocket. As he unwrapped it, he snarled, "I dunno! Stop hassling me, you guys! How the Christ am I supposed to know what to do? Especially with you guys . . . all over my fuckin' back? Maybe we just ought to turn the whole fuckin' thing over! Turn it over . . . to the cops! To the police!"

"Oh, good thinking," said Gladwynne—his voice dripping with sarcasm.

"Yeah, muttered Hens—totally unaware of the put-down. "But, then? How the hell am I gonna tell the cops? Tell 'em how I ever got wind of this?" He appeared to be talking to himself—more than to Gladwynne or Smigelski. "I can't fucking tell 'em! Can't tell 'em . . . that I've got the shithouses bugged!"

"Why not?" asked Smigelski—batting his eyes, his voice even more sarcastic than Gladwynne's had been. "Doesn't everyone? Doesn't everyone bug the ol' shithouses?"

"Some places don't." Hens was totally oblivious of Smigelski's cynicism. "Jesus," he mumbled. "It's a problem all right."

Smigelski turned serious once more: "Not really," he fumed. "Listen Hens! Despite what your pea-brain is telling you . . . you really don't have a choice! If you don't call the police, I fucking will! Can your gnat's brain fathom that? Either you call 'em . . . or I call 'em! One way or another! Either way . . . the law gets called! I don't even know . . . why we're wasting all this time! Here we are! Just chatting about it! It may be a problem for you, Hens, old boy! But it's not . . . for me! If these shitheads go through with this . . . and, let me tell you, they're a committed bunch of assholes . . . there are gonna be one hell of a lot of people! People who're gonna wind up fucking dead! Now . . . you tell me . . . what the hell is there to decide?"

It occurred to Hens that he'd been gesturing with his fresh cigar. He jammed it into his mouth—then, began to rifle through his pockets for matches. Gladwynne tossed him Smigelski's pipe lighter from the top of the battered desk.

"Now, wait just a fuckin' minute," he half-shouted, as he flipped the tiny wheel on the stainless steel lighter. "Just a goddam minute! I'm the one! The one . . . who's in charge here! Ain't no one gonna decide what to do, in here! No one . . . besides me! So, just shut your hole! Both of you!"

"Save your bad breath," sneered Smigelski. "This is too big . . . to be kept in this charming little broom closet! And you fucking know it! The authorities . . . they are gonna know! They're gonna find out! Whether you tell 'em . . . or I tell 'em! Also, period! Also, paragraph! They're gonna fucking know! My only question is . . . do we go to the New York P.D.? The FBI? Maybe the Secret damn Service? The Little Sisters of The Poor? Who?"

"All right!" shouted Hens. "All-fuckin'-right! I've made my decision! I'll fuckin' call the fuckin' cops!"

He bolted toward the door!

"Wait a minute!" growled Smigelski! He stepped between Hens and the exit!

Hens was livid! "Who the fuck do you think you're talkin' to?" he seethed. "Get your Polack ass out of my way! Or I'll fuckin' cut you in half!"

"You don't pack the gear," hissed Smigelski. "But, we can determine that . . . some other time! You're not going anywhere! Not till we decide! Decide who . . . who you're gonna call! And what you're gonna tell 'em! And when! Like fucking now!"

"Who the hell do you think you are?" screamed Hens. "Ain't no one talks to me that way! Just who the fuck do you think you are?"

"You listen to me, Hens," snarled Smigelski. "I've taken all the crap . . . all the shit . . . I'm gonna take, from you! This is something that's bigger . . . than your shit-assed little kingdom here! I don't know if your flea-sized brain is capable of grabbing that or not! Here? Here . . . you may be Almighty God! But, outside of here? Outside of your cozy little colony here? Outside of here . . . you're fucking nothing! You're some kind of a little pissant! That's all! Just a horse's ass . . . tyrannical . . . pissant! Away from here, though? Away from here . . . you're not shit!"

Hens cocked a ham-like, grimy, fist! Then, he apparently thought better of it!

Smigelski ignored the gesture! "Listen, Hens," he growled. "You listen to me! These assholes are making their dainty little bombs . . . in an apartment house! There are six or eight floors . . . in that building! Do you dig? That means that there's a hell of a lot of innocent people! A hell of a lot . . . of innocent people! They're all in danger of being blown to smithereens! Being blown to kingdom come! If these bastards aren't as smart . . . as they think they are!"

"If they screw up," added Gladwynne, "you've got a real catastrophe! Do you remember a few years back? When that town house . . . the one in The Village . . . when that place blew up? That was a bomb factory! And a hell of a lot of people died!"

"Ahhhh," mocked Hens. "There were only four, or five, that kicked off!"

"Only," scoffed Smigelski.

"Yeah?" snapped Gladwynne. "Well, this one has the potential to kill more! Kill dozens more . . . of unsuspecting people! Hundreds of 'em, maybe! Innocent people!"

"Yeah," agreed Smigelski. "So, what you're going to tell the authorities . . . is that these assholes are putting bombs together! Putting together bombs . . . in this particular apartment house! On Fifty-sixth Street!

In <u>Manhattan</u>! You're gonna <u>tell</u> the authorities . . . so they can <u>clear</u> everyone! <u>Get</u> everyone . . . get 'em the hell <u>out</u> of there! Can you <u>understand</u> that?"

Hens' nod was almost imperceptible. "<u>All</u> right," the director finally blurted. "All fucking <u>right</u>! Just give me the fuckin' <u>address</u>! Maybe you better write it <u>down</u>!"

Smigelski didn't move—maintaining his position, between Hens and the door. He spoke the apartment's address to Gladwynne—who wrote the information on a stenographer's pad, lying by the monitor. The latter tore off the sheet—and proffered it to Hens!

The steaming director practically crumpled it—as he snatched it from Gladwynne's hand.

"Now," snarled Hens, "let me get the fuck <u>out</u> of here!" Then, narrowing his stone-like stare on Smigelski, he hissed, "<u>You</u>? You . . . I'll fuckin' <u>deal</u> with . . . later."

"You're not through dealing with me <u>now</u>, Hens! <u>Who</u> are you gonna call?"

"The local <u>precinct</u>! <u>They'll</u> fuckin' know what to do!"

"I think it ought to go <u>higher</u>," observed Gladwynne.

"So do I," agreed Smigelski. "But, they <u>should</u> know . . . at the precinct . . . who to <u>refer</u> the thing to." Turning to Hens, he returned the latter's steel-laden glare! "If the local precinct wants you to call someone <u>else</u>," he warned, "I want your <u>word</u> . . . that you <u>will</u>! I don't want you just simply hanging <u>up</u> . . . and not pursuing it any <u>farther</u>! Just because you'd <u>kept</u> your piece-of-shit word, technically, to the Polack! Kept your <u>promise</u> . . . and called the damn <u>precinct</u>. I want the law <u>involved</u> . . . fucking <u>involved</u> . . . in this thing! Involved right <u>now</u>! And involved . . . right up to their <u>asses</u>! Do you <u>dig</u>?"

Hens nodded—totally deflated. "Yeah," he responded, sighing heavily. His voice was practically inaudible. "I'll fuckin' get' em <u>involved</u>. You and I <u>will</u> tangle assholes! At some other <u>time</u>!"

"Whenever you're <u>ready</u>! But, if you don't get the <u>law</u> involved . . . there won't <u>be</u> any assholes . . . for us to <u>tangle</u> with!"

Once his shift was over, Smigelski immediately found a payphone on Queens Boulevard—and called Leland Nype. He relayed to his employer the entire day's activities—beginning with the conversation between Clark and Frank, and culminating with the vicious, potentially-deadly, confrontation with Donald Hens!

"You did <u>right</u>, Vick! Don't worry about <u>Hens</u>! I'll handle <u>him</u>! He <u>was</u> upset, I'm sure. But, I think that, maybe . . . down <u>deep</u> . . . he was probably <u>grateful</u> to you! He'd never <u>say</u> it. But, I think he's probably <u>grateful</u> to you! As unlikely as that may <u>sound</u>! For making his decision <u>for</u> him! Once he cools <u>off</u>, he may not even hold any <u>animosity</u> toward you!"

"Yeah. And maybe all the king's horses . . . and all the king's men . . . will be able to put Humpty Dumpty back <u>together</u> again."

Nype laughed. "In any case, Vick," he assured, "you don't have to take any <u>crap</u> from him. You work for <u>me</u> . . . not <u>him</u>!"

"Well, I'd be curious, Mister Nype . . . to know if the sonofabitch actually <u>did</u> call the cops! The precinct . . . or anyplace <u>else</u>!"

"I'll check <u>into</u> it. I've got a couple connections down at Police <u>Headquarters</u>. I'll get right on the horn. Find out what's going on. You'd better give me the <u>address</u> . . . of that <u>apartment</u> house on Fifty-sixth! I'll see if I can stir up some <u>manure</u>! What're your immediate <u>plans</u>, Vick?"

"Nothing concrete. Not right <u>now</u>, anyway. I don't want to go <u>home</u>, though. Not with all of <u>this</u> hanging. Especially, if I can be of some <u>help</u> . . . to somebody. Sometime! Somewhere!"

"You'd be available to talk to the police?"

"Of course. Certainly."

"Okay. Fine, Vick. Why don't you give me about an <u>hour</u>? Call me back at, say, six o'clock? Maybe I'll have a <u>handle</u> on things by then."

"I sure <u>hope</u> so," Smigelski murmured, as he hung up the phone. "I sure hope that <u>someone</u> does!"

TWELVE

A T 4:15PM—45 MINUTES BEFORE SMIGELSKI'S troubled call to Leland Nype—the phone, on the desk of Lt. Royce Dane, had rung. The dour-faced, slight-of-build, pencil-line mustached, detective had absently plucked the receiver from its cradle—and jammed it between his left shoulder and ear.

"<u>Bomb</u> Squad," he'd spoken into the instrument. "<u>Dane</u> here."

"Yeah, Lieutenant. I hope to shit <u>you</u> can help me. That, at least, <u>someone</u> can! I've been <u>dicked</u> around! From <u>one</u> goddam department to <u>another</u>!"

"I'll <u>try</u>, Sir. Does it have to do with a <u>bomb</u>? Or a bomb <u>threat</u>?"

"Yeah. At least, I <u>think</u> it does!"

"Who's <u>this</u>?"

"Name's <u>Hens</u>. <u>Donald</u> Hens. I'm Director of Security . . . at **Ballinger's**! In Rego <u>Park</u>!"

"And what's <u>happened</u>, Mister Hens? Has someone made a <u>bomb</u> threat out there?"

"<u>Yes</u>! <u>No</u>! <u>Shit</u>! I mean . . . not <u>yet</u>! What I <u>mean</u> is . . . well, I <u>think</u> we're on to . . . on to . . . on to a whole bunch of <u>bombers</u>! Whole <u>band</u> of 'em! <u>Shit</u>-load of 'em! <u>You</u> know! <u>Terrorists</u>!"

"Is this on the <u>level</u>, Mister Hens? I mean, we've got more and better things to <u>do</u> down here . . . than to fart around with crank <u>calls</u>!"

"I'm <u>telling</u> you! Telling you that it <u>is</u>! That it's on the <u>level</u> . . . goddam it! There are a couple of my <u>employees</u>, over here! Gonna make fucking <u>bombs</u>! Gonna make <u>bombs</u> . . . and put 'em in fuckin' <u>paint</u> cans! Blow up the whole fuckin' <u>store</u>! Is <u>that</u> fucking 'on the level' enough for you?"

"Are you <u>sure</u> . . . that there's not someone pulling your <u>leg</u>, Mister Hens?"

"I'm fucking <u>positive</u>! I have it on the <u>best</u> authority!"

"Oh? And what authority is <u>that</u>?"

"Never <u>mind</u>! I just <u>know</u> . . . that it's fuckin' <u>true</u>!"

"I'm afraid that I'm going to need a little more than <u>that</u>, Mister Hens."

"What the fuck <u>is</u> this?" The phone had practically exploded in Dane's ear. "I've got a fuckin' <u>bomb</u> scare . . . goin' on out here! You guys are <u>supposed</u> to get off your <u>asses</u>! Get off your asses . . . and take <u>care</u> of shit like that! Now . . . <u>you</u> listen to <u>me</u>! I want you to get <u>your</u> ass out <u>here</u>! And start fuckin' takin' <u>care</u>!"

"I thought you said it <u>wasn't</u> a bomb scare! That it <u>was</u> . . . and then it <u>wasn't</u>."

"Well . . . goddam it . . . it <u>is</u>! And it <u>isn't</u>! I . . . <u>listen</u> . . . ! <u>Look</u>, goddam it! You gotta come <u>over</u> here! I'm Director of <u>Security</u>! fourth <u>floor</u>! Rego <u>Park</u> store! Fucking **Ballinger's**! On Queens <u>Boulevard</u>! The <u>receptionist</u> . . . she'll show you in! I've been on this fuckin' <u>phone</u> . . . for twenty-five fuckin' <u>minutes</u>, now! And <u>no</u> one's done a fuckin' <u>thing</u>! Now, get on <u>over</u> here! And fuckin' <u>hurry</u>!"

The phone had popped—loudly! Then, it had gone dead, in Dane's hand!

Thirty-five minutes later, Lt. Dane was shown into Donald Hens' office. The latter rose to greet the Bomb Squad officer. The two men shook hands, rather sloppily—for the briefest of moments—then, seated themselves.

Taking a cigarette, from a pack in his shirt pocket, Dane lit up. "Now," he snapped, "suppose you <u>tell</u> me, Mister Hens, what the hell you've <u>got</u>! I <u>warn</u> you, though! If this is some kind of cockamamie <u>stunt</u> . . . I'll come <u>down</u> on you! With both <u>feet</u>!"

"It ain't no <u>stunt</u>! And it certainly ain't no <u>joke</u>! I <u>promise</u> you that. I only wish to hell it <u>was</u>!"

"Well then, suppose you <u>tell</u> me: How would you <u>know</u> . . . that someone's going to put a <u>bomb</u> in . . . ? In a can of <u>paint</u>? Was <u>that</u> it? Blow up the <u>store</u>? How do you <u>know</u> that?"

Hens' face began to take on the slightest tinge of red! "God <u>damn</u> it," he roared. "Because they fuckin' <u>said</u> . . . they were gonna do it!"

"To <u>whom</u>? Who'd they <u>say</u> that to? To <u>you</u>?"

"No."

"Then to <u>whom</u>? <u>Look</u>, Mister Hens . . . if this statement was made to someone <u>else</u> . . . you'd better trot his or her <u>butt</u> in here! Trot it in here now!

My <u>patience</u> . . . is beginning to run a shade <u>thin</u>, at this point!"

"There . . . there <u>wasn't</u> anyone else."

"Look . . . <u>Hens</u>! I just <u>told</u> you that my patience . . . not my strong suit, under the <u>best</u> of conditions . . . is fast running <u>out</u>! Now, I'm not going to just <u>sit</u> here . . . and play <u>guessing</u> games with you! Let me suggest one more <u>time</u>! Let me <u>ask</u> you. Ask you . . . politely . . . to <u>tell</u> me how you <u>know</u> that there's a bomb threat! And . . . at <u>this</u> point . . . leave out all the stupid <u>games</u>!"

Hens removed his half-smoked cigar—and pointed it at the diminutive detective! "And <u>I'm</u> telling <u>you</u>, Lieutenant," he hissed, "that there's a goddam <u>bomb</u> threat! I'm not purposely tryin' to throw you a fuckin' <u>curve</u>! It's just that . . . it's just that I don't really know if I can <u>tell</u> you. Tell you <u>how</u> I . . . how I <u>know</u> it!"

Dane slammed his fist on Hens' desk—effectively rearranging half the rubble! "Well," he seethed, "you goddam well <u>better</u> tell me how you know! <u>If</u> you know! And <u>what</u> you know! And you'd <u>goddam</u> well better quit jacking me <u>around</u>! I'm at the point where . . . well, it's a real <u>temptation</u> to run your surly ass <u>in</u>! Run it <u>downtown</u>, for questioning! There's a <u>law</u>, y'know, against filing a false <u>police</u> report! Do I make myself <u>clear</u>? I'm all through farting <u>around</u>! Now, you'd goddam <u>well</u> . . . better <u>tell</u> me something! Something <u>quick</u>! And something <u>substantive</u>! That's <u>if</u> you've got anything at <u>all</u> to tell! Something that makes some goddam <u>sense</u> . . . for a change! So far, I haven't heard a goddam <u>thing</u>!"

Hens leaned back in his chair—and studied his soggy, rancid, cigar. It took a Herculean effort for him to avoid Dane's piercing, would-turn-cement-into-chocolate-syrup stare!

Sighing heavily, the director muttered, "I . . . there were <u>two</u> employees. One of 'em fucking <u>told</u> the other."

"Well, <u>thank</u> you! Thank you <u>so</u> much . . . for <u>that</u> little nugget," replied Dane, sarcasm dripping from his voice. "Did <u>you</u> . . . you, <u>yourself</u> . . . did you hear <u>them</u>?"

Hens didn't answer!

Dane rose, and leaned over Hens' desk—much as Smigelski had done earlier! "Maybe," he snarled, "you didn't <u>hear</u> me, Mister Hens! I <u>asked</u> if you . . . you, <u>yourself</u> . . . if <u>you</u> heard them say <u>anything</u>! Anything . . . about a frigging <u>bomb</u>!"

"Well . . . no."

"<u>Shit</u>! Here we go <u>again</u>! Why do I get the feeling I'm in the middle of a George Burns/Gracie <u>Allen</u> bit? Or, possibly, the <u>Marx</u> Brothers? Now, suppose you break <u>down</u> . . . and <u>tell</u> me what you know! And make it goddam <u>quick</u>! I'm at the end of my <u>rope</u>, Hens!"

"I <u>know</u> it's true! True . . . that there's a <u>bomb</u> threat," blurted Hens. "Because we . . . because we . . . we <u>bug</u> the employee's <u>john</u>!"

Dane plopped back down into the chair! "You <u>what</u>?" he asked, incredulously! "You fucking . . . <u>what</u>?"

"We bug the employee's <u>rest</u> rooms!"

"That's what I <u>thought</u> you said! That's the most <u>outrageous</u> . . . most <u>disgusting</u> . . . thing I've ever <u>heard</u> of! At least I can <u>understand</u> . . . why you were so reluctant! So <u>reluctant</u> . . . to let me <u>in</u> on that little caper!"

Hens jammed his cigar back into his face, and leaned forward—staring at Dane! "Look, Lieutenant," he growled, "don't give me any fuckin' <u>lectures</u> . . . on fuckin' <u>morality</u>! We bug the <u>crappers</u>! <u>Period</u>! Fuckin' <u>paragraph</u>! If you <u>approve</u> . . . <u>fine</u>! If you <u>don't</u> . . . why, <u>that's</u> fine too! I could fuckin' care <u>less</u>! I'm tellin' you that we catch a <u>lot</u> of thefts . . . a <u>fucking</u> lot of thefts . . . that way! We're talkin' serious fucking <u>money</u>!"

"I don't give a <u>shit</u>, if you catch people who're . . . who're . . . who're goddam planning to assassinate the <u>president</u>! I've never <u>heard</u> of anything so <u>disgusting</u>! <u>Never</u>! Not in my whole damn <u>life</u>!"

"Well, it's fucking <u>necessary</u>! We need to <u>do</u> it! We save a <u>lot</u> of money . . . that way! <u>Lots</u> of money!"

"There's no <u>way</u> . . . you can justify something like <u>that</u>!" His grimace could've stopped a train! "No <u>way</u>! Not to <u>me</u>, anyway."

"I could fuckin' care <u>less</u>, Lieutenant! I don't have to justify <u>anything</u> to you! So, just fuck <u>off</u>!"

"You're <u>class</u>, Hens! <u>All</u> class!"

"Yeah? Well, I'm sorry if all this . . . <u>offends</u> your delicate fuckin' sense of <u>outrage</u>, Lieutenant! But, <u>that's</u> the way it fucking <u>is</u>!"

Hens picked up two employee reference cards—from the ruins which were the top of his desk—and virtually threw them across his desk, at Dane!

"These two . . . employees of the <u>store</u> . . . they were fuckin' <u>overheard</u>! Overheard, <u>yesterday</u>! By one of our <u>security</u> men at the observation post," he advised the detective, without a trace of remorse.

Without a smattering of emotion. "They were talkin' about what the security man thought were <u>bombs</u>! But, in very <u>general</u> terms! Today, the employees got more <u>specific</u>! A <u>hell</u> of a lot more specific! They said they were gonna put a bomb in a lot of the one-gallon cans of our <u>paint</u>! Then, they were talkin' about . . . how they're gonna bring 'em <u>back</u>! <u>Return</u> 'em . . . back into the store!"

"But, you . . . you, <u>yourself</u> . . . you didn't <u>hear</u> these two employees. Didn't <u>hear</u> 'em . . . say a <u>thing</u>?"

"<u>No</u>, goddam it! I just <u>told</u> you! Told you . . . that it was our <u>security</u> guys! Actually, they're not <u>our</u> employees. They don't actually <u>work</u> for **Ballinger's**! They work for **Tarkenton Security**! One's name is Gladwynne . . . black guy. He's been here a good <u>while</u>. Other one's a <u>new</u> man. Long Polack <u>last</u> name."

"Are they here <u>now</u>?"

"<u>Naw</u>. Gone <u>home</u>! <u>Both</u> of 'em. Left <u>awhile</u> ago. Like, five <u>o'clock</u>. If I hadn't got dicked <u>around</u> . . . like I did . . . on the goddam <u>phone</u> . . . police department transferring me, from <u>one</u> goddam place to <u>another</u> goddam place . . . and, if you'd have got out here a little faster . . . why, they'd probably still fuckin' be <u>here</u>!"

"Uh huh," replied Dane, sneering. "<u>You</u> try fighting the traffic out from <u>Manhattan</u> . . . this time of day! See how fast <u>you'd</u> ever get here! Besides, if your <u>brain</u> wasn't completely up your <u>ass</u> . . . you'd have <u>kept</u> 'em here! <u>One</u> of 'em, anyway! Till I <u>got</u> here!"

"Says <u>you</u>! That's <u>your</u> fuckin' department! I'm just fucking <u>reporting</u> this shit! If <u>I</u> gotta do your fuckin' work for you, Lieutenant, they'd pay me more. I'm sure that . . . if you'll simply pick up the phone, and call **Tarkenton** . . . they can give you those guys' home phone numbers, and addresses! And all such shit as that. Seems to me, though, that the white guy . . . the Polack . . . I think he lives over in Jersey, somewhere."

Dane's smile was one of mock sweetness. "Thank you so much, Mister Hens! Thank you so profusely . . . for telling me how to do my job! All right, I'll get ahold of those guys. Anything else you got? Any more tasteful little gems . . . you got for me?"

"Yeah, I got more! One of the security guys . . . the Polack . . . he followed this employee . . . this guy, Crimmins . . . to an apartment! Did that . . . last night! Let me see, now . . ." He rifled through the piles of papers on his desk. "Here it is," he muttered. "Lemme see. Apartment house . . . at four-sixty-three, East Fifty-sixth. In Manhattan. I think he said it's just off Second Avenue."

"Yeah? Go on," responded Dane—grinding his cigarette out, in the over-full ash tray on Hens' desk. "I'm enchanted!"

"That's it, Lieutenant," answered Hens. "He followed Crimmins to that address. Crimmins doesn't live there, though. Not in that apartment house. He lives in fucking Astoria."

"Well . . . if you don't mind my asking . . . what's the significance of this Fifty-sixth Street apartment?"

"Only that this Polack guy . . . he thinks that's where they might be puttin' bombs together! Said it was a big-assed building! Lots of people livin' there! The Polack was afraid something'd fuck up! Or someone would! And the whole goddam building'd go up! Personally, I think he's full of shit . . . with all due respect. But, I told him . . . promised him . . . I'd tell you! So, I'm fuckin' telling you!"

Dane shook his head—as he lit another cigarette. He allowed himself a mirthless laugh. "Hens," he snarled, "you're all class! All fucking class!"

At 6:00 PM, Smigelski dialed Leland Nype's residence number. The latter snatched up the phone—before the second ring had begun!

"Vick?"

"Yes."

"Where are you?"

"Coffee shop. On Queens Boulevard. Across from the store."

"Good! I figured you'd still be out there . . . somewhere! I just talked with a Lieutenant Dane . . . of the Bomb Squad! He's over there right now! In Hens' office!"

"In Hens' office? Donald Hens?"

"Yes! You may find this difficult to believe . . . but, the good lieutenant and the sweet and cuddly Mister Hens are not getting along very well! I told Dane . . . that I thought you were probably still in the area! And that you'd promised to call me at about six o'clock. He said to tell you that he'd be waiting for you! In Hens' office. Why don't you trot on back across the street . . . and meet him? Meet Lieutenant Dane! Meantime, I'll phone over there . . . and tell him that you're on your way!"

"Fine, Mister Nype. As a matter of fact, I can hardly <u>wait</u>! I'm <u>sure</u> . . . that Hens didn't want to <u>tell</u> the lieutenant anywhere <u>near</u> what I'd <u>wanted</u> him to."

Once Smigelski had arrived at the office of Donald Hens, he learned that the security director had <u>left</u> for the day! And he'd done his best—to convince Dane that the lieutenant should wait for Smigelski in the <u>corridor</u>!

It hadn't <u>worked</u>! Not even <u>close</u>!

Hens had finally instructed his poor, troubled, deeply-frightened, receptionist to seat herself in <u>his</u> sanctified chair! She should "keep an <u>eye</u>" on Dane— till the officer "finally hauls his ass on <u>out</u> of here". Then, charitably, she would be free to go home.

When Smigelski walked in, he was <u>warmly</u> greeted by the distraught woman. As though he was a long-lost cousin. Dane arose, as Smigelski entered.

"You must be the man from **Tarkenton**," he greeted the newcomer. "Smigelski, is it?"

"Right," smiled Smigelski. "And you're Lieutenant Dane?"

"You got it," said Dane—extending his hand.

Once the men had exchanged greetings, Dane observed, "Look, we're keeping this nice lady . . . from her evening meal. Mister Hens . . . quite obviously . . . doesn't have much confidence, in the honesty of his local constabulary. So, he assigned this poor lady . . . to see that I didn't snoop <u>around</u>. Or clean <u>out</u> the joint. Not necessarily in that <u>order</u>."

The woman smiled nervously.

"That being the case," Dane continued, "why don't you accompany me . . . back to Manhattan? That way we can talk. I've got to get back over to what I laughingly refer to as my office . . . pretty damn sudden. Any problem with that?"

"No, Lieutenant. I can leave my car here . . . and take the bus, or the train, out tonight. I live in Metuchen, New Jersey."

"Well," grumped Dane, "at least that was one thing . . . that Hens was on top of."

Once in Dane's car, the officer began to question our hero:

"Vick," he began, "may I call you Vick? I understand that you're one of the guys who has the neat job . . . the honored profession of observing what goes on in the male employee's restroom. Is that correct?"

"Yeah," nodded Smigelski. "A vocation . . . made in heaven."

"I was quite prepared," laughed Dane, nervously, "to meet some kind of a pervert, I guess! You don't act as though you live to watch what happens in there."

"I'm not! I don't! But, I've acquired this bad habit. It's called eating, don'tcha know. I use my glorious paycheck for little luxuries . . . like food and rent. I've even reached a point . . . where I'm considering the purchase of a second shirt."

The officer grinned broadly—and, deftly, shifted lanes, in the busy Queens Blvd. traffic! "The sainted Mister Hens," he advised, "tells me that you overheard . . . overheard a couple of conversations. Between this Crimmins guy . . . and that black dude."

"That's right. Yesterday! Hens didn't want to hear it. I guess, maybe, I can't blame him. I didn't have all that much to go on. Not at that point, anyway. I followed Crimmins, though! Last evening! Followed him to an apartment . . . on East Fifty-sixth Street!"

"So Hens told me."

"He told you that?"

Dane nodded. "Yeah," he replied. "Shouldn't he have?"

"Yes! Of course! I'm glad he did! I just didn't expect that he would! He's pooh-poohed . . . the whole damn thing! From start to finish! Wasn't wanting to . . . wasn't going to . . . get you guys involved! At all! I had to practically threaten him . . . with fisticuffs! And, even then, I wasn't all that sure that he'd so much as even phone you guys! I've so misjudged, the dear boy!"

Smigelski related the entire sequence of events to the officer, as they made their way down Queens Blvd., across the Queensbury Bridge—and into Midtown Manhattan.

"I don't believe this! I jolly well do not believe it!" Dane seethed to Smigelski—as he emerged from a conference room, at Police Headquarters. "I don't fucking <u>believe</u> it! Judge <u>Sinclair</u> is in there! And he just fucking <u>refused</u> . . . to sign a fucking <u>warrant</u>!"

It was 7:50PM! Smigelski had waited outside the conference room, for almost an hour—on the possibility that he <u>might</u> be called upon to testify. Before the judge. It didn't happen.

"He . . . he <u>refused</u>?" asked Smigelski, incredulous. "The judge <u>refused</u>? How could he <u>refuse</u>? Doesn't he <u>realize</u> . . . that the whole damn <u>building</u>, the whole damn <u>place</u> . . . it could go <u>up</u>?" He snapped his fingers—and was startled by the loudness of the exercise. "Could go <u>up</u>! Just like . . . frigging . . . <u>that</u>!"

"Who fucking <u>knows</u>," groused the detective. "I <u>explained</u> it to him! Explained the whole <u>thing</u> to him! <u>Explained</u> it to the man! Very <u>slowly</u>! Very <u>deliberately</u>! In great fucking <u>detail</u>! <u>Elaborate</u> detail! Didn't get . . . <u>couldn't</u> get . . . <u>through</u> to him! I <u>probably</u> didn't even come <u>close</u>!"

Dane slammed his right fist, into his left palm! "I <u>knew</u>," he continued, "that he'd be <u>upset</u> at being called <u>down</u> . . . to even <u>look</u> at a goddam <u>warrant</u>! <u>Any</u> goddam warrant! Blew his <u>dinnertime</u> . . . at home. <u>Some</u> of these bastards . . . they put in a <u>real</u> ass-dragging day! Maybe four whole . . . entire . . . <u>hours</u>! They make more <u>money</u> . . . than you and I do! Put to-fucking-<u>gether</u>! And they <u>work</u> four whole, entire, shittin' hours a <u>day</u>! And people <u>wonder</u> . . . why the stupid dockets, are so damn <u>crowded</u>!"

Smigelski was as upset as Dane! "Well," he snarled, "the good judge wouldn't refuse to <u>sign</u> the damn thing . . . simply <u>because</u> you had the <u>audacity</u> to interrupt his goddam <u>supper</u>! <u>Would</u> he? I mean he . . ."

"I'd like to <u>think</u> that he wouldn't. But, I really don't <u>know</u>. The reason he <u>gave</u> me was . . . ! Well, he <u>said</u> that the <u>manner</u>, in which we <u>got</u> the damn evidence . . . or information or whatever . . . was <u>unconstitutional</u>! Of course . . . from a purely <u>legal</u> standpoint . . . he's probably <u>correct</u>! <u>Dammit</u>!"

"Yeah! But, <u>Lieutenant</u>! There's a whole <u>shitload</u> of innocent <u>people</u> out there! People, that'll . . ."

"You don't have to sell <u>me</u>, Ski! I <u>told</u> him . . . told the estimable <u>judge</u> . . . that I'd brought you <u>down</u> here! Brought you down, <u>personally</u>! Without <u>your</u> having had <u>your</u> supper! In the event that he needed to <u>ask</u> you any pissy-assed questions! Told him to have a real <u>go</u> at you! Didn't make a damn bit of <u>difference</u>! His goddam Honor said he wasn't going to rouse eighty-four <u>families</u>, from their happy hearth and home! Just on the off-chance that <u>something</u> might . . . just <u>might</u> . . . be going <u>on</u>, in the goddam building! Of course, it didn't <u>help</u>, that I had to tell him that I didn't have the foggiest <u>idea</u> . . . as to <u>which</u> apartment all this shit was supposed to be going <u>on</u> in! He flat didn't want to <u>hear</u> anything I had to <u>say</u>! Open and <u>shut</u>! Just like <u>that</u>! De-fucking-<u>clined</u>!"

"What . . . what're you going to <u>do</u>, Lieutenant? I mean . . . you can't just simply turn your <u>back</u> on . . ."

Dane held up his hand—like a traffic cop. He shook his head—emphatically! "You don't want to <u>hear</u> it," he replied. "You don't want to <u>know</u>! You really <u>don't</u>!"

The lieutenant indicated the exit. Smigelski fell in beside him.

Once the pair was outside, Dane spoke: "Look, Ski. I don't intend to sit <u>around</u>! Sit around . . . with my thumb in my bum . . . and let a bunch of <u>assholes</u> blow up a whole goddam <u>building</u>! A building . . . full of innocent <u>people</u>! It's getting <u>late</u> . . . and I know that you live out in <u>Jersey</u>. Do you think, though, that you could stay in <u>town</u>? For a little <u>while</u>, anyway? I don't know <u>exactly</u> . . . what I have in mind! Not <u>precisely</u>! A lot of ad-<u>libbing</u> . . . going to be going on tonight. I'd <u>like</u> for you to be <u>around</u>! In case I should happen to <u>need</u> you! If that's too much of an <u>inconvenience</u> . . . well, I certainly <u>understand</u>! You've done <u>more</u> than your duty . . . as a good citizen! Done <u>that</u> . . . already. If you need to get home, I'll get someone to drive you back out to Rego Park. So you can pick up your car."

"I can be <u>around</u> . . . if you <u>need</u> me. Listen, there's a really big coffee shop . . . *White Palace* . . . over on Fifty-seventh and Second. That's where I ran <u>into</u> all those assholes last night. I can hang out <u>there</u> . . . if you need me."

"<u>Good</u>! That'd be <u>perfect</u>! You'll be close <u>enough</u> . . . if it happens that I <u>do</u> need you. I'll really <u>appreciate</u> it, Ski."

"Need <u>me</u>?" asked Smigelski, nervously. The significance of the word had just sunk in. "What on earth would you need <u>me</u> for?"

"One never <u>knows</u> . . . <u>do</u> one? Probably I <u>won't</u>. I probably won't need you at <u>all</u>! Don't <u>expect</u> I would! I'd just <u>appreciate</u> your being close <u>by</u>! Beyond <u>that</u> . . . I really don't want to <u>say</u> too much."

<u>Now what have I gotten myself into</u>? thought Smigelski. <u>What am I going to tell Junie</u>?

Ten minutes after dropping Smigelski off at the coffee shop, Lt. Dane entered the apartment building on East 56th Street.

Locating the worn button—labeled in faded letters "Supr"—the detective pressed it in! All the way to the wall! And held it in that position!

It took a matter of 20 seconds—before a male voice blasted over the speaker:

"All right! All right . . . for Christ's sakes! Hold your water! I'll be right there!"

Two minutes later, a disheveled young black man opened the door to the lobby. Dane flashed his badge—and strode inside!

"What . . . what can I do for you, Officer?"

"You the super?"

"Yeah."

"What's your name?"

"Jones."

"Jones, huh?"

"Yeah. Jones. And I can prove it. Haven't had a cop yet . . . that believed me."

He fished into his back pocket—and produced a wallet, which had seen better days. Many of them. Extracting a badly-frayed driver's license, he presented it to the detective. Dane took the license. His scowl turned to a slight smile—as he handed it back.

"Not only Jones," he observed, "but, John Jones, hah?"

"Yeah. What can I do for you, Officer?"

"Well, I might as well level with you. We have reason to believe that there might . . . just might, now . . . but, that there might be a bomb factory operating here! Operating . . . as we speak . . . in this building!"

"A . . . a <u>what</u>?"

"You heard me <u>correctly</u>. Now, I don't know which <u>apartment</u> it might be in, but I'm . . ."

"<u>C'mon</u>! Lieutenant is it? Come <u>on</u>! What kind of . . . of <u>bullshit</u> are you trying to <u>lay</u> on me?"

"When they peel what's <u>left</u> your ass off what's left of the ceiling . . . then you won't think it's <u>bullshit</u>! The people . . . the ones that I think I'm <u>on</u> to . . . are primarily <u>young</u> people. Probably male <u>and</u> female. How many <u>people</u> . . . say, under thirty-years-of-age . . . do you have <u>living</u> here?"

"Oh, <u>wow</u>! How the hell should <u>I</u> know? Maybe thirty-<u>five</u>! Maybe <u>fifty</u>! There's a hell of a lot of <u>apartments</u>, in this building, Lieutenant. Everyone keeps pretty much to <u>himself</u>. To <u>herself</u>. Hell, there may be a <u>hundred</u> . . . maybe a hundred-and-<u>fifty</u> . . . people <u>live</u> here. I can't hang any <u>kind</u> of number . . . on under-<u>thirty</u>. I really <u>can't</u>. <u>Honest</u>! I'd probably have to say . . . on a <u>guess</u> . . . that there's maybe a little more than half of the <u>tenants'd</u> fall into that category. There's eighty-four <u>apartments</u> in this building, you know."

Dane nodded. "Yeah, I know," he said. "I'm afraid that's not much <u>help</u>. Let me ask you <u>this</u>: Have you noticed any <u>one</u> tenant . . . one that's had a lot of <u>visitors</u>, lately?"

"Aw <u>c'mon</u>, Lieutenant. I'd really like to <u>help</u> . . . I really <u>would</u> . . . but, I don't hold no one's <u>hand</u>. People <u>come</u> . . . people <u>go</u>. <u>No</u> one pays 'em much never-mind. Least of all <u>me</u>! I don't . . . <u>ever</u> . . . keep track! <u>Never</u> keep track!"

Dane's face was beginning to flush! "Look, goddammit!" he blustered. "There are people in this goddam building . . . right now . . . who could be putting together a goddam bomb! Even as we speak! You dig? A bomb! A goddam bomb! And . . . if they screw up . . . they'll be looking for you . . . and everyone else, in the building . . . over on Forty-seventh Street, somewhere! Now, goddam it, if you know something . . . and I don't give a rat's ass how you know it . . . you'd better tell me! Before someone gets hurt! Hurt really bad!"

"Look! Really! I'm not putting you on, Lieutenant! I'm not! If I could help you . . . I damn well would! I swear to that! I really do! But, I don't hardly know anyone . . . in the place. I haven't been here quite two weeks. I don't know anyone! Not a soul! I haven't seen a bunch of people . . . young or old . . . going into one specific apartment! Honest! I'm telling you! I never watch the door. Never watch the lobby. Someone could be in and out of here . . . fifty times an hour . . . and I'd never know! Each tenant has a key. You're the second time that anyone's . . . ever . . . rung my bell! Only time I ever hear from the tenants . . . any of 'em . . . is when the plumbing gets stopped up or something. Or if something shorts out. The building . . . for its age . . . is in pretty good shape. Hadda put a window in two-oh-six . . . a few days ago. Outside of that? Not much. Not much at all. I'm a writer, actually . . . and this job is ideal. Free pad . . . and they pay the light bill! A couple bucks for groceries, they give me. All I am . . . believe me, Lieutenant . . . is a warm body. I got my boiler-tender's license . . . and that's all I really need. Keep an eye on the <u>furnace</u>. <u>That</u> sort of stuff. Gives me all kinds of <u>time</u> . . . to devote to my <u>writing</u>."

"Okay, Jones. Okay. You've <u>convinced</u> me. I <u>believe</u> you. You don't mind if I nose <u>around</u> a little bit . . . do you?"

"Hell <u>no</u>, Lieutenant. Be my <u>guest</u>! Uh . . . you're not going to be creating any . . . ah . . . <u>hassles</u>! <u>Are</u> you?"

"No. Certainly <u>not</u>. Wouldn't <u>dream</u> of it."

The super departed. Dane waited till the young man was out of sight. Then, reaching into his coat pocket, he produced a stethoscope-looking device— and plugged it into his ears!

Trudging up and down the long corridors—on each <u>floor</u>—he pressed the instrument against the door of <u>each</u> and <u>every</u> apartment!

Methodically, Dane worked his way through the first <u>three</u> floors. Painstakingly, he'd remained at <u>each</u> door—until he could hear enough conversation, or other action, to convince him that there was no <u>bomb factory</u> inside. In two cases, he'd taken great pains to convince himself that, in each instance, the apartment was <u>vacant</u>.

Three different times, people stepped from the elevator—while the detective had his "snooper" pressed up against a door. Fortunately, the clatter and clang of the vintage car had provided ample <u>warning</u>—allowing Dane to appear as though he'd just walked <u>out</u> of one of the apartments, on that floor. No one <u>seemed</u> to pay him much attention.

On the fourth floor, Dane's spirits <u>lifted</u>! Pay dirt seemed <u>imminent</u>! A good deal of noise emanated from the flat, nearest the <u>elevator</u>! Acid rock—<u>blasting</u>

from a stereo, turned up far too loudly—filled, virtually, the entire floor! The racket could be a cover! The occupants could be attempting to drown out certain sounds! Noises which would suggest that there were a goodly number of people inside—most of whom could possess youthful voices!

Pressing his "bug" against the door, the lieutenant listened—intently! He was able to pick up snatches of disjointed conversation! There was one voice, inside, ranting about "capitalist swine"! Another spoke highly of socialism! There were two or three references to "revolution"!

After eavesdropping for almost ten minutes, Dane decided it was a false alarm! The detective became convinced that it was merely a gathering of "wired" students from *City University of New York*. It was the currently-popular "cultural revolution" with which they were so thrilled. Copious amounts of marijuana—and probably a few other "medications"—were being consumed inside!

On the fifth floor—inside the apartment furthest down one of the long hallways—Dane decided that the goings-on inside were positively "spooky"! He could hear people, in the flat—moving about! But, there was virtually no conversation! The lieutenant was able to ascertain that some manner of implements were being clattered from place to place! But, no conversation! Nothing spoken! Eerie!

Finally—after six or eight interminable minutes—the detective heard a woman's voice! A coarse—almost whining—voice: "Be fucking careful . . . with that fucking thing! You want to blow us clear to the fucking moon?"

"Calm <u>down</u>, Annabelle," responded a young male voice. "No <u>sweat</u>!"

"Well," answered Annabelle's grating voice, "somebody <u>else'd</u> better put that fucking <u>cap</u> on, then!"

"I'm <u>telling</u> you . . . to calm fucking <u>down</u>," replied the same male voice—fraught with tension. "Clark can <u>do</u> it! Now, just <u>cool</u> it! Stay <u>off</u> his ass! He doesn't need any more <u>tension</u>!"

"Stay off his <u>ass</u>?" Annabelle's voice had gotten louder—and higher-pitched. "Stay off his <u>ass</u>? <u>Listen</u>! The sonofabitch is gonna blow us <u>all</u> . . . blow us <u>all</u> . . . fucking sky-<u>high</u>! Now, <u>I'm</u> telling <u>you</u>! I want someone <u>else</u> . . . to put that goddam <u>cap</u> on!"

"Clark," beseeched the male voice—his tone reeking of resignation, "maybe you'd <u>better</u> let Jerry do it!"

A nervous smile formed on Dane's lips. He'd recognized the name Clark—from what Smigelski and Donald Hens had told him. And from the employee's record card—that Hens had shown him.

He <u>had</u> his apartment!

<u>Better get in there</u> . . . <u>before someone really screws up! And we really have a problem</u>!

Withdrawing his .38 Police Special revolver, Dane raised his foot—to the point that his knee was pressed, tightly, up against his heaving chest! Then, he unleashed a Herculean <u>kick</u>! The door flew <u>open</u>! It <u>slammed</u> against the inside wall—with a deafening <u>clatter</u>!

Bursting into the living room—pistol at the ready—the detective shouted, "<u>Police</u>! Don't <u>any</u> of you move! Not a goddam <u>twitch</u>!"

All eleven occupants froze!

Dane's eyes opened—to Bette Davis proportions—when he saw the <u>contents</u> of a huge, old fashioned, "Davenport Table", in the center of the living room: <u>Dynamite</u>! <u>Blasting caps</u>! <u>Timing Devices</u>! Reel upon reel of <u>electrical wire</u>! The presence of all this potentially-lethal equipment! The cache <u>shouted</u> the group's chilling, frightening, message! Its <u>devastating</u> intention!

On the coffee table—across the room—sat a pink "Princess" telephone! Seemingly, the only halfway-civilized hunk of "civilian" equipment—in the entire room!

Motioning the group to line up against the far wall—as remote as possible, from the mind-boggling array of explosives, on the long, narrow, table—Dane edged toward the phone!

Three recalcitrant members of the group hesitated: Two white women and a young black man! They, obviously, were <u>not</u> anxious to join their eight compatriots, across the room!

Dane cocked the revolver's hammer! And <u>aimed</u> it—directly, and with great flourish—at the young man's groin!

"Get your ass over <u>there</u>," he seethed! "Or do you want an instant, thirty-eight caliber, <u>vasectomy</u>! Gotta <u>special</u> on 'em . . . going today!"

The young man moved! Followed—much more slowly—by the two women! It took far too <u>many</u> heart-fluttering moments—but, the recalcitrant pair finally <u>did</u> obey!

Dane picked up the receiver—then laid it on the table. He bent over to dial 911, on the keypad. The lightness of the phone made dialing <u>any</u> number difficult! However, the detective managed it! Then, he retrieved the receiver!

When the connection was made to the <u>police dispatcher</u>, Dane spoke gruffly, into the instrument: "<u>Dane</u> . . . <u>Lieutenant</u> Dane, <u>Bomb</u> Squad . . . speaking! <u>Listen</u> to me! I'm at four-sixty-three East Fifty-<u>sixth</u>, in Manhattan. Apartment five-<u>fourteen</u>! You <u>got</u> that? I'm holding <u>eleven</u> people at bay! Send <u>help</u>! Need a goodly number of <u>reinforcements</u>! <u>Fast</u>! Need at least three <u>wagons</u> . . . and God-<u>knows</u>-how-many <u>backup</u> cars! As many as you can <u>get</u> here! And as <u>fast</u> . . . as you can <u>get</u> 'em here! <u>Got</u> that?"

The dispatcher repeated the data—and Dane growled his affirmation! Then, he dropped the receiver back into its cradle!

It was at that moment that one of his prisoners decided to speak <u>up</u>! Dane recognized the rusty-file voice as that of <u>Annabelle</u>! She was an <u>Amazon</u> of a woman! At six-feet, three-inches, she was beautifully <u>proportioned</u>! Highly <u>unusual</u>—for a woman of that height!

"<u>Why</u> the fuck . . . are we standing <u>around</u>?" she courteously entreated her compatriots. "He's just one <u>guy</u>! <u>One</u> fucking guy! And he's got no fucking <u>help</u>! No <u>back</u> up! Not for the next few <u>minutes</u>! That <u>gun</u>! It's only got <u>six</u> bullets in it! Six fucking <u>bullets</u>! If we <u>rush</u> him . . . we've <u>got</u> to be able to <u>take</u> him! Before his fascist pig-<u>buddies</u> can <u>get</u> here!"

Dane's mouth twitched into a nervous smile! "That's <u>right</u>, Annabelle," he snarled. "But . . . if you <u>do</u> rush me . . . the first three or <u>four</u> of you are <u>dead</u>! Fucking <u>dead</u>! Maybe the first <u>five</u>! Maybe, even, the first six! I can get off a round . . . with the best of 'em! Faster'n most! I know that I'm gonna get me . . . at the very least . . . a piece of six of you assholes! At least a piece! You can bet money . . . hated capitalist money . . . on it! And the first one . . . number one . . . to bite the dust will be you, Annabelle-Sweetie! Right in the old left tit! That's right where you'll get it, Sweetheart! Right in the old left tit! You can take it to the goddam bank!"

"He's fucking bluffing," growled Annabelle. "He'd never get that many rounds off!"

"Yeah? Listen, Smart Girl! You know that I'm gonna get you! I'll blow that left tit . . . blow it right off of you! The rest of you piece-of-shit imbeciles? I don't know! I don't know how many of you I'll get! But, I'll get some of you! You shitheads feelin' lucky? Any of you? Come ahead . . . assholes! Spin the wheel!"

The eleven began—ever so slowly—to inch forward!

Dane bent into a semi-crouch, and—both hands on his revolver—aimed at Annabelle's bountiful bosom!

"C'mon ahead, you pissants," he hissed. "C'mon! Who's committed enough? Who's dedicated that much . . . to your shitassed cause? Committed enough . . . that you're willing to give up your pissy-assed life for it? That you're ready to die . . . for the glory of it all? Who's gonna die . . . a glorious hero? I'm sure that there must be five or six of you assholes . . . that're so devoted, that you're not gonna let a little thing like getting your brains splattered all over the room get in your way! C'mon, God damn it! C'mon ahead! Even if you do get me . . . it'll be worth it to me! Well worth it! To take out as many of you dipshits as I can! Well? What're you waiting for . . . assholes? C'mon! What's the matter? Aren't you . . . ?"

At that point, Dane noticed—that a fat, white, youth was sidling toward the table of explosives! Stealthily, the young man began to reach for one of the bombing devices! It appeared to be "live"!

Dane leveled his gun, at the punk! "I wouldn't!" he admonished.

The youth didn't!

Ten seconds later, the sounds of police sirens filled the night!

Within five minutes, the building was crawling with uniformed policemen!

THIRTEEN

THE FOLLOWING MORNING, SMIGELSKI WAS 20 minutes late, getting to work. His appearance showed him—well, confirmed him—to be much the worst for the wear.

"Good God, Gertie," Gladwynne greeting him—with an exaggerated grin. "What the hell happened to you? I've seen my cat drag in better-looking stuff. Hell of a lot better looking than some kind of a washed-out, hung-over, Polack! What the hell <u>happened</u>, Ski?"

Smigelski plopped himself down into his chair. "Well," he groused, "I didn't get any sleep to speak of. And that's for <u>openers</u>!"

"I'd have to believe that."

"All hell broke loose last night, Dick!"

"Yeah? Like what?"

"Well, like the cops <u>busted</u> that apartment on Fifty-sixth last night," replied Smigelski, with a massive sigh.

"They <u>did</u>? <u>Really</u>? They really <u>did</u>? Why wasn't it on the seven o'clock <u>news</u> this morning?"

"Because they either <u>believed</u> me . . . when I told 'em that these assholes were in <u>cahoots</u> with groups in <u>Washington</u> and <u>Chicago</u> and <u>L.A.</u> and who-<u>knows</u>-where-else! Or, more likely, they found some stuff in the <u>apartment</u>! Stuff that <u>linked</u> 'em . . . with those other clowns! All I got . . . was just bits and <u>pieces</u>! And I was <u>around</u>, down there! All damn <u>night</u>! I get the <u>impression</u>, though, that they found names and addresses . . . of a whole lot of <u>people</u>! <u>Many</u> people . . . in, I guess, some other <u>terrorist</u> bands!"

"What's <u>that</u> got to do . . . with the seven o'clock news?"

"Well, if they told God and everybody that they'd <u>captured</u> these scumbags, then their beloved 'brothers and sisters' in the other cities'd probably <u>scatter</u>! Either <u>that</u> . . . or the authorities figured that those assholes'll start <u>detonating</u> things! Blowing <u>up</u> stuff . . . all over the place! Blow the <u>shit</u> . . . out of all these targets that Clark and Frank were <u>talking</u> about! I guess that the cops're trying to keep a <u>lid</u> on the thing! For <u>awhile</u>, anyway! To sneak <u>up</u>! Get the <u>drop</u> . . . on these bastards! <u>All</u> of 'em! Here, there . . . and everywhere <u>else</u>! Snag 'em <u>all</u>! Or, at least, run down as many as <u>possible</u>, anyway!"

"Yeah. But, didn't those <u>guys</u> . . . the ones in the <u>apartment</u> . . . didn't they get to call their <u>attorneys</u>?"

"I guess they were <u>supposed</u> to! But, I don't think they ever <u>did</u>! Hell, I'm not <u>sure</u>! The <u>cops</u> . . . they didn't look to share a whole hell of a <u>lot</u> with me. What I <u>learned</u> . . . or what I <u>think</u> I may have learned . . . was just from <u>snatches</u>, of really-rushed conversation, here and there! And . . . for Christ's <u>sakes</u> . . . keep what I'm telling you under your hat! For one thing, I'm not even sure that I know what the hell I'm talking about!"

"You can count on me not saying anything. But, Jesus Ski, they can't just circumvent the law! I mean, they're supposed to read 'em the Miranda Card . . . and all such shit as that!"

"Hell, Dick. I don't know . . . if they did that or not! And I could really care less. For one thing, I think that their lawyer is none other than William Katzmeyer. You have to know that . . . if these schmucks had gotten hold of him . . . he'd have splattered the whole thing all over television! All three networks! You'd have seen it on the eleven o'clock news . . . last night! Every one of those liberal, so-called, reporters would have had his or her nose . . . so far up Katzmeyer's ass, that they'd have to go to the hospital! To have 'em all surgically removed!"

"Yeah," Gladwynne agreed, glumly. "I can see what you mean. Still . . ."

"It'd blow the whole thing! Blow the entire gig! In all the other cities! They needed to keep a lid on it! Still do! If the good guys are gonna have a shot . . . at getting hold of these bastards! Nailing 'em . . . before anyone gets hurt! As I understand it, Dane flew out to Chicago! And that was last night!"

"Dane?"

"Lieutenant Dane! Bomb Squad! He's the guy who came over here to talk to our sainted poobah . . . Mister Hens. I'd stuck around . . . across the street, at the coffee shop. Hens actually did, though! He actually called the police! Dane came out! I guess Hens . . . oh, he of the sunny countenance . . . didn't get along really <u>well</u>, with Lieutenant Dane. You may find that difficult to believe. So, <u>I</u> got involved! Dane tried to get a <u>warrant</u> . . . to search the entire <u>building</u>! The apartment on Fifty-<u>sixth</u>!"

"<u>God</u>! The whole damn <u>building</u>?"

"Yeah. I <u>guess</u> so! <u>None</u> of us knew what <u>apartment</u> these shitheads were in! But, this asshole <u>judge</u> . . . <u>he</u> wouldn't sign the goddam <u>warrant</u>! <u>Source</u> of the information . . . which came from your friendly neighborhood <u>Polack</u> . . . was not <u>constitutional</u>, I guess! Well, I'm <u>sure</u> that the whole thing was not constitutional, dammit!"

"Because you <u>heard</u> it . . . because <u>we</u> heard it . . . in the ol' <u>shithouse</u>? <u>That's</u> what made it unconstitutional?"

"Yup. But, this guy . . . <u>Dane</u>! He didn't let a little thing like <u>that</u> stop him! Helluva <u>guy</u>, he is! I don't have the foggiest <u>idea</u> how he did it! And <u>he's</u> not real <u>anxious</u> to tell <u>anyone</u> . . . including me! But, he <u>did</u>! He found <u>out</u>! This guy was . . . somehow . . . able to <u>determine</u> what <u>apartment</u> the slimebuckets were <u>in</u>! Not only <u>that</u> . . . but, he kicked down the goddam <u>door</u>! Kicked it right <u>in</u>! Took 'em <u>all</u>! Every damn <u>one</u> of 'em! How 'bout <u>that</u>, sports fans?"

"<u>All</u>? Took 'em <u>all</u>? What's <u>all</u>? How many <u>were</u> there?"

"<u>Eleven</u> . . . so I understand!"

"<u>Eleven</u>? <u>Jesus</u>! Was the glorious <u>Premier</u> there?"

"<u>Yeah</u>! As I understand it, her name is <u>Annabelle</u>! Has some screwy <u>last</u> name! Dane thinks it's <u>false</u>! I guess she's really a <u>huge</u> broad! I didn't <u>see</u> her . . . but, Dane said she was a damn <u>Amazon</u>! And not a drop of <u>fat</u> on her, either! He said she should really have gone straight! Should've tried out . . . for middle linebacker . . . for the Giants or Jets!"

"Where'd she pick up the ginger-peachy moniker? The out-of-this-world 'Premier' deal?"

"Well, apparently, the outfit's called The Freedom People's Nation. So, it's supposed to be, apparently, some kind of apeshit nation! An independent nation! I guess it could be local . . . or nationwide! Hell, it could be international! The cops don't think . . . I don't believe they do, anyway . . . they don't think that there were any more people! Not in the local group! Not outside of the eleven . . . that Dane busted! Hell, I could be wrong about that! If I stop and think, I could be wrong . . . about everything! Like I said, they didn't take me into their confidence! But, this shit-assed group . . . is supposed to be a real-life, bona fide 'nation'! Is that overpowering. or what? The idea, I guess, is that . . . if it's a pissy-assed 'nation' . . . well, then it has to have a premier! Or some kind of head gazink! Cute? Is that clever . . . or what?"

"Hmmmmph," grunted Gladwynne. "Not much of a nation. I'm not impressed!"

"Dane thinks that they're made up of all different 'nations'! Or maybe they're all part of the same one! But, they're in other parts of the country!"

"Holy shit!"

"Let me tell you: This particular 'nation', or whatever in hell it is . . . the one that hung out on Fifty-sixth . . . was, for sure, big enough! Was powerful enough . . . to take out that whole furschlugginer neighborhood! Packed the gear . . . with all the shit, that they had put together there . . . packed the gear to wipe out, literally, blocks, although I guess they'd had smaller, specific, targets! Like, maybe, the Statue of Liberty . . . and maybe the tunnels! And the George Washington Bridge! Possibly Police Headquarters! The Federal Building, maybe! God only <u>knows</u>! It's really <u>frightening</u>! Frightening as <u>hell</u>! Scares <u>me</u>, anyway!"

"So, all these <u>creeps</u> . . . they're all in <u>jail</u>?"

"As far as I <u>know</u>! What Dane did . . . he stuck me in a <u>coffee</u> shop, last night! Before he went out and <u>busted</u> those schmucks! <u>Man</u>! I drank so much <u>coffee</u> . . . that I can't get twenty feet from the can. Wound up . . . like I was drinking <u>Drano</u>! Every time I burp, it <u>percolates</u>. About ten o'<u>clock</u>, . . . maybe a little later . . . he picked me up, from *The White Palace*! Took me down to Police <u>Headquarters</u>! I really don't know <u>why</u>. But, he must've had <u>something</u> in mind. I'm <u>sure</u> he did. There was a hell of a lot of <u>commotion</u> going on, down there! All <u>hell</u>, I'm sure, was breaking loose! But, I really wasn't <u>involved</u> with it! Wasn't involved in <u>any</u> of it! <u>None</u> at all, dammit! <u>Frustrating</u> as hell! I can only <u>guess</u> . . . can only <u>imagine</u> . . . some of the stuff that went on! That <u>must've</u> gone on! Like I said, they weren't really all that <u>anxious</u> . . . to take me into their saintly <u>confidence</u>! Finally, <u>Dane</u> had me driven. Can you believe <u>driven</u>? <u>Chauffeured</u> . . . out to my room, in Jersey. I guess he was getting ready to take off . . . for <u>Chicago</u>!"

"Holy <u>shit</u>, Ski! You really got yourself into the big <u>time</u> . . . with <u>this</u> caper!"

"Yeah." he muttered. "I suppose so. Maybe. The thing that really <u>bothers</u> me, though, is . . . when this idiot Katzmeyer gets <u>himself</u> involved! He's gonna raise forty-'leven hells! Rattle all kinds of cages! Mostly . . . I'm sure . . . about those playful little rascals being held incommunicado!"

"Well, you really don't know . . . not for a fact . . . that they actually were! You don't really know that they were . . . in point of fact . . . held incommunicado! Do you?"

"No. No, I don't! But, did you hear anything about it . . . on the seven o'clock news, this morning?"

"Touché! But, Katzmeyer . . . even as we speak . . . isn't the great man off somewhere? Defending Attila the Hun? Or Bluebeard . . . or Jack The Ripper or somebody?"

"Probably. I think he's still involved in the Attica prison riots thing . . . up in Buffalo! And I think he's also in to some Indian thing going . . . out in New Mexico, or Arizona someplace. I really don't know where the hell he is! Half the time, I don't think he does either!"

"Half the time?"

"Touché . . . to you too, Sir," responded Smigelski with a smile. It just about broke his face. "The guy's always holding some pissy-assed news conference! So he can inform all us great unwashed . . . as to just how screwed up the country is! The networks, of course, they eat that shit up! They love him!"

"I've noticed."

"Yeah," his Polish partner replied, glumly. "But, you're about the only one! The thing that galls me is that he's supposed to be so utterly . . . so beautifully . . . selfless! Dedicated as hell . . . to all these noble, worthy, causes! But, if anyone was to actually stop . . . and to actually think! He always manages to haul in . . . a big fat <u>fee</u>! For <u>himself</u>! From <u>someone</u>! Usually the <u>government</u>! Out of <u>whatever</u> the 'noble cause' is . . . that he <u>involves</u> himself in."

"Yeah, you're right. It usually <u>is</u> from the taxpayers," grunted Gladwynne. "If he was so damn <u>dedicated</u> . . . as he'd have us <u>believe</u> . . . why, he'd be happy, to work for <u>free</u>! You'd <u>think</u> that, anyway! You'd think . . . that he'd be <u>glad</u> to donate his <u>time</u>! If that's what it <u>took</u> . . . to further the cause of <u>fairness</u>! And <u>freedom</u>! And the American <u>way</u>!"

"I understand . . . that he's got a home in Mount Vernon! One that'd dazzle the <u>Rockefellers</u>! He always . . . <u>always</u> . . . manages to get <u>his</u>! Ironic. Ironic as hell."

"Ironic? How's that?"

"He's made himself . . . his-own-<u>self</u> . . . a <u>fortune</u>! Picked up all <u>kinds</u> of loot . . . decrying the plight of the <u>downtrodden</u>! Somehow, though, they always seem to <u>stay</u> downtrodden! But, the esteemed Mister <u>Katzmeyer</u> . . . somehow, he <u>always</u> manages to come <u>out</u> of these things a few hundred thou' to the <u>good</u>! A few hundred thou' <u>here</u>, a few hundred thou' <u>there</u>. Pretty soon it adds <u>up</u>. Eventually, you're talking some serious <u>money</u>."

"You sound like Senator Dirkson," laughed Gladwynne.

"Yeah. Well, it's really not <u>funny</u>, Dick. When <u>he</u> gets wind of the fact, that these poor, downtrodden, little <u>pimps</u> . . . these dedicated little <u>rascals</u>, who were merely going to playfully blow the country to kingdom <u>come</u> . . . have had their <u>rights</u> denied them, he'll <u>really</u> fill up all your newscasts for you."

"I can <u>imagine</u>. I can just <u>imagine</u>. Or maybe I <u>can't</u>."

"He'll tell you all <u>about</u> those poor, misunderstood, assholes! The poor <u>unfortunate</u> ones! These poor wretches . . . who our rotten-to-the-core <u>culture</u> has produced! Who our corrupt . . . needs to be destroyed . . . society has <u>failed</u>! Failed . . . so <u>badly</u>! And, of course the <u>networks</u> . . . why, they're gonna eat that shit <u>up</u>! They always <u>have</u>! Presumably, always <u>will</u>! Get the old <u>nose</u> . . . right to the old <u>ass</u>! <u>Quickly</u>! And <u>firmly</u>!"

"Holy <u>schmolely</u>, Ski! <u>I've</u> never . . . ever . . . <u>liked</u> the bastard! But, I didn't realize <u>you</u> were that <u>uptight</u> about him!"

"Ahhhh. It's not only <u>him</u>! Although he's bad <u>enough</u>! The networks'll . . . <u>they'll</u> interview every goddam left-wing kook they can dredge <u>up</u>! And, of course, they'll act as though these assholes are the last <u>word</u>, on the subject. On <u>any</u> subject."

Smigelski had anticipated the coming media storm—with a paradoxical sense of anticipation and <u>dread</u>! Who could possibly <u>know</u> how it would come out?

That <u>afternoon</u>—things began to <u>break</u>! Big <u>time</u>!

The media was <u>filled</u>! <u>Overwhelmed</u>—with the "<u>outrageous</u>" news that a large number of members of a "non-establishment" group in Chicago—The Free The People Coalition—had been taken into <u>custody</u>! Police—and a half-dozen agents from the Federal Bureau of Investigation—had raided a five-room home in suburban Des Plaines!

The authorities had confiscated substantial amounts of dynamite, timing devices and blasting caps—as well as other materials associated with the manufacture of explosive devices!

In addition, the cops and agents had seized a veritable arsenal! A frightening number of .45 automatic handguns, a dozen carbines, 20 submachine guns—and six hand grenades!

Jailed were nine men and five women! Authorities believed that the 14 people—the individuals that they had taken into custody—had comprised the entire membership of the Chicago group!

Within an hour, a second story broke! District of Columbia police and federal authorities had raided an apparently-deserted office building, on the Nation's Capital's northeast side!

Taken into custody were12 members of The Brotherhood of Hanoi! As had happened in Chicago, a copious number of weapons were confiscated! The group was well known to D.C. police—and to the FBI. The terrorist band had, for months, been suspected of planting two bombs in the Capital Building! Both, fortunately, had been discovered—before they'd detonated!

In addition, the group was thought responsible for the attempted assassination of the admittedly right-wing senior senator from the state of Alabama! The lawmaker had led a Senate-floor fight to expand the death penalty—to include conviction, in a good many instances, involving terrorism! He'd listed some of the more heinous, extremely-deadly, federal crimes! Atrocities that seemed to have been perpetrated—

with greater and greater frequency, over the previous few years—in the far-reaching bill!

As the senator had driven along one of the freeways, in a Maryland suburb, another car had pulled alongside—and a fusillade of bullets had crashed through the window of the driver's door! Somehow, the slugs had missed the senator! But, he'd lost control of the car! The vehicle had spun into the median, had tipped over—and caught <u>fire</u>! The would-be assassins—believing they'd <u>fulfilled</u> their nefarious mission—had, seconds later, sped away!

The solon, though, had, somehow, managed to crawl out of the deceased car—seconds before it had <u>exploded</u>! This—despite having suffered a broken arm, numerous lacerations, as well as a substantial number of painful cuts from the flying shards of glass! In addition, he'd suffered burns over almost 25% of his body! An <u>amazing</u> feat of survival!

As the current day Washington story was breaking, Los Angeles police—along with a copious number of FBI agents—were raiding yet <u>another</u> bomb factory! This one was located in the very shadow of <u>City Hall</u>!

The group—called simply Liberation—consisted of some 20 suspected members. Thirteen were taken into custody—along with the "traditional" overwhelming number of arms and explosives!

Two smaller raids—in Detroit and Atlanta—yielded lesser amounts of bombs and firearms. And a lesser number of arrests!

<u>Where had they gone wrong</u>? wondered Smigelski—who, along with his partner, had sat glued to the small battery-powered radio that he'd "smuggled in"!

All three networks' 6:00PM newscasts were crammed with the raids in Chicago, Washington and Los Angeles! Significantly, it was at that point—that they'd also, <u>spectacularly</u>, broke the story of the previous evening's capture of the 11 put-upon members of The Freedom People's Nation, in New York!

One of *Amalgamated Broadcasting System's* more enterprising reporters had discovered that, in the case involving "The Big Apple", those 11 prisoners had, shockingly, been held <u>incommunicado</u>! <u>Incommunicado</u>—all night! And for most of the current day!

The news anchors always, without fail, went out of their way—to stress that <u>facet</u> of the story. Almost to the <u>exclusion</u> of any other aspect. Much <u>less</u> emphasis was placed upon the potential <u>danger</u>—and the staggering numbers of the <u>dozens</u> of lethal bombs—seized in the spectacular raids! No <u>mention</u> was ever made of the multitude of <u>firearms</u> confiscated! The overwhelming, immense, <u>firepower</u>—of the multitude of in-production bombs, as well as the massive number of "insignificant" weapons involved—seemed to populate the highly-viewed newscasts' "back burners"!

At the close of the *ABS* newscast, the anchor delivered a <u>blistering</u> editorial—decrying the violation of the precious civil rights, of those "unfortunate young people" who'd been "illegally detained"! Who'd been denied their "self-evident civil liberties"—over "such an <u>intolerable</u> amount of time"! Who'd been denied "their constitutional <u>access</u> . . . to our plainly <u>corrupt</u> judicial system"! The "ghastly deprivation" had been attributable, of course—to "our even <u>more</u> hopelessly-corrupt "law-enforcement authorities"!

Viewers were invited to remained tuned—for "A Special *ABS* News Report!

After a seemingly-endless string of commercials—and flashy "promos", extolling the network's up-coming programming—the screen, amid much fanfare, switched to its Buffalo affiliate! From there, they would broadcast a live interview with "famed Defense Attorney William Katzmeyer":

INTERVIEWER: Mister Katzmeyer, I understand you're on your way back to New York City . . . to see about the people that were arrested down there, last night. In what the police are calling a raid on an out and out bomb factory.

KATZMEYER: Well, that's what the <u>police</u> would like you to <u>believe</u>! That's the official <u>line</u>! And they're gonna <u>stick</u> with it! In point of <u>fact</u>, though, the cops <u>illegally</u> invaded a private <u>dwelling</u>! Do you see what I'm <u>saying</u>? A private <u>dwelling</u>! They <u>raided</u> it! <u>Without</u> . . . and I cannot <u>stress</u> this enough . . . they invaded that private <u>dwelling</u>! And <u>without</u> a <u>search</u> warrant! A <u>warrant</u> . . . which. in <u>truth</u>, had been <u>sought</u>! And the judge had . . . <u>properly</u> . . . refused to <u>sign</u> it! So, what you <u>have</u> down there . . . you have eleven American <u>citizens</u>! Eleven of our fellow <u>Americans</u> . . . being held <u>prisoner</u>! Not only are they being held <u>prisoner</u> . . . but, they're <u>all</u> being held prisoner <u>incommunicado</u>! <u>Incommunicado</u>, for God's sake! Well, they <u>were</u>! And for the better part of twenty-four <u>hours</u>! Can you <u>believe</u> that? Twenty-four <u>hours</u>! A few minutes . . . less than a full <u>day</u>! At no <u>time</u> were they permitted to phone their <u>attorney</u>! Now, <u>these</u> are <u>not</u> things . . . that are <u>negotiable</u>! This is the <u>law</u>! The law of the <u>land</u>! We're talking about things, that the police are <u>required</u> . . . required by <u>law</u> . . . to <u>do</u>! To <u>honor</u>! Civil <u>rights</u> . . . that the authorities are duty <u>bound</u> to <u>recognize</u>! Recognize . . . and <u>honor</u>! The <u>police</u> . . . they're <u>obligated</u>! It's their <u>duty</u> . . . to do certain <u>things</u>! <u>Especially</u> . . . in a case such as <u>this</u>! As you can <u>see</u> . . . as <u>anyone</u> can see . . . they did <u>not</u> perform their duties! Did not even <u>try</u>! They out and out <u>flaunted</u> these young people's civil <u>rights</u>! Even a mass-<u>murderer</u> . . . or, damn it, a serial <u>rapist</u> . . . has these rights! But, not <u>these</u> committed, young people! In <u>their</u> case . . . why the <u>Gestapo</u> just simply broke down the <u>door</u>! Herded them off to the <u>stalag</u>! All <u>this</u> . . . without respecting <u>anything</u> even remotely <u>resembling</u> these kids' <u>rights</u>! Rights <u>guaranteed</u>! Guaranteed . . . by our <u>Constitution</u>! Now, I have no idea of what the police <u>say</u> that they found! But, <u>listen</u>! <u>Listen</u> to me! The police have been <u>known</u> . . . they <u>have</u> been known . . . to <u>plant</u> evidence! <u>Evidence</u> . . . so <u>called</u>! Been <u>known</u> to 'throw down' all <u>kinds</u> of fallacious stuff . . . in the <u>past</u>! A <u>lot</u> of things! In an effort to <u>get</u> those . . . those who hold divergent political <u>views</u>! Positions that're <u>contrary</u> to what the <u>establishment</u> would have us hold.

INTERVIEWER: Well, Sir, the police seem to contend that . . . if they'd let the prisoners <u>contact</u> you, or another attorney . . . that they'd have been unable to have <u>accomplished</u> the raids. What the authorities label as 'productive ones' . . . in cities like Los Angeles and Washington and Chicago. Their <u>claim</u> . . . is that the alleged terrorists in those cities . . . as well as in Atlanta and in Detroit . . . would've been <u>forewarned</u>! That they'd have <u>escaped</u>! Or . . . <u>worse</u>, according to the authorities! The authorities . . . they apparently believe that they'd have detonated a number of <u>bombs</u>, in those areas! The authorities . . . they all say that they'd have <u>killed</u> many people! <u>Hundreds</u> of people!

KATZMEYER: (With a patronizing smile) If this didn't pertain to basic civil <u>rights</u>, not only being <u>violated</u> . . . but trampled <u>underfoot</u> . . . I guess I'd think of your Mid-America naiveté as <u>charming</u>! <u>Somewhat</u>, anyway! <u>Listen</u>! We <u>know</u> . . . only what the police <u>tell</u> us! The only <u>fact</u> . . . the one, single, undisputed <u>fact</u>, we have, at this precise <u>moment</u> in time . . . is the fact that eleven <u>people</u> were <u>herded</u>! Rounded up . . . and <u>herded</u>! Like so many <u>cattle</u>! <u>Herded</u> . . . out of a private <u>dwelling</u>! <u>Prodded</u> . . . as it were! Out of a private <u>dwelling</u>! At <u>gunpoint</u>! At virtual <u>gunpoint</u>! Guns <u>drawn</u>! Held . . . in violation of their basic <u>rights</u>! <u>Detained</u> . . . for almost twenty-four <u>hours</u>! With <u>no</u> opportunity . . . not <u>one</u> . . . to consult with an <u>attorney</u>! Even the <u>police</u> admit that! Well . . . as it turns out . . . they <u>had</u> to! So, what you <u>have</u> . . . is the <u>personification</u> of the know-all, hear-all, see-all, the damnable, <u>police</u> state! Wake <u>up</u>! This is the absolute <u>personification</u> of the police state! And you <u>have</u> that . . . in one lousy <u>cop</u>! One corrupt <u>pig</u>! One <u>Nazi</u> pig, who . . . in direct <u>violation</u> of a judge who <u>refused</u> to sign a search warrant . . . takes the law into his own <u>hands</u>! Try and <u>deny</u> that! This police pig . . . with absolutely no <u>regard</u> for anything! No regard for <u>anyone</u>! This is <u>nothing</u> . . . but, a <u>naked</u> display of Gestapo-like <u>police</u> power! I don't know about <u>you</u> . . . but, <u>I</u> consider this to be very <u>frightening</u>! A God-awful . . . terribly <u>frightening</u> . . . situation! Now, if they're <u>allowed</u> to get <u>away</u> with this . . . get away with this <u>ludicrous</u> invasion of <u>privacy</u> and out and out <u>trashing</u> of civil rights . . . there'll be no <u>stopping</u> them! No <u>way</u> of stopping them! We <u>have</u> to take a stand! Take a <u>stand</u>! Here . . . and <u>now</u>! Otherwise, we're going to wind up giving <u>up</u> . . . giving up every <u>freedom</u>, that we've ever <u>gained</u>, in the almost-two-hundred year <u>history</u>, of this great <u>nation</u>!

Two days following the shown-nationwide interview, all charges against the 11 members of The Freedom People's Nation were <u>dismissed</u>!

Manhattan's district attorney stated, simply, that there was no <u>sense</u> going forward—with a case that he <u>could not win</u>! All evidence in Dane's illegal search and seizure would have been ruled to have been <u>inadmissible</u>! Most scholars agreed that this would've been the logical outcome of <u>any</u> such legal action!

The turn of events, of course, cast a shadow over any and all court procedures in Chicago, Washington, Los Angeles, Atlanta and Detroit!

Lt. Royce Dane was—immediately—<u>suspended</u>, albeit with pay! He would, however, have to answer serious departmental charges—for his <u>unauthorized foray</u>, into the apartment on East 56th Street!

FOURTEEN

THE NEXT TWO MONTHS WENT routinely enough for Smigelski. He continued to work at **Ballinger's Department Store**, in Queens.

The gig had settled into an almost-boring routine—of watching each and every day drag its way past. Not much action. Two or three times each week, he—and/or his partner—would turn up some small, nondescript, illegal, transaction, negotiated in the sanctified environs of the men's room. All minor-league stuff—compared to the mind-warping bomb-making exploits of loveable Clark and frightened Frank! The present, non-earthshaking, "difficulties" all managed to get settled—with a minimum of dust being raised (although, the presence of one Donald Hens always promised <u>some</u> adventure!)

His hoped-for, potentially-wondrous, promotion had not yet come to pass—although Leland Nype had advised him (continually) to "hang in there". In our hero's mind, his superior had not forgotten him.

He and Gladwynne had, by then, become fast friends. He had even begun getting along—passably well—with Donald Hens. "Only you . . . and Saint Francis of Assisi," Gladwynne had quipped—numerous times.

Days and weeks passed—and, as indicated, nothing untoward seemed to occur.

Well, there had been that one red-letter day—when Gladwynne had been required to monitor the ladies' room. Neither of the two women, assigned to that duty had reported to work. However, within two hours, **Tarkenton** had sent over another <u>woman</u> to assume the watch—and Gladwynne was safely returned, unscathed, to his billet with Smigelski.

Even June Bodner had come to accept, more or less, the latter's position—albeit with an abundance of grudging, good grace. With Smigelski's hours leveling off at a steady, dependable, 8:00 AM to 5:00 PM shift, the couple was able to settle into a more routine—much less hectic—lifestyle. That value alone, seemingly, was sufficient for June to "pull in her horns".

They'd even set a wedding date! Something <u>neither</u> of them had thought possible—for the longest while!

Then, in May of 1975, Smigelski's world came crashing down!

The phone rang, in the little cubicle office he'd shared with Gladwynne. It was late afternoon—4:45PM. The black man picked up the phone. "Gladwynne here."

"My. Don't we sound official today."

"Oh, Hi Junie. How the hell are you?"

"Well, except for people . . . who spout obscenities into the phone at me . . . I'm fine."

"Hey! I don't know about you . . . but, obscene calls are the only thrill I get nowadays."

"You do them rather well," she replied, with her patented warm laugh, "How-some-ever, if you don't put a certain Polack on, this'll <u>really</u> turn into an obscene call."

"Don't hit me, Junie," laughed Gladwynne. "I'm a yellow cabdriver!"

"You're also an idiot."

"Yes. Quite so. But, enough about me." Doing his best to imitate Ed Sullivan, Gladwynne continued, "Let's hear it now . . . for Victor B. Smigelski! Fresh from a successful appearance in Donald Hens' office! Coming to you live! From our lofty perch . . . overlooking the ever-so-scenic, lavish, men's john! Take it away, Vick-Sweetie!"

Smigelski snatched the receiver from the chortling Gladwynne. "I think someone'll be taking <u>you</u> away, one of these days," he ribbed his partner. "Hello, Junie?" he said into the phone. "How the hell are you?"

"You guys have been working too closely . . . for far too long," answered his fiancée "And, I'm sure, watching the men's privy hasn't helped any. But . . . that to the side . . . I'm fine. How the hell are you?"

Smigelski grinned and half-covered the mouthpiece—allowing his muffled voice to bleed through to June—and reproached Gladwynne: "What the hell kind of friend are you? To go ahead . . . and give me an obscene phone call?"

"Will you two rubby-dubs knock it off?" barked June, in mock-anger. "This is costing me an arm and a leg. Jersey is long distance, y'know."

Removing his hand from the receiver, Smigelski chuckled. "It sho' is," he replied.

"C'mon, Honey," pleaded June. "I just wanted to ask you if you'd be home on time. I still can't get used to your being here every night for din."

"Yeah. Sure. Unless you know something I don't."

"No. I just wanted to be sure. Tonight, I'm gonna really dazzle you with my footwork!"

"Oh yeah? How so?"

"How does scalloped potatoes and pork chops grab you?"

"Wunderbar! Who'd you rob? I didn't think that . . . if you and I pooled our vast resources . . . I don't think we'd be able to come up with a satisfactory downstroke, for pork chops."

"Well, I've been saving my money . . . in a little tin box, don'tcha know." June was parodying a humorous—and slightly Ribald—song from the fifties Broadway show, _Fiarello_.

"I wouldn't touch that line with a ten-foot pole . . . or an eleven-foot Swede," replied Smigelski.

"Yeah," responded June. "Really led with the ol' chin there, didn't I? Sometimes a six-foot Pole . . . like yourself . . . is more than I can handle. Anyhoo, I was just checking. I'll put the stuff on now, and . . ."

The blast at the other end was deafening!

"Junie! Junie? Oh, my God!!!"

"What . . . what happened?" shouted Gladwynne. "That was a hell of a noise!"

Smigelski simply stared at the dead phone in his suddenly-clammy hand! "Oh, my <u>God</u>," he rasped again. "Oh, my <u>God</u>!"

Gladwynne bounded out of his chair! "What . . . what <u>is</u> it, Ski? What <u>is</u> it?"

Ignoring Gladwynne, Smigelski mashed the phone back into its cradle—and slumped back into his chair!

Then, he snatched the instrument up—and frantically dialed the number of his former wife, in New Brunswick, New Jersey! After two rings, his call was answered!

"<u>Inez</u>? Inez, is that <u>you</u>?"

"Yes, Vick. What's the <u>matter</u>?"

"I didn't expect you to be <u>home</u>! <u>Thought</u> I'd get one of the <u>kids</u>!"

"I was sick today. Phoned in, and . . ."

"<u>Look</u>! <u>Inez</u>! Don't ask any <u>questions</u>! Just get the kids! <u>All</u> of 'em! Get the <u>kids</u> and . . . <u>all</u> of you . . . get out of the <u>house</u>! <u>Now</u>! I <u>doubt</u> that you've got much more than a <u>minute</u> or two! <u>Everyone</u>! <u>All</u>! Get everyone . . . get 'em the hell <u>out</u> of there! Do you <u>understand</u>? Then, get to a <u>phone</u>! Get to a <u>phone</u> . . . and call the <u>police</u>! Tell 'em someone <u>called</u> you! Told you there was a <u>bomb</u> planted! A <u>bomb</u> planted! In your <u>house</u>! <u>Hurry</u>, Inez! For <u>God's</u> sakes . . . <u>hurry</u>! Get everyone <u>out</u>! <u>Everyone</u>! <u>Out</u>!"

"All <u>right</u>! All <u>right</u>, Vick! I'll get . . ."

Smigelski broke the connection!

Immediately, he dialed "O"—and when the local phone company's operator came on the line, he barked into the instrument:

"<u>Operator</u>! This is an <u>emergency</u>! My name is <u>Smigelski</u>! S-M-I-G-E-L-S-K-I! It's absolutely <u>vital</u> . . .

absolutely <u>critical</u> . . . that you get through to police <u>headquarters</u>, in Metuchen, New <u>Jersey</u>! It's in the two-oh-one <u>area</u> code . . . but, I don't have the <u>number</u>!"

"I'll get you Directory Assistance, Sir."

"<u>NO</u>! We don't have <u>time</u>, goddam it! Now . . . <u>listen</u> to me! <u>Please</u>! Please, <u>listen</u>! Get the Metuchen <u>Police</u>! Tell 'em that I live <u>upstairs</u> . . . over the *Paddock <u>Bar</u>*! On <u>Hillside</u>! Name's <u>Smigelski</u>! Tell 'em I have reason to believe . . . that a <u>bomb</u> is going to explode! At my <u>room</u>! Room <u>Three</u>! Over the *Paddock Bar*! Maybe the bomb'll be <u>downstairs</u>! In the bar <u>itself</u>! It <u>might</u> go off within <u>minutes</u>! Within <u>minutes</u>! For Christ's <u>sakes</u>, Operator . . . <u>please</u>! <u>Please</u> get the police over there! <u>Please</u>!"

"Yes, <u>Sir</u>! Right <u>away</u>!"

The connection was broken!

Smigelski stared at the phone—for about 10 seconds! Stunned! Dazed! Disbelieving!

"<u>Christ</u>, Ski!" Gladwynne's voice seemed to be coming from some nether world—through a coarse, grainy, shroud of shock! "Jesus <u>Christ</u>! Did what I <u>think</u> happened . . . did it really <u>happen</u>?"

"I . . . I'm afraid so!" His voice was overflowing with abject dejection. He stared off—absently locking his gaze on the doorway to the little cubbyhole! "I . . . I can't . . . I can't <u>believe</u> this! I mean, it's <u>got</u> to be a . . . to be a <u>dream</u>! A fucking <u>dream</u>! A goddam <u>nightmare</u>! It <u>couldn't</u> have . . . ! I mean . . ."

He began to sob!

"<u>God</u>, Ski! What can I <u>do</u>? What can <u>anyone</u> do?"

Smigelski struggled to his feet—practically knocking the ratty chair over onto its side! "Tell <u>Hens</u>!

Oh, and call Mister <u>Nype</u>! <u>Tell</u> 'em . . . <u>both</u> of 'em . . . that I'm <u>gone</u>! Tell Mister <u>Nype</u> . . . tell him, what just <u>must've</u> happened!"

Still stunned—from head to toe—he had to force himself to walk to the door! His knees resembled two-way hinges!

Once in the car, Smigelski had to do his best to clear away the tears! He knew that, otherwise, he'd never make the long drive back to Central New Jersey! Not with such badly blurred vision! Not as thoroughly as his eyes had hazed over! He swabbed at them—frantically—with a couple paper napkins! Ones that June had left on the front seat of his car—a couple of nights previously, when they'd negotiated the drive-thru at **McDonalds**.

<u>Junie</u>! He increased his speed!

Somehow managing to swerve in and out of the heavy traffic, he sped down Queens Blvd.—and over the 59th Street Bridge! He cursed the bumper-to-bumper traffic on Second Avenue—and the endless series of lights on 42nd Street, as he made his way across Manhattan!

He got to the Lincoln Tunnel! Finally! Once through the tube, he barreled toward the New Jersey Turnpike! After entering the Pike, he floored the tired old Dodge! A slow-moving eternity ground its way by—before he reached the Metuchen exit! The quickest way to North Plainfield happened to go through Metuchen!

Exiting from the toll road, he handed the cashier a $5.00 bill—and didn't bother to wait for his change! He roared to the center of the town—the one he'd called home! As he swept in and out of the moderate traffic on Main Street, he was able to note that the building, in which his room was located—two blocks up Hillside—was still <u>intact</u>!

<u>Thank God</u>!

Three police cruisers loomed in front of the bar—their red lights flashing and rotating! The situation seemed to be well in hand. He <u>hoped</u> so, anyway! He <u>fervently</u> hoped so!

Smigelski sped past the scene—on through South Plainfield and Plainfield, to June's apartment! He'd not been halted by police—in <u>any</u> of those municipalities! A source of <u>wonderment</u>!

Within a block-and-a-half of June's building, he was confronted by the <u>inevitable</u> row of police cars! Their flashing red lights shouted—<u>screamed</u> incessantly—the ominous <u>news</u>! The heart-breaking, gut-wrenching, mind-boggling, undeniable, <u>bulletin</u>!

Abandoning the Dodge, behind one of the police cruisers, he rushed to the building! What was <u>left</u> of the building!

The store downstairs <u>had been completely blown out</u>! The <u>ceiling</u> above—the floor of <u>June's</u> apartment—did <u>not</u> exist! There was a monumental <u>hole</u> in the roof—of what once had been a two-story building!

On the ground floor—what was <u>left</u> of it: A <u>mountain of rubble</u>! Plaster! Wood! Tile! Mortar! Remnants of what had once been various pieces of unrecognizable furniture! Badly-warped display cases! Twisted light fixtures! Food stuffs—equally unrecognizable! And <u>bodies</u>! Dear <u>Lord</u>! <u>Three</u> bodies! Three <u>mangled</u> bodies!

Eight or nine uniformed policemen milled about—holding a dozen curiosity-seekers at bay!

Approaching one of the cops, Smigelski tearfully rasped, "Could I please speak to . . . to whoever . . . to whoever's in charge?"

The officer was about to order him to move along—then, saw the grief and agony contorting his face! "Who're <u>you</u>?" asked the policeman.

"My . . . my fiancée . . . she lived . . . she lived upstairs." He'd been barely able to answer. "She lived up there . . . with her two kids!"

The cop shook his head, sadly. "I'm sorry, Sir," he said. "It <u>looks</u> awfully <u>bad</u>! You'd be wantin' to talk to Inspector Normandin." He pointed at three men—standing close by what was left of the building. "Inspector Normandin's the one in the tan coat . . . and the grey fedora," he advised. "The chunky little guy."

Smigelski hurried toward the group! Inspector Normandin—seeing him approach—held up his hand! "I'm sorry, Sir," the detective half-shouted. "<u>No</u> one's allowed inside the police line! You're going to have to . . ."

"<u>Inspector</u>! My fiancée lived <u>upstairs</u>! With her two <u>children</u>! I was <u>talking</u> to her! Talking to her . . . on the <u>phone</u>! When the <u>explosion</u> . . . when the <u>explosion</u> . . ." He put his hand on the inspector's shoulder. "<u>Inspector</u>," he pleaded, "you've <u>got</u> to help me!"

"Your name?"

"Smigelski, Inspector. Victor Smigelski. I work in Queens . . . at **Ballinger's Department Store**. Live in Metuchen. We were on the phone! Junie and I! I was talking . . . talking right to her when . . . when . . . when . . ."

"What was her name . . . your fiancée?" asked another plainclothesman. "What did you say her name was?"

"June," replied Smigelski, removing his hand from Normandin's shoulder. "June Bodner."

The cop nodded at Normandin. "That checks," he said.

The inspector reached inside his coat—and fished a package of *Marlboros* from his shirt pocket. Lighting one, he stared straight into the distraught Smigelski's eyes.

"There's not really very much we can tell you, Mister Smigelski," he advised. "We've only been here twenty . . . maybe twenty-five . . . minutes now. Squad cars got here little over a half-an-hour ago . . . maybe forty minutes ago. No sign of life! Blast was tremendous! Must've been! Took the whole damn building! Well, you can see that! Blew out windows in the next four . . . maybe five, maybe six . . . buildings! We don't actually know who might've been in there! In any part of the building! Don't know who could've been inside . . . when the sonofabitch went off! Apparently, there was no warning! Near as we can tell, anyway! We've got a crew . . . on the way over! To sift through all this!" He put his hand on Smigelski's shoulder. "I really can't offer you much hope, Mister Smigelski. Of course, there's always the possibility of a miracle! If you believe in such things."

The stocky little detective sighed heavily—
and removed his hand. A third officer joined the
conversation:

"I'm Detective Crowder, Mister Smigelski. We
don't have an official <u>theory</u>. Not <u>yet</u>, anyway. We
have to think that <u>someone</u> had a <u>hard</u>-on . . . a <u>real</u>
hard-on . . . for the <u>storeowner</u>! The guy that <u>owned</u>
the store, downstairs. Uh . . . there wouldn't be any
reason for someone to try and do in Miss <u>Bodner</u> . . .
would there?"

"Yeah! No! I <u>dunno</u>! Maybe! Yeah . . . possibly!"

"You say your fiancée had two <u>kids</u>?" asked
Normandin. "Were <u>they</u> at home? Were <u>they</u>
home . . . with her? Or do you <u>know</u>?"

"I . . . I don't <u>know</u>! Dammit, I don't really <u>know</u>! I
was . . . I was under the <u>impression</u> that they <u>were</u>!
They usually <u>are</u> . . . around this time of day! I don't
<u>remember</u> her saying anything about the kids! Not
one way or <u>another</u>! We hadn't been on the phone . . .
not for all that <u>long</u>! I'm trying to <u>think</u>! Think . . . if I
can remember <u>hearing</u> 'em! <u>Hearing</u> 'em . . . in the
<u>background</u>, y'know! But, shit! It's all a goddam . . . all
a goddam <u>blank</u>!"

"Does she have any <u>relatives</u> . . . or <u>friends</u> . . .
close by?" asked Crowder. "Somewhere the kids
might <u>be</u>?"

"Um . . . her <u>mother</u>! Millicent Gladzell! <u>She</u>
lives . . . uh . . . she lives just a couple blocks <u>away</u>!
<u>She</u> watches the kids . . . during the day! While Junie
<u>works</u>!"

Crowder's face brightened, slightly. "Well, <u>that's</u>
the first halfway <u>encouraging</u> thing we've run into," he
observed, "since we <u>got</u> here!"

"Look, Inspector," said Smigelski. "I told you that I wasn't sure if anyone would want to do anything like that to <u>Junie</u>! That's not quite <u>true</u>!"

"Not quite <u>true</u>?"

"Getting to <u>her</u> is . . . well . . . it's a way of getting to <u>me</u>!"

"Mister Smigelski?" scowled Normandin. "Just what the hell are you <u>talking</u> about?"

Smigelski explained to the three detectives the significance of his collaboration with Royce Dane, in New York.

After the lengthy dissertation, Normandin removed his hat and scratched his head. "Sonofabitch," he muttered. "So <u>you</u> were involved . . . in <u>that</u> magilla? The one with those Freedom <u>Nation</u> assholes? Or whatever the hell they <u>called</u> themselves?"

"Yeah," nodded Smigelski. "That's me. Look . . . is there any way you can find out . . . if my <u>wife</u> and <u>kids</u>? If <u>they're</u> all right? If <u>they</u> made it?"

He gave Crowder Inez's address—and the officer hurried to his cruiser, and grabbed up the police radio. After a seemingly endless wait, the detective returned to the group!

"Apparently," he reported, "there was no <u>explosion</u> over in Brunswick. Your ex called the <u>cops</u>! They're over there <u>now</u>! Over at <u>her</u> house! Dispatcher said he didn't know if they'd found a <u>bomb</u> . . . or not! Said that . . . if there'd have <u>been</u> an explosion . . . he'd damn well <u>know</u> about it! So listen, <u>that</u> sounds pretty encouraging!"

"Anything about the bomb . . . in Metuchen?" queried Normandin.

"Apparently, they <u>found</u> one! A bomb in the <u>bar</u> . . . underneath this gentleman's <u>room</u>! Explosive, in the <u>men's</u> room, as I understand it. The guy . . . at headquarters, over there . . . he said he thinks that they've gotten it all pretty well <u>defused</u> by now! But, their guy can't be <u>certain</u> of that either!"

Smigelski nodded absently. His fevered mind was awash—in a raging, turbulent, churning, sea of troubling, half-answered, totally-devastating, questions: Nobody, for instance, seemed to know how many people may have been in the grocery store—at the time of the blast! Any poor soul who might have been unfortunate enough, to have been inside—well, they could <u>never</u> have survived! And, of course, neither could <u>June</u>! Or the <u>kids</u>! Not <u>realistically</u>!

The <u>kids</u>! <u>Oh</u>, <u>my God</u>! <u>The kids</u>!

"Look, Inspector," he began. "About Junie's <u>kids</u>, I . . ."

"Yeah. We were just going to ask you if you could take a ride . . . with Detective Crowder, here. Over to the kids' <u>grandmother's</u> house. Over to Mrs. <u>Gladzell's</u> house. See if . . . <u>hopefully</u> . . . they might be over <u>there</u>!"

Again, Smigelski nodded, absently—and accompanied Crowder, to his police car!

No one was home at June's mother's residence! Crowder went to six or seven neighbors—inquiring as to when the woman had left. And whether she'd had her grandchildren in tow.

Returning to the cruiser, the officer advised the grieving Smigelski, "Well, one lady says she <u>thinks</u> that Miss Bodner's mother went to the shopping mall! Over on Route Twenty-two! Saw her getting into a <u>cab</u>! Lady . . . in the yellow <u>house</u>, over there . . . said she didn't <u>think</u> that the kids were <u>with</u> her. <u>Another</u> lady . . . next <u>door</u> to the old girl's house . . . said she hasn't <u>seen</u> the kids! Not all <u>day</u>! I'm <u>sorry</u>, Mister Smigelski!"

Back at the scene of the explosion, Smigelski and Crowder found that the promised crew had just arrived—to begin the macabre task, of sifting through the literal tons of rubble!

Smigelski accompanied Normandin and the other officer back to Police Headquarters—leaving Crowder in charge. The latter promised to contact Normandin—the minute he was able to determine whether the children had been among the victims. If it would be possible that <u>anything</u> could be determined!

Other officers were dispatched to the shopping mall on U.S. Route 22—in an attempt to locate June's mother.

Finally—almost 90-minutes later—the dreaded call came:

"Mister Smigelski," began Normandin with a massive sigh, "I <u>hate</u> to have to <u>tell</u> you this . . . but, the <u>worst</u> of what we feared is exactly what <u>happened</u>! The <u>bodies</u> . . . of <u>both</u> children . . . have been <u>found</u>! Along with that, of Miss <u>Bodner</u>!" The words were clipped—almost as though he'd spat them. "Along with the bodies of <u>four</u> people . . . who were apparently in the <u>grocery</u> store, at the time," the inspector groused. "<u>Motherfuckers</u>!"

Smigelski sat—transfixed! His only response was to clench and unclench his fists—and mutter: "The sons of <u>bitches</u>! The sons of <u>bitches</u>! The sons of <u>bitches</u>!"

FIFTEEN

THE NEXT FEW WEEKS WERE, quite obviously, a living hell for Smigelski.

To help dilute some of the grief, from June Bodner's mother, he'd taken over all funeral arrangements—after first identifying the almost-<u>unrecognizable</u> bodies of his fiancée and both of her children. After having left the morgue, he had vomited, non-stop, for almost two hours! Once the siege had finally finished, he'd had to acknowledge, to himself, that he'd never experienced a situation, in which he'd been so thoroughly devastated! So emotionally drained! Not in his entire life! Mentally! Emotionally! Physically! Or in any <u>other</u> way!

It would be a little over a <u>week</u>—before he'd be able to keep anything in his stomach! A period—during which he'd, noticeably, lost 18 pounds!

With the cooperation of the FBI, his former wife and his children were given new identities! Armed with these new, much different, personas—they were relocated, to Albuquerque, New Mexico.

A without-a-doubt, lethal, bomb had been found attached to the rear outside wall, of their residence, in New Brunswick. The deadly device had been mere <u>seconds</u> from <u>detonation</u>—when it had been disarmed! An extremely potent explosive, it was estimated to have had the potential to have taken out—a half-dozen neighboring houses! At least! The mind-boggling death potential was, of course, <u>devastating</u>!

The specter of having his family wiped out—along with the actual loss of June and her children—had Smigelski, literally, on the edge of the bleak, dark, deeply-emotional, world of <u>suicide</u>! Only the highly-emotional realization, that his family <u>did</u> survive, kept him from going "over the edge"! He was absolutely <u>convinced</u> that—had Inez, and the kids, <u>not</u> beaten "The Grim Reaper"—he was certain that he'd have <u>followed</u> them! Would have "reunited" with them—as well as with June, and her children—in <u>eternity</u>!

The police had guarded the family—24/7—for the next 11 arduous days! Up until the moment that they'd left—for New Mexico!

The relocation of his kids—had become an especially <u>bitter</u> pill! He and Inez, of course, had always remained very <u>close</u>—despite their marital difficulties! Her death would've been a horrible situation! Smigelski could not <u>imagine</u> the loss of <u>both</u> Inez <u>and</u> June! The shattering thought of how close his <u>own</u> children had come—to being "blown to smithereens"—continued to cause him head-to-toe <u>shivers</u>! He didn't even want to <u>think</u>—of the heartbreaking deaths of <u>June's</u> son and daughter! He'd come to be a father figure to <u>both</u>! God <u>awful</u>!

The entire state of tragic-in-spades affairs—were God awful!

He'd found himself becoming much closer to June's constantly-distraught, always-in-tears, mother! Much closer!

Having come so close to losing his children, Smigelski had—immediately—begun spending practically every practicable waking hour, at Inez' home! Interacting—nonstop—with the children! Now they were gone! Gone! Almost a full-continent away! Dear Lord!

He dared not contact them. Who knew who could be watching? Or listening? That—when all was said and done—seemed, logically or otherwise, to be the cruelest blow of all!

My life has turned to shit!

That always-present, inescapable, never-letting-up, thought remained behind—or in front of—his every thought!

The FBI proposed that Smigelski also remove himself from the area! One of the agents, in the New York City office—with whom he'd, almost instantly, formed a close association—had mentioned Fargo, North Dakota.

"That ought to be just about right," the agent had observed. "You'd really be away from the mainstream! Way away from the mainstream," he'd advised. "Yet, you wouldn't be an overwhelming distance . . . from Inez and the kids."

Smigelski—after much soul searching—had declined! He would wonder—<u>forever</u>, he was sure—whether it had been the right decision!

He did, though—at the Bureau's insistence—move to another residence! While the bar's owner—downstairs—had, repeatedly, stated otherwise, the man had been <u>noticeably</u> relieved, once his "star tenant" had, actually, <u>relocated</u>!

With the help of Leland Nype, he was able to relocate to a nice apartment, in Madison, New Jersey—about 40 miles from Metuchen. He'd found himself situated, in a large complex—under an assumed name. ("Someone else's name", as he'd constantly described it.) The accommodations, of course, were eons nicer—much more opulent—than had been his little cubbyhole of a room over the bar. A definite upgrade!

Nype had "ground his way, though a bunch of red tape" to have gotten Smigelski a "substantial" raise in pay! His employer had advised the grief-stricken employee—to take as much time off, as he would need!

"As much as you'll <u>ever</u> need," he'd urged. "When you feel . . . as though you're able to return, Vick, we'll talk about something, in a totally-<u>supervisory</u> capacity. Under your new . . . and different . . . <u>name</u>. With a good deal <u>less</u> public exposure! And at a good deal <u>more</u> money! More than you're taking home now!"

"Don't hold your <u>breath</u>, Mister Nype," Smigelski had snarled. "Don't hold your breath!" His superior—a most understanding man—had merely smiled! And patted his still-mourning employee, on the back!

Smigelski was reaching a point—where he was far from the picture of health! Splotches of sickly-looking pinks had broken out all over his body! He ate little! He began to walk, in a slightly-bent-over posture! Not unlike an old man! He spent hour after hour after hour after hour—"holed up", in his apartment! Sitting! No television! No radio! No stereo! Nothing! Just sitting! Staring off into space!

He'd even stopped visiting Mrs. Gladzell! June's mother had remained in North Plainfield—and the trip had reached a point, where it was "too much like work".

From time to time—with absolutely no warning— he would burst into tears! His entire body would wrack—convulsively—from head to toe! Overcome— with debilitating, spastic, sobs! And, as time was passing, the situation was not improving!

Smigelski's "new civilian life" seemed to consist of nothing—other than phoning the various law enforcement agencies: North Plainfield Police, Metuchen Police, New Brunswick Police, New York City Police, the FBI. And a federal agent—at some Washington agency. He never had understood the national body's function. But, he had maintained contact with "Agent Harvey"—"for whatever reason".

Nothing! No progress! No word! No clues! No arrests! No encouragement! Absolutely nothing! Would any of these animals—these sub-humans—ever realize any form of justice? For the savage, heartless, slaughter of June—and her kids? Or for the near-deaths of Inez—and his own children? Would they ever be brought to justice? Any of them? Ever?

The above-mentioned local and federal agencies—in every case, he was convinced—had come to consider him "a royal pain in the ass"!

Too fucking bad!

Things, eventually, reached a point—where the only person who would deign to even speak to Smigelski—was the recently-reinstated Lt. Royce Dane.

"It's almost impossible to pin these dipshits down, Ski," he'd advised, on more than one occasion. "No one knows . . . for sure . . . when the bombs were actually set! We think we know! Hell, we do know! But, proving it . . . any of it . . . that's a whole 'nother thing! And . . . with the estimable Mister Katzmeyer, as their sainted attorney . . . there's no one down here, with balls enough to make him unhappy! Sorry to have to put it to you like that . . . but, that's the way it fucking is! Face it! Those pissants are almost above the law!"

"Almost?" groused Smigelski. "Fucking almost?"

Eight weeks, after the tragic explosion, Smigelski—expectedly or not—returned to work, at **Tarkenton**.

"I had to do <u>something</u>!" he'd lamented, sadly, to Leland Nype.

He was <u>transferred</u>, back to Captain Fox's division—and given the rank of <u>lieutenant</u>! At, as promised, a <u>substantial</u> raise in pay! At Nype's <u>insistence</u>, the "serious" salary increase was made retroactive! The more-than-generous stipend provided the still-grief-stricken man, with a substantial amount of <u>money</u>, in his first "kinder, gentler" paycheck! He'd long since reached a point—where he'd doubted he'd <u>ever</u> see that much money! Especially in one lump sum!

<u>I've got all this money</u>! <u>Great</u>! <u>But</u>, <u>shit</u>! <u>What the hell good is it</u>? <u>What the hell good does it do</u>?

Smigelski's new primary professional responsibility consisted of touring the dozen-or-so **Tarkenton**-controlled locations in The Bronx—checking on the many and varied security guards deployed therein.

The new situation gave him a goodly amount of leisure time. More than he could ever have imagined. More than he'd really <u>wanted</u>. Especially given his still present, seemingly never-ending, stress-laden, mental/emotional anguish! <u>Much</u> more off-site time! That was due to the fact that there were not that many <u>sites</u>—to "supervise". He could see <u>Nype's</u> finger—in the entire arrangement.

With such an excessive amount of time on his hands, he'd begun meeting with Lt. Dane—virtually on a daily basis. Most usually at a mid-town Manhattan coffee shop. (No—not <u>that</u> one!)

Dane, he knew, was making an heroic effort to get something accomplished, insofar as bringing some— or, hopefully, all—of the 11 members, of the hated Freedom People's Nation, to justice! Most especially where the unlawfulness pertained to the deaths in North Plainfield! The lieutenant's magnificent—his tireless—effort had remained horribly <u>frustrating</u>! For <u>both</u> men!

Despite the fact that the diminutive officer had been pulled off that specific case—reassigned, for the most part, to "massaging paperwork"— Smigelski knew that he'd spent night after night after night, shadowing various members of "The Nation". Following—in the shadows—these non-incarcerated "victims of injustice"! Or frequenting their various public hangouts!

It was obvious that Dane was carrying a heavy burden of self <u>guilt</u>—with respect to the deaths of June Bodner and the children! In addition, the media's continuing, unrelenting, never-ending, attack on him—which remained in high gear—was having a profound effect, on the troubled officer! And the relentless, ruthless, campaign—by virtually <u>every</u> left-wing "leader"—was extracting an enormous emotional and psychological price!

Smigelski was convinced that he was witnessing the deterioration—"the evaporation"—of the man! Before his very eyes!

"I'm convinced, Vick," Dane had lamented, on more than one occasion, "that I did the right goddam thing! The only thing I could've done! What the hell was I gonna do? Sit around? Just sit on my ass? Let those assholes blow up all manner of shit? Blow up the whole damn neighborhood? Or a shitload of other places? I'm convinced . . . that I saved the lives of dozens of people! Maybe hundreds! Especially when you factor in D.C. . . . and Chicago and L.A. and Detroit and Atlanta! The authorities put the kibosh . . . on all of those! Every damn one of 'em!" Then, looking at the crestfallen Smigelski, he'd always added, "With three obvious exceptions!"

"I know, Lieutenant," sighed Smigelski. "I know. You probably saved millions of dollars too! To say nothing of so many . . . of our national treasures! All the stuff . . . that those sons of bitches were going to blow up! National landmarks! And you . . . you, and you alone . . . you are the one, who preserved 'em!"

"And for that," grumped Dane, "the media crucifies me! The mayor of our fair city . . . himself . . . he dictated a letter of reprimand! No one . . . not a fucking soul . . . none of them, will come anywhere near me! Not down . . . at Headquarters! Or a half-a-million other places! It'd be curtains for them! End of the line . . . career-wise! My duties . . . so called . . . are not unlike the proverbial guy who's paid to wind a goddam eight-day clock."

"Yeah," sighed Smigelski. "That about sums up my glorious job description."

As time passed, the FPN members—obviously upset with being constantly followed by Dane—intensified their campaign to discredit the detective:

Clark appeared on three different television programs to complain that his phone had been bugged! He even furnished an electronics expert to "verify" the fact. He never failed to launch into his normal venomous diatribe—concerning "the creep who busted in on us . . . without a search warrant, of course! He's been following me all over the place! All the time! He never stops! He's always there! It's out-and-out police harassment, of course! What else could it be? But, who cares? Who the hell cares? No one cares! That's who! Not a soul!"

To which the interviewer—without exception—would always respond, "Well, I care! And I'm sure . . . that our many viewers care! They care! I assure you of that! There are thousands . . . tens of thousands, probably millions! All . . . who care! I know that . . . from the huge amount of mail, I get!"

"Yeah, well," Clark would mutter, "this whole thing is caused . . . because I happen to hold opposing views! Opposing views . . . from our corrupt establishment! In what's supposed to be a free country!"

Two other members of the FPN, in newspaper interviews, proclaimed themselves the innocent victims of "a concerted campaign . . . of relentless police harassment"! Courtesy of Royce Dane, of course!

Dane, himself, was, three times, "called upon the carpet"! Reprimanded—again and again! Ordered to "cease and desist" such "obvious harassment"!

With almost each and every FPN interview—topped off, of course, by the, "traditional", the requisite, official reprimand—the needle had, each time, dug further into Dane! Had gouged—with each interview, and resultant reprimand—a little deeper! There were times when, he would advise Smigelski, the continuing abuse "is becoming damn nigh impossible, for me"!

"I suppose I should <u>resign</u>," he'd continually grumped. "That's <u>really</u> what they <u>want</u> me to do. They all <u>claim</u> . . . all the powers that <u>be</u>, they all <u>insist</u> . . . that I'm giving the department a black <u>eye</u>! But, goddam it, I'm <u>not</u>! I <u>know</u> I'm not!"

"Not going to resign? Or not giving the exalted department a black eye?"

"<u>Both</u>! <u>Neither</u>! Anyway, I'm <u>not</u> going to! <u>Resign</u> that is! To me, that'd amount to unconditional fucking <u>surrender</u>! I figure that, as long as I'm <u>here</u> . . . as long as I'm halfway on <u>top</u> of it . . . something <u>might</u> turn up! And <u>maybe</u> . . . just <u>maybe</u> . . . I can be in <u>position</u>! In position . . . <u>legally</u> . . . to be able to <u>handle</u> it! To actually <u>do</u> something to throw these pieces of shit into the goddam <u>slammer</u>! I'm probably <u>dreaming</u>, y'know, but . . ."

"No, Lieutenant," Smigelski had replied. "I can see what you're <u>saying</u>! See it as clear as <u>day</u>! I . . . really and truly . . . know where you're coming from!"

"I keep telling you to call me <u>Royce</u>," the detective had replied, with a cryptic laugh. "We <u>are</u> friends. Are we <u>not</u>?"

Smigelski had nodded—and sighed. "God help us if we're <u>not</u>," he'd groused. "I guess that we're probably all we've <u>got</u>. I don't know, Royce. I'm so goddam <u>depressed</u>! Even <u>now</u>. Even <u>still</u>! Even <u>yet</u>! And it's been over <u>three</u> months, now. More than three goddam <u>months</u>! Pushing <u>four</u>! And I <u>still</u> can't . . . can't get my <u>head</u> together! I can't get over losing <u>Junie</u>! And . . . dear Lord . . . those two <u>kids</u>! Two innocent little <u>kids</u>! And <u>shit</u>! There's <u>Inez</u> . . . and my <u>own</u> kids! They're <u>alive</u> . . . thank God! But, I can't ever <u>see</u> 'em! Why, I've . . ."

"Listen, Vick! I know it'll sound <u>trite</u>! Anything I'd <u>say</u> would sound trite! But, you <u>will</u> get over it! <u>Eventually</u>! Not a hundred-<u>percent</u>, maybe! Not a hundred-percent, <u>probably</u>! I <u>doubt</u> that you'll get over it . . . a hundred-<u>percent</u>! <u>Never</u> a hundred-percent! But, you <u>will</u> get over it! <u>Eventually</u>!"

Smigelski had shaken his head slowly—and sighed once again. The epitome of gloom! "Look," he muttered, "there's <u>nothing</u> . . . nothing that we can <u>do</u> about it! Do about <u>any</u> of it! <u>You</u> or <u>me</u>! <u>Nothing</u>! Not one goddam <u>thing</u>!"

"Not a fucking <u>thing</u>," affirmed Dane. "Not one fucking <u>thing</u>! They've all got <u>alibis</u> . . . for the killings! No one can pin 'em <u>down</u>! Pin <u>any</u> of the bastards down! Not even fucking <u>close</u>! <u>No</u> one can <u>prove</u> . . . where these animals <u>were</u>! Where the shitheads <u>were</u> . . . when the <u>bombs</u> were set! Probably because . . . well, <u>definitely</u> because no one can say, with any kind of authority . . . <u>when</u> the goddam bombs were even <u>set</u>! Probably <u>hours</u> . . . hell, maybe <u>days</u> . . . before the fucking things ever would've <u>exploded</u>!"

"God <u>damn</u> it, Royce! There's no fucking <u>justice</u>! <u>None</u>!"

"You're telling me? I'm the guy who put the kibosh on a whole bunch of mayhem! And I'm the guy who's had the wrath of God come down on his young ass! The wrath of God! And, of course, the left wing media! Which they think is a wonderful thing!"

"Well," Smigelski had snarled, "something's gonna have to be fucking done! It's driving me nuts! Fucking nuts! Those sons of bitches! They're running around scott-fucking-free! Free! And with the great, good, capability . . . of flipping us the finger! At every turn!"

"I know, Vick. I fucking know! It flies in the face of everything! Everything we've ever been taught! You know what I'm saying! From the time we were little kids, we were taught that right always prevails! And all such shit as that! But, in real life . . . out here in the real world . . . that's not the way it works! Just about everything that's been legislated, over the past few years . . . state, local, national, it doesn't make a shit! All the laws they've passed . . . over the past fifteen, or twenty, years . . . they've all always favored the bad guys! Have fucking tied the hands of the cops! Always hampered the good guys! Without exception! And those asshole appeals courts! Those shitheads . . . are just sitting up there! Just waiting . . . to trip up any convictions that we ever have the audacity to snarf in!"

"You're telling me?"

Dane had built up a full head of steam! "Throw the goddam thing out! Always on some trumped up . . . some asshole . . . legal technicality! The old court reporter happened to fart or something! Out! Throw the goddam case fucking out! Throw the sonofabitch out! And they've got all these apeshit laws . . . to fucking back 'em up! Like you say, goddam it, there isn't any justice! Just fucking law!"

"You sure give me lots of hope!"

"I'm sorry, Vick. But, why should I try and shit you? I can't hold out much hope! But, there is some! Some little bit . . . damn little bit . . . of hope! Whatever chance we have, though . . . is we have to trip those creeps up! Listen . . . I'm gonna be on top of it! Rest assured! Stay on top of it! I'm not gonna let 'em have an inch! Not one fucking inch! Not if I can help it! Key phrase there . . . is 'if I can help it'."

Smigelski had finished his coffee. "Royce, I really have to go. Something about earning my salary. It's been a million laughs." He reached across the table—and shook the officer's hand. "All kidding aside," he continued, "I really and truly do appreciate what you've done! What you've tried to do! I know that you'd like nothing better . . . than to see these hyenas, in the goddam jail!"

"Or . . . better yet . . . in the grave!"

"Yeah. That makes two of us, Royce! That makes two of us!"

Two weeks after the bleak conversation mentioned above, Lt. Dane was set upon, as he'd exited from a restaurant—his favorite "eatin' place"—in his native Brooklyn!

The time was 10:25PM. He'd felt a certain unease—as he'd walked the half-block to his car! Then, much as Smigelski had done, in the warehouse—which, at that point, had seemed to have occurred eons before—Dane had dismissed the creepy feeling of foreboding!

"Getting' spooked in your old age, Royce-Baby," he'd murmured to himself!

As he'd inserted the key in the driver's door-lock, he was <u>hit</u>—from behind! With a 30-inch length of two-by-four! The force of the vicious blow had propelled him—crazily—forward! His forehead had then plastered—into the door's window! The collision had the almost-unbelievable force—of actually <u>cracking</u> the safety glass! The result caused Dane's <u>head</u> to ricochet—violently—backward!

As he was falling to the sidewalk, the board had smashed him again! This time, just above his left ear!

"<u>Scatter</u>!" he heard one of his assailants shout! "There's a fucking <u>crowd</u> . . . gonna be gathering! Let's get the hell <u>outta</u> here!"

The three men took off—on foot!

Dane was able to <u>recognize</u> his attackers! All <u>three</u> assailants were men he'd <u>arrested</u>, on that fateful night! In the <u>apartment</u> on East 56th Street! Of <u>that</u>, he was sure!

One of the ambushers, he knew, was <u>Clark</u>! The black man! One of the two white men was named <u>Jerry</u>! Dane couldn't remember the name of the <u>third</u> assailant. It didn't <u>matter</u>, by then. At least it didn't <u>seem</u> to matter!

The diminutive detective was, by that time, fast losing consciousness!

Six hours later, Lt. Dane awoke, in an antiseptic hospital room! Alone! No visitors! No one at his bedside—to counsel him! Or to console him! He had no family! Smigelski, Dane had always imagined, was probably as close to being a relative, as could ever be expected. And, of course, Smigelski had no way of knowing the detective had been so mercilessly set upon!

The feisty little man hung between life and death—for almost 36 hours!

No one had advised Smigelski of the lieutenant's situation. When Dane hadn't shown up at the coffee shop—for the third day in a row—Smigelski called the Police Department. He was advised that Lt. Dane was "not at work today". Nothing further! A programmed, totally pedestrian, response!

It took two additional days before Smigelski was able to pin down one of the police dispatchers! Pin her down enough—to learn of Royce Dane's outrageous misfortune!

By that time, the detective had been discharged from the hospital! He was rehabilitating—at home! Nursing a "world class concussion . . . and an all-universe headache"!

SIXTEEN

S EVEN LONG, MOURNFUL, MONTHS—AFTER THE damnable bomb had blown June Bodner, and her children, into eternity, four young people sat talking, in the rear-most booth of *The White Palace* coffee shop on 2nd Avenue and 57th Street, in Manhattan.

The quartet—two men and two women—were engrossed in an animated, hoarsely-whispered, conversation. It was obvious—that they were totally oblivious, of the comings-and-goings about them.

"Well," snarled a young black girl, "this is one time I don't <u>agree</u> with the Premier! I think she's waited too damn <u>long</u>! Let it get <u>away</u>! The moment's <u>passed</u>! <u>Gone</u>! <u>Long</u> fucking gone!"

"Oh, <u>Norma</u>," replied one of the young men—Mathew, a white youth, in his early-twenties. "You <u>know</u> how . . . how <u>everyone's</u> been <u>watching</u> us! Like a bunch of fucking <u>hawks</u>! Especially that shit-ass, <u>Dane</u>! He just fucking won't let <u>go</u>! There's still a few pigs left, you know . . . that're still loyal to his no-good ass! They'd <u>love</u> to catch us with our pants down!"

Norma wasn't having any. "<u>Bullshit</u>," she spat. "The heat's been <u>off</u>, now! Off . . . for three or four <u>months</u>! No one's even <u>seen</u> Dane! Not for freaking <u>ages</u>! Not since he met his . . . ah . . . 'unfortunate <u>accident</u>'! Not since he bit the <u>cement</u> . . . outside of that restaurant, that night. I understand that they <u>transferred</u> his hard-on ass! Transferred him to <u>Brooklyn</u> . . . or someplace! Gave him a <u>desk</u> job! Let him <u>rehab</u> . . . from his little tussle . . . in a nice comfortable office! Told him . . . in no uncertain terms . . . to keep his freaking nose <u>out</u> of our business! Told him, that he'd be a hell of a lot better <u>off</u> . . . just minding his own <u>shit</u>! He's <u>really</u> not a concern anymore! Not one freaking <u>bit</u> . . . of a concern! Past fuckin' <u>tense</u>!"

The other young woman—a youthful 20-years-old, whose bountiful bosom was straining against the token restraint of a tiny, extremely-tight, hot-pink-and-chartreuse, paisley, halter—joined the conversation: "Look," she insisted, "we've come this <u>far</u> with the Premier. I say we should go all the <u>way</u>! All the way . . . with <u>her</u>! She's <u>always</u> been there! Been there . . . for <u>us</u>! <u>We</u> ought to be there for <u>her</u>!"

Norma wouldn't budge. "<u>Yeah</u>? Oh <u>yeah</u>? Well, just where are we gonna get the <u>money</u>? <u>Any</u> fucking money? The damn money . . . to even freaking <u>live</u> on? <u>Used</u> to be . . . we never had to <u>worry</u> about it! There was <u>always</u> money! If nothing <u>else</u>, there was still . . . <u>always</u> . . . the goddam <u>money</u>! <u>Now</u>? Now, we're <u>all</u> freaking hand-to-<u>mouth</u>! Every damn <u>one</u> of us! People <u>love</u> us! But, <u>none</u> of us can find work! <u>No</u> one'll hire us! <u>Any</u> of us! Fucking <u>capitalist swine</u>!

"You been reading too many <u>pamphlets</u>," offered the young lady with the colorful halter. "Take a <u>strain</u>, \Norma!"

"She's right, you know," observed the fourth youth—nodding toward Norma. "She's absolutely spot-on!"

He was a young black man—who, when standing, resembled a flagpole. He measured six-feet, seven-inches, in height—and tipped the scales at less than 165 pounds.

Norma placed her hand on top of his.

"Well," replied Mathew, the white youth—with an overdone sigh, "you guys can do whatever you damn <u>please</u>! But, Shirley and I . . . we're sticking with the <u>Premier</u>. If you guys want to <u>split</u> . . . well, I guess that's your <u>choice</u>! But, as for <u>me</u>, I wouldn't . . ."

It was at that moment that the four noticed the fortyish white man—looming in front of their table!

Mathew looked up at the interloper. "What you <u>want</u>, Man?" he sneered.

"Just <u>this</u>," replied the intruder—smiling down at the quartet.

He withdrew a .45 automatic handgun from his topcoat pocket!

The hamburger joint was filled with the <u>seven</u> explosions!

The first bullet struck <u>Norma</u>! In the <u>face</u>! At the bridge of her <u>nose</u>! It <u>exited</u>—at the back of her head! Taking a third of her <u>skull</u>, with it! The massive amount of splattering blood <u>inundated</u> the wall behind the booth! <u>Immediately</u>! The young woman toppled to her right—against Mathew! A crumpled, lifeless, <u>mass</u>!

Two bullets ripped through the upper part of the tall, skinny, black man's stomach—plastering his intestines against the cushions behind him! His body lurched backward—before ricocheting forward! It came to rest—against Norma's death-stilled body!

Another slug slammed into Mathew's right eye—ripping away a goodly portion of his skull, as it blew out through the back of his head! He waggled back and forth—not unlike some kind of, out-of-control, runaway, pendulum! He slumped forward—his head banging onto the table!

The fourth target—the young woman in the halter—screamed! An inhuman, ethereal, sound! Her petrified eyes widened to traffic-light proportions! As she stared up at the barrel of the automatic! The weapon must have looked like a howitzer to her!

Taking careful—and deliberate—aim, the stranger pumped a hollowed-out slug into each of the young woman's breasts! Her body wrenched—seemingly, in all directions at once! Her bosom had—instantaneously—become past tense!

Noting that the black string bean was still writhing, the gunman leveled the immense weapon once more—pumping another bullet into the top of the youth's head! He writhed no more!

Calmly returning the heated, smoking—now empty—gun to his coat pocket, the assassin walked, swiftly, out of the coffee shop! And into the throng—on busy, crowded, in-a-hurry, 2nd Avenue!

The grisly killings, of course, filled the 6:00PM and the 11:00PM newscasts! Yard upon yard upon yard of videotape, displaying the grisly, blood-splattered, scene—in exacting, grim, grotesque, detail—poured, virtually non-stop, from millions of TV sets! Locally—and nationally! The networks <u>rushed</u> hordes of the stomach-wrenching pictures—thoroughly detailing the incredible, terrifying, visions, from every angle! The airways were <u>overflowing</u>—with the electronic "portraits", depicting the incredible murders—traversing the nation, to each of the webs' outlets, across the country!

Witnesses, at the scene, were interviewed! Literally every one of these people offered vastly-conflicting descriptions, of the gunman! <u>None</u> of them seemed able to agree upon <u>anything</u>! One lady wasn't even positive that the assassin was male! The <u>sequence</u> of events was heavily, consistently, in heated question! Excited, top-of-the-lungs, arguments persisted—over the number of gunshots! One of the witnesses—a portly man, seated easily <u>30 feet</u>, from the bloody booth—proclaimed that two bullets had narrowly <u>missed</u> his own head!

Of course, the many frenzied witnesses were totally unable to keep from, vehemently, rendering terribly-conflicting descriptions of the assassin:

One lady described the assailant as a man who stood "a mile high"! Another woman said the murderer was "about average height and weight". Two men chimed in, with the statement that, in their view, the man was almost seven-feet tall. "Probably a basketball player," as one described him.

One of the waitresses wasn't sure it was even a man! "Looked like a woman, to me," she maintained. "Wearing a man's coat! For a disguise," she went on to theorize.

Some thought the assassin was a pale Caucasian. Others thought he was white—but, of "swarthy" coloring. The terrified woman—who'd been seated in the next booth—swore that the gunman was "a smallish Negro"!

The mayor chimed in—striking his favorite theme: "If we only had decent . . . sensible, logical . . . gun control laws, throughout the entire country . . . not just here, in New York . . . you can bet, that we'd never see such outrageous carnage! Nothing . . . like the violence that we saw this afternoon!"

It was one of *Amalgamated's* more enterprising investigative reporters—who first determined that the four victims were members of the Freedom People's Nation!

Indeed, "they were among the eleven young people," intoned one of the network's anchors. "These individuals were herded . . . yes, herded, like so many head of cattle . . . off to jail! Incarcerated, in the infamous . . . and spectacularly illegal . . . raid! The mind-numbing outrage . . . that was conducted by none other, than Lieutenant Royce Dane! Royce Dane! You remember him! Formerly of the NYPD Bomb Squad!"

One of the victims, Shirley—the young white girl—had come from Port Huron, Michigan. She had left home, three years before—after having renounced her parents, and "everything they stand for". She'd gained a measure of local notoriety—when she'd thrown one of the beauty contest trophies she'd won, through the window of the mayor's office! A week later, the other one got flung into the high school's lobby—barely missing the assistant principal!

Her grieving, forty-something, parents had not seen—nor heard from—their daughter, in the ensuing three-year period! Obviously, a time of terrible worry and great fear, for the distraught couple!

A reporter from the *ABS* outlet in Detroit had—ceremoniously—driven up to Shirley's parents' home and had shown them—with a macabre, overdone, circus-like, for-the-television-camera's-benefit, flourish—three of the highly-detailed, <u>hideous</u>, <u>photographs</u>, of their unfortunate daughter's death-twisted corpse! The pictures depicted—in grievous, terribly-graphic, grotesque, blood-splattered, detail—the stomach-churning, remains, of what had been the young woman's <u>bosom</u>! These were <u>not</u> the "fuzzed out" photos (the "decent" ones) that had—so continuously—been shown on the net's affiliates!

During the ensuing "interview", the girl's badly-shocked folks had both been given to uncontrolled <u>gasping</u>! Both had then begun <u>vomiting</u>—violently! Somewhere—in amongst all this anguish-producing confrontation, the mother had launched into a bone-rattling series of blood-chilling <u>screams</u>! At the top of her lungs! The father <u>sobbed</u>—unendingly! He'd staggered to the sofa, and had <u>continued</u> to cry! Like a <u>baby</u>! Neither parent, of course, was <u>close</u> to being capable—of even <u>attempting</u> to answer <u>any</u> of the withering barrage of highly-<u>insensitive</u> questions, hurled at them!

The father's heart-rending <u>sobs</u>, however, had wound up making for a "really <u>great</u>" sound bite! They were featured—time after time—on the network's subsequent newscasts! The "interview" had been termed "a rousing <u>success</u>"—by the web's brass!

Hey! That's show biz!

Between the 6:00 PM and the 11:00 PM newscasts, Annabelle Best—Exalted Premier of the Freedom People's Nation—appeared at *ABS's* studios in Midtown Manhattan! From where she taped another heart-warming, rewarding, fulfilling, "politically neutral", interview! <u>This</u> classic—with the network's number-one anchor.

The newscaster, Leon Almas, did nothing to hide his obvious sympathy—toward the still—"distraught" Amazon:

> ALMAS: Now, Ms. Best, I'm given to understand that you are the <u>leader</u> of this group . . . the Freedom People's Nation. Is that true?

> BEST: Yes, Sir. <u>Now</u> look . . . <u>look</u> at what we have! Just <u>look</u>! To have those four <u>vital</u> young people . . . my dearest <u>friends</u> . . . to have 'em <u>shot</u>! Shot <u>down</u>! Shot <u>dead</u>! <u>Assassinated</u>! Shot <u>down</u>! <u>Shot</u> . . . like poor, helpless, <u>animals</u>!

ALMAS: Well, we know that Shirley Mortson was from a little town . . . north of Detroit. But, we don't have much background on the rest. Can you fill us in as to the other three?

BEST: Well, the young black man . . . Marshall Phillips . . . he was from Harlem. He won All-City . . . in high school basketball. That was four or five years back. He was . . . <u>believe</u> me, Mister Almas . . . he was a <u>great</u> athlete! A great <u>man</u>. <u>Great</u> man! Simply <u>great</u>! Totally <u>dedicated</u>, he was! Simply <u>devoted</u> . . . to <u>rectifying</u> the many, many <u>wrongs</u>! The countless, unforgivable, <u>injustices</u> . . . done to his <u>people</u>! The <u>incredible</u> tortures, that his people had to <u>endure</u> . . . throughout the bloody <u>history</u>, of this racist <u>nation</u>! And Norma <u>Hamill</u>! She was even <u>more</u> dedicated! She was born in <u>Newark</u>! <u>Lived</u> there . . . all her <u>life</u>. She became a member of the <u>FPN</u> about a <u>year</u> . . . maybe eighteen <u>months</u> . . . ago!

ALMAS: And the young <u>white</u> man? <u>His</u> name was Mathew Finney? Where was <u>he</u> from?

BEST: <u>Nebraska</u>! Little town called Grand <u>Island</u>. His parents . . . <u>they</u> own a lot of <u>land</u> out there! His <u>father</u> was some kind of a big <u>noise</u>, in town politics, out there. Mathew <u>saw</u> . . . could <u>see</u> . . . how his father's heavy-handed <u>treatment</u> of the poor, was doing terrible <u>things</u> to them! <u>Unforgivable</u> things! And he just got to the point . . . where he simply could not <u>stomach</u> it any longer! <u>None</u> of it! <u>Listen</u>! He came to New <u>York</u> . . . like a lot of <u>other</u> people . . . looking for something <u>better</u>! Some place . . . some kind of <u>organization</u>, maybe! One that'd stand <u>up</u> . . . against man's inhumanity to <u>man</u>! He found <u>us</u>! <u>That's</u> why he joined us. And <u>now</u>? Now, he's <u>dead</u>!"

ALMAS: Now, Ms. Best, the big <u>question</u>: <u>Who</u> . . . who, on the face of this <u>earth</u> . . . who would want to <u>do</u> such a <u>terrible</u> . . . such a <u>horrible</u>, such a <u>despicable</u> . . . <u>thing</u>? Such a vile <u>thing</u> . . . to these four young people? To <u>wipe</u> 'em . . . wipe 'em, off the face of the <u>earth</u>? <u>Why</u>? Why was this <u>done</u>? Who would have such a demented <u>reason</u> . . . any <u>kind</u> of warped reasoning . . . to have done such an <u>incalculable</u> thing? Who <u>could</u> have done such a thing?

BEST: Mister Almas, <u>you</u> know the answer as well as <u>I</u> do! There's only <u>one</u> name . . . that comes to mind. As you know, there's this one pig <u>cop</u>! A <u>pig</u> . . . who's been out to <u>get</u> us! Out to <u>get</u> us! And . . . for a good long <u>time</u>! I've always <u>felt</u> that . . . sooner or <u>later</u> . . . something inside him would just simply <u>snap</u>! But, of course, I <u>never</u> expected <u>anything</u> like this! Not like <u>this</u>! Even from <u>him</u>! I mean who could <u>expect</u>? Expect anything . . . like <u>this</u>?

ALMAS: That would . . . obviously . . . be Lieutenant Royce Dane, about whom you speak! Late of the police bomb squad! Obviously!

BEST: You're the one who said it! You were the one . . . who said the lieutenant's name! I didn't!

ALMAS: But, according to the witnesses, none of the victims . . . none of them . . . seemed to recognize their slayer! Of course, there were so many horribly conflicting descriptions! Far-flung descriptions . . . of the entire scene! They were all over the place! Still, according to most of the witnesses, none of your colleagues seemed to recognize their assassin! How would one explain that?

BEST: Listen! None of those witnesses knows what they saw! None of 'em! Not a damn one of 'em! Or maybe they do . . . and, maybe, they're just not being frank! Who knows? Who could know . . . what threats might've been made against 'em? Those pigs? Well, they're capable of . . . capable of jolly well anything! I wouldn't put anything past 'em! Not any of 'em! I mean . . . just look! Look . . . just look . . . at what happened to these four people! To my four associates! My four friends! They're dead! All of 'em! Dead!

ALMAS: Yes, but Lieutenant Dane was supposed to have been in a meeting! With at least fourteen <u>other</u> officers . . . at the <u>time</u>, of the ghastly shootings!

BEST: <u>Yeah</u>! If you can <u>believe</u> . . . fourteen other <u>pigs</u>! Cops are <u>liars</u>! Every damn <u>one</u> of 'em! We <u>all</u> know that! <u>All</u> of 'em! What do you <u>think</u> they'd say? Of <u>course</u> they're going to cover for one of their own! Would you expect anything <u>else</u>? <u>Look</u>! Even if he didn't actually <u>do</u> the actual killing . . . he, most certainly, could've <u>had</u> it done! And <u>that'd</u> give him fourteen certifiable <u>alibis</u>! For . . . you know . . . when the murders were actually <u>committed</u>! And all <u>this</u> . . . just because he couldn't get away with taking the law, into his own <u>hands</u>! I <u>knew</u> . . . that he'd positively flip <u>out</u>! Sooner or <u>later</u>! Some people had <u>said</u> . . . that he was, already, on the <u>edge</u>! <u>Been</u> on the brink! Ever since his unfortunate <u>accident</u> . . . some months ago! A <u>lot</u> of people have said . . . that he'd been unable . . . to <u>cope</u> with what <u>happened</u>, to him, that night . . . in Brooklyn! But . . . my <u>God</u>! As I said <u>before</u> . . . I'd never <u>expected</u> it would come to . . . to come to <u>this</u>! The petty <u>harassment</u>? Well, we could handle <u>that</u>! We <u>did</u> handle it! We <u>did</u>! We <u>dealt</u> with it! We weren't <u>happy</u> with it, of course! But, we could . . . and we <u>did</u> . . . <u>cope</u> with it! Living in a fascist <u>society</u> . . . like <u>this</u> one is . . . well, you've got to <u>expect</u> it! But, c'mon! A <u>massacre</u>? A cold-blooded <u>massacre</u>? The merciless gunning <u>down</u> . . . of four innocent <u>people</u>? <u>Four</u> people? Just <u>sitting</u> there? <u>Sitting</u> there?

Eating? Minding their own business? (Snapping her fingers—loudly!) And now . . . they're dead? Just like that? No one is safe! Not in this rotten society! No one! Absolutely no one!

ALMAS: Isn't that rather a strong statement? I mean . . . aren't you worried? About a possible defamation of character suit?

BEST: You brought his name up! I didn't! But, as long as we were talking about him, I thought that I'd better level! Level . . . with your viewers! Besides, what can they do . . . to me? Revoke my driver's license? I don't have any money! I'm broke! And . . . the way things are . . . I don't figure to have any money! Not soon, anyway! This corrupt society . . . this fascist culture . . . it sees to that! Always sees to that!

Annabelle, then, launched into her well-rehearsed, 12-minute, diatribe—describing, in infinite detail, the many inequities and ills, fostered by the "corrupt society"! And the "fascist culture"! Uninterrupted— and unchallenged—of course!

Leon Almas wound up thanking the woman— profusely—for her "insightful" interview. Further, he allowed as how he was certain that her willingness to take a stand—for those things, to which she was so obviously committed—would be, he was sure, well-received by *Amalgamated's* many viewers.

"A breath of fresh air," according the celebrated anchor.

The wire services inundated newspapers, across the country, with descriptions—and stark, detailed, photographs of the grizzly mass murders! Editorial upon editorial—in New York and nationally—decried the use "of such naked force . . . in a horribly misguided attempt, to control political mavericks". Most of these publications went on to proclaim: "No one should have to suffer the hideous fate of being put to death . . . for merely holding an opinion. One deemed not proper".

One paper—in Greenwich Village—claimed to have proof that Lt. Dane had, personally, hired a Mafia hit man, "paying him $20,000 for the rub-out"! The "carefully planned-out carnage" was scheduled for a time when Dane would be in full view—of a bountiful number of law enforcement personnel. They didn't deign to offer an explanation as to how Dane and/or the hit man could've known that the four would've been in *The White Palace*—at the specific time that Dane would've been involved with those many officers.

Dane steadfastly refused to be interviewed by the media! "You don't want to hear <u>anything</u> I've got to say," he'd snarled—<u>continually</u>. "As more than one person has said . . . factually . . . you clowns aren't going to let a few facts get in the way of a good story."

Ten days later, the media-sustained impact of the spectacular murders was only beginning to fade. Ever-so-slightly—but the repercussions from the multi-assassinations were, noticeably, beginning to lessen. Smigelski, himself, had noticed that he was being "shadowed", by the media (and not particularly efficiently) less often!

Each of the investigations—launched by NYPD, the District Attorney's Office, and the Federal Bureau of Investigation, had turned up absolutely no leads! Spokesmen and spokeswomen for the various law enforcement agencies appeared to be running out of well-worn platitudes!

"What'd you <u>expect</u>?" asked Annabelle, cryptically—every time a microphone was shoved in her face. "The <u>pigs</u>? <u>They're</u> certainly not going to go after one of their <u>own</u>! Get <u>real</u>!"

On the twelfth day, after the spectacular shootings—a bright day, in which the sun had bathed the sky in a breathtaking portrait of vibrant yellows and a few soft purples—a young black man pulled his four-year-old Chevrolet Nova up beneath the ornate canopy, of the mammoth *Berrigan Hotel*, in Windsor Locks, Connecticut. Parking next to the multi-doored lobby entrance, he sauntered inside.

The room clerk looked up from his *Playboy* magazine—and smiled.

"My name is Clark Valo," announced the newcomer. "My wife should've already registered. I was to meet her here this afternoon. I'm a little bit early . . . but, I'm sure she's here by now."

"Oh yes, Mister Valo. She told me you'd be asking. She's in number seven-twenty-seven. Just drive up to the end of the last building, in this line . . . and turn left. Seven-twenty-seven is the fourth room from the very end. Ground floor."

"Thank you. Oh! Could I please have a key to the room? Just in case she's napping or something."

The clerk handed Clark a key—and bade him have a nice stay.

The new arrival drove back to 727—and parked just outside the door. He removed his "overnighter" from the back seat—and made his way to the room. Unlocking the door, he silently let himself in—closing the door softly. The room was empty.

Tip-toeing the length of the quarters—to the bathroom—he pushed open the door to the lavatory! Pushed it firmly! It crashed against the toilet!

The bone-rattling clatter caused the white woman—who'd been languishing, in the tub—to jump the proverbial "mile"! She'd been humming—and soaping her beautifully-firm, coral-tipped, breasts with a fluffy blue washcloth.

Standing in the doorway, Clark smiled broadly. "<u>Wow</u>," he enthused. "What a perfect <u>spot</u>! Perfect environment . . . for a warped, demented, perverted, <u>voyeur</u>! Like <u>me</u>, for instance!"

"<u>OH</u>! Oh, <u>Clark</u>! <u>OH</u>! Gee <u>God</u>!" She was just beginning to come down! To slowly recover! "You <u>scared</u> me," she sighed—loudly! She was also smiling—broadly! "Two year's <u>growth</u> . . . shot to <u>hell</u>!

Shot . . . <u>completely</u> . . . to hell! I didn't <u>hear</u> you! I'll be out in a <u>minute</u>!"

Dropping his suitcase, Clark held up his hand. "Don't get <u>out</u>," he admonished. "I'll get <u>in</u>."

"What . . . what're you <u>doing</u>?"

"I'm taking off my <u>clothes</u>, Silly! What does it <u>look</u> like I'm doing? I <u>promised</u> myself . . . when I was but a <u>child</u> . . . that I'd <u>never</u> get into the bathtub! Not with my <u>clothes</u> on. Leastways . . . not one that's full of <u>water</u>."

"We can't <u>both</u> fit in here! <u>Can</u> we?"

"Of <u>course</u> we can! If one's on the <u>top</u> . . . and the other one's on the <u>bottom</u>!"

"Well, <u>I'm</u> not gonna be the one . . . on the <u>bottom</u> . . . Lover Man. You'll <u>drown</u> me!"

"<u>Yeah</u>! But, what a way to <u>go</u>! I <u>promise</u> you . . . that you'll have the broadest <u>smile</u>, on any corpse . . . in the <u>history</u> of mankind! Well, in the whole damn <u>funeral</u> parlor, anyway."

She became serious. "I wish you wouldn't <u>do</u> that, Clark! I sure wish you wouldn't talk . . . you know . . . about <u>corpses</u>! <u>Especially</u> after what happened to Mathew and Norma and Shirley and Rob!"

"Aw c'mon. Buck <u>up</u>! I was just <u>zinging</u> you! Now, I'm fixing to <u>screw</u> you!"

"Not . . . not in the <u>bathtub</u>, Clark!"

"Why? Why <u>not</u>?"

"Well . . ."

"Well, <u>what</u>?"

"I've . . . I've never gotten it . . . in the <u>bathtub</u> before!"

"Ah <u>HAH</u>! A fabulous <u>first</u>! Coming <u>up</u>! And that's not the <u>only</u> thing that's coming up! Well, in point of fact, it is up! Up . . . all the way! Good and hard! Has been . . . for some good while now!"

"You really are . . . aren't you!"

"Really are . . . what?"

"Really are . . . going to screw me! In the tub!"

"Actually, I'm going to screw you in your box! Your box happens to be . . . in the tub!"

"I wish you wouldn't use that word! You know that I detest it!"

"What word? 'Screw'?"

"No. Of course not. You know me . . . better than that!" Her eyes assumed a dreamy, far-away look—and her mouth curled into a smile! "I rather like the word 'screw'," she advised. "Love the word 'screw'! It's 'box' . . . that I detest!"

"Aw relax, Honey! You're all wound up!"

He deposited his shirt on the toilet seat. Undoing his belt, unhooking the waistband and unzipping his fly, he let his trousers drop to the floor. He stood before her—as though posing for a sculpture—in his yellow-satin, low-rise, briefs!

"Oh my God, Clark! I've never seen those before!"

"Yeah? Well, look quick! You're not going to be seeing much of 'em now! Not for long, anyway! I'm fixing . . . to take 'em off!"

"How will you ever get 'em . . . over that huge rod?"

He laughed. "I wish," he said, "that you wouldn't use that word. You know how I detest it."

"What word is that? 'Rod'?"

"No. Of course not. It's 'how'. You know how much I detest it."

She broke up! The water, in which she was lying, splattered slightly, against the sides of the tub. "Clark," she managed to say, between chortles, "you're impossible!"

"No, Ma'am. Just highly improbable," he replied—laughing as heartily as his quarry, while he was pulling off his shoes and socks.

Then, he stepped out of his slacks—and bent down, over the tub. "That's my girl," he said, taking her chin in his hand. "I love to hear you laugh."

He peeled down the flamboyant shorts—to mid-thigh! He was immense!

She reached up and caressed his swollen, throbbing, member! "You shore talk big, Pardner," she rasped. "But talk ain't the only thing, around here, that's big!" She gave an extra tug, on his massive organ—then, kissed the tip! "Ain't the only big thing . . . in this room!"

He let his undershorts drop to the floor—and stepped out of them.

"Oh, Clark!" She pulled herself up—to kiss him there, again and again! "My God!" she exclaimed, after planting six or eight additional busses, on his pulsating appendage. "I just can't get over the size of you!"

"You don't have to get over the size of me! You've just got to get around the size of me!"

"My pleasure, Sir." She slouched back down into the water. "Seriously, though . . . all kidding aside . . . are all black men that well-endowed?"

"I don't rightly know. Never took a survey! Prepare yourself!"

"Prepare myself? Like, how?"

"Well, you might . . . ah . . . spread your legs."

"Like this?"

"Hey! For a <u>white</u> girl, you catch on <u>quick</u>!"

He climbed into the tub. Kneeling between her spread-wide legs, he gazed down at the lovely young woman.

"<u>Jesus</u>, Rita! The water sure is <u>hot</u>!"

"So am <u>I</u>! I <u>like</u> it! Like it <u>hot</u>! Like it . . . <u>really</u> hot!"

"I'm sure you <u>do</u>! I'm sure you <u>are</u>! <u>Hot</u>, I mean!"

"I <u>really</u> wasn't expecting to entertain <u>company</u> in here, Mister Valo. Besides, all you've <u>done</u>, so far . . . is <u>talk</u>! If I <u>remember</u> correctly, I was <u>promised</u> a screwing! A proper <u>screwing</u>! An industrial-<u>strength</u> screwing! And . . . so far . . . I'm not too <u>thrilled</u>!"

"We'll have to remedy <u>that</u>," he said, huskily—as he lowered his body onto that of the beautiful young woman! "Remedy the <u>hell</u> out of it! <u>Won't</u> we?"

She tensed slightly—as she felt the hot water trickle up inside her! He was pressing his massive organ against—then, slightly inside—her vagina!

"Oh, <u>Clark</u>! <u>Clark</u>!" She half-shouted his name— as he entered her, all the way! She unleashed a sensuous half-sigh/half-moan—as the hot water fully gushed inside! Almost as though some out-of-control, turbulent, rapids, in some far-flung, exceedingly-wild, country waterfall had been unleashed!

Slowly—ever so slowly—he began to rise up, then lower himself, as he pushed his overgrown manhood into, and out of her! As the tempo, of the beginning-to-be-frenzied love-making increased—heading toward its inevitable "earth-shaking" crescendo—a significant amount of water was splashing onto the sides of the tub, then out onto the floor!

His naked, muscular, buttocks would break the surface of the water—then, submerge, once more, as he drove himself ever-deeper into the subterranean depths of her! With each beneath-the-surface penetration, massive gales, of the steaming water, would cascade deep into her overwrought channel! The constant, swirling, whirlpool-type, sensation had been an immediate—and consistent—turn-on for her! The overwhelming, highly-intense, full-to-the-brink, sense of "drowning", down there, was causing her to begin to wriggle—to writhe, frantically—beneath the handsome young stud! Her moaning filled the small bathroom—to overflowing! Not unlike the (fortunately) firmly-anchored tub—in which the resounding, earthquake-like, love-making was taking place!

He was <u>pistoning</u> into and out of her—faster now! Faster yet! Even faster! Faster and faster! He could almost imagine the bathwater—what little seemed to be remaining—producing a multitude of whitecaps! He'd become a veritable <u>jackhammer</u>! Water cascaded out of the tub—in even greater amounts!

Her body was <u>trembling</u>! From tip to toe! <u>Uncontrollably</u>! Her eyes rolled back toward the top of her head—as wave upon wave of ecstasy absolutely <u>consumed</u> her! Her <u>passion</u>—was fast reaching its <u>crest</u>!

"<u>OH</u>! Oh, <u>Jesus</u>! Oh, <u>Clark</u>! I'm . . . I'm . . . I'm <u>coming</u>! It's . . . <u>unnngghhh</u>!"

"Come <u>on</u>, Baby," he whispered, his lips mere inches from her ear. "Come <u>to</u> me!"

Her body stiffened, and began to quake—violently—beneath him! Her frenzied fingers gouged into his <u>shoulders</u>! <u>Deeply</u> into his shoulders! Her body <u>temperature</u> was such—that it should've sent the scant amount of water remaining, in the tub, to the <u>boiling point</u>!

The two lovers—furiously caught up in the throes of Rita's <u>climax</u>—were totally unaware of the added <u>presence</u>, in the room! The looming <u>third</u> figure—in the water-drenched bathroom!

The gasping, heaving, Rita was, of course, totally immersed in the tidal wave, of overwhelming <u>ecstasy</u>! The frenzied, volcanic, sensation was, obviously, consuming her! The writhing, moaning, woman—was even poised at the threshold of an unanticipated <u>encore</u>! A <u>second</u> orgasmic delight, when Clark—for some inexplicable reason—looked back over his right shoulder!

<u>He</u> was the one who gasped! At the <u>sight</u> of the stranger! The <u>interloper</u>! Standing on the saturated floor—of the <u>bathroom</u>! The <u>intruder</u>! Staring <u>down</u>—at the frenetically-thrashing couple!

This uninvited <u>late</u>-<u>comer</u> was pointing a monstrous .45 automatic <u>handgun</u>! Was <u>aiming</u> the firearm—directly at Clark's <u>back</u>!

The black man tried to get off an earth-shaking shriek! It never got past his turned-to-cement throat!

The handgun <u>blasted</u>! The bullet <u>ripped</u> into Clark—between his shoulder blades! In <u>addition</u>, the slug imbedded itself—in <u>Rita's</u> abdomen! Blood <u>gushed</u> from the gaping excavation in Clark's back!

The .45 exploded <u>again</u>! The hollowed-out projectile slammed through Clark's <u>neck</u>! And lodged—in Rita's right <u>breast</u>!

The water—what was left of it—turned, almost instantly, to a violent, stomach-turning, crimson!

The interloper took careful <u>aim</u>! And sent a third shot slamming into Rita's <u>forehead</u>! The bullet pounded through her <u>skull</u>—then, clanged against the porcelain tub behind the woman's instantly-disfigured head!

Returning the smoking automatic to his pocket, the assassin calmly walked out of the room, across the parking lot—and disappeared into the massive field behind the hotel!

Despite the thundering, deafening, reports from the monstrous firearm—no one seemed to have heard <u>any</u> of the devastating shots!

Rita—who was not married to Clark, or to anyone else—had requested a rear room, at the posh hotel. She'd not wanted to draw unnecessary attention to her black/white relationship with the now-lifeless man, lying atop her corpse! The rear part of the hotel had—at that time of day—been almost totally deserted!

It befell the unfortunate—shocked into incoherency—maid to come across the two grotesquely-positioned bodies! <u>That</u> frightening discovery did not take place—until the following <u>morning</u>!

The head of the Homicide Detail termed the God-awful scene, "The most <u>sickening</u> thing I've ever seen! And I've seen a <u>few</u>! Including a <u>hatchet</u> murder, or two!"

The investigation disclosed that Clark Valo—a former employee of **Ballinger's Department Store**, in Rego Park, had been a charter member of the Freedom People's Nation.

Rita Ridinger—born and raised in nearby Hartford—had joined the FPN 15 months before her death.

Each, of course, had been part of the eleven who'd been held, incommunicado, the night of Lt. Dane's raid!

Six of those eleven were—at that macabre point—dead!

SEVENTEEN

THREE WEEKS AFTER CLARK AND Rita had been so spectacularly—so horribly—discovered in Windsor Locks, Lt. Royce Dane wheeled, slowly, into the illuminated basement garage, of his apartment building, in Brooklyn.

Easing his three-year-old Oldsmobile Cutlass into the "too damn narrow" stall—one designated for his "overpriced" apartment—he killed the engine, lifted himself out of the car—and hurried across the massive facility, to the narrow entrance of the basement lobby.

Once inside, he made his way to the elevator and pressed the black "UP" button. He waited 15 or 20 seconds—for the illuminated car to become visible, through the frosted glass door. The feisty little officer glanced at his wristwatch, while the door opened. 2:25 AM.

Dane entered the car, pressed the button for the 7ᵗʰ floor and looked at his watch again—as the door closed and the elevator began to lurch upward.

At the same instant, three people—two women and a man—huddled on the second floor, pressed up against the wall opposite the elevator shaft. Each of them brandished a <u>submachine</u> gun!

"How do you <u>know</u> it's gonna be <u>him</u>?" asked one of the women—a heavyset lady, in her mid-twenties. "How can we <u>tell</u> it's <u>him</u>?"

"C'mon! Alice <u>saw</u> him," answered the lone male. "<u>Saw</u> him . . . pull in! That <u>window's</u> right over the entrance to the damn garage! She's <u>sure</u>! Sure it's <u>him</u>! <u>Aren't</u> you, Alice?"

The other woman—a tall, lithe, slender female of 21 nodded emphatically. "It's <u>him</u>, all right," she confirmed. "He just pulled <u>in</u>! Couple <u>minutes</u> ago! Jesus <u>Christ</u>! It's two-<u>thirty</u> in the fucking <u>morning</u>! How many goddam people . . . do you <u>think</u> . . . are gonna be schlepping in and out, at <u>this</u> fucking hour? Now, shut your <u>hole</u> . . . and fucking pay <u>attention</u>! We don't want no <u>fuck</u>-ups! You <u>set</u>, Frank?"

The obviously-nervous young man hesitated, then nodded! Nodded—tentatively! Exceptionally timidly!

Alice stared at the portly woman. "How 'bout <u>you</u>, Lorna," she pressed.

The other woman nodded—much more emphatically than had been the case with the obviously-distressed Frank.

At that moment, the top of the lighted car began to appear—at the bottom of the frosted glass doors, on the second floor! The three <u>aimed</u> their firearms—at the door!

"<u>Now</u>, goddam it!" shouted Alice. "Fucking <u>now</u>!"

The trio proceeded to pump <u>round</u>—after <u>round</u>, after <u>round</u>, after <u>round</u>—into the elevator! Glass shards <u>exploded</u> in every direction—as the merciless, endless, <u>rain</u> of hot lead <u>poured</u> into the car!

Dane <u>staggered</u> against the back wall! His body <u>convulsed</u>—unrelentingly—as bullet upon bullet <u>pierced</u> its way through him! Then, once the hailstorm of slugs had finally <u>stopped</u>, he slumped forward! The trio's target dropped to the <u>floor</u> of the car! Torrent upon torrent of blood <u>spewed</u>—from his badly-riddled, lifeless, <u>body</u>!

The elevator had—by then—come to an eerie halt!

The three assassins <u>sprinted</u> to the stairs, at the end of the corridor! They trundled, helter-skelter, down the steps—two and three stairs, at a time! Bursting out of the stairwell, they <u>barreled</u> across the lobby—and out through the front <u>door</u>! Out into the <u>street</u>!

A <u>fourth</u> member of the group waited, in a huge Chrysler New Yorker—the engine purring silently! The driver dropped the gear-selector into "Drive"—almost before the three assassins had gotten completely inside the car! The quartet roared <u>off</u>—into the night!

The media, of course, overflowed with "fair, straight-down-the-middle," coverage of the spectacular assassination!

It took no time for the multitudes—to tie the merciless gunning down of Dane, with the gruesome, grotesque, murders, in Windsor Locks! And, of course, to the "broad-daylight" shootings at *The White Palace*, in New York!

As expected, the mayor appeared, once again—all over the radio and television dials—to plead his case for a national gun control law! "A strong one . . . one with very little room for exemptions"!

The print media rushed to join the mayor, editorially—claiming, for the most part, that "an armed citizenry is proving to be as bloodthirsty . . . as our armed constabulary has been ineffective". One editor added, cryptically, "And equally as unprincipled".

A Greenwich Village daily paper hinted, darkly, that Dane "had been sacrificed"—in a warped, loathsome, conspiracy, by "the far-right loons", in a ruthless effort to cast "the dedicated young 'radicals', of the Freedom People's Nation, in the most unfavorable of lights".

William Katzmeyer picked up the baton—and ran with it! Interviewed on virtually every radio and television outlet in the city—as well as each of the three national networks—the attorney proclaimed, to the waiting world, that he had urged the five remaining FPN members to go into hiding!

"It's their only way! Their only chance! Their only shot . . . at surviving, this whole horrible thing," he'd pontificated. Endlessly!

"I don't know who killed Dane," he'd proclaimed to Leon Almas, the *Amalgamated* anchor. "But, obviously, the reasoning behind it has been . . . to turn public sentiment! Turn it . . . against my clients! It's to turn public sentiment against my already decimated clients! Even more foreboding, they want to set it up . . . to where my clients can now be shot down! Can literally be executed! As has already happened! So many times now! Literally shot! On

<u>sight</u>! Now, apparently, the right-wingers feel it can be done . . . <u>legally</u>! No questions <u>asked</u>! <u>Another</u> revolutionary . . . <u>gone</u>! Who <u>cares</u>?"

The situation grew even more tense—when the "underground" newspapers got into the act:

One editorialized, "The five remaining members of the FPN will surely be able to breathe a little easier—now that the pig, Dane, has been sent on to the big precinct house in the sky."

Another wrote, "We can shed no tears for a man who trampled upon so many peoples' rights, for so long. We believe Royce Dane got exactly what was coming to him—quite possibly too late. <u>Undoubtedly</u> too late. Had he been 'taken out' earlier—much earlier—six dedicated young members of the Freedom People's Nation would probably still be alive today—despite what the establishment would have you believe."

A third paper proclaimed, "If the Freedom People's Nation thought they had problems before, just wait until the revenge-bent police force gets through with them. Can you imagine one pig cop in town—who doesn't have it in for the FPN? These people will not rest—until they've gunned down every member of this dedicated group! All to be done—in the name of justice. Of course. What else? If you thought the pigs were impossible before, just wait until the oncoming campaign of police retaliation hits full-force! And, believe us, it will! Anybody holding views contrary to those of the establishment, will—sooner or later—be ground under the relentless police jackboot!

If the media was in a frenzy—and it was—the entire Police Department <u>appeared</u> to have become completely unhinged!

Opinion, among those on the force, appeared split down the middle! Many officers felt that Dane had brought discredit upon the force—making his or her already-difficult job almost impossible. As time went on, though, a significant number of officers were coming around to the <u>unspoken</u> position—that "the brass" might have "sold out" the all-too-controversial Dane! Still, <u>many</u> were relieved—that he'd been "dropped"! Like the proverbial "hot potato"!

Five weeks later—shortly after midnight—Smigelski tooled his brand new Ford Torino into the parking lot, outside his apartment in Madison, New Jersey.

As he coasted into his assigned slot, beneath the corrugated aluminum roofing, a queasy sensation began to overtake him! A feeling of <u>menace</u>! Of <u>doom</u>! Not unlike the <u>original</u> sense of foreboding! That uneasiness that he'd experienced—just prior to having been jumped that night at the **General Appliance** warehouse!

Had <u>that</u> happened—so <u>long</u> ago? Had so many mind-boggling events taken place—<u>since</u> then? So <u>many</u>?

He reached to turn off the ignition—then, abruptly <u>stopped</u>! Instead, he pushed the gear-selector into "Reverse"—and began to back, slowly, out of the parking slot!

Obey that impulse!

Once he'd made his 90-degree turn—and had dropped the selector into "Drive"—three murky figures bounded out of the corrugated aluminum shadows! Directly in front of his car!

Two women and one man! Each carried a submachine gun!

As the trio raised their weapons, Smigelski floored the gas pedal! The Torino lurched forward—then, roared ahead! Before any of the three would-be assassins could squeeze off a round, the car had slammed—into two of them!

One—a heavyset white woman—was thrown 20-feet to the right!

Another—a white man—found himself catapulted up onto the hood! He crashed—face-first—into the windshield! The dazed man froze, in that position! For the briefest of instants! Then, he was rocketed off the side of the hood, by the sheer physics—arising from dynamics of the speeding car! He wound up, literally, splattered—face down—on the black top!

Smigelski had—immediately—recognized the frightened, the battered, contorted, face! It was that—of Frank Crimmins! He'd had good reason—as it turned out—to be scared!

The third member of the hit party—a slender white woman—managed to get off three or four shots, as she'd fallen! Smigelski was barreling past her! The bullets had ripped through the window in the passenger's door—and had imbedded themselves in the center of the headliner, close by the windshield!

Unhurt, she'd arisen—immediately—and aimed her weapon at the fleeing Torino!

Keeping his head low, the crouched Smigelski headed for the entrance/exit of the complex!

Once again, the woman opened <u>fire</u>—with the deadly weapon! <u>Dozens</u> of bullets <u>penetrated</u> the trunk and the rear window of the automobile! <u>Shattering</u> the latter! Most of the slugs lodged in the back of the front seat! A few buzzed a mere few <u>inches</u> to the right of Smigelski's <u>ear</u>! They'd exited through the <u>windshield</u>! Two more bullets wound up lodged in the <u>dashboard</u>!

The frantic Smigelski swerved out into the street—literally on two wheels—then, roared off toward the center of town! Running the stop sign at the first intersection, he'd lurched the battered Torino around the corner—and headed toward <u>Police Headquarters</u>!

After speeding 3½ blocks—in his mad dash toward police protection—Smigelski came up with <u>another</u> thought! A <u>radical</u> thought!

Wheeling the vehicle around—in a deafening screech—he snapped off a highly-efficient U-turn! Without hesitation, he sped back—toward his apartment complex!

"Dumb <u>asshole</u>," he muttered to himself—over and over! "Dumb Polack <u>asshole</u>!"

Killing the headlights, he dropped his foot off the accelerator—and coasted around the final corner. onto his street, and into the complex!

A huge Chrysler New Yorker had driven to the spot where he'd encountered the trio of would-be assassins! Two figures were bent over the fallen, throbbing-head-to-toe, pain-wracked, woman! Frank

Crimmins remained lying—in a twisted heap—about 25 feet away!

"Must've had a driver! Had a damn driver! Waiting for 'em," muttered Smigelski, under his breath. "What a fucking set-up!"

He floored the Torino once more! The ear-splitting roar of the engine—as it kicked into a passing gear—overwhelmed the deathly quiet! The graveyard-like silence—which had inundated the entire parking area! It also overwhelmed the "angels of mercy"! The high-octane warning came far too late for Smigelski's proposed targets!

The Torino sliced across the parking lot's floor—at well over 55 miles per hour! The vehicle slammed into all three!

Two macabre "thumps" gave testimony to the fact that Smigelski had run over the still-prone gunwoman! Again! The other woman—and the driver of the Chrysler—were both thrown 30 or 35 feet! The latter had splattered (that word again)—head-first—into a heavy, metal, garbage dumpster! He'd, upon the devastating collision, had come to a complete—and emphatic—halt!

Smigelski frantically backed up! He wheeled the bullet-riddled car around! Spying the lifeless body of Frank Crimmins, he jammed the selector into "Drive"—and headed toward him! Two additional thumps! They seemed louder—than any of the others! The car screeched to a stop! Smigelski crammed the selector into "Reverse", once more, and zoomed back! Across Frank's body! Once again!

He wheeled the newly-ventilated Torino around, once again! And made another frenzied run, at the heavyset Lorna—who had not <u>moved</u>! Not since he'd bowled her over the <u>first</u> time! Two additional thumps! Even much <u>more</u> pronounced thumps! <u>Satisfying</u> noises!

<u>She sure was a big 'un</u>!

Again, he pulled the selector into "Reverse"—and backed over Lorna's corpse! "For good <u>measure</u>! And one to <u>grow</u> on! And all such shit as <u>that</u>!"

He had to look—<u>carefully</u>—for Alice! She, as noted, had been thrown about 30 feet! Once he'd spied her, he could see her agony-filled attempt to <u>crawl</u>! To <u>drag</u> herself—in between two parked <u>cars</u>!

She didn't make it! Smigelski smashed into her once <u>again</u>! After she'd been flattened—a fulfilling second time—he rolled <u>over</u> her! Then, he <u>backed</u> over her! Then, he double-<u>thumped</u> across her, once more!

As he'd barreled over her lifeless form—for the final time—two police cruisers <u>stormed</u> into the complex! The newly-legislated red-and-blue flashing lights just about blinded Smigelski! He'd heard no sirens!

The two officers who'd been "riding shotgun" in their respective squad cars leaped—<u>revolvers drawn</u>—from the cruisers! Practically before the cars had come to a stop!

Cautiously, approaching the battle-scarred Torino, both ordered Smigelski out of the vehicle—with his hands up! He complied—as the two police drivers joined their partners!

While one of the officers began to pat him down, Smigelski was, suddenly, <u>consumed</u>—by spasm, upon spasm, upon spasm! He found himself shaking—uncontrollably!

Satisfied that their quarry was "clean", the cops attempted to question the badly-shaken man! However, Smigelski could not stop trembling! He was unable to utter anything! Anything—even remotely coherent!

Three or four minutes later, a third cruiser careened—siren screaming—into the parking lot! Lights were snapping on—in every building of the, till-then-mostly-darkened, complex! The third squad car contained Inspector Douglas Daniels—the senior officer on duty!

Daniels listened, impatiently, while the four patrolmen described the situation—as it had been, when they'd so hurriedly arrived! The cops, dutifully, followed the inspector from one body to another—leaving the statue-like Smigelski to stand, unattended, next to his highly-ventilated Torino! The officers continued their running, non-stop, highly-emotional, commentary—as Daniels made his macabre tour!

All four would-be assassins were, of course, dead! Definitely no longer with us! Rapidly "assuming room temperature"!

Daniels barked an order—over his dashboard radio: "Send for the meat wagon! Get 'em here . . . like yesterday!"

Then, he confronted the badly-shaken "suspect"!

One of the officers had, by then, wrapped a blanket around the still-shivering Smigelski's shoulders. "Are . . . are any of them alive?" he was finally able to ask.

"No," responded Daniels, glumly. "Not a damn one! You did quite a job! A tidy job . . . on each one of 'em! My compliments! I'm assuming, now, they were the ones . . . the ones, with all the hardware! Now, suppose you tell me! What the hell went on here?"

The following day, another—albeit slightly more reserved—media circus erupted! The reaction to Smigelski's encounter with the four Freedom People's Nation was substantially more subdued!

Three or four network anchors—and more than a few politicians were asking, primarily, the same rhetorical question: "Was the environment becoming so jaded . . . that the media, and the public, were beginning to assume a regrettably more blasé attitude?

"Are such desecrated, God-awful, scenes as this . . . are they becoming the norm?" Daniels had asked the rhetorical question, aloud—to no one in particular! He'd posed the query—at the scene—the night before. That was—to those, trying to analyze the carnage—a most frightening prospect!

Or could it have been, simply, that the evidence all seemed to point to the fact that the FPN members were clearly trying to assassinate Smigelski?

"Not all that much there . . . to sink their teeth into," was the intended victim's opinion.

The citizens of Madison, New Jersey, though, refused to take quite so nonchalant an attitude! The town was aflame! Smigelski became something of a celebrity! Especially within his apartment complex! With one notable exception:

The elderly lady, who'd lived directly across the hallway from him, chased him down the following day—as Smigelski was exiting the small alcove, in which the building's mailboxes were located.

"I saw what you did . . . last night!" she snarled. Smigelski had smiled at her—and was about to reply, when she screamed at him: "Don't give me that stupid grin, Mister! I saw! Saw what you did! You took off! You got away! You did get away! You could've stayed gone! But, no! Not you! You had to go . . . and come back! Had to run down . . . all those people! Run 'em right over! Deliberately run 'em over! I saw it all! Saw everything! They didn't have a chance . . . those people! Not one chance in hell! And you just kept on! Kept on . . . running 'em over! And running 'em over! And running 'em over! My God, Man!"

"Well, if you saw it all . . . then, you saw that they were trying to goddam kill me! Shoot me . . . full of holes!"

"Sure! They shot at you! But, you . . . you got away! You got stark away! You should've stayed gone! Should've gone to the cops . . . or something! But, no! Not you! You had to come back! Had to hit 'em! Knock 'em all down! Knock 'em all over! Every one of 'em! That wasn't bad enough! Well, not good enough! Not for you! You had to go and run 'em over . . . again! Run 'em over . . . time and time and time and time again! Just kept running over 'em! Over and over! God, Man! Over and over! I think you're sick! A very sick man! Only someone who was terribly sick . . . only someone like <u>that</u> . . . would <u>do</u> that kind of <u>horrible</u> thing! You're <u>sick</u>, Mister! <u>Sick</u>!"

"You're goddam <u>right</u>! I'm <u>sick</u>, all right! I'm sick to <u>death</u> . . . of bleeding-hearts, like <u>you</u>! Like <u>you</u> . . . you dippy old <u>broad</u>! You make me want to <u>vomit</u>! Those bastards were <u>there</u> . . . for one <u>reason</u>! One <u>purpose</u>! To <u>shoot</u> my Polack ass! To shoot it . . . full of <u>holes</u>! To <u>kill</u> me! Do you <u>understand</u> that, you old windbag? Can you figure <u>out</u> . . . what I'm <u>saying</u>? They were going to goddam <u>kill</u> me! As in 'Bang! Bang! You're <u>dead</u>!' You'll have to pardon the <u>hell</u> out of me . . . if I tend to get just a wee bit <u>upset</u>, about such things."

He waggled his index finger—about three inches from her nose! "You're damn <u>right</u>," he seethed. "You're damn <u>right</u> . . . I ran over 'em! Ran over <u>all</u> of 'em! And I'd do it <u>again</u>! In a goddam <u>heartbeat</u>! Without giving it another <u>thought</u>! Go to <u>lunch</u> . . . right after squishing the <u>shit</u> out of each <u>one</u> 'em! They're all <u>dead</u>! And do you know <u>what</u>? It doesn't break my <u>heart</u>! Not one <u>bit</u>! On the <u>contrary</u> . . ."

"You . . . you <u>scum</u>! You unfeeling <u>scum</u>!"

He seemed surprised that he had his finger in her face—and, promptly, pulled his hand back. "Chew on <u>this</u>, Frumpy Lady," he snapped. "Chew on <u>this</u>! I'm <u>glad</u>! Happy as <u>hell</u> . . . that they're <u>dead</u>! Each and every <u>one</u> of 'em! At least there's four <u>people</u> . . . <u>four</u> people . . . that I don't have to <u>worry</u> about them trying it again! I don't have to sweat <u>those</u> schmucks . . . blowing my Polack <u>ass</u>, off the face of the goddam <u>earth</u>!"

"Trying it <u>again</u>? They would <u>never</u> have tried it again! <u>Certainly</u> . . . not after you hit those <u>first</u> two people! Injured <u>them</u> . . . so bad! Not when you hit that <u>man</u> . . . and that <u>woman</u> . . . so bad! Hit <u>them</u> so bad . . . right at <u>first</u>, there!"

"Don't tell <u>me</u> . . . what they would and wouldn't <u>do</u>! I've got a <u>bulletin</u> for you . . . you old busybody! Those are the <u>sonsofbitches</u> . . . the <u>bastards</u> . . . that blew up my <u>fiancée</u>! <u>Killed</u> my fiancée! And her two <u>kids</u>! Two <u>kids</u>! Blew 'em . . . to kingdom <u>come</u>! Blew 'em all <u>up</u>! They <u>killed</u> Junie! <u>Junie</u> . . . and her two wonderful <u>kids</u>! You wanna <u>talk</u> . . . about not having a goddam <u>chance</u>? <u>Junie</u> . . . and the <u>kids</u>! <u>They</u> never had a goddam chance! Can you get <u>that</u> . . . through your lard-assed <u>brain</u>? They fucking <u>killed</u> the woman! The lady . . . that I was going to <u>marry</u>! Get <u>that</u> . . . through that asshole <u>brain</u> of yours! <u>Killed</u> her . . . and two innocent little <u>kids</u>! Blew 'em fucking <u>away</u>!"

Tears began to stream down his cheeks! "They blew up <u>Junie</u> . . . and her <u>kids</u>!" he screamed. "They never had a goddam <u>chance</u>! Never knew what fucking <u>hit</u> 'em! Even a goddam <u>rattlesnake'll</u> warn you . . . before it <u>strikes</u>! But, not <u>those</u> bastards! Not <u>those</u> creeps! Not <u>those</u> sonofabitches! And let me tell you something <u>else</u>, you old fart! Let me tell you something <u>else</u>: There's <u>one</u> more! One more <u>scumbag</u>! One left in that goddam <u>outfit</u>! I'm only sorry that <u>she</u> wasn't there last night! I'd have taken <u>her</u> down too! I'd have <u>killed</u> her no-good ass! Just like <u>that</u>!" He snapped his fingers! The sound was surprisingly loud! Seemed to ricochet off all three walls of the little enclosure! "I'd have taken great <u>delight</u> . . . in <u>killing</u> her ass! Would've enjoyed the <u>hell</u> out of it! Would've loved nothing <u>better</u> . . . than to have <u>splattered</u> the bitch! Splattered her . . . all over the goddam <u>parking</u> lot! Do you dig what I'm <u>saying</u>? You <u>got</u> that . . . you old bat?"

"<u>You</u>," she seethed, as she headed back to her apartment. "You're nothing but an . . . nothing but an . . . an <u>animal</u>!"

The Middlesex County grand jury launched an investigation and—despite various not-so-veiled threats, from numerous liberal groups—concluded that <u>no charges</u> would be filed against Smigelski!

It came as no surprise that the many slugs removed from the Torino were shown to have come from one of the submachine guns that had been used—in the bloody assassination, of Lt. Royce Dane, in Brooklyn!

Of the eleven FPN members—who'd been herded into the police vans on that fateful night, only one remained: Annabelle Best! The Premier!

In addition to the hair's breadth escape from death, Smigelski found himself with other problems: His car, for instance.

The Torino had been the proud recipient of 28 bullets! The front end turned out to be, virtually, crushed! The price one pays—for sending four would-be assassins to their reward! The one window with no bullet damage was, miraculously, the one in the driver's door! The car, of course, was an obvious total loss!

The sainted insurance company took the position that their coverage did not provide for such "outside the norm" situations. Especially, announced the adjuster (and then his supervisor) when the facts document that Smigelski had, nefariously, <u>returned</u> to the scene—"bent on even more mayhem".

"If you'd have stayed <u>gone</u>," pontificated the supervisor, "why, we might've could've <u>talked</u>! But, to come <u>back</u> . . . and then, to run those people <u>down</u>, the way you did . . . was <u>unforgivable</u>! Oh <u>yes</u>! I <u>saw</u> the write-up in the paper! No matter what other <u>issues</u> may have entered into the situation, you <u>returned</u>! You <u>did</u> return! Returned with only <u>one</u> motive! To <u>kill</u> those people! Or . . . at the very <u>least</u> . . . to cause them great bodily <u>harm</u>! To cause them <u>immense</u> pain! I'm sorry, Mister Smi-jell-ski, but we can <u>not</u> help you! Case <u>closed</u>!"

"I'm not <u>believing</u> this," Smigelski had ranted—loudly enough that the entire claims office could hear. "I just joined the book-of-the-<u>month</u> club . . . with the <u>payments</u>, on the damn car! Haven't even made the second <u>payment</u>! And <u>you're</u> telling <u>me</u> . . . that I'm stuck with thirty-five more <u>payments</u>? At a hundred-and-sixty-four <u>bucks</u> . . . and change?"

"I'm <u>sorry</u>, Mister Smi-jell-ski," the supervisor had replied. "But, that's just about <u>it</u>. <u>Next</u> time, you might want to stop and <u>think</u>! Stop . . . and <u>think</u>! About what you're <u>doing</u>! <u>About</u> to do!"

"Yeah," snarled Smigelski, "and the next time I want a <u>sermon</u>, I'll go to church!

A ray of sunshine: The Ford dealer who'd sold him the Torino got wind of Smigelski's problem and—not unmindful of the publicity value which would surround a vehicle such as Smigelski's—traded him a brand new Ford LTD for the bullet-riddled Torino! The badly-damaged automobile would be prominently displayed in the dealer's showroom! Our hero was overjoyed!

Now, if only I can find an insurance company that doesn't have its corporate head up its corporate ass!

EIGHTEEN

A WEEK LATER, SMIGELSKI RESIGNED FROM Tarkenton Security Services.

Sitting in one of Captain Fox's fabled, garish-blue, plastic, chairs, he explained, to the feisty little man, that he'd simply had <u>enough</u>! <u>More</u> than enough:

"I'm not blaming **Tarkenton**, Captain. But, since I came to work here . . . all <u>sorts</u> of things have happened to me! Very <u>few</u> of 'em were good!" He sighed deeply. "I felt," he went on—talking to himself, as much as the man behind the desk, "I'd really <u>thought</u> . . . that I'd lived a rather eventful life before. Felt I'd met more than my <u>share</u> . . . of nuts, and weirdoes . . . in the car rental business. But, <u>God</u>! <u>Everything</u> that's happened to me . . . ever since I've <u>been</u> here . . . has brought me nothing but <u>trouble</u>! <u>Everything</u>! Every damn <u>thing</u>! I didn't mind so much getting beat <u>up</u>. Wasn't <u>thrilled</u> with it, of course. But . . . like you always say . . . the pain'll eventually go <u>away</u>. <u>Eventually</u>!"

"That's right, Ski," the little man replied—beaming broadly. "I always felt that . . . if I didn't teach a man anything else, if I taught him that . . . then, I wouldn't be a failure."

Smigelski nodded—and sighed, heavily, once more. "See, Captain? You were talking about <u>physical</u> pain. The <u>emotional</u> pain . . . that's something <u>else</u>! I just can't get over Junie's <u>death</u>! Well, her . . . and her <u>kids</u>!" Tears welled in his eyes. "And," he muttered, "and . . . dear Lord . . . those two <u>kids</u> of hers! Her two innocent <u>kids</u>! <u>Dying</u>! Before they even had a chance to <u>live</u>! <u>Junie</u>! The <u>kids</u>! <u>God</u>! It's all too <u>much</u>! I could <u>never</u> . . ."

Captain Fox started to interrupt—but, Smigelski held up his hand.

"I <u>know</u> what you're going to say, Captain. Time's the great <u>healer</u>! Probably <u>true</u>! <u>Eventually</u> . . . you'll tell me . . . I'll get <u>over</u> it! Maybe <u>so</u>. <u>Probably</u>. Probably <u>will</u>. <u>Eventually</u>. But . . . believe me when I <u>say</u> this . . . it's going to take a long <u>time</u>! A <u>hellishly</u> long time! It's gotten so that everything I <u>do</u> . . . every damn <u>thing</u> that I ever <u>do</u> . . . around here, <u>reminds</u> me of Junie! Of the <u>kids</u>! I've become <u>convinced</u> . . . convinced, that I <u>won't</u> get over it! I'll <u>never</u> get over it! Not until, at least, I go ahead . . . and sever my ties <u>here</u>! I really <u>have</u> to resign, Captain! I've . . . really and truly . . . fought a thousand <u>battles</u> with myself. You'll never <u>know</u> . . . how I've <u>anguished</u> over this! Over <u>everything</u>! And I just simply cannot go <u>on</u>! Not at **Tarkenton**! Can't <u>do</u> it! Cannot <u>do</u> it!"

"Well, Vick, you know how I hate to lose a good man . . . a good man like you. You're one of the <u>best</u>, Vick. And . . . just between us girls . . . I know that Mister Nype had it in his mind that, someday, you'd have <u>his</u> job! Even though they went and sent you back to my division! He thinks of you . . . almost like a son! Always askin' how you're doin', y'know . . . and stuff like that! I know that he's gonna be disappointed too!"

"Well, I was going to go up and talk to him . . . if you don't mind. I realize that I do work for you . . . have worked for you . . . and I don't want to get crossways, with whatever protocol there is, that exists between the two of you. And I felt that I owed you the courtesy of telling you . . . before I talked with him."

"That's right, Vick. That's the way to do it. You got class, Vick! Like I say, I really hate to lose you. But, I guess there's nothin' I can do about it. I just want you to know, that if you ever change your mind . . . or, if sometime down the road, you decide that you want to come back . . . as far as I'm concerned, you always got a job here!"

Fifteen minutes later, seated in Leland Nype's posh office, Smigelski informed the older man of his decision.

"I can't say I haven't been expecting it, Vick," Nype said. "I knew, of course, that everything . . . was really getting to you! Well, hell, it had to. Even though my path didn't cross hers . . . not all that often . . . I could see how Miss Bodner's death was eating at you! How it was . . . out and out . . . consuming you!"

"Yeah. Junie . . . and the kids," moped the erstwhile employee.

"It's certainly understandable! Perfectly understandable! What're you going to do now?"

"I don't <u>know</u>." Smigelski let go another in a seemingly endless series of sighs. "I don't really <u>know</u>," he repeated. "I've been able to put <u>back</u> a few bucks . . . over the past few months. Thought maybe I'd just take a <u>vacation</u> . . . so to speak. Possibly, a <u>long</u> vacation. Just get my Polack ass <u>away</u>! Away . . . from <u>everything</u>! For who-knows-<u>how</u>-long!"

"Probably the best <u>therapy</u>," agreed Nype. "I sure can't think of anything more <u>intelligent</u>."

"I was going to <u>say</u> . . . that I don't remember the last time I <u>took</u> a vacation. But . . . thinking <u>back</u> . . . I guess I've had a <u>few</u> of 'em, over the past couple years. <u>More</u> than a few."

"You know and I know, Vick, that <u>those</u> weren't vacations. Were <u>not</u> vacations! What're you going to do <u>now</u>? Go see your <u>kids</u>? Your ex-<u>wife</u>?"

The question surprised Smigelski! "How . . . how the hell did you know <u>that</u>, Mister Nype?"

"What could be more <u>natural</u>? I'd just <u>advise</u> you, though . . . be <u>careful</u>! Be awfully damn <u>careful</u>, Vick. There's only <u>one</u> of those FPN's left! But, she was the <u>leader</u>, y'know! And, I guess, she's a real <u>doozer</u>! Fucking <u>deadly</u>!"

"Yeah. You got <u>that</u> right!"

"What was her <u>name</u>? Annabelle . . . Annabelle . . . ?"

"<u>Best</u>. Dane always thought that it was a <u>phony</u> name. Don't know if anyone ever looked <u>into</u> it. Best!" He spat the woman's last name, once again! "<u>Best</u>! HAH!"

"How could I forget <u>that</u>", Nype responded, offering a wry smile. "A name like <u>that</u>? Listen . . . be awfully <u>careful</u>, Vick. That bitch is still <u>around</u>! <u>Someplace</u>!

Lying in the goddam <u>weeds</u>! I guess no one's <u>seen</u> her . . . not in awhile! But, vermin like <u>her</u> . . . they don't <u>ever</u> go away. According to my little voices, down at Police <u>Headquarters</u>, though, she's pretty well dropped out of <u>sight</u>!"

"So I understand."

Nype picked up a lethal-looking letter opener from his desk—and made an exaggerated swipe at an imaginary victim! "You know that old Myron Cohen joke," he said, with a mirthless laugh. "Everybody gotta be <u>someplace</u>."

"Mister Nype, I've made myself <u>sick</u>! Actually, physically, <u>sick</u>! Worrying . . . and wondering . . . where she <u>was</u>! Where the hell she <u>is</u>! Worrying if she's going to <u>surface</u>! Worrying <u>when</u> she's going to surface! I've, finally, <u>decided</u> that . . . well, the only thing I can <u>do</u>, is to simply try and put her out of my <u>mind</u>! If she <u>tries</u> something with me . . . well, I'll <u>deal</u> with it then! Cope with the damn thing . . . <u>then</u>! Don't really have a helluva lot of <u>choice</u>, in the matter!"

"Yeah. But, <u>listen</u>, Vick! We're talking about your <u>kids</u>! Your <u>kids</u>, dammit! If she <u>thought</u> . . . that the only way to <u>get</u> at you was through the <u>kids</u>, why, . . ."

"I know," Smigelski rasped. "I <u>know</u>! And I'll be <u>careful</u>! <u>Bet</u> on it! <u>Damn</u> careful!"

"<u>Do</u>, Vick! Do be <u>awfully</u> damn careful! You have no way of <u>knowing</u> . . . <u>none</u> of us do . . . we don't know <u>who</u> she may have <u>aligned</u> herself with, by this time! She <u>could</u> be, y'know, heading up <u>another</u> band of cutthroats! Maybe <u>twice</u> as many assholes . . . as that stupid little <u>FPN</u>! Maybe even <u>twice</u> as bloodthirsty! People we don't even <u>know</u> about! <u>Can't</u>

know about! Don't even know that they even <u>exist</u> . . . if they <u>do</u> exist! Who can <u>tell</u>?"

"I don't know how <u>anybody</u> . . . anybody, on <u>earth</u> . . . could be more <u>bloodthirsty</u>, than those goddam pieces of FPN shit!"

"I don't <u>either</u>! But, it's awfully hard to <u>say</u>. As I understand it, ol' Annabelle had just simply dropped <u>out</u>! <u>Poof</u>! She'd, supposedly, dropped <u>out</u>, actually . . . <u>before</u> those other four tried to take <u>you</u> out! Maybe even before <u>Dane</u>! The police don't really <u>know</u>! <u>None</u> of us know! The cops doubt that she's even in the <u>area</u> any longer! But, hell, <u>they</u> don't know!"

"She could've <u>supervised</u> it, y'know! Coulda supervised <u>Dane's</u> murder! And <u>mine</u>! Could've put the whole thing together . . . by remote <u>control</u>! She's fucking <u>deadly</u>!"

"I <u>guess</u>! <u>Maybe</u>! <u>Apparently</u>! Who the hell <u>knows</u>? Just be awfully damn <u>careful</u>, Vick! <u>Awfully</u> damn careful! Okay?"

"I <u>will</u>, Mister Nype. Rest <u>assured</u>! I <u>will</u>! It's nice of you to be <u>concerned</u>!"

"Well, I feel somewhat <u>responsible</u> . . . for what's <u>happened</u>! All the God-awful things that've <u>happened</u>! All the <u>shit</u> that's come down . . . in your <u>life</u>! Not only <u>that</u> . . . but, look. Listen, Vick. I've never <u>had</u> a son. We couldn't <u>have</u> children . . . my wife and I. So," he sighed deeply, "as corny as this <u>sounds</u>, you've become like a <u>son</u> to me! A <u>son</u> . . . more or less!"

"I'm <u>honored</u>."

"Well, anyway, give Inez and the kids my <u>best</u>. I'm <u>sorry</u> . . . that they're so far <u>away</u> from you now. But, really, it <u>was</u> the only way! Oh! There's something else you should probably <u>know</u>. I never <u>told</u> you this . . . and I'd asked <u>Inez</u> not to . . . but, **Tarkenton** has been putting a little something <u>extra</u>, in her bank account, every month."

"<u>What</u>? How come you didn't <u>tell</u> me? Never <u>told</u> me?"

"Wasn't any <u>need</u> to. Down deep, I've been <u>expecting</u> this day! And I didn't want the arrangement to seem like . . . well, seem like . . . like some kind of <u>hammer</u>, over your head! We'll still send it . . . still deposit the money . . . whether you're still <u>employed</u> here, or not! It's really not all that <u>much</u>! We've <u>done</u> it through the FBI! <u>That</u> way, no one <u>here</u> . . . including <u>me</u> . . . knows their address! They . . . the folks, at 'the Bureau' . . . they <u>always</u> see that, every month, it gets <u>deposited</u> into her account!"

"Yes, but . . . I had no <u>idea</u> that . . . ! Do you <u>know</u> something, Mister Nype? When I first <u>came</u> here, I thought that the security business was the absolute <u>dregs</u>. Thought **Tarkenton** was the . . . was, well, the <u>asshole</u> of the whole goddam <u>universe</u>! I really <u>did</u>! I thought that everyone <u>here</u> . . . I didn't <u>know</u> you at that point . . . but, I thought that <u>everyone</u> was an insensitive <u>clod</u>! That <u>nobody</u> gave a damn! <u>Ever</u>! I thought that <u>everybody</u> did absolutely <u>nothing</u>! Nothing . . . but screw everything <u>up</u>! I <u>even</u> thought that Captain Fox was an ignorant <u>slob</u>! I know <u>better</u> now, of course, but . . ."

Nype laughed. "Captain Fox is a special <u>guy</u>," he replied. "A <u>very</u> special guy! <u>Some</u> people they <u>laugh</u> at him . . . the way he sometimes comes <u>across</u>! But, he's one of the most <u>principled</u> men I've ever <u>met</u>! Totally <u>devoted</u> to his work. And to his <u>employees</u>!

I guess the <u>mentality</u>, of some of the men they put on . . . and <u>keep</u> on, as guards . . . well, I guess <u>that</u> leaves a little to be <u>desired</u>. That's the nature of the <u>beast</u>. But, they do the best they <u>can</u> . . . down there. Poor Captain Fox . . . he gets so many <u>stiffs</u>, schlepping through down there. And he <u>deals</u> with all of it! Deals with <u>them</u>! Every damn <u>day</u>! <u>Amazing</u>! I can't <u>imagine</u> . . . how he keeps from pulling his <u>hair</u> out! I could <u>never</u> do his job!"

A massive shudder, overtook Leland Nype—and his face contorted into a massive grimace! "<u>Never</u>," he continued. "Never in a million <u>years</u>!"

NINETEEN

IN BUFFALO, NEW YORK, THERE is a street, which is approximately six blocks long—and is located smack, in the heart of downtown: It is the infamous Chippewa Street.

While not nearly as world-renowned as so many other celebrated sites—Baltimore's "Block", New York City's Time Square area, or Boston's "Combat Zone" of the mid-seventies—Chippewa Street probably had as many hookers per-square-inch as any of those other, more celebrated, "sidewalk stewardess" locations.

Seven months after Smigelski had left **Tarkenton Security Services**—and on one of the darkest nights imaginable—three white prostitutes and six black "ladies of the evening" were plying their trade, on the northwest corner, where Chippewa and Franklin Streets meet. The other three extensions of the intersection were equally densely populated, with "providers of horizontal pleasure".

Pimps rolled, slowly, up and down the street—showing off their flamboyant, ermine-upholstered, pink and/or lavender, Cadillacs and Lincolns. All of this—despite the lateness of the hour.

At about 2:30 AM, a young-appearing white male—decked out in a surprisingly loose-fitting paisley shirt, but sporting exceptionally tight jeans—approached one of the above-mentioned ladies of loose moral standing. He sported an immense beard—and the proverbial "fourteen pounds of hair"! Each and every one, of the latter, seemed to have a mind of its own.

The prostitute—easily the tallest of the "working girls"—smiled at the prospective "john".

"Hi." Her voice was a nasal whine—and clouded somewhat. The result of a battle, to the death, with a horrible cold. A malady that she'd been, frustratingly, unable to shake. "Wanna go out?" she asked.

She went on to nod her head rapidly—obviously, answering her own question, for him.

"Well," he replied. "Yeah. I guess so. Uh . . . how much is it going to cost me?"

"Depends on what kind of date you want to have."

"Uh . . . well . . . you see . . . I don't have much money."

"Oh Christ! Where have I heard that before? All right," she added—with an overdone sigh. "How much you got?" Her smile had long vanished. "Jesus," she spat. "If ever I saw a goddam nickel-and-dime town . . . this is it!"

"I got twenty-five or thirty bucks."

Her face brightened somewhat. "Look, Honey," she said, "tell you what I'll do. I usually charge at least fifty. Rock bottom. But, it's been a slow night. Damn slow! And . . . as you can see . . . I'm up to my ass!

Up to my ass . . . in <u>competition</u>! So, I'll tell you what. It'll <u>only</u> cost you the thirty! But, <u>listen</u>! That's just for a straight <u>fuck</u>! No <u>exotic</u> shit. No <u>perversion</u> shit."

He nodded. "Yeah," he answered. "That'll be okay, I guess,"

"Good. Now, where's your car?"

"Up on Washington Street. About three blocks from here."

"Okay, listen. Whyn't you go get it . . . and pick me up <u>here</u>? Right <u>here</u>! What kind of car you got, Sweetie?"

"White Ford. LTD. Jersey plates. Four door."

She patted him on his backside. "Okay," she instructed. "You go ahead . . . and you get it. I'll be <u>waiting</u> . . . right here." She sniffled, then sneezed! "Don't be long, now," she admonished.

He hurried back up Chippewa to Washington, unlocked the LTD, and climbed in. The engine sprang to life, on the first twist of the key.

He tooled down to Franklin Street—certain that the hooker would've gotten a better offer, by then! Would have stood him up! She was, after all, a real "looker". Prettier than any of her competition—or so it appeared. On the other hand, there <u>was</u> plenty of that erotic competition in evidence.

Not to worry! The tall whore—was still standing on the corner! She smiled, when she recognized him. He pulled to a stop—and stretched to reach across the front seat—and grunted, loudly, as he opened the passenger's door.

She slid into the front seat, close beside him—displaying a copious amount of lithe, long, shapely leg. Immediately, she placed her left hand—on the inside of his right thigh! Within seconds, she was nestling the side of her hand—tightly—against his testicles! He was beginning to perspire, slightly! Apparently, the precise reaction—for which she was looking!

"Where . . . where to?" he asked nervously.

"Oh, Honey! You're not gonna get scared, <u>now</u>! <u>Are</u> you?"

Nuzzling his testicles—even more firmly—she directed him out Franklin Street. Some six blocks later, she instructed him to turn left onto Virginia Street. As they rode along the parked cars on Virginia Street, she nudged him, down there—nudged him, emphatically—once again!

"<u>God</u>, Honey," she exclaimed. "A man driving a nice car? A <u>beautiful</u> car . . . like <u>this</u>? You'd <u>think</u> that . . . a man driving a nice car like <u>this</u> . . . you'd <u>think</u> that he'd have more <u>money</u>! More dough . . . than <u>that</u>! Than just a lousy thirty <u>dollars</u>!"

"Do you have any <u>idea</u>? Any <u>clue</u> . . . what the payments are? The <u>payments</u> . . . on this bucket? <u>That's</u> why . . . that's the main <u>reason</u> . . . I'm lucky to have even a lousy thirty <u>bucks</u>!"

After proceeding another six or seven blocks, she sent him through a withering maze, of right and left turns—eventually winding up on a short, narrow, one-block-in-length, pockmarked, street. Plymouth Street. The neighborhood had, at one time, been quite affluent. But, at that point, the entire area appeared to be in the second or third stage, of "going to seed"! (A charitable evaluation.)

At her direction, he pulled up in front of what had been, at one time, a huge, rather opulent, single-family home. However, the place had been, for some years, sectioned off into three small apartments on the first floor and three slightly-larger flats on the second level. (No lobby.) On the third floor—at one time, the attic—the place afforded three exceptionally small, single rooms, and a tiny, coed, community bathroom.

The couple disembarked from the LTD—and walked up the steps to the porch. She fumbled around in her huge over-the-shoulder bag—and finally flushed out a key. The lock, on the front door, fought her tooth and nail—but, she finally managed to cause it, reluctantly, to turn. Heaving a relief-filled sigh, she pushed open the ponderous, ultra-reluctant, obstacle.

They entered the rather tiny lobby. She turned and kicked the heavy door shut—resulting in an ear-splitting, thunderous, slam!

"Up the stairs, Sweetheart," she said, huskily, patting him on his bottom.

The nasal whine seemed to have <u>abated</u>—once she'd entered the car. By the time the pair had climbed to the third floor—of the old domicile—her voice had become downright <u>earthy</u>!

"We call it <u>Cardiac Heights</u>," she huffed, as they reached the top of the second staircase. The highly-remote third floor! "I only <u>have</u> one room. Have to share the <u>john</u>, up here . . . with two other people. One's the caretaker. He's in bed . . . alone . . . by nine o'clock every night. He's a nice enough old fart, I guess. A bit of a busybody. But, he never really bothers me. Then, there's a waitress. Works at an all-night diner. She lives right across the hall. She never gets in . . . till, like, eight o'clock in the morning. We both sleep all day. And the caretaker? Hell, he doesn't make much noise. So, it works out pretty well. Except for the fucking <u>stairs</u>!"

She unlocked the door. They entered a dank, bleak, room—furnished with a single bed, a tiny, warped-wood, desk, and a lamp table (complete with cheap lamp—which was eternally lit, he assumed). Other "amenities" included a ponderous old wooden wardrobe, a battle-scarred dresser, and an ancient bathroom-type sink. The latter was attached to one of the rather-scruffy walls. The sort-of-rancid place presented an "interesting" mixture of odors: From mustiness, to cheap perfume—to the unmistakably-womanly smell, of the hooker herself.

The single lamp had been left, in its constantly-lit function, of course. But, the small-wattage, of the laboring bulb, wasn't making much of a dent—in the pervasive gloom.

His "hostess" locked the door—and turned to face him. "I <u>do</u> need the thirty, Honey," she advised. "In <u>advance</u>."

He reached into his back pocket. It took a major effort—to pry his old, frayed, wallet from the overly-tight jeans. Removing three bills, he handed her a twenty and a ten. Then, he replaced the surviving five—back into his billfold.

She jammed the two bills into her oversized purse. "You sure you don't want to spring for the thirty-<u>five</u>?" she asked, her voice even more languid. "We could have even <u>more</u> fun."

"I really can't afford the <u>thirty</u>! Can't <u>really</u> afford . . . all the fun we're going to <u>have</u>."

She laughed. For some reason, he'd believed that he'd never hear her laugh! <u>Ever</u>! "Well," she replied, patting him, once more, on his backside, "I saw the five <u>in</u> there. <u>Thought</u> that . . . if you wanted a little something extra <u>special</u> . . . we could . . ."

He began to undress—removing his oversized shirt. Seeing no place else to put it, he laid it, with great care, on top of the old wooden wardrobe—close by where she was standing.

"Naw," he responded, at length. "Thirty's gonna have to just about <u>do</u> it."

"Okay," she sighed. "You're the <u>boss</u>."

She began to remove her own clothing.

"I guess that <u>you're</u> . . . about the tallest woman I've ever <u>seen</u>," he informed her.

"Tall <u>girls</u>! Are they a <u>turn</u>-on for you?" she asked—pulling her peasant blouse over her head, and kicking off her seen-better-days penny loafers.

"Yeah. I <u>guess</u>. I guess they <u>are</u>. They <u>must</u> be. Not that I go down to <u>Chippewa</u>! Well, not all that <u>often</u>, anyway. Once or twice a <u>month</u>, I guess. That's about all I can <u>afford</u>. Not even <u>that</u> often, I imagine. But, I don't remember seeing <u>you</u>, down there! Pretty lady like <u>you</u> are . . . and so <u>tall</u> . . . I'd have <u>remembered</u> you. I sure <u>would</u> have!"

She'd been braless. As she hung her blouse, on an "elephant hook"—located inside of the wardrobe's door—her ample, firm, gloriously pink-tipped, breasts undulated, in a most erotic, sensuous, manner! A symphony in overdone, highly-exaggerated, almost unbelievable, series of blatantly-sensual movements!

Stripped to the waist, she presented an Amazon beauty, almost undreamed of! Especially, in a woman so tall! And so beautifully proportioned! Her breasts were huge! But, not to the point of grotesqueness! Not even close! The lush, pink nipples stood erect— as if making a statement of their own! An eloquent statement!

She pulled her skirt up—and struggled to get it over her head! Then, she hung it over the blouse— displaying, once more, a pair of beautifully-shaped legs! Turning her back, she peeled a pair of black lace panties down—over her glorious, very shapely, bottom! As was the case—with everything else, about this woman—her beauteous behind was perfectly proportioned! Perfectly!

He stood there! Stripped to the waist! Transfixed! The woman was out and out gorgeous!

Completely naked, except for a pair of white cotton anklets, the hooker threw her panties across the back of the chair—then, sat down on the creaky bed!

"C'mon, Honey," she urged, while removing her socks. "Take your pants off! I really don't have all night! Literally!"

She laid down on the undersized, narrow, bed— her heels dangling off of the bottom part.

He undid his belt and waistband—then, unzipped his fly. Pulling his jeans down to mid-thigh, he seated himself next to her, on the bed, and began to remove his shoes.

"I can't imagine a line more corny . . . than this one," he rasped. "But, what's a nice girl like you . . . doing in a business, like this? If you don't mind my saying so, you're . . . well . . . you're different! It's like you're really not a . . . not a . . . a . . ."

"A whore?"

"Well . . . no. I wasn't going to use <u>that</u> word."

"Why <u>not</u>? That's what I <u>am</u>! Might as well <u>say</u> it! Fucking <u>use</u> the word! I'm a <u>whore</u>! I <u>know</u> it! I <u>accept</u> it. I make my <u>living</u> . . . by going to <u>bed</u>, with men! Letting 'em <u>fuck</u> me! <u>That</u> makes me a damn <u>whore</u>! But, it's <u>nice</u> of you . . . to <u>say</u> that! To say . . . that I'm <u>different</u>!"

She laughed once more. Her bosom quaked, once again—sensuously! "Can you begin . . . begin to <u>imagine</u> . . . how many <u>times</u>?" she continued. "How many times I've <u>heard</u> that line? Can you <u>imagine</u>? Listen . . . I'd much <u>rather</u> just go ahead! Let the guy <u>fuck</u> me! Collect my <u>money</u>! And go on my <u>way</u>! Let the guy go on <u>his</u>! I'd be a hell of a lot better <u>off</u> . . . if I could just <u>do</u> that."

"But . . . you <u>can't</u>?"

She lowered her eyes. They seemed to take on a <u>softness</u>! A dimension that he could never have imagined. She shook her head, slowly.

"No," she answered, at length. "Not really. I get really <u>wound</u> up . . . too many times! Get myself all <u>involved</u> . . . half the time! I wind up . . . wanting to know who his <u>wife</u> is, for instance! How many <u>kids</u> he's got, for God's sake! Why he's <u>here</u>! Here . . . with <u>me</u>! Instead of <u>home</u>! Home . . . with <u>her</u>! The whole <u>bullshit</u>! I made up my mind that . . . with <u>you</u> . . . I wasn't going to get into that whole <u>thing</u> again! I wasn't going to <u>ask</u> you . . . about <u>anything</u>! Not a fucking <u>thing</u>! Of course, I said the same <u>thing</u> . . . about the guy right <u>before</u> you! And I couldn't make it stick <u>then</u>, either. This particular guy, <u>he</u> likes kinky sex! And his wife won't <u>indulge</u> him! So? So, he goes to a <u>whore</u>! Tonight, he happened to get <u>me</u>! Guy's got four <u>kids</u>! And he's <u>petrified</u> . . . that anyone'd ever find out that he came to <u>me</u>! Or to anyone <u>else</u> . . . down on Chippewa Street!"

She shifted up onto her elbow, reached over—and began to stroke his back. The caresses sent a shudder through him—from head to toe! More so—than he'd expected! It was all involuntary! She <u>seemed</u> to not notice! Or maybe it was simply a reaction she'd grown quite used to!

"I guess," she continued, with a sardonic laugh, "I just can't make any sort of resolution stick. I've probably only made <u>that</u> one . . . about seven-trillion times."

He placed his shoes under the bed—breaking away from her seductive touch—and stood up. Looking down at her, he smiled. "That's why I say that you're not the <u>type</u>," he advised. "A true <u>whore</u> . . . would just lay back. Think about her <u>grocery</u> list. Or a darling little <u>dress</u> . . . she saw at **Hens & Kelly**, or something. That's why . . . well, it's why . . . it's why you're <u>different</u>!"

He slithered out of his jeans! Then, his white briefs! He dropped them, in a pile, on the floor. Naked, he sat back down on the bed, once more.

"I'm not looking for anything <u>special</u>," he advised her. "It's just that, when I see someone, who's a little special . . . especially in a business, like the one <u>you're</u> in . . . I guess I'm just naturally a little bit curious, myself. In most cases . . . hell, in every <u>case</u>, till now . . . I could care <u>less</u>. I'm simply here . . . to get my <u>ashes</u> hauled. You should <u>excuse</u> the expression. And that's about <u>it</u>! But, <u>you</u>! You're <u>different</u>! Even to the point that, with a <u>regular</u> whore . . . if we'd have talked, even this long . . . she'd have already raised all kinds of hell, with me! Would've told me to get it over with! So that she could get back out . . . back out, on the street! But . . . with you . . . I feel as though I could talk to you! Talk to you . . . all night."

She started to say something—but, he raised his hand! "Don't worry," he assured. "I'm not going to. I'm not going to talk to you all night. But . . . I feel like I could! And I feel . . . that you wouldn't get all bent out of shape! That's what I'm getting at! You're just so . . . so nice!"

She began to stroke the top of his naked left buttock.

"Well," she replied, "so are you! You're sweet. Even in such a cold-blooded business . . . like this one . . . it's nice to know that someone thinks you're more than . . . more than, well, just a . . . a . . . a damn receptacle! And take your time, Honey! With all those broads, out there . . . I doubt I'd be able to turn another trick tonight, anyway! I feel really lucky . . . really lucky, that I got you! Tall girls aren't all that much of a turn-on! Not for a lot of fellas! The ones who do like big girls, well . . . the ones I've encountered . . . they all want me to just dominate them! Whip them, sometimes! Whip them . . . most times! No . . . I'm pretty well in, for the night."

"Well, I like big girls . . . and I certainly don't want to be whipped! But, that to the side, I've just never met anyone like you! Never! Look, Miss. I hope you don't think I'm too damn nosy! But, what's your real interest? Your real ambition? In life, I mean! And don't tell me it's whoring! Or working for world peace! I'll never believe that! Any of that!"

She sat up—and began to massage his shoulders. He managed to control his reaction! He could tell that she was deep in thought. Probably trying to formulate her response.

"Well," she answered, after a ponderous minute or two, "mostly my concern is in . . . in the political arena! I'm concerned . . . about the less fortunate, among us! The plight of the unfortunate! The plight of the poor, I guess you could say! I worked in a couple organizations . . . you might say! But, it was all volunteer stuff! No money! Never any real money!" She reached around in front of him—and took his semi-erect member into her hand. "And," she went on, "a girl has to make a living, y'know!"

"Would . . . would you tell me your name, Miss? Your real name? Every woman I've ever met . . . met this way . . . well, they always have a stupid French name. Even the black girl . . . that I'd had a couple weeks ago. She told me that her name was . . . Yvonne Duval or something."

She laughed. "I should tell you that my name is . . . is Vickie Duval. Something like that. Because, you'll never believe my real name."

"Sure, I would. Try me."

"Would you believe it's actually . . . Annabelle?"

"Really? Annabelle?"

"Yeah. Isn't that a piss-cutter? Named after a maiden-aunt . . . on my father's side. She was a real bitch!"

He arose! Picking up his jeans and undershorts, he walked across to the wardrobe—where he'd placed his shirt, so fastidiously.

"Where are you <u>going</u>, Honey?" she asked. "Is the name <u>that</u> bad? So <u>bad</u> . . . that you can't <u>fuck</u> me?"

"You <u>told</u> me," he replied, darkly, "that I could have a little more <u>fun</u>! More <u>fun</u> . . . if I invested a little more <u>money</u>! I've got <u>something</u>, here in my shirt, that . . ."

She laid back down. "Aw . . . <u>forget</u> it," she answered. "Hell, I <u>saw</u> how much you had. I <u>doubt</u> that I'd have actually had the <u>balls</u> . . . to have taken your last five <u>bucks</u>! Even though I'd <u>asked</u> for it. Unless, of course, you've some more <u>dough</u>—stashed in that <u>shirt</u>! Otherwise, I couldn't . . ."

"No," he said, firmly. "This is something I really <u>want</u> you to <u>have</u>!"

He extracted a small .22 caliber pistol from the pocket of his bulky shirt! Then, he quickly turned! And aimed it—directly at the naked woman, on the bed!

She sat bolt upright! "<u>Hey</u>!" she gasped. "What the fuck <u>is</u> this? You sure didn't <u>seem</u> like the type . . . to try and <u>rob</u> a girl! <u>Look</u>! I don't have all that <u>much</u> up here! Maybe seventy-five <u>bucks</u>! Maybe <u>eighty</u>! It's all I've <u>got</u>! <u>Please</u> . . . don't take <u>that</u>! I make <u>shit</u> . . . absolute <u>shit</u> . . . at this profession! Absolutely <u>shit</u>! You've <u>seen</u> the competition! <u>No</u> money . . . at fucking <u>all</u>! <u>Believe</u> me! What little money I've actually <u>got</u> . . ."

"I'm not <u>interested</u> in your goddam <u>money</u>! Do you know who I <u>am</u>? Underneath all this <u>hair</u>?"

"<u>Should</u> I?"

"Does the name Victor B. <u>Smigelski</u> . . . does <u>that</u> name . . . ring any kind of goddam <u>bell</u>?"

Her eyes opened—to undreamed of proportions! "<u>You</u>! But . . . but, <u>why</u>? Fucking <u>why</u>?"

"Oh, I dunno. I guess I'm just an old <u>sorehead</u>! When you blew up the woman I <u>love</u> . . . the woman I <u>loved</u>, <u>and</u> her two <u>kids</u> . . . why, I tend to get a little pissed <u>off</u>! And then, when you try the same damn <u>thing</u> with my <u>own</u> kids, and my ex-<u>wife</u> . . . to say nothing of trying to rub my <u>own</u> Polack ass out . . . well then, I get just a little bit <u>upset</u>! <u>Finicky</u> bastard, that I am! Finicky as <u>hell</u>! But, what're you gonna <u>do</u>? I must be getting just a wee bit <u>cantankerous</u> . . . in my old age! Just can't take a <u>joke</u>! Not like I <u>used</u> to!"

He aimed the pistol—right between Annabelle's eyes! His finger tightened on the trigger! "I can't <u>tell</u> you," he rasped, "how I've <u>waited</u> for this moment!"

"What <u>moment</u>? What . . . what're you going to . . . going to <u>do</u>? Her voice had taken on that irksome, nasal, quality once again.

"Come <u>off</u> it! "What am I going to <u>do</u>?" He mimicked her high-pitched whine.

She began to shiver! Her entire body was—instantly—<u>quaking</u>! The bed, beneath her, was almost rocking!

"You know damn <u>well</u> . . . what I'm going to do," he hissed. "It's become a goddam <u>obsession</u> with me! An <u>obsession</u>! I've <u>thought</u> of hardly anything <u>else</u>! For so goddam <u>long</u>! I've <u>ruminated</u> over so many ways . . . an endless number of <u>ways</u> . . . that I'd like to <u>use</u>! Would <u>love</u> to use! To <u>kill</u> you! To <u>kill</u> your demented, no good, ass! The <u>early</u> favorite was . . . well, it was that I was going to take a goddam <u>axe</u> to you! Chop off your <u>fingers</u>! One by fucking <u>one</u>! And then your <u>toes</u>! Then, your <u>hands</u>! Then, your <u>feet</u>! Just keep <u>going</u> . . . like <u>that</u>! But . . . sentimental fool that I <u>am</u> . . . I actually can't <u>bring</u> myself to <u>do</u> that!

Even to you! If I had a nickel, though, for every time I've fantasized about it . . . I'd be a rich man! Hell of a rich man!'

"Oh, come on!" She'd stopped shivering—apparently sensing a chink, in Smigelski's armor. "What good would killing me do? It's not going to bring back your girlfriend! Or even that asshole detective!"

"You're right! It won't! Let's just chalk it up to my being a small . . . a spiteful . . . person! Obviously, a terrible flaw, in my character! There was also another fantasy I'd had! Had to do . . . with luring you to bed! This was long before I ever found out that you'd taken to whoring as a career path! I was going to get you into bed! Do my best to get you to an orgasm! Then, right at the height, of your climax . . . I was gonna blow your goddam brains out! There were times, when I fantasized about tying you to the bed! And sticking my gun up your ass! Or up your snatch! Oh, listen! I've got a million of 'em! As you can see . . . you were seldom out of my thoughts!"

"That's . . . why that's sick!"

He nodded. "Probably," he replied. His voice, by then, had grown exceptionally husky. "You're probably right! But, ain't it fun?"

He padded—naked, except for his socks—back to the bed! He waggled the gun two—or three-inches from the tip of her nose!

"You're the last one . . . the last one in the whole fucking world . . . to judge what's sick," he seethed. "Or who's sick! Last one . . . in the whole goddam world!"

"Fuck you," she spat.

He straightened up—the pistol still aimed at her head!

"<u>Speaking</u> of such things," he snarled, "when I actually <u>found</u> you tonight . . . <u>downtown</u> . . . I thought, 'How <u>delicious</u>! How <u>gloriously</u> delicious! First, I'll <u>fuck</u> her! Then, I'll <u>kill</u> her!' More or less like having my <u>cake</u>! And <u>eating</u> it too . . . you should excuse the expression! I think <u>that's</u> what I was <u>goin'</u> to do . . . when I came <u>up</u> here with you! But, <u>now</u>? Now I find that I . . . that I <u>can't</u>!"

She heaved a massive sigh. "Well," she answered, "<u>that's</u> a relief!"

"I wouldn't get all that <u>comfortable</u>, Bitch! What I <u>meant</u> . . . is that I couldn't have <u>sex</u> with you! Every time . . . every goddam <u>time</u>, you <u>touched</u> me . . . I wanted to throw <u>up</u>! I should've <u>known</u>! Sex is an act of <u>love</u>! And <u>no</u> one could possibly <u>hate</u> anyone . . . not as much as <u>I</u> hate <u>you</u>!"

"There's . . . there's a thin <u>line</u>, y'know!" Her voice had become a nasal almost-shudder! It betrayed the unaffected image she was trying so desperately to convey! "An <u>awful</u> thin line," she continued. "Between <u>love</u> . . . and <u>hate</u>!"

"I <u>used</u> to believe <u>that</u> too! I really <u>did</u>! But, take my <u>word</u> for it . . . it's not even <u>close</u>! Junie? Junie, I <u>loved</u>! You? I <u>hate</u> you! <u>Loath</u> you! <u>Despise</u> you! <u>Abhor</u> you! You make me want to <u>puke</u>! Even the very <u>thought</u> of you . . . makes me want to <u>puke</u>! Not <u>close</u>!"

She'd lost her grip—and she <u>knew</u> it! She was <u>trembling</u> again! <u>Badly</u>! She made an Herculean attempt to continue speaking! It was taking more and more effort, Smigelski noted.

"I . . . I don't see what you . . . what you . . . what you hope to accomplish." Her voice was, by then, paper thin—and even more whining!

"First and foremost," he sneered, "I get revenge! Sweet revenge! Like I told you before, I'm a small, hateful, person! But, a side benefit . . . an important bonus . . . is that no one else'll ever have to worry about you! Worry about you . . . blowing them to smithereens! Not fucking ever!"

"Well . . . well, I'm not, you know! Not with the FPN anymore!"

"That's not hard to believe! There is no more fucking FPN! I'm heartbroken! Trying . . . desperately, y'know . . . to control my grief!"

"But, even if there were," she added, frantically— her voice even more whimpering, "even if they were still around . . . I'm not into that shit! Not any longer! Not into that kind of shit!"

"Bullshit! You've still got friends . . . in the 'movement'! Friends in Chicago! And Washington! And L.A. . . . and probably a zillion other places!"

"No! No . . . really! When we blew that whole thing . . . that whole plan . . . when Dane broke into that apartment! He got all that shit! And all those names, and the addresses . . . of our brothers and sisters! In all those other places! All those other cities! They . . . well, they . . . they cut me off! My colleagues . . . in the movement! They cut me right off! They don't know me, anymore! Don't want to know me! No one does! I'm like poison to them! Why . . . why do you think I became a damn whore? It was not my chosen profession, y'know. But, none of those people . . . none of the other revolutionaries . . .

none of 'em'll have <u>anything</u> to <u>do</u> with me! <u>Nothing</u>! Nothing . . . not <u>one</u> goddam <u>thing</u> . . . will they have to <u>do</u> with me!"

"Well, <u>that's</u> good to know! Gratifying as <u>hell</u>! I'd <u>hate</u> . . . to have 'em sniffing <u>around</u>! Trying to avenge your <u>death</u>!"

She was shaking—badly, by then! Almost <u>convulsing</u>! Perspiration was <u>pouring</u> out of her gorgeous, Amazon, body! Her face was utterly <u>contorted</u>! Her eyes—despite being overwhelmed with <u>fear</u>—still had a slight bit of room! For stark, out and out, <u>hatred</u>!

"Why on earth are you <u>shaking</u> like that?" he asked—contempt coating every word. "What's the <u>matter</u>, Premier-Baby? Not nearly so <u>brave</u> now . . . <u>are</u> you? It's all <u>right</u> . . . for <u>you</u>, to rub out entire families! Just blow 'em <u>away</u>! No big <u>deal</u>! With one wave of your fucking <u>hand</u>! Just like <u>that</u>! (He snapped his fingers—loudly!) <u>Boom</u>! But, when the <u>crunch</u> comes . . . when you're <u>positive</u>, that <u>you're</u> going to be the one, to vacate the <u>planet</u> . . . why, then <u>life</u> becomes a little more <u>important</u>! Does it <u>not</u>? A little more <u>valuable</u>! <u>Right</u>? I could <u>puke</u>! <u>Bitch</u>!"

He returned his attention to where his gun was aimed! It hadn't strayed more than an inch or two! The weapon remained pointed at the narrow area—between her eyes!

Slowly—tantalizingly—he squeezed on the trigger, once again!

Before Smigelski could fire off the round, Annabelle cut loose with an animal-like <u>shriek</u>! It had to have awakened every dog in the neighborhood!

Her hand swept—with blinding speed—under her pillow!

The open switchblade knife that she pulled from its confinement was almost a blur—as she lunged up, and sprang off the bed!

She plunged the long, lethal-looking, blade into the biceps of Smigelski's left arm—as the gun in his right hand exploded!

The bullet caught Annabelle—flush in the mouth!

The small-sized slug, though, slowed her only slightly! She attempted—with all her Amazon strength—to pull the knife loose, from her assailant's arm!

The second bullet plastered in—goring her, in her neck!

She wound up on the floor! On her stomach!

Shrieking—and thrashing wildly—she attempted to rise! She'd gotten to her hands and knees—when the third bullet slammed through the small of her back!

The .22 caliber slug being so little—and Annabelle's strength so great—the latest penetration merely sent her back, writhing furiously, onto the floor! Blood, by then, was gushing from all three wounds! The ponderous amount, of pure gore, was shocking—given the smallness of the caliber of the slugs!

Smigelski transferred the firearm to his left hand, and—gritting his teeth—managed to yank the switchblade from the bloody wound in his left arm! The knife clanked to the antiquated linoleum!

Instantly, the pistol was returned to his right hand! He stood—looming over the fallen Amazon! Even as she was, steadfastly, writhing toward the spot—where the knife had dropped!

He leveled the gun once more! Calmly, he aimed—and fired! The bullet entered her lean, muscular, statuesque, left buttock—sending her careening, over onto her back!

Taking careful aim, once again, Smigelski pulled the trigger The lead payload pounded into Annabelle's body—inches above her vagina!

Her torso <u>wrenched</u>—fiercely! One final <u>convulsion</u>! One last <u>spasm</u>! She was all through!

He knelt beside her! "I only have one bullet <u>left</u>, Annabelle-Baby," he rasped. "Do you know where it's <u>going</u>? Do you have any <u>idea</u>? I purposely bought a small <u>gun</u>, you know! Did that on fucking <u>purpose</u>! First, it doesn't make all that much <u>noise</u>! But . . . more <u>importantly</u> . . . I wanted you to <u>suffer</u>! I wanted to <u>see</u> you! <u>Watch</u> you . . . as you fucking <u>suffer</u>! Now, this <u>last</u> one . . . it's going in your <u>ear</u>! Right in your fucking <u>ear</u>!"

She was reduced to gurgling! Her body still undulated! Sometimes, <u>wildly</u>! Gyrating, it was—in mortal <u>agony</u>! Only not to the extent—of mere seconds previously!

She'd <u>understood</u>, though! Had heard every <u>word</u>! Her head <u>shook</u>—virtually <u>shouting</u> the word "<u>NO</u>!" She shook her head—as violently as was possible, given her situation! Shook it—from side to side! Her lips pursed!

Smigelski put his ear to her mouth! "What <u>say</u>?" he asked.

"No!" Her voice was barely audible—but, she <u>had</u> managed to utter the word! Sheer Amazon strength!

Raising back up, he calmly pressed the nose of the gun against her right ear! Only her crazed eyes, at that point, were capable of bespeaking the depth—of her horror!

He squeezed the trigger! The gun barked! Annabelle's body stiffened—one final time! Then, it went limp! She was <u>dead</u>!

Smigelski pulled himself to his feet. He was soaked with—among other things—perspiration!

It was at that point that he was able to focus his attention on the crimson gore—cascading down his left arm! He could never have imagined—that it had been bleeding so profusely!

Then, he began wondering—exactly how long the sirens had been blaring, in the distance! They were getting louder! By the second!

He dropped the empty pistol onto the bed!

Ripping violently at one of the bed sheets, he tore a strip of material—about two-feet long and six—or seven-inches wide! Using his good hand—and his teeth—he <u>bound</u> up his wound, as best he could! And as quickly as he could! The finished product—a rather inept dressing—would make no one forget Florence Nightingale!

He kicked his undershorts under the bed—as he frantically tugged the tight jeans up his legs and over his buttocks! He jammed his stockinged feet into his shoes! Then, he picked up the still-warm handgun from the bed—and slipped it into his shirt pocket!

Donning the shirt, as he scrambled down the two flights of stairs, he made the front door and porch—at precisely the same moment, as a police cruiser careened around the corner! A half-block away!

Smigelski leaped over the porch railing—landing, he thanked heaven, on his feet!

He sprinted along the narrow, broken, sidewalk which ran alongside the huge house! Hesitating not one second, he barreled into the backyard, past the garage—and out into the alley!

He was slamming the gate—as the patrol car screeched to a halt, in front of the house! Sirens—wailing from every direction—indicated, emphatically, the fact that other squad cars would be at the scene! Shortly! And in great numbers!

Smigelski dashed down the alley—in the direction, opposite that from which the police car had come! It was no help! Two other cruisers were roaring up the cross-street—onto which the alley exited! They blew past the opening—to join their associates, in front!

"Oh, shit!" he muttered to himself, as he was about to exit from the dark, gravel-laden, alley. "Your <u>car</u>! Your fucking <u>car</u>! It's <u>parked</u> . . . right out in <u>front</u>! How could you be so damn <u>stupid</u>? So goddam <u>stupid</u>? You've got your head <u>stuck</u>! Stuck . . . clear up your <u>ass</u>!"

Panic began to set in!

He'd always felt that he'd been so <u>calm</u>—till then! A veritable <u>rock</u>—till that moment! Throughout all the other <u>murders</u>: The four at *The White Palace*! Clark and Rita in the bathtub in Windsor Locks! Even the encounter—with those four late FPN members—in the parking lot, at his apartment complex, in New Jersey! Well, he'd wound up somewhat a basket case, after the latter adventure! Just not <u>during</u> the "entertainment"!

But, <u>tonight</u>! Tonight had been <u>different</u>! <u>Vastly</u> different! Despite the fact—that he'd <u>seemed</u> under control! Even through the moment—when he'd sent that final bullet crashing into the Amazon's <u>ear</u>!

Annabelle! She had been the last <u>one</u>! The final <u>curtain</u>! Everything was to have been <u>settled</u>! There would nothing <u>more</u>! Nothing left to <u>do</u>! <u>No</u> one remained! No one left—with whom to <u>settle</u>! A clean <u>slate</u>! What the shrinks call "<u>closure</u>"!

June had been <u>avenged</u>! <u>That</u> was the main thing! Had always <u>been</u> the main thing! Her—and the <u>kids</u>! It had been Smigelski's demented "Quest For The Holy Grail"! The glorious <u>mission</u>—the <u>sanctified</u> mission—had, at long last, been <u>accomplished</u>!

Maybe they'd <u>all</u> be able to rest a little easier now! June and her children! <u>Rest in peace</u>, <u>guys</u>! Mission <u>accomplished</u>!

Why, then, did he not feel exhilarated? Why was he—so obviously—<u>panicking</u>? Why <u>now</u>? He began to feel sick to his <u>stomach</u>!

What to <u>do</u>? What—on <u>earth</u>—to do? What—on <u>earth</u>—<u>could</u> he do? <u>Why</u>—on <u>earth</u>—had he left that damn LTD, in front of the <u>house</u>? Surely, the police will <u>find</u> it! <u>Trace</u> it to him! <u>Stupid</u>! <u>Stupid</u>! <u>Stupid</u>!

"Where else <u>could</u> you have put it, Asshole?" he muttered aloud.

Certainly, it would've been terribly difficult to have parked the automobile anywhere else! Most certainly, he'd have aroused Annabelle's suspicion! It probably wouldn't have taken <u>much</u>! At that <u>moment</u>, anyway!

"What're you gonna do now?" His voice was too loud! Was he <u>losing</u> it? Going totally <u>bonkers</u>—now that he'd accomplished that, over which he'd obsessed for so long? Having satisfied his <u>mania</u>—his <u>fixation</u>, his <u>obsession</u>—that of <u>avenging angel</u>? Having avenged his fiancée, and her children, was he now <u>unraveling</u>? With a <u>rush</u>? Going completely to <u>pot</u>?

"What're you fucking gonna <u>do</u>?" His voice was <u>still</u> too loud! <u>Everything</u> seemed to be too loud! Everything was closing <u>in</u> on him!

Fortunately, no other police cars seemed to be converging on the area! He was certain that the officers would be busily engaged—inside the house! Probably for the next few minutes! Hopefully, for the next few <u>hours</u>!

Should he make a run for it? Or try and find a hiding place for the duration? He stood transfixed! Dumbstruck!

At that moment, a current-year Pontiac Bonneville screeched to a stop—blocking his exit from the alley! "<u>Great</u>," muttered Smigelski. "Now they've fucking got me hemmed <u>in</u>!"

TWENTY

S MIGELSKI STOOD THERE—DUMBFOUNDED! STARING AT the idling Pontiac—blocking the exit from the alley!

What to <u>do</u>? <u>Run</u> for it? But, <u>where</u>? Back up the <u>alley</u>? Down the <u>street</u>? The street—on which the <u>Bonneville</u> was sitting! Run in the <u>opposite</u> direction—from which the car was heading? So that the cops would have to turn the Pontiac <u>around</u>—to pursue him? Or? Or maybe they'd simply just go ahead—<u>shoot</u> him! Why <u>not</u>?

Maybe he should head back into the shadows! Try and take advantage of the darkness, that the alley afforded! Would <u>that</u> not be best?

He took one what-he'd-thought-was "a final look around"! The person in the Bonneville—apparently a male—seemed to be dressed in a suit and tie! Seemed <u>not</u> to be clad—in a uniform!

<u>Christ</u>! <u>They've even got plainclothes guys on the case! So soon</u>?

He stood—as though a pillar of salt! He seemed unable to move! Even an <u>arm</u>! Let alone, a <u>leg</u>!

The driver's door, of the Pontiac, shot open—and a silver-haired man shouted, as loudly as he'd dared, "Vick! It's me! Quick! Get in!"

Smigelski recognized the voice immediately! It was Leland Nype! In an instant, he was inside the car—with the older man! The latter dropped the gear selector into "Drive"—and, slowly, the car eased away. Tantalizingly slowly!

"Looks like you've got a bit of a wound there," observed Nype.

"Knife! Sonofabitch hurts! Hurts like hell! Got me in the goddam muscle!"

"Well, I don't recommend that you go to a doctor tonight! Not around here, anyhow!"

"Where . . . where are you taking me?"

"You'll see."

Nype drove—five miles under the speed limit—to Porter Avenue, three blocks away. After having meticulously obeyed the stop sign, he wheeled to the right—headed for *Kleinhan's Music Hall*, another three blocks down Porter. Neither man spoke.

As they approached the *Music Hall*, Smigelski almost swallowed his tongue! There—in the parking lot—sat his LTD!

He looked at his erstwhile employer. "I . . . I don't understand, Mister Nype. Where . . . where did you come from? How'd my car . . . how'd it get there? What the hell's going on?"

"Vick," Nype replied, with a broad, warm smile, "I could never hope . . . never hope to ever repay you! Repay you . . . for your loss! Your loss . . . of Miss Bodner! Or . . . God help us . . . for the terrible death, of her kids! Could never come close . . . to repaying you. I've <u>always</u> felt that . . . in a very real <u>way</u> . . . it was my <u>fault</u>! The whole <u>thing</u>! Well, <u>partly</u> my fault, anyway! That I always shared a goodly portion of the <u>responsibility</u> . . . that she was so horribly <u>murdered</u>!" He shuddered—head to toe! "Her . . . and her <u>kids</u>! Even <u>more</u> frightening . . . it was more good <u>luck</u>, than anything <u>else</u> . . . that <u>your</u> <u>own</u> kids weren't blown up! Them . . . and <u>Inez</u>! <u>That</u> would've been the <u>end</u> . . . the very <u>end</u> . . . for you! I'm <u>certain</u>! I <u>know</u>, though . . . trite as this may <u>sound</u> . . . I <u>do</u> know what Miss Bodner's <u>death</u> . . . what it <u>did</u> to you!"

"Yes, but . . ."

"Let me <u>finish</u>! I've kept my <u>eye</u> on you! I really <u>have</u>! <u>Closely</u>! <u>Very</u> closely! Much <u>closer</u> . . . than you could ever <u>know</u>!"

"You <u>what</u>?"

"<u>You</u> heard me! Do you think I didn't <u>know</u> . . . <u>don't</u> know . . . who took <u>out</u> those four? That little group . . . in the <u>coffee</u> shop? And that highly-affectionate <u>couple</u>? Those lovers . . . up in <u>Connecticut</u>? Have to <u>admit</u> . . . that I dropped the goddam <u>ball</u>, on the thing! Screwed <u>up</u> . . . <u>completely</u> . . . when those four <u>shitheads</u> tried to machine gun you <u>down</u>, in Madison! I'd actually <u>had</u> people out there! Watching <u>out</u> for you! Out <u>there</u>! <u>Really</u>! I <u>did</u>! On a fulltime <u>basis</u>! But, when the dipshits assassinated <u>Dane</u>, I wound up figuring that they'd had <u>him</u> pegged . . . for all those <u>killings</u>! So . . . like some kind of <u>idiot</u> . . . I just pulled my people <u>away</u>! Away . . . from your <u>complex</u>! A <u>mistake</u>! <u>Obviously</u>! Bad, bad, <u>bad</u>, mistake! Almost cost you your <u>life</u>! I'd <u>really</u> have felt guilty . . . if <u>that</u> had happened! Couldn't have <u>lived</u> with myself . . . I don't think!"

Nype pulled to a stop—next to Smigelski's LTD—and shifted into "Park".

Leaning back against the luxurious seat cushions, he asked, "How the hell did you <u>ever</u> find her? Find <u>Annabelle</u>?"

"<u>That</u>? That was just shithouse <u>luck</u>! I've got a couple or three <u>friends</u> . . . up here in Buffalo. One of 'em was trying to con me into <u>moving</u> up here. He thought it'd be <u>best</u> for me. Best <u>thing</u> . . . to just <u>remove</u> my Polack ass, from New Jersey. There'd be only memories of <u>Junie</u> . . . and the <u>kids</u> . . . down there!"

"I can sure see the logic in <u>that</u>."

"So could I . . . to a point. Anyway, this guy . . . he got me a <u>subscription</u>. A subscription . . . to *The Buffalo Evening News*. Well, about the second or third week, that I was getting the paper, they did a <u>series</u>, the paper did. About <u>prostitution</u> . . . in Buffalo! Most especially . . . on <u>Chippewa</u> Street! Obviously!"

I noted that this was where you picked her up.

"Yeah. That's where it all <u>happens</u>! Prostition-wise! Pretty much the center of <u>operations</u>, for whores! <u>Everybody</u> knows that! Everyone in Western New <u>York</u>, anyway! The paper . . . they'd taken a hell of a lot of <u>pictures</u>! <u>All</u> of 'em on Chippewa Street! And . . . in the <u>background</u>, of one of those <u>photos</u> . . . there was this <u>woman</u>! She <u>looked</u> . . . for all the <u>world</u> . . . looked like <u>Annabelle</u>! You couldn't tell . . . for <u>sure</u>! Leastways, <u>I</u> couldn't! But, <u>listen</u>! There aren't <u>that</u> many girls . . . black <u>or</u> white . . . that are her <u>size</u>!"

"Yeah. <u>That</u>, I can believe."

"So, I look a flyer! Headed the ol' LTD <u>up</u> here! Speaking of my car . . . what the hell is <u>it</u> doing over here?"

"Well . . . when you and Annabelle went <u>upstairs</u> . . . on Plymouth Street . . . I <u>figured</u> that you might not be looking far enough <u>ahead</u>! Thought maybe you'd . . . quite possibly . . . <u>need</u> it to be <u>away</u> from there! So . . . talented little old me . . . I <u>hotwired</u> it! Brought it over <u>here</u>! Walked back . . . and picked up my <u>Pontiac</u>! Fortunately, I got <u>back</u> . . . before a whole lot had <u>happened</u>! Not as <u>young</u> . . . as I used to be! Took me a hell of a lot <u>longer</u> . . . to get back . . . than I <u>thought</u> it would!"

"Before a whole lot <u>happened</u>? You did <u>that</u> . . . before all <u>hell</u> broke loose?"

"Of <u>course</u>! Fortunately, I <u>did</u> get back! <u>Winded</u> as hell . . . but, I <u>did</u> get back! Was sitting in my <u>car</u> . . . across the street, the no-<u>parking</u> side . . . when all the <u>shooting</u> started! I could <u>hear</u> it! Could even <u>tell</u> that it wasn't a high-powered gun! Sounded more like <u>firecrackers</u> popping, or something! She must've, maybe, left a <u>window</u> open, or something!"

"Yeah. There were . . . I think . . . <u>two</u> small windows up there. And . . . if I'm remembering right . . . <u>both</u> were open! Stuffy as hell, it was . . . up there!"

"Whatever. In any case, I could hear all that <u>hell</u> . . . breaking loose! Could hear it . . . all the way down, on the <u>street</u>!

"I'm glad you <u>did</u>! But, <u>how</u> . . . how'd you come to be <u>up</u> here . . . in the <u>first</u> damn place?"

"Obviously, I've had <u>people</u> . . . a good <u>many</u> people . . . <u>watching</u> you! We've got a <u>subsidiary</u> up here! Well, we've got 'em all over the state, you know! But . . ."

"Really? I didn't know that."

"Well, we don't go out of our way to publicize it. But, when you came up here . . . I knew that you were on to something! The people I'd had on you . . . in Jersey . . . one of them followed you! Tailed you . . . all the way up here!"

"I'm not believing this."

"Believe it! Listen, Vick. I know you! Know you, well enough . . . to know that you'd never give up! Not until you'd taken out . . . good ol' Annabelle! Till she was past tense!"

"Yeah," muttered Smigelski. "You've got that right. Didn't take too many smarts to . . ."

"The people . . . up here . . . they kept telling me! Talking to me . . . about how you were growing a stupid-assed beard! Letting your hair get a hell of a lot longer! You look like shit, by the way! Just thought I'd pass that unsolicited evaluation along! They told me that you'd dropped all kinds . . . of stupid weight! The way they were talking, I figured you as dropping . . . oh, maybe . . . ten or twelve pounds! Maybe fifteen! God, Vick! It must be nearer to twenty-five . . . or, maybe even, thirty!"

"Little over thirty-five . . . truth to tell! Figured that I had to change . . . really change . . . my appearance! Critical as hell . . . that I look different! A helluva lot different! As much as possible, anyway!"

"Well, you sure did a helluva job! I'd never have recognized you! Fortunately, Glenn Hayes . . . the agent I'd finally sent up here . . . he'd watched you! For a couple or three weeks, now! He was able to see you . . . as you'd <u>changed</u>! So, <u>him</u>? Him, you <u>didn't</u> fool!"

"<u>Glenn</u>? Glenn <u>Hayes</u>? I only met him <u>once</u>. Only the one <u>time</u>. But, I <u>knew</u> . . . knew that he was one of your high-powered <u>guys</u>. You had <u>him</u> . . . following me around? No <u>wonder</u> I never caught on!"

"Yeah. Well, when you started stalking up and down <u>Chippewa</u> Street . . . the night before <u>last</u> . . . he <u>figured</u>, that you were about ready to make your <u>move</u>! He figured that <u>you</u> felt as though you'd succeeded . . . in changing your <u>appearance</u>! That you'd changed it . . . <u>sufficiently</u>! He figured . . . correctly, obviously . . . that you were about ready to <u>pounce</u>! So, I drove up . . . <u>yesterday</u>, as a matter of fact! I've been kind of keeping <u>my</u> eye on you too! A little <u>bit</u>, anyway! Me and Glenn! I <u>saw</u> her! Saw <u>Annabelle</u>! Saw her . . . probably before <u>you</u> did! <u>Tonight</u>, anyway! I <u>knew</u> . . . knew damn <u>well</u>, knew <u>exactly</u> . . . what was going to <u>happen</u>! Be just a matter of <u>time</u>! But, I <u>knew</u> it! I <u>followed</u> you two crazy kids . . . out to <u>her</u> little base of operations!"

"Thank <u>God</u>," mused Smigelski. "Thank <u>God</u>!"

"I'm <u>assuming</u> that our lady friend . . . that she's no longer <u>with</u> us! <u>Dead</u>, is she?"

Smigelski grinned! Broadly! "<u>Yeah</u>! She sure <u>is</u>! Sure as hell <u>is</u>! But, it took some <u>doing</u>! I emptied the whole goddam <u>gun</u>! Put every round I <u>had</u>! Pumped every <u>bullet</u> . . . <u>into</u> her! She's strong as a <u>horse</u>! The <u>last</u> one . . . went right into her goddam <u>ear</u>!"

"<u>Was</u> . . . as strong as a horse," corrected Nype. "She's on her way to the good ol' <u>glue</u> factory now! Even as we <u>speak</u>. Poor <u>thing</u>! I can just <u>see</u> us all! See us <u>all</u> . . . wearing black <u>armbands</u>!"

"Look, Mister Nype. I can't <u>thank</u> you enough! Can't <u>tell</u> you . . . how <u>grateful</u> I am! For pulling my <u>chestnuts</u> . . . out of the fire! I <u>wonder</u> . . . wonder what would've <u>happened</u>, though! What'd happened . . . If I'd have come, <u>tearing</u>-ass, out of the place! Come barreling <u>out</u> . . . hell bent on <u>escape</u> . . . and then found my <u>car</u> missing!"

Nype laughed. "Well, if <u>that'd</u> happened, I was right <u>there</u>," he answered. "<u>I'd</u> have whisked you away! The only thing that really <u>worried</u> me . . . was that I wouldn't get <u>back</u>, over there! Wouldn't <u>get</u> back over to Plymouth Street! Wouldn't get <u>back</u> . . . not before the <u>fun</u> began! Then, you really <u>would've</u> had a problem."

Smigelski nodded. He appeared to deflate. It seemed as if he was shrinking—becoming even <u>smaller</u>—as he sat in the front seat of Nype's car! In addition, his complexion was <u>paling</u>! <u>Noticeably</u>!!

"Vick? Vick are you all right?"

"Yeah," he answered weakly. "I . . . I guess that it's all, finally, catching <u>up</u> with me! What I'd been <u>doing</u>! What I've just <u>done</u>! Well, there <u>were</u> the ones . . . at *The White Palace*! And the couple . . . up in <u>Connecticut</u>! <u>Those</u> actions were . . . obviously . . . cold-<u>blooded</u>! <u>Purely</u> cold-blooded! The ones . . . those bastards with the <u>machine</u> guns, in Madison . . . <u>that</u> was, pretty much, a case of self-<u>defense</u>! <u>That's</u> what I've always <u>thought</u>, anyway! What I just <u>did</u> though . . . eradicating <u>Annabelle</u> . . . <u>that</u> was cold-blooded too! Same as the <u>hamburger</u> joint . . . and the <u>hotel</u>, in Connecticut! But, somehow, <u>this</u> . . . this thing with <u>Annabelle</u> . . . well, <u>it</u> was <u>different</u>! Different as <u>hell</u>!"

"I <u>think</u> I can understand that, Vick. In effect, this . . . what you just <u>did</u>, with Annabelle . . . <u>this</u> was what you might call "The Final Curtain"! It's all <u>over</u> now! <u>Done</u>!"

"Yeah. I <u>guess</u>."

"Plus, consider <u>this</u>! You may or may <u>not</u> have been naked . . . when you dealt with Annabelle! I'm <u>guessing</u> that <u>she</u> would've been unclothed! If you were unclothed . . . either one of you, or both . . . <u>that</u> would've added a whole different dimension! Hell, I'm just <u>guessing</u>!"

"Well, your guess is pretty much . . . right <u>on</u>! Probably!"

"Whatever! No matter <u>which</u> way you want to <u>look</u> at it . . . there <u>had</u> to have been <u>some</u> matter of <u>intimacy</u> there! Clothed . . . or unclothed! No matter how <u>repugnant</u> that intimacy might've been! It <u>was</u> . . . <u>believe</u> me . . . <u>there</u>! That <u>has</u> to have <u>some</u> effect, on your present state of mind! <u>Has</u> to!"

"Yeah. I . . . I guess. I suppose so. You're probably right. You're <u>undoubtedly</u> right. As per usual!"

"Well, you know, Vick, that I really <u>don't</u> condone what you've done! Well, I <u>can't</u>! Not <u>supposed</u> to, anyway. Obviously, in a way I <u>do</u>, though! <u>Obviously</u>! One way or <u>another</u>, Vick, I have to <u>admire</u> you! Admire the <u>hell</u> out of you! Admire you . . . for simply having <u>balls</u> enough! <u>Balls</u> enough . . . to <u>do</u> it! To do <u>any</u> of it! Let alone . . . <u>all</u> of it! I <u>know</u> that <u>I'd</u> have been tempted . . . <u>sorely</u> tempted . . . to do the same damn <u>thing</u>! I just don't know . . . if I'd have had <u>balls</u>, enough, to follow <u>through</u> on the thing! To go ahead . . . and <u>do</u> the deed!"

"I wonder if it was <u>balls</u>, Mister Nype. <u>Stupidity</u> might be more accurate."

"Not so! What're you going to do <u>now</u>?"

Smigelski seemed to deflate even further! He appeared to be hunched over! Permanently? He'd begun to wriggle—almost uncontrollably—in the passenger's seat. His entire body seemed just a shudder or two—from being caught up, in a series of convulsions!

"I really don't <u>know</u>, Mister Nype," he was able to respond—through clattering teeth. "I really don't <u>know</u> . . . <u>what</u> I'm gonna do. I haven't really <u>thought</u> much about it! Much . . . about <u>anything</u>! Except <u>getting</u> those sons of bitches! It's <u>crazy</u>! I <u>know</u> that it's <u>nuts</u> . . . but, I never really looked any <u>further</u>! No further . . . than <u>Annabelle</u>! <u>Especially</u> after all the <u>others</u> . . . once <u>they</u> all wound up, biting the dust! Never gave life . . . after <u>Annabelle</u> . . . never <u>really</u> gave it a <u>thought</u>! I dunno. I'll probably wander back down, to <u>Jersey</u>! Kind of <u>afraid</u> to move to Albuquerque. Afraid of putting Inez and the kids . . . in any <u>kind</u> of danger! Maybe . . . I dunno . . . might even move to <u>Detroit</u>! Have a cousin . . . and his wife . . . living there. Hell, I might even . . ."

"Do you think <u>Jersey</u> is a good idea? As you mentioned, there are <u>mountains</u> . . . mountains of <u>memories</u> . . . down there, Vick! So damn <u>many</u> memories! <u>None</u> of 'em good!"

"Yeah. I s'pose. Still, Jersey seems to be the <u>simplest</u> . . ."

"Besides, if the Buffalo <u>police</u> . . . if they happen to figure <u>out</u>, just who Annabelle <u>is</u> . . . who Annabelle <u>was</u> . . . they could, somehow, link her to <u>you</u>! I just think you'd, probably be <u>much</u> better off . . . in a place, where they can't lay their <u>hands</u> on you! Not <u>immediately</u>, anyway. Of course, if they <u>do</u> find out who she actually <u>is</u> . . . who she actually <u>was</u> . . . I have a sneaky <u>feeling</u>, that the cops aren't going to move heaven and earth to track <u>down</u> her killer!"

Bemused, Smigelski shook his head slowly. His face—normally exceptionally animated and expressive—had become a total blank page.

"<u>Shit</u>," he finally muttered. "I really don't <u>know</u>, Mister Nype. Maybe you're <u>right</u>!" He sighed deeply—reawakening the pain in his arm! "Yeah, I guess you're <u>right</u>! There's really not anything <u>for</u> me . . . back in Jersey! But, I <u>really</u> don't think I want to stay up here either!"

Nype reached into his inside suit coat pocket.

Smigelski tensed—as the older man withdrew a packet of papers!

"<u>Here</u>," he said, handing them to Smigelski. "Here, Vick. There's a whole set of <u>identity</u> papers in here! A whole <u>shit</u>-load of 'em!"

"<u>Identity</u> papers? Why would . . . ?"

"Driver's license, social security card, voter's registration card . . . even a stupid damn library card. That sort of stuff."

"I don't <u>understand</u>!"

"You will. There's also the name and address and phone number of my <u>brother</u>-in-law! He's in Charlotte, North <u>Carolina</u>! His name is Alec Wakefield! He owns an <u>Oldsmobile</u> dealership down there."

"Yeah. But, what has all this . . . ?"

"Well, he needs a **lease** manager! I <u>know</u> that you did that same thing . . . did that exact same thing . . .

out at **Avis**, in Piscataway. He'll pay you a good salary! He'll even give you a piece of the leasing profits! He knows who you are! And what you are! But, as far as he's concerned, you are whoever the driver's license says you are!"

"Who my . . . my driver's license . . . who it says I am?"

"Precisely! Your new name is Hawthorne! Or maybe it's Hathaway . . . or some damn thing! Also, there's five hundred bucks . . . all in twenties . . . in there. I figure that you can't be too awfully solvent."

Smigelski was beginning to bounce back! He sat up erect! Color, surprisingly, began to seep back into his pasty complexion! He was even able to contain the winces (to a point, anyway)—as he moved, gingerly, about!

"But . . . but why, Mister Nype?"

"Let's just say that I like you. You're a hell of a guy, Vick. But, mostly, I guess that I'd just like to think that I've been a part . . . how-ever-minor . . . of seeing that those bastards got theirs! We both know that they never would've paid . . . for all the shit they did! Not without someone like you! Not without someone like you . . . the headsman . . . taking their unprincipled asses out! Who knows how many more people would've been killed? Sacrificed? For their glorious cause? Who knows what would've happened . . . had those schmucks been allowed to continue on their merry way? Of course, we all owe a debt of gratitude . . . to Lieutenant Dane!"

"Well, all I know is that I'll never be able to repay you, Mister Nype."

"You've already <u>repaid</u> me, Vick. You've repaid <u>me</u> . . . and anyone <u>else</u> who'd ever had the same thing happen to <u>them</u>! Or their <u>loved</u> ones! The same <u>thing</u> . . . as happened to Miss <u>Bodner</u> and her <u>children</u>! Now, you'd better <u>get</u>! Are you going back to your <u>room</u> . . . in Cheektowaga?" He was referring to a Buffalo suburb.

"Yeah," Smigelski answered, sighing heavily, once again. "I guess I <u>will</u>. I'm in no <u>shape</u> . . . to try and <u>drive</u>, to North <u>Carolina</u>! Not <u>tonight</u>, anyway!"

"My <u>suggestion</u> . . . my <u>advice</u> . . . would be, that you should stop at a *Seven-Eleven*, or someplace. Get some peroxide! A hell of a lot of peroxide! Ten . . . maybe twelve . . . bottles! Then, when you get to your room, start <u>pouring</u> the stuff . . . <u>literally</u> pouring the stuff . . . into that <u>wound</u>! It'll <u>bite</u> . . . bite like <u>hell</u> . . . but, you're gonna want to clean <u>out</u> the damn wound! Clean it the hell <u>out</u>! Also, I think I'd get <u>rid</u> of the stupid <u>beard</u>. I'd get my <u>hair</u> cut, too! And I think I'd eat every damn piece of whipped cream <u>cake</u> . . . in Erie County! Get some of your <u>weight</u> back! As <u>much</u> as possible! As <u>quick</u> as possible! And act . . . like you'd never <u>lost</u> it!"

Smigelski smiled—and extended his right hand. Nype took it—in both of his.

"Mister Nype," Smigelski rasped, "I can't thank you <u>enough</u>."

"Vick . . . it's been a pleasure <u>knowing</u> you. Take <u>care</u> . . . in your new <u>life</u>! I <u>hope</u> . . . I really <u>hope</u> . . . it'll be a happier one! A <u>much</u> happier one! <u>Much</u> happier . . . than your <u>old</u> one!"

"I'm sure it <u>will</u> be! <u>Thank</u> you, Sir! Thank you . . . for <u>everything</u>!"

Smigelski got, even more gingerly, out of the Pontiac. He crossed over to his LTD, got in—and fired up the engine.

Nype waited until the Ford had exited the parking lot. Then, he dropped the gear selector into "Drive"— and eased his Pontiac out into the street. At the first red light, he pulled up beside Smigelski—and waved a final, highly-emotional, <u>farewell</u> to his former employee.

As the light turned green—and Smigelski's LTD lurched forward—Nype rubbed his chin and sighed! Smiling, he muttered to himself, "As Fibber McGee used to always say about Molly . . . 'There goes a good kid'."

THE END

ABOUT THE AUTHOR

George was born in Detroit, Michigan, in the early 1930s—and grew up during a time before the micro-waved dinner was eaten in front of the TV, expired nuclear-powered spy satellites dropped back to earth, or violence from half the world away was posted on You Tube, two seconds after it occurred. It was a time when boys played baseball in sandlots, girls played house, teenagers went to family-rated movies, families enjoyed the same radio programs, and nothing was better than a great Mystery Novel. How things changed! In what is laughingly referred to as his "adult life", our boy has lived in Detroit, Central New Jersey, Western New York's Niagara Frontier—And San Marcos, San Antonio and Houston, in Texas. He is the proud papa of seven kids!